Also by Bruce Macbain

Odin's Child: Book One of Odd Tangle-Hair's Saga
The Ice Queen: Book Two of Odd Tangle-Hair's Saga

Roman Games: A Plinius Secundus Mystery (Book 1)
The Bull Slayer: A Plinius Secundus Mystery (Book 2)

THE
VARANGIAN

A NOVEL

BRUCE MACBAIN

Blank Slate Press | Saint Louis, MO

Blank Slate Press
Saint Louis, MO 63116

For information, contact
Blank Slate Press at 4168 Hartford Street, Saint Louis, MO 63116
www.blankslatepress.com
www.brucemacbain.com

Blank Slate Press is an imprint of Amphorae Publishing Group, LLC

Manufactured in the United States of America
Cover and Interior Illustrations by Anthony Macbain
Cover and Interior Layout by Kristina Blank Makansi
Set in Adobe Caslon Pro and Viking

Library of Congress Control Number:

ISBN: 9781943075249

To Carol with love and gratitude

THE
VARANGIAN

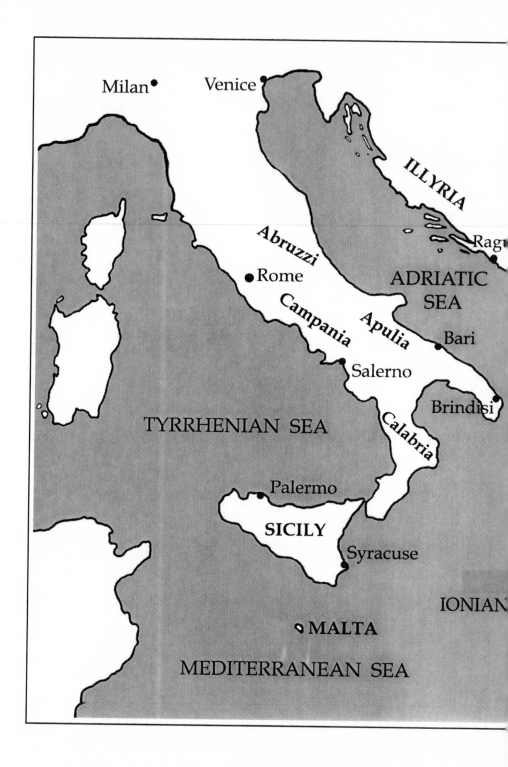

CENTRAL MEDITERRANEAN

MILES

0   100   200

MACEDONIA

THRACE

Dyrrachium

Constantinople •

Orchrid •

Prusa •

Thessaloniki •

Nicaea •

Valona

EPIRUS

Dorylaeum •

Larissa •

AEGEAN SEA

ORFU

ANATOLIA

Athens •

Cephalonia

SEA

CRETE

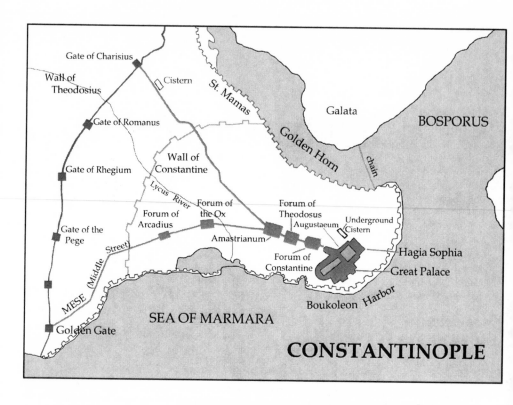

CONSTANTINOPLE

Gate of Charisius
Wall of Theodosius
Cistern
St. Mamas
Galata
BOSPORUS
Gate of Romanus
Golden Horn
chain
Gate of Rhegium
Wall of Constantine
Lycus River
Forum of the Ox
Forum of Theodosus
Forum of Arcadius
Augustaeum
Underground Cistern
Gate of the Pege
Amastrianum
Forum of Constantine
Hagia Sophia
Great Palace
MESE (Middle Street)
Boukoleon Harbor
Golden Gate
SEA OF MARMARA

SICILY

TYRRHENIAN SEA
LIPARI ISLES
Palermo
Messina
Rometta
Erice
Trapani
NEBRODI MOUNTAINS
MONE
VAL
DE
Alcantara River
MT. ETNA
Taormina
Mistretta
Marsala
Troina
Simeto River
Mazara
Enna
Catania
Miles
0   10   20   30
Agrigento
Salso River
CAPE SCROCE
Butera
Syracuse
PANTELLERIA
Noto
MEDITERRANEAN SEA

CASC OF CHARACCERS

VARANGIANS
Bolli Bollason: Icelander, son-in-law of Snorri-godi
Gorm Rolfsson: Swede, brother of Glum the berserker
Halldor Snorrason: Icelander, son of Snorri-godi
Harald Sigurdsson: half-brother to Saint Olaf, later king of Norway
Sveinn Gudleifsson: Commandant of the Varangian Guard
Ulf Ospaksson: a Varangian from Iceland

GREEKS (Members of the Imperial household)
Constantine IX Monomachus: Emperor (1042 – 1055),
    Zoe's third husband
Constantine Paphlagon: a eunuch, Commander in Chief of the army;
    John's brother
George Paphlagon: a eunuch in charge of the Imperial wardrobe; John's
    brother
John Paphlagon: a eunuch, Guardian of Orphans
Maria Paphlagon: sister of John, Constantine, and Michael IV;
    mother of Michael V
Michael IV Paphlagon: Emperor (1034-1041), Zoe's second husband
Michael V Calaphates: Emperor, (1041-1042), son of Maria and Stephen
Romanus III Argyrus: Emperor (1028-1034), Zoe's first husband
Sclerena: mistress of Constantine IX
Stephen: "The Caulker", husband of Maria, father of Michael V
Theodora: former nun, then Empress reigning jointly with Zoe
Zoe Porphyrogenita: Empress (1028-1050), daughter of Constantine VIII

OTHER GREEKS
Alexius: Patriarch of Constantinople
Alypius: a wealthy citizen of Constantinople
Constantine (Michael) Psellus: bureaucrat, historian, orator and teacher
Eustathius: Logothete (minister of the post and foreign affairs)
George Maniakes: general
Loucas: an orphan, one of John's spies

Melampus: an alchemist, father of Selene
Olympia: Psellus's wife
Selene: Odd's wife

RUS

Ingigerd: wife of Grand Prince Yaroslav of Kievan Rus
Stavko Ulanovich: a Rus slave trader
Vladimir Yaroslavich: son of Yaroslav and Ingigerd
Yaroslav Vladimirovich: Grand Prince of Kievan Rus
Yelisaveta Yaroslavna: daughter of Yaroslav and Ingigerd, later wife
of Harald

OTHERS

Arduin: a leader of the Italian Lombards
Gizur Isleifsson: priest, older brother of Teit Isleifsson
Moses the Hawk: Khazar captain of Maniakes's bodyguard
Snorri-godi: powerful Christian Icelandic chieftain, enemy of
Odd's father
Stig No One's Son: vagabond, viking, Odd's mentor
Teit Isleifsson: a young deacon, the recorder of Odd's saga
William de Hauteville: a Norman freebooter

THE BYZANTINE IMPERIAL HOUSE
The Later Macedonian Dynasty (simplified)

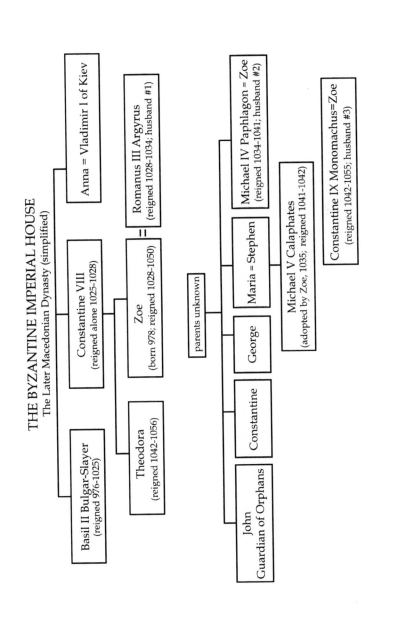

Basil II Bulgar-Slayer
(reigned 976-1025)

Constantine VIII
(reigned alone 1025-1028)

Anna = Vladimir I of Kiev

Theodora
(reigned 1042-1056)

Zoe
(born 978; reigned 1028-1050)

Romanus III Argyrus
(reigned 1028-1034; husband #1)

=

parents unknown

John
Guardian of Orphans

Constantine

George

Maria = Stephen

Michael IV Paphlagon = Zoe
(reigned 1034-1041; husband #2)

Michael V Calaphates
(adopted by Zoe, 1035; reigned 1041-1042)

Constantine IX Monomachus=Zoe
(reigned 1042-1055; husband #3)

PROLOGUE

ICELAND, MOUNT HEKLA
ANNO DOMINI 1080

Here begins the third book in the saga of Odd Tangle-Hair.

A year ago, Bishop Isleif, my father, brought me to this old heathen's tumbledown farmhouse to record his reminiscences of young Prince Harald, who, as all the world knows, became King of Norway and has been dead now for over a decade. Odd served the prince as his skald in Gardariki and in Golden Miklagard when they were both young men. But where Harald went on to a life of glorious conquest and splendid fame, Odd returned years later, penniless and alone, to the ruins of his family home at the foot of this slumbering volcano. (The reason for this is still a mystery to me.) And here he has stayed, speaking to no one until my father dispatched me, much against my will, armed with food, ale, and bundles of parchment to take down the old man's words.

This I have dutifully done, and it has been an education to me, which perhaps my father in his wisdom foresaw. For I have learned that Harald of Norway was not quite the paragon we thought he was, and that Odd Tangle-Hair, for all his violence and blasphemy, is not the monster that he first appeared to my innocent eyes. He has wrapped me in the web of his life—me, the pious young deacon—and opened to me a world I never dreamt of. It has been a long journey and we are not yet at the end of it. But, one grudging step at a time, I have come to feel for this old man—what shall I call it? Is love too strong a word? Of course, I would never say so to him.

Two weeks ago, my elder brother Gizur, who is in charge of the cathedral while our father is away in Rome, tried to drag me home. I went with him but only long enough to replenish my supplies of ink and parchment; of ale, flatbread, and dried fish (for the poor old man lives on practically nothing). My brother gave me an angry stare as I rode away from our hall, leading the pack horses, but he didn't try to stop me. And now here I am again, knocking on the weather-beaten door. And here is Odd, bent, sparse-haired, bleary-eyed because he seldom sleeps, but still powerful in the shoulders; still dangerous if he were pushed. With a grunt he acknowledges me and stands aside. And now, while he drains a horn of ale, and then another, and I spread out my parchment and quills in the dusty half-light, I review in my mind the story so far.

In the autumn of 1031, Odd, after many adventures, gave up the viking life and made his way to Novgorod to join Harald at the court of Prince Yaroslav the Wise and his consort, Princess Ingigerd. It didn't take him long to realize that he had fallen into a snake pit. Ingigerd, a woman of fierce passion, had secretly loved the late King Olaf of Norway and now fostered his little son, Magnus. Olaf had died at the battle of Stiklestad and his younger half-brother Harald, only fifteen then, had barely escaped the carnage and now sought shelter at the Rus court. Prince Yaroslav—elderly, pedantic and oblivious to his wife's feelings—welcomed Harald and honored him with a high position in his druzhina. But Ingigerd saw Harald, quite rightly, as a threat to Magnus, whom she was determined someday to place on his father's throne. To make matters worse, Yaroslav and Ingigerd had a daughter, Yelisaveta, a headstrong, defiant girl, always battling with her mother. Harald made the foolish girl fall in love with him and claimed he would have her to wife one day. This drove Ingigerd wild and she vowed to destroy Harald. The unwitting weapon she chose was young Odd Tangle-Hair. The shameless woman seduced Odd and for two years they carried on an affair right under the noses of Yaroslav and Harald. A foolish and sinful business, but Odd was young and easily beguiled by this beautiful woman. Odd, it seems, always learns his lessons too late. Meanwhile Ingigerd tried one stratagem after another to kill Harald, all without success.

Harald was riding high until suddenly everything collapsed. Magnus was named Olaf's successor by the Norwegian jarls and Odd's affair with Ingigerd was exposed. Harald, feeling understandably betrayed, flung himself on Odd and tried to kill him. Novgorod erupted in civil war. Ingigerd's enemies among the Rus boyars seized this opportunity to attack her, while her Swedish kinsman, Yngvar, and his warriors defended her. Odd was thrown into prison and Harald escaped in the confusion with everything he could steal. In the end, Odd too managed to escape. Taking the identity of Churillo Igorevich, he joined Yngvar's expedition to the East. Sadly, it ended in disaster and Odd spent four bitter years as a slave of the Mohammedans, chained to a Greek sailor. The only good he got of it was that he learned to speak this man's language.

Finally, in 1037, at Kiev, where he was brought by his master, Odd slipped his chain. And who should be in Kiev, Yaroslav's new capital, but Ingigerd, once again securely on her throne and as determined as ever to destroy Harald. For Harald, it appeared, had made his way to Miklagard where he joined the illustrious Varangian Guard. Now, he was sending rich gifts to Yaroslav and love letters to their daughter. Once again, Ingigerd chose Odd as her weapon. He must follow Harald to Byzantium and bring her back his head. And for this she would reward him with enough money to return to Iceland, which he had fled so long ago, to take vengeance on the murderers of his family. Odd agreed and soon he, together with Stavko Ulanovich, a slave-dealer and Ingigerd's agent, were sailing with the Rus trading fleet to the capital of the Roman Empire.

With these words Odd takes up his story...

"Sir, if you keep looking at my eyes instead of the board,
you will never learn a thing.

PART ONE:
CONSTANTINOPLE
AD 1037 - 1038

1

GOLDEN MIKLAGARD

The size of it! The Romans call it Constantinople, Byzantium, New Rome, or simply The City. We Norse call it Miklagard, 'Big Town.' How puny the words seem. As the late afternoon sun broke through the clouds, there lay spread out before me across the sparkling water a sight dazzling to the eyes: a series of rising terraces clothed in alabaster, acres of it—walls, columns, arches, steps, piled one atop the other and everywhere crowned with golden domes, touched to sudden life by the fire from above.

It was all true, those boasts of Leonidas, the Greek sea captain I had spent four years chained to; and I had thought he was a liar or just crazy. But no words could have prepared me for this, just as no words of mine are big enough for it now. The sight of it came like rain to my barren spirit. Curiosity and wonder—feelings I had forgotten I possessed—stirred in me again like seeds in the damp earth. To walk those avenues, to enter those cool marble towers and hear the whisper of silk along their secret corridors...

After weeks of rowing down the Dnieper and across the sea with our cargo of furs, honey, wax, caviar, and hides, the Rus fleet of a hundred river boats flanked by Greek warships, sailed past the twin guard towers and into the Golden Horn—a long, winding inlet, a kind of fjord, that divides the city proper from the hinterland. Our destination was the Harbor of Saint Mamas on the northern shore of the Horn. For only here, according to treaty, were we Rus allowed to camp. I say 'we' because I was one of them now: gospodin Churillo Igorevich of Novgorod; dressed in a fur hat with a red tassel, a long blue coat, wide striped trousers tucked into soft red leather boots, and a pigeon-blood ruby in my ear. From my belt hung a fat purse of gold and in my hand I held a letter from Yaroslav the Wise naming me his boyar and ambassador to the court of his dear 'brother' Michael, Emperor of the Romans. I was empowered to negotiate a marriage for his daughter Yelisaveta—a marvel of beauty, prudence, and affability—with some lucky Greek princeling. Needless to say, all this had been concocted by Ingigerd without 'Wise' Yaroslav being any the wiser. She counted on rumor of my business reaching Harald's ears, wherever he might be, and bringing him out in the open. Then all I had to do was kill him.

All along the quay our boats—dugouts hollowed from a single giant tree trunk—were tying up and unlading in front of a crowd of curious onlookers. The Greeks never tired of watching us—we fearsome, shaggy savages of the North, who three times in their history had attacked them from the sea and nearly captured their city. For this reason, though our trade goods were welcome, we were closely guarded, confined to one region of the city, and disarmed before being allowed ashore.

"Eh? Eh? Odd Tang—excuse me, Chu*rillo*…" Stavko winked hugely, laughed with a spray of saliva, and shook his head so that the lead balls swung at the ends of his greasy braids. The slave trader was to be my guide, my minder, my go-between with Ingigerd. "Eh? Does Stavko exaggerate? You are impressed?"

I wouldn't tell him so. The man gave me the shivers. He clapped me on the shoulder, then quickly pulled back his hand, seeing me wince. "Sorry, gospodin. How is wound?"

We had sailed into a Pecheneg ambush on the river a week ago, and I'd taken an arrow in my right shoulder. It was still plenty sore and I couldn't raise my arm above my head.

"Well, gospodin, I go see to the gifts. Such treasures we are bringing to Emperor! Then we—"

"I say, who's in charge here?" The words were in heavily accented Slavonic. "I'm looking for your, ah, *voi—voivode*." He stumbled over the word for commander. I looked around the crowd to see who had spoken and saw a slender young man—nineteen or twenty, I guessed—pushing his way through the crowd with a couple of soldiers in tow. His skin was olive, his eyes black under heavy brows that met in the middle; his head was round as a nut and covered with short brown bristles that extended downward over his cheeks, chin, and throat. His ears were large. He had a twitchy expression that reminded me of a squirrel. He was clearly some sort of official: his collar, belt, and cape indicated that much, even to a stranger like me.

Vyshata Ostromirovich, who was our commodore, turned round and looked down on the little fellow. "Who by the Devil's mother are you? They send me someone new?"

"Constantine Psellus, sir, Office of Barbarians …"

"Whoever." Vyshata turned away to scream abuse at a couple of sailors who had dropped a cask of mead.

The young man scowled, bounced on the balls of his feet, looked around for someone else to address. Behind his back one soldier grinned at the other. I stepped forward and introduced myself in Greek.

"What? A barbarian speaks our language?" He blinked in surprise.

"I do, sir." (Calling him *kyrios* in Greek, as Leonidas had taught me to do.) "Of a rough sort, anyway. I am Prince Yaroslav's ambassador, come to offer the hand of his daughter to a suitable noble youth."

"What's that? We had no idea, no one told us you were coming."

"I think it was a sudden decision."

He scowled again—to cover his nervousness, I supposed. A junior official suddenly confronted with a situation above his pay grade. "Well, the Logothete must be informed at once and you will accompany me to the hostel, the ambassadors' lodgings."

"Gladly," I smiled and we gripped forearms. For such a small fellow his grip was surprisingly strong. And that is how I met Psellus, who would change my life.

"Have you a man servant?" he asked.

I indicated Piotr, who was standing nearby, with his hair, as usual, in his eyes.

"Then come along both of you." Psellus plunged into the crowd without looking back. It was a characteristic of his that I came to know well: he bustled everywhere as though he were perpetually late for an appointment. *A young man in a hurry,* I thought to myself. He led us to a small boat, very prettily painted, that was tied up some distance down the quay. The rowers raised their oars in salute when they saw us approaching.

"We're crossing the Horn," Psellus called over his shoulder. The hostel is near the Great Palace."

Well, this is progress, thought I to myself. *And how long will it be before I cross swords with Harald?*

Just then a chill wind ruffled the surface of the water and a shiver ran through me. Of excitement—or fear?

2

I AM A BARBARIAN

I opened my eyes at dawn on my first morning in Miklagard, awakened by the cooing of doves outside my window. Young Piotr was already up and laying out my clothes. He was a good lad, lent to me by Ingigerd, of course. Was part of his job to spy on me? Probably.

The ambassadors' hostel was a big stone pile built around a courtyard, and we occupied one small room on the second floor. Other rooms housed a miscellany of men whose clothes and speech alike were foreign to me. I had met a few of them at dinner last night. (Dinner was a skimpy affair of cold lamb, a few limp vegetables, and some vile tasting wine that they call retsina. God knows what they put in it.)

Yesterday, on the way to the hostel, which lay near the Forum of Constantine, Psellus had led me and Piotr at a fast clip down the Mese, the central avenue of the city, where an immense stream of humanity—more people than I had thought lived in all the world together—flowed and eddied through one vast plaza after another. Columns taller than pine trees. Enormous bronze and marble statues so lifelike that they looked as though they might speak. Immense jets of water that shot into the air like the geysers of my homeland and fell back into wide marble basins. My jaw, I'm embarrassed to say, hung open the whole way, while my guide rattled off the names of this and that emperor, this and that saint, at a mile a minute. Psellus, as I was to learn, was an enthusiastic teacher—of anything to anyone—who, in all the years I knew him, never stopped talking except to draw breath.

I was half dressed when Piotr motioned me to sit so he could change the dressing on my wounded shoulder. He had barely begun when our minder knocked upon our door, bustled in without waiting to be invited, and began to speak. "Off to the palace, Gospodin Churillo." (He spoke Greek to me but seemed to take enormous pride in dropping in the occasional Slavonic word.) "Had your breakfast yet? No? Never mind we'll get something from a stall. Mustn't keep the Logothete waiting."

"The log—?"

"*The Logothetes tou dromou.*" He pronounced the words slowly with exaggerated movements of his mouth as if speaking to a child or an idiot. And this was only the first of dozens of unpronounceable titles that I must learn to wrap my tongue around. "Minister of the Post and Foreign Minister all in one," he explained. "His department includes the Interpreters' Bureau and the Office of Barbarians, and a great deal more besides. An important man. My superior." His pride was unmistakable. "He will need to examine your credentials and schedule your audience with the Emperor."

"Barbarians, sir?"

"Yes, well, ah, that is to say, you." He made a wry face and looked slightly uncomfortable.

Leonidas, my fellow slave, had called me that, and always with a sneer. For you must understand that the Greeks divide the world into two halves—themselves and everyone else. And everyone else is *barbaros*. When it was only Leonidas, I could ignore it. Now I was in the midst of a city where the meanest inhabitant might consider me only one rung higher than an ape or a performing bear.

"Come on, then." Psellus was already out the door.

It's a longish walk from the Forum of Constantine to the Brazen Gate—the domed guard house with its three massive bronze gates which forms the entrance to the Great Palace on its landward side. A score of scowling blond warriors clad in scarlet tunics with long-handled axes on their shoulders mounted guard on either side of the entrance. The Varangians! Suddenly my heart was in my mouth. Was he here—the man I must kill? I stared at the impassive, helmeted heads. That tall fellow? Him? No, no, not him.

"Come along, gospodin," Psellus said impatiently and shot me a quizzical look. What did he see in my face? Obediently, I followed him through the vestibule, watched from above by the glittering eyes of two vast faces shaped from bits of shining glass. "Justinian and Theodora," Psellus named them, leaving me to wonder who they were. And then we emerged into the palace grounds.

The *Mega Palation*, the Great Palace of Constantinople. How can I describe it to you, this city within a city? Five square miles of palaces and pavilions linked by lush gardens and tree-lined walks, where exotic plants grew and plumed birds strutted, where more of those astonishing geysers leapt and splashed. Everywhere were guards in gilded armor; everywhere secretaries and messengers hurried on nameless errands; everywhere officials robed in silk swept along, their juniors swimming behind them like schools of brilliantly-colored fish; everywhere the echo of footsteps and a constant susurrus of whispered conversation. We followed a twisting, turning path through this confusion of color and sound—Psellus with chest thrust out and head high, looking neither right nor left and me stumbling along behind, my head on a swivel, trying to see everything at once. The memory flashed through my mind of that long-ago day when, a lonely Iceland farm boy of sixteen, I had gone to the Althing and been astonished by the crowd. You could drop the Althing into a corner of these grounds and never notice it.

We came at last to a two-story building of pink and blue veined marble surrounded by a quiet garden and Psellus ushered me inside. The Logothete's office was spacious but very plain. The walls on three sides were lined with books. On the fourth wall hung cases where butterflies were fixed behind panes of glass. One window was open to the fresh spring air. Behind an ebony desk inlaid with ivory plaques, the Logothete sat, bending to his work. A small man, dressed in a plain brown tunic, he was balding with a great expanse of forehead, a small beard on his chin, fifty years old perhaps. With long delicate fingers he was pinning a large specimen, brilliant with black and orange wings, to a board. Only when he had got it to his satisfaction did he look up. "A beauty isn't it? From my own garden. One of the boys caught it yesterday evening."

Psellus cleared his throat and launched into a preamble little of which I understood. It came as a rude shock that the Greek these educated men spoke to each other was a far cry from the rough sailor's Greek I knew. Psellus had been talking baby talk to me, the barbarian. After a moment, the Logothete waved him to silence and favored me with an inquiring smile. I determined to make the best impression I could and began my carefully rehearsed speech detailing the virtues of the sweet-tempered, affable, and beautiful Princess Yelisaveta (the vicious little bitch!) and how her loving parents, though heartbroken at the thought of parting from her, desired a suitable marriage for her. I drew from my wallet a small painted portrait of her, which considerably softened her needle-sharp nose and chin. The Logothete took it in his long fingers, looked at it a moment and set it down beside the butterfly: two lifeless specimens side by side. I produced also a list of the gifts that would accompany her when the happy day should arrive.

The Logothete looked at me long and hard until I had to lower my eyes. "You're young to be entrusted with such a mission. I wonder they didn't send old Oleg who visits us often." I had a story prepared for this but he didn't give me a chance. "Never mind. Your audience is scheduled for a week from today, although one can never be certain. Sometimes circumstances…" He left the thought unfinished. "Young Psellus here will tell you everything you need to know. I leave you in his capable hands. A pleasure to have met you, gospodin. We'll see each other again, I'm sure. And that leaves only the small matter of the douceur." He used a word I didn't know.

"Excuse me, Excellency?"

"The douceur, the gratuity. Good God, how plainly must I say it, the *gift*."

"Allow me to explain, Excellency," Psellus broke in. "Gifts that open doors, Churillo. Surely you understand. Without a gift nothing happens. It's how things work."

"A bribe!" I exclaimed, using a low word I did know. They both had the grace to look embarrassed. I emptied my purse on the Logothete's desk; I only had some thirty or forty pieces of silver. "If that's not enough I can go back to my rooms."

"This will be quite sufficient," the Logothete said in his precise way. "Thank you."

"And it all goes to you?"

"Not at all. It goes up, it goes down, it spreads itself around. It is the oil that lubricates this great machine. Stay among us long enough, Churillo Igorevich, and you will understand."

"I hope I will."

I felt his eyes on my back as I left the room.

3

The Throne of Solomon

During the week that followed, I saw little of Stavko or any of the other Rus I had traveled with; their days were taken up with buying and selling in the markets. I spent those days in a waking dream. Each morning Piotr and I set out to explore the 'Queen of Cities,' anxiously careful to note landmarks as we went so that we could find our way back to the hostel at night. I can only liken the city to a forest where the trees are columns, the clearings are plazas, the lakes are fountains, the hills are the domes of churches. But here my simile breaks down, for it is not a green forest but a white and golden one—white with dazzling marble, golden with crosses flashing in the sun on the domes of churches. For you must know that Miklagard is a city saturated with religion. Everywhere are churches and monasteries, everywhere hordes of black-robed monks, everywhere holy men, bearded and filthy, clad in sackcloth, hung with chains, squatting on the tops of pillars. Young Piotr bowed and crossed himself at every holy man and priest we encountered, and looked reproachfully at me when I didn't. But he would avert his eyes from those astonishing statues of the old gods, which equally inhabit the city, for he assured me that demons lived inside them.

The city was filled with wonders. In the great square they call the Augusteum is a huge mechanical clock with twenty-four doors around the top which open at the appointed hours. Near it rises a lofty tower, intricately carved, surmounted by the bronze statue of a woman that revolves to show the direction of the wind. Here, too, is the Milion, a great arch above a milestone from which the distance to every city in the empire is measured. On one side of the square is the great domed pile of the Church of the Holy Wisdom, and, stretching away from that, the hippodrome, where a hundred thousand people can gather to watch chariot races and wild beast hunts. Overlooking all, the Emperor Justinian sits astride his horse, a bronze masterpiece so tall herons build nests on his head. Piotr and I spent a whole day in open-mouthed wonder exploring this single square; and it is only one of many.

But Miklagard is also a city of cruel contrasts. On the great thoroughfares noblemen in silk robes ride on Arabian horses and noble women peer out from gilded carriages, street musicians stroll, money-changers sit amidst heaps of coin, the balconied mansions of the rich rise up on either hand, and the porticoes enclose shops that offer delicacies, jewelry, fine stuffs and perfumes from every corner of the world to the dense throngs of plump and well-dressed citizens who pass by. But turn the corner and you are in another world—a world where the poor—so many of them!—live in squalor where the lanes are quagmires of filth, where the corpses of animals and unwanted children lie crawling with worms, heaps of refuse buzz with flies, wild dogs prowl, and beggars reach out bony arms and snatch at your cloak as you pass by. The smell is enough to turn your stomach. Only in my years as a slave had I seen such human misery.

Every day I wandered farther afield: to the edge of the city where the massive walls rise up, to the great harbor on the Bosporus whose soaring lighthouse looks down on the ships plying back and forth between Europe and Asia, and again to the Great Palace where I was soon to make my appearance. The guard was changing at the Brazen Gate—a company of Varangians going off duty and another coming on, looking splendid in their white leggings and scarlet cloaks, marching in step as their officer called the cadence. My fascination with the city these past days had nearly driven Harald from my mind. Now I looked, I stared, but saw no giant Harald towering above the rest—this man I had been ordered to kill, *wanted* to kill because he had foully betrayed me. Was Stavko wrong, then? Was this all a fool's errand after all? Had I come all this way to kill a man who wasn't here?

✝

On the day of the audience, the streets were hung with garlands and strewn with carpets as a jostling crowd of onlookers lined our route to the palace. We three ambassadors—envoys of the Caliph of Cairo, the Lombard prince of Salerno, and myself—rode on white stallions, led by servants in white livery. Behind us trundled wagons loaded with gifts. Vyshata and Stavko and twenty sailors from the Rus trading fleet were on hand to manage ours, which overflowed with marten pelts, casks of honey, and immense candles, enough to light half the churches of the city. Stavko was giving me such winks and oily smiles that I finally had to look away. I'd never been the center of so much attention in all my young life and I confess my heart was thumping. I had hardly slept the night before.

Our destination was the Magnaura, one of many distinct palaces that together make up the Great Palace. It housed the fabled Throne of Solomon, seated on which Michael, Emperor of the Romans, would receive us.

In the forecourt we dismounted and were greeted by the Master of Ceremonies, a handsome man with grey, ringletted hair, his body draped in maroon silk with gold brocade. He led us and our interpreters inside and down a series of vaulted galleries to the gilded doors of the throne room. My two fellow envoys walked at ease beside me, chatting to each other in low voices, looking slightly bored, like men who had been through this before and were no longer impressed. But I—my head swung this way and that, from one wall to another, all of them populated with the glowing images of saints. More than anything it was the faces I couldn't tear my eyes from. The Romans (for this is what the Greeks like to call themselves; I will use both names for them) build these faces from tiny cubes of glass of every hue, thousands of them stuck together, the labor of the endeavor beyond belief. But none of these faces smile. The men especially: pale-skinned, black-bearded, angry, with compressed, down-curving mouths and wide, staring eyes that seem to follow you as you pass by. With a sudden shock of memory, I saw the face of my father, Black Thorvald, on that morning long ago when I found myself looking into his dead, staring eyes. Not a comforting thought.

Then the gilded doors swung open upon the antechamber of the throne room and here was the Logothete. I almost didn't recognize him. I had last seen him dressed in a plain tunic with no ornament, now he was gorgeously robed and wore a gold collar set with pearls around his neck. We bowed deeply to him. He spoke a few words to my two companions through their interpreters and then to me in Greek. "Churillo Igorevich, your gifts are most welcome as is your proposal for the princess's marriage. The Emperor will consider it carefully. Of course, these arrangements are never simple. Psellus tells me that you will address the Emperor in your own words. Admirable. So rare that an envoy troubles to know our tongue. Although in your case I gather the trouble was involuntary."

So he had learned my story from Psellus. I had decided that I would speak in my own voice. Call it showing off, but what is a story-teller if not a performer? At least, so I had thought a few days ago. Since then I had made Psellus coach me until I knew my piece perfectly. Now, as I felt my throat go dry with fear, I wished mightily that I hadn't. Still time to turn it over to Psellus, who was lurking somewhere behind me. But no. I was too proud, or too vain, to give up my chance to address the Emperor. And, as it turned out, much depended on that decision. More than I could have guessed.

"So," said the Logothete, turning away. "I hope you have a good strong voice." I wondered what he meant by that. I would soon find out.

We passed now from the antechamber into the throne room, a stupendous pillared hall of three aisles. Overhead swung huge crystal chandeliers, shedding just enough light for us to find our way but not enough to expose what the Greeks perhaps did not want us to see. As we entered, the courtiers in their various colored costumes, who stood in ranks along the walls, began a rhythmic chanting—the words I could not catch—and, at the same moment, the hall shook to an avalanche of sound, a thundering bass that filled the air all around us and shook up my guts. It was like standing next to some great waterfall. I could not even guess what produced it. Then the curtains parted and I saw the Emperor, a small figure at a distance of some seventy paces, seated on a dais, flanked by the ax-bearing Varangians. And what I will tell now, I don't expect anyone to believe, but it is the truth: on either side of the dais were great golden lions that opened their mouths and roared and beat the ground with their tails and also a golden tree upon which tiny golden birds chirped and moved their wings. I turned with a questioning look to

Psellus, who had come to stand beside me. Nothing he'd told me ahead of time had prepared me for this.

The Master of Ceremonies touched the shoulder of the Saracen ambassador and led him forward. At three places, where there were discs of purple marble set into the paving stones, the man threw himself flat on his face and groveled. Then the curtain closed around him, leaving him face to face with the Emperor. And all the time, the courtiers kept up their chanting, those indescribable musical notes rumbled through the hall, the lions roared and the birds sang. After some minutes, during which I felt a peculiar vibration in the floor beneath my feet, the curtains parted, the ambassador of the Caliph returned to his place and the whole thing was repeated with the ambassador of the Prince of Salerno.

And then it was my turn.

If any Icelander ever hears this history of mine, I beg him to forgive me. Our little country has not even a king, let alone an emperor who claims to speak with the voice of God. But you must understand what was at stake. I had come to kill my enemy, and if this was what I must do to accomplish that, then I would do it and gladly. So, yes, I threw myself down on those purple discs—clumsily—groveled with my face pressed against that cold marble and all the time imagined my father, my dead brother, my old crewmen from the Viper hooting and laughing at me. Now I was at the foot of the dais, close enough to feel the rush of air from the lions' mouths and see the sapphires in the eyes of the golden birds. To one side was an extraordinary contraption of golden pipes and levers, with four men laboring at it, from which the music poured, and directly in front of me was Michael, Emperor of the Romans, seated on his throne, almost near enough to touch. He was not an old man—I'd been told he was still in his twenties—and his features were well-formed. But his color was sickly and his eyes, filmy and unfocussed, looked listlessly out into the middle distance. On his head was a diadem with pearl pendants that hung over his ears. His body was swathed in some indescribable wrapping of gold brocade crusted with sapphires and rubies that looked as if it could stand by itself, and his boots were of purple leather sewn with pearls. His hands were jeweled to the fingertips. Motionless, expressionless, vacant-eyed, he seemed hardly a living man at all.

One last time, the Master of Ceremonies forced me onto my belly while in a loud voice, pitched above all the roaring and rumbling, he announced me. And then—and I know no one will believe this but I swear it is true—he tapped me on the back with his staff, and I looked up and up and up. And the Throne of Solomon was floating, unsupported, near the ceiling, twenty feet above my head. The man's lips curved in a little smile. How many times, I suppose, he had watched barbarian simpletons like me astonished by this magic. But was it magic? Could this Emperor truly command the power of a god greater than Black-Browed Odin and all the rest of them put together? What else could I think? But no, no, a small voice inside me said. No. There is a trick to it. I looked hard and could see no ropes or chains—nothing. But *something moves it*, I told myself, and if I live long enough I may learn its secret.

"You may address His Majesty," the Master of Ceremonies commanded.

I backed away until I was touching the curtain and could, at that angle, at least see the Emperor's distant face. And in my loudest voice I bellowed my little speech in Greek, garbling it, forgetting half of it. After a few moments of this sorry performance, the Master of Ceremonies motioned me to silence and led me out.

4

AN UNEXPECTED VISITOR

That night I sat in my room downing a jug of wine while young Piotr snored in a corner. Images of this extraordinary day swirled in my mind, but there was no particular direction to my thoughts. The excitement had worn off, leaving me depressed. Psellus had disappeared after the audience. Stavko and some of his mates had taken me to their lodgings in Saint Mamas for dinner. It was meant to be a celebration, but I wasn't in the mood for it—what was there to celebrate, after all?—and soon excused myself. I was just thinking about going to sleep when there came a blow upon my door like a battering ram. The door flew open and there stood Harald. His huge bulk filled the door frame. Gods, he was even bigger than I remembered! He must have grown another two inches, and was deeper in the chest. He towered head and shoulders over me. His height was what you always noticed about him first. From the time I first saw him as a fifteen-year-old at the Battle of Stiklestad, he was taller than anyone else around, a child who looked like a grown man and was expected to behave like one. It had shaped his character, made him a bully and a braggart. What was he now, twenty-three? Two years younger than me. He looked a lot older. His long yellow mustaches hung to his chest like walrus tusks.

And he was in a rage.

"I knew it was you, Tangle-Hair, no mistaking that ugly face. Why have you taken a new name? What is all this about?" He thrust himself inside, stooping under the lintel.

"You!" I took a step backward, my hand on my dagger hilt. I could hardly breathe.

"What, didn't see me there, standing right by the throne? Well, you had a lot to distract you. You like their little tricks? Oh, the Greeks are full of tricks." He laughed harshly.

All I could think of to say at that moment was, "How does it fly?"

He blinked in surprise. "What, the throne? How the devil should I know? Who cares how it flies? That's not what I'm here to talk about." His voice was thick with drink and anger. Piotr woke up with a cry and was trying to make himself small in the corner. Harald banged a fist on my table, making the cups jump. "Sit down, Tangle-Hair." He sat himself down opposite me and glowered. "Ambassador from Yaroslav? Liar! I've paid that old fool too well, he wouldn't betray me. No, I smell the wife here. Inge sent you, didn't she? To barter away my *bride*—and what else? *Kill* me? By God, of course! That's why you're here. Well, here I am. You'll never have a better chance." He leveled his stone-gray eyes at me. "Shall we fight now? Or what did you have in mind? A knife in the back? An arrow through the window? Or poison? Come now, that's not your style, Tangle-Hair, I know you too well, you're no assassin. And you deserve a better mistress than Ingigerd."

While he talked my thoughts raced. *If I fight him now, with my shoulder almost useless, he'll kill me for sure, and I'll join my dead ones in Hel with my vengeance untaken. No, I must wait. I must plan. In the meantime, I must speak softly and think how I will kill him. But am I an assassin truly, a snake that crawls on its belly and strikes from cover?* Suddenly I didn't like the feeling.

He brought his face close to mine and studied me as though he was reading my thoughts. He took a deep breath through his nostrils. "How does Inge know about me?"

I explained about the Norseman who was traveling in our convoy from Novgorod, posing as a merchant. How Stavko had recognized him as the one who had brought a casket of gems to Yaroslav and a bundle of letters addressed to Yelisaveta, which he had mistakenly given to Ingigerd instead. Which was why I was here now.

"Ulf, that idiot," Harald snarled. "I'll have the balls off him! And how much has she paid you to kill me? Not enough, I'm sure."

She had promised me five thousand *grivny*, enough to send me home to Iceland a rich man, in exchange for Harald's head pickled in a barrel. I shrugged and said nothing.

He stroked his mustaches and smiled sourly. "I've never understood why that woman hates me, prefers sniveling Magnus to me just because he was King Olaf's bastard and I only the half-brother. But you don't hate me do you, Tangle-Hair? I mean why should you? Old comrades like us!" He slapped the table.

It seemed that he had forgotten, or wanted to pretend he'd forgotten, how he had given me up to be tortured at the bishop's tribunal. How typical.

"Well, goddammit, if we aren't going to draw our swords right now, let's have a drink." He helped himself to the jug, swirled the wine in his mouth and spat it out on the floor. "How do you drink this piss? Look, dine with me tomorrow in our barracks. The provender's better than what you're getting here. And we've got women, too—Greek, Armenian, African, whatever's your pleasure. Hah! I expect it's been a while since you've plowed Ingigerd's furrow. How was she in bed, Tangle-Hair? I always wondered. Give you orders? Touch me here, kiss me there? Ha, ha."

I said nothing. He wasn't actually so far off the mark.

"Come, Tangle-Hair, let us be friends again. I don't want us to fight." Now he looked at me narrowly. "I heard you speak Greek today. Very impressive. I can't get my tongue around the filthy language any more than I could Slavonic. I needed you then—before you decided to take up with Inge, that is. I might need you again. Odd, you can't imagine how much wealth there is here, ripe for the taking, and I am going to take as much as I can, and if you don't do the same, you're a fool. Money! Money's the thing. Being the half-brother of a king means nothing if I have no gold to buy allegiance. Money will buy me fair Yelisaveta. Money will buy me Norway."

"You were always greedy, Harald."

He laughed again. "I make no bones of it. I know my worth down to the last silver penny. Any man who doesn't is an ass." Despite not liking my wine, he poured himself some more and watched me over the rim of the cup. We were both silent for a moment. Then, "Your hands," he said. He grabbed my wrist and pushed up my sleeve. "Damn me, where have you been and had that done? All this just to pose as a Rus? Well, you'll be right at home with the Varangians, they all have 'em. Don't care for it myself." He was looking at the tattoos, the intricate whorls and spirals that Lyudmila, Putscha's mother, had decorated me with when she gave me her husband's clothes and his name—Churillo Igorevich.

I took my arm back. "I, too, had to escape," I said. "I joined up with Yngvar and his Swedes. We fared eastwards into Serkland. It ended badly. I was—"

He waved his hand dismissively. "Sad, no doubt. Water over the dam."

Harald was never interested in anyone else's story. *Well, I thought, let's hear his; I'm sure it's a good one.* I asked him how he came to be here.

"Don't mind telling you," he grinned. He took another drink. "After that small civil war we had, when you were tossed in prison—didn't like to do that to you, Tangle-Hair, but, damn me, what choice did I have? And it was you who betrayed me first, you know. Anyway, glad to see you escaped, you're a clever bastard, always said so. Well anyway, with Ingigerd back in control of things—the damned woman has more lives than a cat—well, I needed to get away, didn't I? No friends left in Novgorod. I mean I could hardly go back to Yaroslav after calling his wife a whore, not right away anyhow. So I collected a few druzhiniks who were willing to throw in with me, we stole some horses, took whatever loose cash we found in the barracks—I suppose some of it might've been yours—and looted a couple of the boyars' houses too. With the city ablaze, no one paid us any mind. Then we took off for deep woods. That was an adventure! We were in that stinking forest for weeks, working our way south, avoiding the towns where my name might be known, breaking into farmhouses when we needed food. Gangs of brigands joined up with us along the way—forest is thick with 'em—and before long I commanded a small army of desperate men. And then there was the steppe to cross and bands of Pechenegs on the prowl. Oh, how they would've loved to get their hands on me, who carved their high chief in half with an ax. Thanks be to God and His Mother, we avoided 'em. But it was a tiresome long way we had to go to reach the sea. Broiling in the sun by day, freezing at night, our clothes turning to rags. Had to toss away most of the silver we'd stolen. Horses all eaten up by ourselves or the wolves. Finally, we reached the coast near Kherson. With the little money we had left, I bought us new clothes and presented myself to the governor of the place, calling myself Nordbrigt, Prince of Norway. From then on things improved. The governor signed us on as marines to protect a merchant convoy bound for Miklagard, even gave me a letter of introduction to George Maniakes, the general, who was on his way to retake Edessa from the Saracens. I don't like to brag, you know me, but before long I was promoted captain of a bandon—a company—and had gathered enough loot to pay for my commission in the Varangians, which isn't cheap, I can tell you. After that, why, they sent me to Jerusalem, escorting a team of masons to restore the Church of the Holy Sepulcher there. I bathed in the Jordan, Tangle-Hair, though I don't expect a heathen like you to care about that, and came back with a shipload of relics that I sold for a fortune. And that just about brings us to the present."

I'm sure most of this was true. Say what you want about Harald, there was never a better soldier. "And those druzhiniks who escaped with you," I asked, "are they in the Guard too?"

Harald shrugged. "Some got killed, some drifted away. They weren't worth much; I soon parted company with them." He pushed his hair aside and showed me a long, wine-colored scar on his forehead. "Saracen *ghazi* cut me with his saber, fighting around Edessa. I broke his neck. Scars—I've got quite a collection. He leaned toward me, peering. "You seem to have come through life with a whole skin."

This made me even angrier. "They're on my back, Harald. A slaver's lash."

"But none in battle?"

I would not mention my wounded shoulder: never show an enemy your weakness. "I've been lucky," I said.

He threw back his head and laughed. "Luck's a great thing, may it never fail you, Odd Tangle-Hair." He stood up suddenly. "Until tomorrow. Our barracks is in Saint Mamas. Get one of your Rus friends to show you the way. We have some Icelanders in the Guard, good fighters and good poets, except for Ulf, that is, who's a blockhead. You'll want to meet 'em. And after that, if you've still a mind to kill me ... well, we'll see."

And with that he was gone.

I sat staring at the empty doorway. I wanted to get drunk, but Harald had drained the jug. In a sudden fit of rage I flung it against the wall with all my strength. Pieces flew everywhere. Piotr, crouching in his corner, cried out in fear. I went over and stroked the boy's head, then threw myself down and wrapped myself in my covers. My brain teemed. Did I still hate Harald? Yes, with a cold anger. He would not even admit that he had wronged me and ask my pardon. But could I kill him with honor—or at all—surrounded by all his men? How simple it had sounded when I was a thousand versts away. Well, I would have to accept his invitation to dinner and see what I was up against. The old proverb came to my mind: The foolish man lies awake all night thinking of his problems. When the morning comes he is worn out, and his problems are still there.

But sleep wouldn't come.

5

my past
overtakes me

Towards dawn I fell asleep and dreamt: my brother Gunnar and I up at the shieling in the sheep pasture, slaughtered sheep everywhere, huge white masses, gushing blood, and my sister Gudrun screaming and screaming, men without faces surrounding her as she lay helpless in the grass as I try to run toward her, my legs like lead, not moving. Too late. Too late. And now her screams become the screams of little Ainikki, the girl from Kalevala whom I loved. Too late. Again too late! Her savaged head on a stake, and next to it, it seems to me, my mother's head. How can that be? And then our house—the walls a mass of flame, the roof exploding, my mother's hair afire, my brother bleeding out his life on the floor. And me running, running. *Run away Odd, run!* That's what you always do. The voice of my father. I turn and draw my sword. And a huge warrior charges at me out of the smoke. Harald! I strike at him but my arm is boneless, my blade slides away, useless, as he throws back his head and laughs at me.

I wrenched myself awake and lay gasping for breath, the sweat pouring from me. Piotr was watching me from his corner, his eyes like saucers; I must have cried out in my sleep. After that, the hours crept by. I sat with my arms around my knees, rocking back and forth, unable to shake off the feeling of despair that my dream had stirred in me. It was Midsummer's Day, warm and sunny, with people carousing in the streets, dancing and jumping over bonfires. I let Piotr go out and enjoy himself while I sat alone at the window until I couldn't stand it anymore. Our room was beginning to feel like a prison. There was no one else at the hostel I shared a language with. At last, I dressed and went out to look for Stavko.

After wandering about for half the day I finally found him in the big, crowded slave market near Saint Mamas harbor: touching the women, fondling them, haggling over prices.

"Odd Tang ... Churillo, I mean, Churillo, over here." Chuckling and spitting, he folded me in a woolly bear hug and kissed my cheeks. So good to see you. Ah. The Imperial audience. What excitement! And what have you been doing since then?" His eyes narrowed. "You have seen Harald maybe?"

"I've seen him. Last night. He came looking for me at the hostel."

"So our little plan is working, eh? We draw him into the open, we cut off his head!" He chopped the air with his arm and grinned wetly.

"Stavko, I'm not sure I can."

"Eh? I can't hear you, too noisy here. Come with me, we'll drink some wine." I followed him to a wine shop nearby; it was nearly empty at that time of day. "Now what do you mean you can't?" Dismay, reproach in his little slivers of eyes.

"He's too well protected. You were right, he's a Varangian Guardsman, a captain of a company, no less. How am I to get at him? I'll be cut to pieces before I get close."

He leaned back from the table and fingered his scrappy beard. "There are always ways, my friend. We'll hire cutthroats, ambush him somewhere."

"No. no, not like that."

He made a noise with his lips. "This is no time for scruples, Churillo. Listen to me. If you don't kill him, Ingigerd won't give up. She will send someone else, keep trying until finally someone succeeds, but you won't have your reward, which, I remind you, is a big one. You want to go home before enemies of your family die of old age, yes? Then we must think. Where can you meet him again?"

"I'm invited to their barracks tonight."

"Excellent! You scout them out, eh?"

"I suppose so. Tell me about these Varangians, Stavko. Who are they, how many?"

He took a drink and drew his sleeve across his lips. "Vladimir the Great, Yaroslav's father, after he converted to True Faith, gave present of six thousand mercenaries, all Rus and Northmen—mostly Swedes—to Emperor Basil Bulgar-Slayer. Many years ago this was."

"Six *thousand?*"

"Oh, but not so many nowadays. Five or six hundred, I think. Not everyone can join. Very expensive. 'Emperor's Wineskins' they are called. Pampered. Better paid than regular troops. Wherever Emperor goes, they go too. Stand closest to his throne. They are divided into six banda of about one hundred men. One bandon a week does sentry duty in palace and sleeps at Brazen Gate. Others stay in barracks here in Saint Mamas, not far from us, living like kings, so people say. And young Harald already commands a bandon? Not bad." He made a face.

"Who commands the whole Guard?"

"The Commandant is Swede named Sveinn Gudleifsson. Old, fat, rich, doesn't stir himself much anymore but has powerful friends. No one goes up against him."

"And, knowing Harald, he's planning to step into Sveinn's shoes. Maybe there's something here we can use."

"Exactly! See? You are thinking." Stavko reached across and punched my shoulder encouragingly. The wounded one. "Ach, sorry! Look, drink up. Time for you to go visit Varangians. I show you the way."

✝

The barracks was a looming three-story building with an iron fence around it that filled a whole city block. We could hear the sounds of a carouse in full-swing before we even turned the corner.

"I leave you here," said Stavko, "and I go to church now and pray to all the saints for you."

I didn't find this remark as encouraging as he meant it to be. I gave my name to the sentry, who led me up a broad staircase to the second floor and down a corridor. Along the way, we passed dormitories, where the men lived ten to a room and slept two to a bed, and an enormous, smoky kitchen. The dining hall—what can I compare it to? Like the hall of some powerful chieftain at home, only twice the size and made of marble instead of timber and thatch. Long trestle tables occupied the middle of it; shields, axes and banners hung on the walls. But it was a pigsty. Puddles of wine on the floor, dogs snarling over bones, servants running back and forth with steaming platters and bowls. Dozens of the Emperor's Wineskins (plainly the name was well-earned) drinking, laughing, shouting; some of them already passed out. And not only the men. There were a fair number of women, all seeming as drunk as their menfolk and a few of them half-naked. The din was enormous.

And in their midst, Harald, a head taller than all the rest—just raising a goblet to his lips when he saw me come through the door.

"Churillo." He waved me over. "Clear a space here." He shoved a sleeping man off the bench beside him. "Sit down. Pour yourself something to drink. Churillo, these are my men, the Fourth Bandon." He took in half the room with a sweep of his arm. "Mates, this is Ambassador Churillo Igor—Ig—what was it?" Then he laughed and shook his head. "Damn me, I'm not the smooth liar that you are, Odd, I can't carry it off. Never mind, your secret's safe with us. We don't talk to the Greeks and they don't talk to us, except to give us orders. My friends, meet Odd Thorvaldsson, known as 'Tangle-Hair', which just look at that shaggy head of his and you'll see why. Known each other for ages, Odd and me. A fine poet and a good friend, served with me at old Yaroslav's court. Odd, say hello to my men—Norwegians, Swedes, Danes, Rus, and a few Icelanders like yourself. Maybe you know some of these lads from home? Halldor, Bolli? Or Ulf?"

Indeed, I did recognize Ulf, though I shook my head, no. Stavko had pointed him out to me on our journey down the Dnieper. Young Ulf, I was to learn, was not overly bright but had a doglike loyalty to Harald. And he looked hangdog at the moment; Harald had obviously berated him for his recent stupidity.

"Pleased to meet you," Ulf muttered, gazing at me from under beetling brows.

"Thorvaldsson, you say? Where from in Iceland?" This was the man called Halldor, suddenly leaning forward and putting his face close to mine.

"From the South Quarter," I answered. "Rangriver under Hekla."

"Black Thorvald's son? The heathen? Christ, with those dark looks you must be."

My skin went cold. "And you, friend?" I said in a low voice.

"No friend of yours. I am Halldor of Helgafel, son of Snorri-godi. And this," he touched the man sitting beside him, a short, balding man with a pointed beard, "is Bolli Bollason, his son-in-law."

Before the thought even formed in my brain, I pulled my knife and climbed across the table to get at him, knocking cups and plates everywhere. I heard the howl of a wild animal in my ears: it was me. We rolled over on the floor, clawing at each other while men jumped out of our way, giving us room. Bolli hit me from behind with something heavy and dragged me off Halldor but I brought my elbow back in his face and he staggered away streaming blood from his nose. Then Halldor was up and had his sword out. I had no sword—the Greeks don't let foreigners carry arms in the city—but I picked up a bench to protect myself. He slashed, hacking off a leg of it, slashed again making splinters fly, while I backed up step by step. Wielding his sword with two hands, he swung low, missing my leg by a whisker. He drew back for another blow, which might have killed me when suddenly Harald stood between us. Halldor was a strong man but Harald seized his wrist and twisted it until he cried out and dropped his sword. I, in my frenzy, threw down the bench and ran in again with my knife but Harald's long arm shot out, and delivered a blow to my chest that sent me staggering back. Two of his men grabbed me from behind, threw me down and sat on me, as I cursed and screamed.

"Enough!" Harald roared. "Tangle-Hair, you troll, have you gone clean out of your mind?"

My chest was heaving, tears of rage filled my eyes, blood pounded in my temples. Halldor, panting, glared at me with murder in his eyes, but he obeyed when Harald ordered him to back away.

"What's this all this about?" Harald demanded.

Between sobs of breath I tried to explain. Back in Gardariki I'd never said much to him about my past and he, caring nothing for anyone's problems but his own, had never asked me. But now I told him how Strife-Hrut Ivarsson and his men had raped and murdered my sister, Gudrun Night-Sun, and how I had killed one of his sons in revenge. How Hrut had retaliated by charging my brother Gunnar and me with murder at the Althing, and was backed up in his suit by the powerful Snorri of Helgafel, a man who hated my father because he would not turn Christman when all the other Iceland chieftains did. How they won a verdict of banishment against us and then, before we could even leave the country, came to burn us out—and Snorri was there to watch it, oh yes, though he tried to hide himself. And only I lived to get away and now my dead ones waited in Hel for the day when I would avenge them. This day!

Meanwhile, Halldor and Bolli kept screaming, "Liar! Burn you out? Snorri couldn't be bothered to piss on you, you heathen filth, you devil's child. You deserved what you got."

Harald rounded on them angrily. "Stop it, the both of you. That is an order. You too, Odd. Let Iceland feuds stay in Iceland. Kill each other at home if you want to, not here."

"He'll go for us again," Halldor shot back. "You see what he's like. You can order us but you can't order him."

"Let go of him," Harald told the men who were holding me down. He squatted down beside me and laid a heavy hand on my shoulder, where blood was seeping through my tunic. "What's this, did Halldor do this? Goddammit, if there's blood drawn then I don't know what to—"

"Pecheneg arrow, two weeks ago. It went deep."

"And you thought you wouldn't mention that to me?"

"Never tell an enemy your weakness."

"And I'm your enemy, is that is?" He shook his head. "I'll have one of our surgeons look at it, they know their business. Tangle-Hair, I don't know if you're brave or just stupid. D'you understand that you're alone here, friendless, no comrades at your back. Halldor and Bolli are tough men, and so are Ulf and Kolskegg and Mar and the other Icelanders here, who probably don't like your family either. Someday, if the Norns will it, you'll settle scores with them, but right now you're of no use to me dead and perhaps very useful alive. You think I can't tell you what to do? One word from me to the Logothete that you're not who you say you are and you're liable to find yourself in a dungeon cell. Your trouble, Tangle-Hair, is that you want to kill everyone. Choose your enemies more carefully. Promise me you'll let this business go." He looked at me hard. "By Christ, I know what it feels like to want to kill a man you hate. But sometimes you have to wait. Come now, I want your word on it."

I nodded. It was the most I could do.

"Now then, if we can all behave ourselves," he looked around the room and met everyone's eye, "we'll forget this little unpleasantness and have dinner."

Well, he was right, I suppose. And this wasn't my finest hour.

The food was good, as promised, although still strange-tasting to my palate; a casserole of meat, cheese and vegetables doused with fish sauce and pungent spices. Halldor and Bolli stalked off and sat at another table, surrounded by their mates. Every now and then I saw them looking in my direction. "What exactly am I useful for?" I asked Harald.

"That's for another time. One thing you learn in this fucking city is to watch what you say within four walls; someone's always listening. In the meantime, you go on playing the ambassador as long as Inge's paying you. I don't mind. Let her wait and wonder and stew. Yelisaveta will marry me when I'm ready to take her to Norway and claim my throne. Nothing you do will change that."

"Why go back at all?" I looked around at all this luxury. "What has Norway got to compare with all this? Let little Magnus have it. You're already a captain, you say you've got plenty of money. What else do you want?"

"You only see a part of it, Tangle-Hair," he said with a frown. "Endless hours of sentry duty in that mausoleum of a palace. Months, years can go by between campaigns. The Greeks are insufferable, they despise us and don't make a secret of it though we spill our blood for them. Little things start to bother you: no beer, no butter, everything tastes of olive oil—I hate the filthy stuff." This was a rather different story than he'd told me last night. "Still," he went on, "there are plenty who do spend their whole lives in the Guard—and you know what happens to them at last? When they're too old and too crippled to serve anymore and they've squandered all their money they're thrown out in the street to beg. That's not for me. The smart ones go home while they can still walk and chew their food, and they live like kings. And I will not only live like a king, I will *be* a king."

"Then go home now. What keeps you here?"

"No, not yet. I'm not nearly as rich as I aim to be."

"And what will make you so rich?"

"As I said, we'll talk again when we're alone. Need you—make you rich. You're a good fellow, Odd. Need someone I can trust." He was drinking deeply, his tongue was loosening.

"You don't trust your Varangians?"

"Of course I do. Trust 'em with my life, but they don't see farther than the tips of their noses. Haven't got your wits."

I didn't like where this conversation was heading. I had come to kill Harald, not become his cat's paw again in some mad and dangerous scheme. And now I had Halldor and Bolli to worry about too. I didn't doubt they'd try to kill me if they saw their chance. I needed to go away and think. At that moment a pretty young woman, naked to the waist, pushed between us and sat on Harald's lap. "You don't pay no attention to me," she pouted.

He bounced her tits in his hands and kissed her neck. "Tangle-hair, you want a girl? Help yourself."

I shook my head. "I'll say goodnight now."

"Heh? So soon? Go on, then. We'll talk again." With that, he buried his face in the hollow of the girl's neck and made her squeal.

By this time the crowd in the hall had grown less, as men staggered off to their sleeping quarters with their arms around their women, or just slumped over where they sat. I was fastening my cloak around me when a Varangian tapped my shoulder. "A moment of your time, friend?" he said. (Where had I heard that shy, husky whisper before?) "I thought I heard Harald say you fought with his army at Stiklestad? And I just wondered if maybe you knew my brother."

I looked at him closer. By the raven! The resemblance was uncanny. The same thick neck and massive shoulders; the same broad, meaty face, with a bow of a mouth, and yet the eyes, bright blue and cheerful, lacked that haunted, animal look I remembered so well. "He went off with King Olaf's army when they marched through Sweden—six, seven years ago— and we never heard from him again. Finally, our old father put up a stone with his name on it."

"Glum?"

"The same. You knew him, then! I'm Gorm—Gorm Rolfsson, his older brother." He gave me an open, cheerful smile, in which his two front teeth were missing.

I gripped his arm. "How glad I am to meet you. Who would've thought—yes, he served aboard my ship. He's dead, I'm sorry to tell you. Struck by lightning in a storm while he howled and brandished his ax. What a fighter he was. I say, you aren't ... I mean—"

"A berserker? No," Gorm smiled apologetically, "Odin's spear touched only him. Just as well, too. No family could afford two of those. The blood money we had to pay for his killings just about ruined us, and we weren't very popular with our neighbors. That's why he left when he got the chance. Dead, you say? But feasting and fighting now in One-Eyed Odin's great hall. Well, it's a relief to know it. He was always more suited to Asgard than to Midgard."

"You talk like a believer in the old gods, friend Gorm."

He lowered his voice. "A lot of us Swedes still are, though we keep quiet about it. A word of warning to you: it don't suit to have Odin too much in your mouth here."

"I'll remember it. And what is your own story, Gorm?"

"Oh, I'm one of six brothers—well, five after Glum left home—but still too many of us to divide up our father's little farm. Like Glum, I had the wanderlust and so I joined up with some other fellows of the district, some of them are here now—Eystein, Thorir, Ermund, Ingimund, and some others—and we fared East to seek our fortunes, following the Varangian Way, first to Gardariki and then to Miklagard, like yourself. And we've done well, those of us who are still alive. There's plenty of silver for the taking here if you have a strong arm."

"And Harald's your captain?"

"He is. He's a good man in a fight and he looks after us well. But as for all his airs and boasting about how he's the rightful king of Norway and he's going to marry a princess of Rus, well we're all sick and tired of hearing about that. And there are plenty of the older men who resent how fast he's risen in rank and grumble that someone higher up is doing him favors, though we don't really know."

"The Icelanders support him?"

"They're Christmen. Take it pretty seriously, some of them, like Halldor. And Harald is always going on about how his half-brother's practically a saint. But that cuts no ice with Swedes or Danes."

"And Norwegians in the Guard?"

"Not very many altogether. Three or four in the Fourth Bandon, which is us, and they don't seem to care much for Harald."

"Interesting."

He looked into my eyes. "Odd Thorvaldsson, you were a friend to Glum. Let me be your friend. If you stay here long you will need one."

"With all my heart, friend Gorm."

I left the Varangians' hall with my head in a whirl of emotions. To have come so close to taking vengeance for my slaughtered family and then to have it snatched away. And then to meet Glum's brother here at the ends of the earth. And what memories that brought back! Stig and Kalf Slender-Leg and Einar Tree-Foot and all the rest of them, sailing away in our own ship bound for the viking life. Never mind that it ended in disaster. And all of them dead or vanished. Would I ever see them again? And what should I do now? Harald was right; I had too many enemies, and maybe Harald not the worst of them. My brain grew weary just thinking about it. I wandered back to the hostel through streets still thronged with revelers and drank until I passed out.

6

A VISIT TO THE PERFUMERY

I had fallen asleep in a state of weary confusion. I awoke to one of the most remarkable days of my life. I opened my eyes to find an old man bending over me, prodding me to wakefulness with a bony hand. He was richly dressed in a long, silk caftan with pearls at the collar and cuffs. A dry brown leaf of a man, his skin was the color of tallow and infinitely wrinkled, and his chin was hairless. I had learned by now to recognize such creatures as eunuchs—half men. (I will tell more about them in another place.) Seeing me wake, he introduced himself as Sgouritzes, an attendant of the Sacred Bedchamber of the Empress Zoe. He produced from his sleeve a scroll of purple vellum covered with writing in silver ink and, in a piping voice, read that I was requested to call upon the Empress this morning in her apartment in the Daphne palace. Groggy and ill-tempered as I was, it took Sgouritzes and Piotr between them to get me washed and dressed and fed to where I looked presentable and felt almost human.

The Daphne is the heart of the Great Palace, reached by paths that wind endlessly through gardens and pavilions, watered by fountains and shaded by poplars. It is a lovely building where the Emperor and Empress each keep a suite of rooms. Few outsiders ever see it. The mosaics that cover its walls and floors are not the pained faces of saints but rather fields of flowers bursting with color, and scenes of hunting and of children playing. But the closer we got to the Empress's rooms the stronger grew the smell—heavy, cloying, sweet, almost physically sticky, hanging in the air like a fine mist of honey. The eunuch smiled at me with a look of anticipation—an aged grandparent taking a child to see some secret treat. Two beardless guards flanked the silver-paneled door. They stood aside for us and we entered upon a scene indescribably bizarre. It was a huge room, dimly lit, and filled with steaming copper cauldrons sitting on charcoal braziers, each one big enough to boil a sheep in. The heat hit me like a blast from an oven, the air was unbreathable. Men and women, dripping with sweat, stirred these cauldrons while others ladled out the content—some of it amber-colored and thin, some of it white and viscous—sniffed it or rubbed it between their fingertips, and either poured it back or took it to a long table where other workers decanted it into little flasks, careful not to waste a drop. Still others sealed the flasks with glass stoppers and melted wax and attached labels to them. Over our head hung baskets and bunches of dried herbs and flowers. One of the women set aside her ladle and turned toward us. She was plump, short, aged about forty, I guessed, with a generous bosom. Her brown eyes were large and set wide apart, her skin was as smooth as a ripe apricot, and her blonde hair hung in damp tendrils on her neck. She drew a sleeve across heavy eyebrows of dark gold. She wore only a sheer cotton shift that clung to her body. I found myself staring at her nipples. Sgouritzes dropped to his ancient knees and touched his forehead to the floor. I did the same.

"Please," she said in a voice that sounded like a little girl's. "We're quite informal here, as you see. Do stand up."

"Majesty, I present Ambassador Churillo Igorevich who—"

"I know who he is. Thank you, Sgouritzes, you may withdraw."

With an expression that looked like relief, the eunuch bowed himself out.

"And what do you think of our factory, ambassador? Back to work, everyone." She clapped her hands. (They had all stopped momentarily to look at me.) "Spikenard," she said, taking a bunch of some dried stuff and dropping it into one of the cauldrons, "and aloes and attar of roses and musk and cassia. Do you like it?"

A memory flashed through my mind. The first day that I visited Princess Ingigerd in Novgorod she had opened a tiny bottle and flooded her bedroom with the scent of roses: my first experience of perfume. That little bottle seemed like a priceless treasure—and probably was. But here were vats, oceans of the stuff. It was too much to take in.

"Why?" I stammered. "What is it all for? Do you sell it?"

"Certainly not." There was amusement in the eyes. "I worship God with sweet-smelling perfumes and unguents. They drive away evil spirits, you know. And I apply them to my person, why shouldn't I? Suddenly, she was uncomfortably close to me. She took my hand and held it under her chin. Her flesh had an unnaturally buttery feel to it. "Still firm, is it not?" she simpered. "How old do you think I am, Churillo Igorevich?"

Oh, by the One-Eyed Odin, I thought to myself, backing away, *this is how I got mixed up with Inge, and look how that turned out! Not again.* "Your Majesty, I'm very bad at guessing ages—"

"How old?" she demanded. "And you may call me Zoe."

"Thirty-five?" I mumbled, hoping to err on the side of youth.

"Sixty next month. And not a wrinkle anywhere on my body. *Anywhere* on my body, Churillo, thanks to these lotions of mine. And," she went on, "I do give a lot of it away to my women and my friends. I delight in generosity. Here." She took a stoppered flask from its rack. "For your sweetheart. You have one, I hope? No? A handsome young barbarian like you? Well, you soon will, I'm sure. I'm fond of barbarians. So different from our men." She placed the little bottle in my hand and squeezed my fingers around it. *If she simpers and squeezes my hand again, I will bolt for the door.* But she was too fast for me. "Does the heat bother you?" Taking my arm in hers, she led me out into the garden. A small dog, a bundle of brown fluff, trotted after us, its nails tapping on the marble. Two of her women and a young eunuch followed at a discreet distance. Although a hot sun blazed overhead, the change in temperature from that stifling room sent a chill through me. Zoe seated herself on a marble bench and pulled me down beside her so that our thighs touched. The dog leapt into her lap. Nearby, a peacock dragged its gorgeous tail and, above us, bright-colored birds chattered in the branches. I kept finding it hard not to look at Zoe's breasts, which, if she was telling the truth about her age, were perfect miracles of firmness.

"A word of advice while you're here, ambassador. Never say anything within four walls that you don't want overheard and reported." This was exactly what Harald had said to me last night.

"Reported to whom, Majesty?" (I was not about to call her 'Zoe'.)

"John." The word came as a whisper and her lips twisted as if from a bad taste.

Something told me I shouldn't pursue this, but my curiosity was piqued. "It's a common name. Which John do you mean?" She looked hard at me for a moment and I thought she wanted to say more, but she changed her mind. "So," she smiled, "I'm told that you're here to arrange a marriage for Grand Prince Yaroslav's daughter with some young man of our family. You're very young to be an ambassador. We haven't had the pleasure of your company here before, have we? Forgive me for not knowing, I'm afraid I don't participate in court life as much as I used to."

"You prefer solitude, then?"

"Prefer! It is *not* what I prefer." Her voice was suddenly shrill, her eyes flashed with anger, or—even more dangerous—hate. Her little dog, with an animal's sensitivity, fled under the bench. She looked away and fought to get herself under control. After a few deep breaths, she continued in a more conversational tone. "I have a great fondness for the Rus, Churillo. My aunt Anna, who was sister to the Emperor Basil, was given in marriage to Vladimir, Prince of Kiev. It was she who persuaded him to adopt the True Faith and she herself founded many churches and monasteries. I was only ten when she went away, but she wrote me letters saying how wonderful and beautiful everything was in Gardariki. I was a lonely child; they meant much to me, those letters."

I doubted that a Greek princess really found Vladimir's log-hewn hall and his rough, hard-drinking Rus warriors all that charming, but I smiled encouragingly.

"Well," she concluded, "I am sure Yelisaveta is a lovely girl. You should realize, though, that our Emperor is not in good health and has much on his mind, so you must be patient. But you have me on your side. I like to do favors for my friends. I hope I may consider you one?" She looked at me under her lashes and touched my hand again. The hairs stood up on the back of my neck. I didn't move. Whoever this woman's enemies were, whoever the dreaded John might be, I wanted nothing to do with any of them. After a moment, she drew back her hand and stood up. "Let me show you around my little realm, Churillo."

One of her women, grey-haired and thin-lipped, approached with a warning look. "Is that wise, Majesty? If the man stays here too long, people—"

Zoe stamped her foot. "Am I not to be my own mistress even here?" The woman bowed and retreated. Zoe led me out of the garden and down a short path to a small, domed building with a pillared forecourt. Its doors swung open on silver hinges; inside was a rainbow of colored marble. At the back of it sat an altar encrusted with rubies and carnelians. "The Chapel of the Holy Virgin of Pharos," Zoe breathed. She bowed low to the altar and I, of course, did the same. (With every passing day these pretenses were getting easier.)

"Churillo, you cannot imagine the power that dwells here. It is not for the eyes of just anyone. Two pieces of the True Cross, the Crown of Thorns, the cloth with the imprint of Our Savior's face, as well as his sandals and tunic and a phial of his sacred blood." She pointed each one out to me—nondescript lumps of wood and who-knows-what-else encased in gold and silver settings. "And the right arm of John the Baptist, and, oh, much more. This is our strength, ambassador, not ships, not engines of war. *This* is why our empire will endure to the end of time. When you return to your country this is what you must tell them." She had drawn herself up to her full height, and I understood that I was hearing the voice of an Empress—the wife, the daughter, the grand-daughter of Emperors—speaking with the unquenchable pride of a thousand years of history. Who was I to doubt the magic in these things? "And one thing more I will show you—and I show it to very few." Upon the altar, wrapped in a piece of purple silk was the small figurine of a man only a little bigger than my hand. Lovingly, she unwrapped it, put it to her lips and kissed it, then held it to her bosom and sighed. I cannot say what the thing was made of; at one moment it looked like gold, and then again like silver. I could almost swear that it changed color while I stared at it. "Christ," she murmured. "My own Christ. I speak to him and he answers me. He warns me, Churillo, when danger is near. When he turns blood red then I know I must act."

"And has he done that, Majesty?"

"Oh, yes, Churillo. He has. And he will again."

She set the figurine back gently on the altar and we went out into the sunlight.

Back in the perfumery she gave me her hand to kiss. "Come again, Churillo Igorevich, whenever you like. Think of me as a friend. And I will see what can be done about your young princess. And here, don't forget your bottle of scent and take another one too. It's all I have to give nowadays."

Sgouritzes walked me to the palace gate. My clothes were wet with sweat and the smell of perfume seemed to follow me like a fog. I would need a bath to get it out of my hair.

"You've served the Empress a long time?" I asked him.

"Nearly all her life."

"I sense there is something, some—difficulty in her affairs?"

"That is none of your concern, ambassador. God will protect her from her enemies."

And that was all he would say.

All the rest of that day I couldn't get Zoe out of my thoughts. What was she? A lonely, pathetic eccentric? A dangerous lunatic? Who were her enemies? Who was this man John? What might she do if that little statue of her god should turn red? What had she done already that had brought her to this sad state? Was there some smell there that all the perfumes in the world could not forever disguise?

7

ZOE'S TALE[†]

DECEMBER, A.D. 988, AGED TEN

The din is nearly unbearable—drums and flutes and voices, raucous, thick with wine, belt out songs from the pantomime stage, mingling with the laughter of men and women. Pretty Zoe and her two younger sisters—homely, timid little things she despises—are led in by their nurse and made to stand in a row in front of the banquet table with its wreckage of food and spilled drink. Her father, Constantine VIII, co-Emperor of Rome, just thirty years old but already grossly fat, belches, loosens his sash, and waves his guests to silence. The room is full of charioteers, actresses, and slim young eunuchs, powdered and rouged. They pay little attention to him. They know he is Emperor in name only. At this moment his grim, blood-soaked brother Basil, the real ruler of the empire, is marching across some distant frontier, slaughtering Bulgars, or is it Pechenegs? But here stand the three little girls, commanded to recite some verses of Homer they have memorized for the amusement of their father and his friends. The two younger ones are tongue-tied, almost in tears. Zoe,

---

[†]Reader, some of what Odd told me—stories that he heard from Psellus and others that do not fit neatly into his narrative—I have thought to present in these separate 'tales,' the better to help you understand certain things that Odd learned only later, sometimes much later. Previously I have been a mere grudging recorder of Odd's story but somehow, during the weeks and months of our acquaintance, my feelings toward him have undergone a change and I want to contribute my own small effort toward making this a better book. - Teit the Deacon

in a trembling voice, begins, but suddenly her mother, Helena, bursts into the room, weeping, screaming, her hair down, half-hiding her face. But not hiding enough of it. Her husband hates her, hates her hideous face ravaged by smallpox. He has not slept with her in years. What man would want to put his lips on skin like rhinoceros hide? Helena curses. Constantine laughs. The guests look away. Helena stands her ground for a moment, then rushes out again, colliding with the doorjamb, almost knocking herself senseless. Zoe runs after her, down the corridor, into the bedroom—gorgeous, hung with purple silk—climbs up on the bed to comfort her mother. Helena holds the girl's smooth, tear-wet cheek to her own rough one and Zoe, even Zoe, who loves her, shrinks from the touch of it. Never, Zoe swears to herself, never will she let herself look like this.

✝

JANUARY, A.D. 1002
AGED 24

Bari, Apulia. The mansion with its whitewashed walls and red tile roof, formerly the home of a Saracen grandee, commands a view of the harbor. Zoe gazes from the balcony at the ships riding at anchor: the flotilla of transports and warships that have brought her, her retinue of women, eunuchs, guards and priests, and her immense dowry here to the heel of Italy. So eager is her uncle Basil to consummate this union that they have braved the storms of winter in the Aegean and Adriatic and God has granted them a safe voyage. Today is cold, gusty, spitting rain, but nothing can dampen Zoe's joy. In another day or two she will meet her husband-to-be. Otto the Third, King of Germany, King of Italy, Holy Roman Emperor. He is only nineteen years old and already his fame has spread across Europe. She has seen a portrait of him—a beautiful young man with large eyes and a firm mouth. And, of course, he has seen a portrait of her and fallen in love with her at once, they assure her. When they wed she will be queen of a realm that reaches from the Rhine to the Tiber. But politics doesn't interest her. Simply to be free! Away from Constantinople, away from the disgusting spectacle of her father's debauchery and her mother's sour despair. To be her own woman at last, embarked on this new adventure.

Sgouritzes, the young eunuch who loves her with a canine devotion, is busy laying out her jewelry. Zoe is by far the most important visitor this little city has ever entertained, and a long line of tradesmen waits outside, eager to show her their wares. A dark-skinned Saracen merchant with a curling beard is admitted, a dealer in unguents and perfumes. Zoe has studied her mirror and is not entirely pleased with what she sees; the salt air, the raw winter wind has dried her skin on their long voyage out. At twenty-four she is still young and beautiful, but ever since childhood she has been haunted by the fear of losing her looks. What if her bridegroom is disappointed in what he sees? She is already three years older than he is. The Saracen proffers a jar of unguent. She rubs a little of it into her cheeks. It comes all the way from India, he tells her. She loves the feel of it. She has nothing so fine at home. He has perfumes, too, like nothing she has ever smelled before. She must have more of it. She will make him tell her the ingredients. If he is unwilling, she'll threaten him with blinding.

Now what is all that racket down below? A clatter of hooves in the courtyard. Half a dozen armed men, mud spattered on sweating horses, one of them carrying Otto's banner. They've come to take her to him. Quick, pour wine, lay out food. Make them welcome. But these men, as they crowd into her chamber, are not smiling. Their captain kneels before her with tears in his eyes. They have ridden from Viterbo, day and night without resting, to bring her the tragic news. Otto is dead. A sudden fever—or poison—no one is sure. That young, strong, vibrant youth, dead within twenty-four hours of falling ill.

Hands reach out to catch Zoe as she falls. Darkness closes around her.

✝

AUGUST, A.D. 1030
AGED FIFTY-TWO

Zoe, naked, lies on her bed, her arms crossed over her breasts, trembling. The air is cold at this hour of the night, between midnight and cockcrow, when spells have their greatest potency. A sudden draft makes the candles gutter and flare. There is no sound save for the hissing and moaning of the witch who recites the *xemetrima*, the incantations, in a mumbling sing-song. While she sings, the old woman touches Zoe's arms, her belly, her thighs, between her thighs, placing the smooth pebbles, the bits of chain, the tufts of wool soaked in the milk of a farrow sow, the splinters of holy wood, the pieces of stale Communion bread, all the charms and amulets for conception that she has brought with her tonight.

Zoe's father, is two years dead. Likewise gone are her mother and her uncle Basil. On his deathbed Constantine had commanded Romanus Argyrus, the City Prefect, a shriveled old man of seventy years with patchy hair and a dripping nose, to divorce his wife and marry Zoe, his spinster daughter. The punishment for refusal was blinding. Naturally, the Prefect agreed and, as Constantine gurgled his last breath, he became Emperor Romanus III. There was no other way to perpetuate the dynasty. Of Zoe's two sisters, one was dead and the other a nun. There was no male heir. After her sad return from Italy thirty years ago, Constantine had been so careless a father as to never arrange another marriage for his eldest daughter when she was young enough to bear a child. Possibly it was because she *looked* so young that the passage of years had not quite registered on the foolish man. And now plainly it was too late. The dynasty would end here. Romanus had done his best in the beginning, played his manly part as well as he could, but it had been pointless, and not only pointless but ridiculous. He knew he was laughed at behind his back and it drove him wild with anger. Like any man, he blamed his wife, not himself for their failure to produce a child. And now he treated Zoe like an enemy, couldn't stand to be in the same room with her, forbade her to draw money from the treasury to lavish on her friends and flatterers.

So now poor Zoe, desperate and abandoned, lies shivering on her bed in the dark while the wise woman labors over her with her spells and charms. "Will it work?" Zoe whispers at last. But the wise woman, who is more honest than she is wise, shakes her grey head and replies: "Empress, nature can only be forced to far."

Zoe screams, leaps up in a shower of pebbles and bits and pieces, snatches up a jeweled belt from her heap of clothes, and strikes at the woman, cutting her on the face. The woman flees and Zoe falls back, burying her face—her preternaturally youthful face—in her pillow.

✝

MAY, A.D. 1033
AGED 55

Zoe is excited. She loves the chariot races: one of the few occasions nowadays that she is permitted by her husband to appear outside the palace, except to go to church. She sits in the Imperial box and looks out over the vast oval track of the hippodrome, its central spine bristling with statues and obelisks, its stands filled with thousands of cheering spectators. It is intermission. Four courses have been run, there will be four more. Meanwhile, acrobats and trick riders perform on the track and the circus factions, each in their color—blue, green, red and white--stand up in their seats, chanting and waving their colored handkerchiefs. Romanus Argyrus, her husband, sits as far away from her as the confines of the box allow. Racing bores him. He is eating a pomegranate, spitting the seeds on the floor, the juice running down his chin while a servant hovers over him with a giant white napkin. Romanus no longer cares if his whiskers are stained, or his coat front. Around them stand the grandees of the court wearing spotless white cloaks, pinned at the shoulder with golden brooches.

And who is approaching now? Oh, Christ in heaven! Zoe thinks. *That man.* He makes her flesh crawl. John, the Guardian of Orphans, dressed in his black robe and hood. He bows deeply before the Emperor, who favors him with a toothless smile. Romanus *likes* the man, or finds him useful anyway, as did Constantine before him and Basil before him. Oh, John is a man of many parts—none of them, however, a pair of testicles. (Zoe is surprised at her own witticism; a pity she can't share it.)

But John has someone with him, a youth whom he is pushing towards her. Zoe has been talking to the patriarch, making a small wager on the next race. She glances up. "Empress," John says, forcing his thin eunuch's voice down to its lowest register, as he always does, "may I present to you Michael, my youngest brother, just up from the country, from our village in Paphlagonia, so anxious to see the races. He is hoping for a place at court. Bow to the Empress." He pinches the boy's arm. The youth ducks his head at her and smiles—a bold, confident smile, almost insolent. And, for a moment, her breath catches. His hair is black and oiled, his skin white as milk, his cheeks rosy, his clothes decently cut, though cheap; his boots are scuffed, he wears a ring on his finger with a vulgarly large stone, surely fake. His chin is smooth. She holds out her hand for him to kiss. He doesn't merely brush it with his lips and release it. He holds her fingers tightly, longer than he should, and presses his lips hard to her plump, unwrinkled flesh. She is momentarily flustered.

"Are you a eunuch, Michael?"

"No, Lady."

"How old are you?"

"Sixteen."

"Sixteen, a sweet age. What a good-looking boy you are, and you know it too, don't you? I'm sure you have many conquests among the village girls." She's *flirting* with him, she realizes with a shock. A boy young enough to be her son.

Michael lowers his eyes becomingly, his cheeks flush. And then again that bold smile.

"Oh, he has the looks in the family, he has," John interposes, attempting a laugh. John's laughter is blood-chilling.

Zoe ignores the Guardian of Orphans. "Michael, what would you like to do in the palace? What education have you had?"

For the first time the boy looks unsure of himself. "I can read."

"And what do you like to read?"

Michael is silent.

"He's a very bright young man," John breaks in hastily. "Writes a good hand, he'll make an excellent clerk. He can work for me for a start. I'm overwhelmed with work, as you must know, Empress. The accounts, the tax registers—"

"Michael," she interrupts John without looking at him, "I am sure the Emperor will find something suitable for you and, in the meantime, you may come and visit me in my chambers, if you like."

"In her Chamber of Stinks, if you can stand it, I swear I can't." Her husband's harsh laugh startles her. She didn't think he was listening. His cackle subsides into a phlegmy cough.

And now the crowd roars as the next four chariots approach the starting gate. John bows himself away, pulling his young brother with him. She follows them with her eyes. Just that morning she had taken out her little figurine of Christ to pray to it, and it had turned from silver to gold in her hand! A good omen, she was sure of it. And now this beautiful boy kisses her hand as if he would devour it. She pulls her attention back to the chariots, but her heart is beating fast.

†

ᚷOOᚦ FRᛁᚦAᚤ, A.ᚦ. 1034
AᚷᛖᚦFᛁFᚦᚤ-sᛁx

It is still early morning and already the Golden Hall is jammed with officials, senators, clerks, messengers, guards; the women of the court fill the rotunda above. The proclamation went out at dawn in the Empress's name. Psellus and his friend, another young clerk in the Logothete's office, elbow their way as close to the dais as they can. (Rude, but Psellus has only been in the palace a month and everything excites him. Whatever this is about, he's determined not to miss a thing.) Snatches of hushed conversation echo from the glittering walls. He stands close to two officials, senior men judging from their jeweled collars, and strains his ears.

Romanus dead? Yes, some time yesterday. Went for his bath, I heard, and they drowned him. Well, tried to. They pulled him out, half-dead, he lasted a little while, couldn't speak, coughing up blood, and then he died.

Who? Who tried to drown him?

Michael's friends, who else? Well, I mean, everyone knows they've been poisoning him for months now, Michael and Zoe. Finally got tired of waiting for the old codger to die.

Careful, keep your voice down, you want some Varangian to overhear you?

Those brutes, they don't know what we're saying. Anyway, everyone's saying it.

Well, he has looked like a walking corpse these past months. Face swollen like a blood sausage, hair and beard all fallen out. Where is he now?

On his bier in the chapel, already forgotten, like a piece of rotten fruit, which is what he looks like.

Shocking, the way they've carried on, the two of them. Kissing and petting and making love right under the old man's nose, what was the stupid bitch thinking of? Sex-mad is what she is, and at her age!

And Romanus, well either he didn't know or didn't want to; more likely the latter, because didn't people try to warn him?

Of course, there was no love lost between him and Zoe, so what did he expect?

Hush! What's happening now?

The organ thunders. The golden doors swing open. A troop of the Emperor's Wineskins race in and form up on either side of the dais, holding their long-handled axes across their chests. Other Guards regiments follow them, driving the crowd back. Psellus is elbowed in the chest, his foot is trodden on, but he manages to hold his place near the front.

The Empress Zoe appears in the doorway, seeming tiny in that huge space. On her head is the diadem with its ropes of pearls hanging down either side, and in her hand, the scepter. Over her shoulders, she wears the brocaded robe crusted with gems, and one step behind her comes her lover, young Michael Paphlagon. Psellus listens to the whispers.

A nobody, from a family of nobodies.

Good-looking boy, though, give him that.

Yes, but not quite right in the head. You've heard the talk. Has fits, falls down in a faint, foams at the mouth, they try to keep it quiet.

Shush!

Zoe has seated Michael on the throne next to her. They wait. The crowd waits. Some delay. What is it now? His Holiness Alexius, the Patriarch of Constantinople, is coming in. His robes are askew, he looks like his legs won't hold him up. The poor man is frightened to death. Two of his deacons half-carry him to the foot of the dais. Psellus presses closer to see. The patriarch is shaking his head, saying something. And now Zoe is saying something, but Psellus can't make out the words. Zoe stands. One of her people holds out a diadem, she takes it, holds it high for all to see, and places it on the head of Michael, her child lover. The organ pours out its thunderous sound. The Guardsmen clash their weapons on their shields. The courtiers, who know their parts well, begin to chant, "Worthy, worthy. Many years, many years." The echoes bouncing back and forth until it is all one roar. The Roman Empire has a new master: Michael the Fourth, may Christ protect him. Now the patriarch joins Zoe's and Michael's hands together in holy—or is it unholy?—matrimony.

And now the senior courtiers, the Grand Chamberlain, the Logothete, the Master of the Wardrobe, the Grand Domestic, dozens of others, are being brought forward one by one to fall on their faces before Zoe and to kiss Michael's right hand. This will go on for an hour, and finally even Psellus, near the end of the line, will have his turn. Psellus risks a long look; he has never been this close to royalty before. Their new Emperor is no more than a boy, younger than himself. His face is expressionless, a mask—what thoughts are swirling behind it? But Zoe's face is radiant, supremely happy. Hard to believe she is old enough to be her husband's mother. But what a brief time that happiness will last. Poor Zoe, so unlucky in her men.

8

GAMES
[Odd resumes his narrative]

Three days had passed since my interview with Zoe. Since then, there had been no new summons from the palace, nor had Harald tried to contact me. I was bored and restless; the novelty of the city beginning to pall. I was finding Piotr's company irritating, too, and Stavko's even more so. I spent much of my time simply walking by myself, trying to work things out in my mind. Thoughts of Harald and Zoe occupied my every waking moment and even invaded my dreams. What did they want with me? How would I fend off the Mistress of Perfumes, who seemed to have her sights set on me? How would I defend myself against Halldor and Bolli, who surely were planning to kill me before I killed them? How would I strike Harald down—if I still meant to? I was troubled by the feeling that I might be here much longer than I had intended and that these people were playing at games of which I did not even begin to grasp the rules. How long could this go on?

Towards sunset on a soft afternoon, I found myself walking on the quayside that stretched along the Horn between the sea-wall and the water, smelling the sharp, salt air that reminded me of home and listening to the foreign babble of the sailors whose ships were moored here. I wore plain clothes and no jewelry, not wanting to look conspicuously rich in this quarter of the city and, obedient to the law, carried no sword. I felt naked without it; but I did have a knife in my boot, Rus fashion. I decided to stop for a bite of dinner at a waterside tavern where I had been once or twice before. The food wasn't anything special but it made a change from the stew that was served up every day at the hostel, and at night it was a lively place with sailors and girls dancing to the flute and tambourine and clapping of hands. And I'd spent a pleasant half-hour there in the upstairs room with one of the serving girls. Maybe I would again—I was feeling the urge.

Abgar the host, a genial, fat Armenian, seated me on a bench at one end of the long table and set before me a jug of retsina, (I was starting to like its sharp, pine sap taste). I ordered a plate of grilled mackerel with beans and black bread. It was early yet. The last rays of the sun slanted through the open door and the place wasn't crowded. At the far end of the table sat four sailors, swarthy and black-bearded, drinking deeply and talking in a language I didn't understand, with a lot of laughter and slapping of shoulders. I supposed they'd just gotten paid off from their ship. And then, as I waited for my food to come, a young man came through the door, carrying under his arm a narrow box of lacquered wood with brass hinges and clasps. He was slightly built with close-cropped black hair and a pale, triangular, beardless face. An intelligent face, I thought, and yet intentionally blank. A face that was hiding something? He wore a blowsy tunic of plain, dark linen and baggy trousers of the same fabric. Abgar gave him a smile and called him Andreas.

Andreas sat at the table, about half way between me and the sailors, asked for a cup of wine, and unlatched his box. The two halves of it opened out on their hinges and I saw that it contained two leather dice cups with some dice and a heap of round, flat stones, some black and some white. The bottom of the box, clearly the playing board, was decorated with two rows of alternating black and white triangles that met together at their points. It wasn't chess or our Norse *hnefatafl*. I'd never seen anything like it.

The youth looked in my direction as if inviting me to play. I shook my head no. I'd just been cogitating that only a fool plays a game whose rules he doesn't understand. This was, no doubt, a harmless way to lose a few pennies, but even so. First, I would watch. Then one of the sailors, with encouraging grunts from his mates, slid over on the bench until he was facing the boy and said, "I play you, kid."

"Twenty *folles* a game," the boy replied without looking up, busying himself arranging the pieces on the triangles. His voice was rough as though he were trying to force it into a lower register.

"Lemme see you money. You gonna lose it."

Andreas unhooked a purse from his belt and spilled out a mixture of copper and small silver coins. "And yours?" The sailor slapped a fistful of coins on the table. I was beginning not to like his manners. But the boy seemed unperturbed. The other sailors came over and stood behind their friend. One of them handed him the wine bottle and he took a long pull at it. They began to play, shaking a pair of dice in the cup, and throwing them on the board. I can only give a hint of the play, not understanding it myself. They played very fast, the boy especially, his slender fingers hovering and darting like dragonflies over the board, moving his black pieces around, pursuing the white ones. The corners of his mouth turned down in concentration, he never took his eyes from the board, and he allowed himself only small sips from his wine cup. In a few minutes the first game was over. The sailor laughed, belched, and slid some of Andreas's coins over to his side. His mates slapped him on the back.

"We go again," he said. "Forty *folles*, yeah?"

The boy smiled and nodded.

But the next game didn't go so well for the sailor, or the one after that. As the dice rattled and clattered, the boy kept sending his opponents pieces back to their starting place while, one by one, he removed his own pieces from the board and stacked them neatly beside it. And the money began to go the other way. And every time the boy scooped up his winnings there was a flash of fire in his slanting green eyes. It's not just the money, I thought, it's the winning. He loves this. Meanwhile, the sailor's color thickened and his jaw muscles bulged. He drank off the bottle and demanded another one. Abgar, who had been watching without seeming to, shook his head. "Time to move on, my friends."

"The little shit's cheating!" the sailor yelled. He swept the board off the table and threw a vicious punch at Andreas, striking him square in the face, knocking him off the bench. Instantly, Abgar was in the middle of them, swinging a belaying pin, and I at the same moment jerked my knife from my boot. (I hadn't realized until that moment how much I'd been longing to get into a fight with *somebody*.) But it was all over in a second and no blood was shed. The sailor's friends dragged him away and Abgar hustled them all out the door.

We turned back to Andreas, who was sitting on the floor, holding a bloody sleeve to his nose. While Abgar gathered up the board and pieces,

I helped the boy to stand and steadied him on his feet with one arm around his back and my other hand on his chest and made the interesting discovery that 'Andreas' was quite unmistakably a young woman.

With a sudden jerk she broke away from me, snatched her game box from Apgar's hands, and ran out the door. I followed her, running half way down the street, but she vanished in the gathering dusk. I returned to the taverna where Abgar greeted me with an expressive shrug. "The boy comes around once or twice a week. I think he circulates around all the waterfront places."

"And he always wins?" I asked. I was careful to say 'he'; obviously, the girl wanted her secret kept.

"Usually."

"And it ends in a fight?"

"Not often. Customers know I won't put up with that. Those fellows were new here."

"But who is he, where does he live?"

Abgar allowed that he had no idea, had never asked and didn't think it any of his business.

I sat down and finished my meal and soon the place was full of neighborhood characters and girls who were passably attractive. One of them filled my wine cup, asked me to dance, kissed me, named her price, and for the next few hours I was happy to think of nothing.

9

TOO MANY QUESTIONS

"Churillo Igorevich, a pleasure to see you again."

"And you, Constantine Psellus."

"I trust you will enjoy the evening's festivities," he said in his serious, stilted fashion. We lay side by side on gilded dining couches, linen napkins tied around our necks. Behind us hovered carvers and cupbearers in scarlet livery. "And what have you been doing with yourself?" he asked.

"Nothing. Waiting and wondering." Which was true enough but something told me not to mention my conversation with Harald or my brawl with the Varangians, Halldor and Bolli.

"You must understand that nothing happens here quickly. Are you comfortable in the hostel."

"Not very."

"Dear me, I seem to find you in a bad mood. Well, let us hope it won't be much longer."

One set of platters with the remains of a saddle of venison were being taken away while other plates were set before us laden with lamb laced with cloves and cardamom, a grilled turbot, loaves of white bread. Our long-stemmed goblets were filled again. The golden plates, the glassware, the jewels and gold thread of the costumes, the mosaics of flowers and birds that covered the walls, all gleamed and twinkled in the light of massed candelabra. The music of lutes and woodwinds from a small orchestra competed with the clatter of plates and the hum of conversation. I found that eating while lying on my side was uncomfortable—it is a custom that the Romans themselves seldom practice any more—but in the Hall of Nineteen Couches, where state dinners are held, it is obligatory for a few of the most favored guests, of which I was one. All the others in the vast high-ceilinged hall sat on chairs around small tables. The occasion this evening was to honor the ambassadors, most of whom, their missions accomplished, would soon be going home. But not me.

A herald had come to the hostel that morning with our invitations. I left Piotr to his own devices and went among the Rus shops in Saint Mamas looking for something to freshen my wardrobe. I looked at boots and bought myself a pair of yellow leather ones; looked at caps and bought a tall one with a turned-up brim of marten fur and a spray of pheasant plumes pinned to the front. I looked quite handsome in it, or so the shopkeeper assured me. Along the way I asked after Stavko, but no one seemed to know where he was. After that, I spent a couple of hours just loafing along the waterfront, gazing across the wind-ruffled water to the Galata shore and watching the fishermen unload their catch. A powerful yearning to be at sea again came over me, and my heart felt heavy in my breast. How many more days must I idle away in this alien city? Where would I be a year from now? What fate had the Norns in store for me? Too many questions with too few answers.

I re-crossed the Horn and went into Apgar's taverna, hoping to find 'Andreas', but he—she—wasn't there. I was sorry. Something about her had stirred my feelings. Maybe it was just the fact that we were each, in our own way, imposters, or maybe that I admired her courage. I had a vague feeling that I had dreamt something about her, but I couldn't remember what it was. I stayed and drank a jug of wine and half-listened while Apgar enlightened me as to the virtues of the Armenian race and how the empire couldn't exist without it, and pumped me for my own story, about which I told him some lies, until finally it was time to go back and dress for the banquet.

I rode to the palace along with the other ambassadors. As before, we were given horses and a mounted escort of Khazar cavalry. I exchanged smiles with them but that was the limit of our communication. I wondered if they were as anxious to be quit of this place as I was. Piotr rode beside me; my rank required that I have at least one servant in my train. The poor boy was homesick and just as impatient to leave here as I was now that the novelty of the big city had worn off. The difference between us being that Piotr actually had a home and parents to go back to, and I did not. I was homesick for I knew not where. How much longer, gospodin, he kept asking until I lost my temper with him.

It was hot in the Hall despite all the windows being thrown open and the drapes tied back. I dabbed at my chin with my napkin while I studied my fellow guests. Of the ambassadors, only the Saracens in their sheer, white robes and headdresses looked comfortable. The ambassador from Salerno, a Lombard named Arduin, was dressed in northern fashion, with a cloak of lynx skins hanging from one shoulder. I had heard him speaking fluent Greek earlier and we exchanged a few words.

Next to each ambassador was his interpreter from the Office of Barbarians. Psellus, whom I had not seen since the day of the audience, reclined alongside me, ready to translate, although it was clear that my Greek was better than his Slavonic.

The Emperor and Empress were at a separate table together with the Patriarch, the Grand Chamberlain, the Logothete, and a few others, including the only other woman in the room besides Zoe. "The Emperor's sister, Maria," Psellus whispered in my ear; a hatchet-faced woman with dead white skin, a red gash of a mouth, and several pounds of jewelry hanging on her. Her laugh was loud and raucous and often, it seemed, directed at Zoe, who never glanced at her. And as for Zoe, how different she looked from when I had last seen her in her linen shift. Now she was cocooned in layers of silk and wore a cloth over her head that hung down to her shoulders, covering her hair and half her face. She looked uncomfortable and unhappy, staring straight ahead of her, not speaking, and spoken to by none. I noticed that she barely touched her food. I had tried to catch her eye but she looked right past me without a sign of recognition.

One other figure at their table was a monk, or so I took him to be. In an unadorned black robe, his very plainness made him stand out from all the others. I watched the Emperor over the rim of my goblet. Having more time to observe him than I had before, I was struck by the puffiness around his eyes, as if he had slept badly, and noticed his hands were swollen making his rings cut into his fingers. He spent most of the evening talking to the monk. It wasn't possible to overhear their words, but the Emperor looked weary, distracted.

Since no one was talking to me, I let my eyes roam over the room. Standing behind the Emperor's couch were a squad of Varangians, still as statues, in burnished armor, their axes over their shoulders. Was one of them Halldor or Bolli? With their masked helmets on I couldn't be sure. I felt their eyes on me and it made me tense. Of the guests there must have been two hundred or more, each in his distinctive regalia. In their midst I saw Harald—who could mistake that great bulk and leonine head? He wore civilian clothes and was sitting at a table with some other yellow-haired men, Scandinavians or Rus, who I assumed were also Guards officers. Did he see me? I was certain he did, yet he gave no sign. This was beginning to bother me: Zoe and now Harald, both so anxious to meet me just a few days ago and now both of them pretending that I didn't exist? What was it all about? I decided to concentrate on my food, which was delicious. I wiped up the last drop of gravy with my bread.

When the plates had been cleared away, dessert was served in a remarkable fashion. Enormous golden platters, heaped with peaches and apricots and other fruits that I had never tasted before, were wheeled out on carts while, at the same time, gilded chains descended from holes in the ceiling. Servants attached hooks at the ends of these chains to the handles of the platters and some invisible mechanism in the roof hoisted them up and swung them around just over our heads so that we could help ourselves to the fruit. Instantly, I thought of the soaring Throne of Solomon. Was that all it was, then—a pulley? Were my eyes so easily fooled? But no. No. There were no chains attached to the throne, couldn't have been without my seeing them, just as I saw these now. No, I was still without an explanation for that miracle.

The Logothete, taking the time to have a word with each ambassador in turn, arrived at my couch. "Sir," I asked, "can you tell me anything about the progress of my mission? May I tell Grand Prince Yaroslav that his prayers have been answered and his daughter will soon be wed?"

Not that I gave a damn about Yelisaveta, you understand. Harald was welcome to her. But, as I have said, I was finding this charade unbearably tiresome. The Logothete looked uncomfortable. Objections had been raised in certain quarters. When pressed, he shook his head. No, he couldn't say why, only that the matter was still under discussion. I murmured something about not wanting to impose on their hospitality much longer. He smiled noncommittally and passed on.

I turned to Psellus but he only shrugged and claimed to know nothing about it. He seemed uncharacteristically quiet. I made up my mind to press him hard, for I had a great many questions in mind and I was sure that he had, at least, some of the answers. But just then the Master of Ceremonies stood up, tapped the floor with his golden staff, and announced the evening's entertainment. And so we were treated, in succession, to troupes of acrobats and mimes, dancing girls in tall turbans and swirling skirts, trained apes and dogs, and other amusing nonsense that went on for nearly an hour.

"And finally," the Master of Ceremonies spoke again, "to round off the night's festivities and send us to our beds with heavenly voices sounding in our ears, John the Guardian of Orphans has prepared a special treat for us." He nodded in the direction of the black-robed figure. The man got heavily to his feet and turned an oily smile on us all, showing a gold front tooth. I'd been watching him on-and-off all evening. He hadn't eaten much, but had drunk a remarkable amount, though he seemed able to hold it. He was very tall, stoop-shouldered, with a bulbous forehead, pouched eyes, and a mouth set crookedly in his face. His cheeks were smooth, moist and oily like slabs of fat—a eunuch, of course, though this was nothing unusual. Half the men in the palace were eunuchs. I remembered Zoe said she feared a certain 'John'. Could this big, soft-handed, baby-faced capon be him?

He clapped his hands and, at once, a side door opened and in trooped a couple of dozen children, boys and girls in separate lines, in age from about eight to sixteen, dressed all in white cassocks. They bowed to the Imperial couch. Michael smiled at them. "Sweet children," he said. "They do you credit, brother John. You have lifted them out of wretchedness and taught them to sing with the voices of angels." John acknowledged this with an unctuous smile. "You, Your Majesties, are their mother and father." The words dripped from his lips like thick oil dripping from a jar. Michael brightened at this but Zoe, as she had all evening, stared straight ahead, her eyes perfect blanks.

The children began to sing and it was lovely. I noticed Psellus brush away a tear. It did seem to me, however, that these children were not overfed: their faces were white and thin, their hair lusterless. They finished one song, a hymn to the Virgin or some such, and were beginning another when pandemonium broke out. Michael lurched to his feet, knocking over his wine glass, clutching at his throat and making strangling noises, his eyes wide and staring, foam at the corners of his mouth. The children's voices faltered but John, looking desperate himself, motioned them to keep it up. The Varangians rushed up and surrounded the Emperor, and from somewhere a purple curtain appeared which two of them held in front of him. The whole room was on its feet now with a great clatter of chairs and a commotion of shocked, anxious voices. The Master of Ceremonies, who was visibly shaking, told us all to leave quickly, assuring us that the Emperor was perfectly well, nothing to fear. The choristers were herded out the side door, followed by Zoe, John, and the others, with the Varangians carrying Michael under his purple sheet. As the hall began to empty I tugged Psellus's sleeve and held him back.

"What is it? Let go of me." He looked at me in alarm and tried to pull away.

"I want to talk to you."

"Hardly the time."

"No better time. Just give me a few minutes. I'm full of questions. Walk out in the garden with me. Please."

He shook his round, brown nut of a head and squinted at me under his heavy brows. "What sort of questions?"

I sensed his suspicion, but I thought I knew what would work with him. From the little contact we'd had, when he coached me for the Imperial audience, it was clear that he was a vain young fellow, inordinately proud of his knowledge. I only had to appeal to that. "You're my mentor. Who else can instruct me?"

Outside, a full moon cast a ghostly light on the statues of gods frozen, like trolls, in mid-step. The torchieres had burned themselves out. The palace, I had learned, was nearly deserted after dark. Almost no one actually slept there. We found a bench in a shadowy corner where the only sound was the splashing of a fountain.

"Has the Emperor been poisoned?"

"What? No, not poisoned. God forbid! He's ill. He's been like this for a year, the fits, the fainting. And it's getting worse. The doctors have done all they can. He's given a fortune to the shrines of Cosmas and Damian, he washes the sores of holy men, he endows refuges for harlots, but nothing seems to help."

"So young to be so ill. And that's another thing that puzzles me,

Psellus. Zoe must be three times his age. How in the world did that marriage come about?"

Psellus looked more nervous than usual, and he always looked nervous. "Now, Churillo, you're treading on dangerous ground. I don't know you, I don't know who else you're talking to. I'm not going to put my head on the chopping block just to entertain you with backstairs gossip." He made to stand up. "Goodnight to you."

"I've met Zoe, you know." That stopped him. I couldn't see his expression, but I heard him inhale. He was silent for a long moment.

"She invited you to her apartment? Well, you wouldn't be the first good-looking young swain. And what is your impression of her, if I may ask?"

"Extraordinary. The perfume, all of that… I don't know what to say. Is she crazy, weak-minded?"

He shook his head. "She's a woman who's seen much sorrow. Some of it her own fault, some of it not. She wants desperately to be loved, and can't find anyone to love her. Her father treated her with contempt, so did her first husband, Romanus, and so, it appears now, does Michael. Whether he ever loved her, who can say? But lately he's made her virtually a prisoner in the Daphne."

"One thing I know, she's frightened. I could see that. She mentioned a man called John. Is that the same—"

"The *Orphanotrophos*, the Guardian of Orphans, yes."

"Michael called him 'brother John.' He's a monk?"

"He isn't actually, though it amuses him to dress as one. He is, in fact, Emperor Michael's brother. An exceedingly clever, enormously powerful, unforgiving man. He is the real head of the family—a family of upstarts, of nobodies from the wilds of Paphlagonia. He introduced young Michael to Zoe, promoted their affair. There are two other brothers, Constantine and George, both eunuchs like John, and a sister Maria, who is married to Stephen, the *Droungarios*, that is, Admiral of the Fleet. They have a son, an unintelligent young man also named Michael. Altogether, quite a crew. They were all at the head table tonight. Consider yourself lucky if you never meet any of them. The Emperor is the only one of them who's worth anything. He's turned out better than anyone had a right to expect, considering how he came to the throne."

"Which was..?"

"No, no, my friend. Now I'm talking too much, straying onto dangerous ground. Such things are not for your ears. And, if I may offer you some advice," he gave me a knowing smile, "don't accept any more invitations from Zoe. There are certainly spies in her apartment, and some people will not be pleased that you are talking to her."

"Meaning John? Michael?"

"I'll say no more."

"All right, then, let me ask a different question. All of this," I spread my arms wide, "all of this, how does it work?"

He regarded me skeptically. "What are you talking about?"

"I'm talking about *this*. The palace. All these people, with their different colored costumes and their unpronounceable titles. What do they all do? Teach me, Psellus. I need to know."

"But why?"

"Because I'm beginning to think that I'm going to be here for a while. Listen, I'll tell you a story. Some years ago I was a, well, a pirate."

"You don't say. How exciting."

"And my men and I were captured in Finland and held prisoner by a tribe of savages. They cut off the heads of some of us and put them on stakes. The rest of us they treated like slaves. To save us I had to learn their language. I was able to make an ally, a young girl who was also a prisoner—" I thought with a pang of sweet Ainikki and the life we might have had—"and made contact with her people, and finally we got away."

"But, my dear fellow, you're not a prisoner here."

"I'm no better than a prisoner if I'm ignorant. So teach me what I need to know to sail these strange waters."

He peered into my face as if really seeing me for the first time, and then spoke softly. "You are certainly the strangest barbarian that I have ever met. How does it work, you ask? It works by intimidation and fear, by flattery in the right places, by telling lies when necessary, by trading favors, by having the right friends, and by information, the most precious currency of all. One must collect it, save it, never share it without getting something in return. It has very little to do with neat little boxes on a chart. All the important rules are unwritten ones. I've been here nearly three years and I'm still learning them. Is any of this making sense to you?"

This was a subject dear to his heart, as I knew it would be. He was a bureaucrat to his fingertips, and a born teacher to boot. And for the next hour, talking without stop, the words crowding on each other, as he paced back and forth and waved his arms about, he lectured me on his favorite subject. "We're a bureaucracy of merit, not of birth. Few of us come from great wealth. Most of us are new men who hope to retire as rich ones. Now the *protovestiarios* is the Master of the Wardrobe, a most important post. The *kanikleios*, is keeper of the Imperial inkstand, but he does much more than that. There are the *kouropalates* and *spatharokandidatos*, those are ranks, not jobs, you mustn't confuse the two, and the Grand Chamberlain we call *parakoimomenos*. *Para-koi-mo-men-os*, accent on the *men*. It means 'he who sleeps alongside.' Say it after me now, that's right. And he's always a eunuch … and the *Logothetes tou dromou*, minister of the post, my boss, who oversees our foreign diplomacy. You'll find that titles have little to do with the responsibilities of the job. Who would guess that the Guardian of Orphans has taken charge of all the state finances? Anyway, the Logothete is sometimes a eunuch but sometimes isn't, Eustathius isn't—"

You may imagine that all this detail was tedious, more than I'd asked for, more than I wanted or needed to know. You would be wrong. I felt as though the corner of a curtain was being lifted to give me just a peek at a vast and complicated machine, more complex, more subtle in its workings than anything my life had prepared me for. These were things for which there were no words in my language. I began to understand how these courtiers carried in their heads a living map of the ever-shifting terrain through which they moved, just as a steersman knows every shoal and current of his home waters. They had to know hundreds of their fellow-bureaucrats, by name, title, and rank, some of them moving up the ladder, some down, in a complex dance of power and advantage. I felt the same excitement that I had when Stig No-One's Son explained the mysteries of navigation to me on our voyage to Norway. And it wasn't only a matter of satisfying idle curiosity. A few days earlier, Harald had boasted of all the power and wealth an ambitious man could put his hands on here. But it was only now that his words fully sank in. With Psellus as my guide through this labyrinth, I saw a path open before me. Other barbarians had done well for themselves here, and not only the Emperor's Wineskins. Apgar had been telling me of countrymen of his who had become great generals, even emperors. I was clever, brave. Couldn't I aim as high? Of course, there was one serious stumbling block in my case: I was here under false pretenses. How long could I keep that up and what would happen if I were exposed? Well, I would face that when the time came.

"—there are eighteen ranks of bearded men," Psellus rattled on, "and eight of eunuchs ..."

"Eunuchs, Psellus," I broke in on his monologue. "Tell me why must a man give up his balls to serve your Emperor? You aren't..?"

"Me? Certainly not." He was offended. "Why eunuchs? I suppose the idea is that a eunuch, having no progeny, will not scheme to advance them. Nonsense, of course. One only has to look at John, who schemes to advance his brothers. Some people claim that eunuchs are like angels, both being sexless. On the other hand, they say that once a viper bit a eunuch and it was the viper that died."

"And you, Psellus, how do you come to work here?"

"Oh, my story is the usual one. My parents were ambitious for me and could afford to hire the best teachers. For a young gentleman to get ahead in the world, it's either the army, the Church, or the palace. I wasn't built to be a soldier, I'm afraid I haven't faith enough for the Church. That leaves the palace. From childhood I excelled in rhetoric and every branch of leaning. Certain contacts were made. And here I am, doing exactly what my talents—my considerable talents, if I may say so without boasting—suit me for. I have high aspirations, you know, and my prospects are excellent. I'm not yet twenty and I'm already well advanced. I will be someone to reckon with one day."

The fellow's smugness was almost too much to bear, and yet, in spite of it, I was starting to like him. I had still one more question. "Psellus, in God's name, how does the throne fly?"

"What, you're still worrying yourself about that? *Magic.*" He grinned and waggled his fingers in my face.

"I don't believe you."

"No? But, Churillo, you must allow us to have *some* secrets."

At last, the hour grew late; we were both tired. "Psellus, I feel like I've taken only the first step. Will you give me more of your knowledge another day?"

"All right. In return for which you will improve my Slavonic—which, I confess, is not all it should be—and tell me more about your northern world. Gardariki, Finland. Witches!"

We laughed together. It was a good moment. I felt, finally, that I was making a friend among the Greeks. He stifled a yawn. "Where do you go now?" I asked him.

"Home. Or, I might just sleep here. To tell the truth, I don't like walking the streets alone at this hour of the night."

I took his arm. His house was on a narrow lane off the Mese, about a mile from the palace, in the shadow of the Aqueduct of Valens. Like all the houses around it, it was a two-story brick structure that turned a blank face to the street. The door was of heavy oak, studded with bronze nails.

"I'll leave you here, then," I said, "unless you'd like to offer me a bed for the night, it's a long walk back to the hostel.

He looked suddenly alarmed and drew back. "No, I'm sorry, it's impossible."

"Because I'm a barbarian?"

"Not that, Churillo. My home—gloomy place. My mother is—well, never mind. You'd be uncomfortable. I'm sorry."

"Quite all right," I shrugged. "Good night, then."

Then I realized I'd entirely forgotten about Piotr. Cursing the boy, I made my way back to the palace and collected him from the kitchen where he had found a corner and gone to sleep after being fed on some very tasty scraps. We walked to the hostel, groping our way through the echoing streets.

"Well," he demanded grumpily, "have they said any more about the princess's marriage? Will we be going home soon?"

"You may be if you like," I told him. "I may not."

10

JOHN'S TALE

A VILLAGE NEAR GANGRA, PAPHLAGONIA
A.D. 1004 - AGED SEVEN

"I'm a big boy, Mama, I can bathe myself."

The iron washtub sits in the middle of the kitchen. His mother takes another kettle off the hearth and pours in more water; steam rises in the cold air.

"A special treat, then, for my big boy," she says.

But why doesn't she smile? Why does she avoid his eyes? He puts a foot in the water. "Too hot, mama!"

"Hush," she says. "Not too hot. Get all the way in. In a minute it will be cold. Get in, I say." She presses down on his shoulders, sinking him up to his neck while he squirms. But in a few moments it does feel lovely, not too hot, not too cold; he relaxes, leans back, how nice to be treated like a baby again. He closes his eyes, waiting for his mother to scrub him. He hears footsteps, heavy ones. He opens his eyes and sees his father standing over him. What is he doing home in the middle of the day? His father scowls. Well, nothing strange about that, his father always scowls.

"Good afternoon, Papa," he says in a small voice, suddenly—why?—frightened by this big man, who is rolling his sleeves up to the elbows, showing the black hairs on his thick forearms, flexing his fingers.

"No!" cries his mother in a strangled voice, but he pushes her aside and plunges his arms into the water, forcing his hands between John's legs. John thrashes, flails his arms, kicks, water goes everywhere. "Hold his arms, goddammit! It's safer than cutting, you want blood everywhere?"

He grasps his son's scrotum in his left fist. With his other hand he pinches one little testicle between thumb and forefinger and crushes it like a grape, then the other, while John shrieks until he has no more breath left—piercing cries that can be heard all over the village. But no one is going to come and rescue him. This is simply what Paphlagonians do. They're famous for it all over Anatolia. The child faints.

When he wakes up, it's dark outside. He's in bed and a cloth is wrapped tightly around his waist and between his legs. The ache there! Waves of nausea sweep over him, his skin is icy. He's afraid to move. He hears his mother crying in the next room, hears his father talking, his voice thick with wine. "He'll make our fortune," his father is saying. "Don't say you didn't agree to it. He's a smart boy, the priest said so, already knows his letters. We'll get him more schooling, in Heraclea maybe."

"On what, you foolish man? You, nothing but a village money-changer."

"You shut your mouth. There are ways."

His mother keeps crying until there is the sound of a palm hitting a face, and then silence. John faints again. It will be weeks before he can walk without pain.

✝

THE BLACHERNAE PALACE, A. D. 1014
AGED SEVENTEEN

Constantine VIII, Co-Emperor of Rome, prefers this small palace tucked away in a far corner of the city for his more private affairs, away from his tiresome, scar-faced wife and his daughters, away from his fierce brother Basil, who lords it over him. Tonight he is entertaining Romanus Argyrus, an elderly senator who is angling for promotion to City Prefect. And what will Romanus give him in return? Something special has been promised. The senator is shown into the bedroom, where Constantine lies propped on cushions, his robe carelessly open, exposing his belly. And behind the senator another figure—a slender, beardless boy made up to look almost like a girl: powdered and perfumed, lips and cheeks rouged, hair dressed in oiled ringlets, earrings in both ears, wearing a lavender-colored cloak pinned at the shoulder and a pale blue silk tunic that reaches only to mid-thigh, showing bare, smooth legs.

"Majesty, may I present John," says Romanus Argyrus.

Constantine is disappointed; he has eunuchs by the dozen who feed him, bathe him, tuck him in at night. What novelty is there here?

"John is a young man of many talents," Romanus goes on quickly, "writes a fine hand, brilliant with figures. But those are not his most interesting abilities, oh, far from it." Romanus winks, one lecher to another, the men understand each other. "Skin like a baby's ass. Lips and tongue educated, shall I say, beyond the ordinary. He comes from my home district. I plucked him out of a stinking village and trained him myself. I make you a present of him, Majesty, though I will be sorry to lose him. Perhaps you'd like to be alone with him, get acquainted?"

John approaches, kneels at the Emperor's bedside, licks his lips, smiles expectantly. He has no sexual feelings but he has studied how to arouse them in other men. And he has learned to master his horror of being touched. He will do anything, *suffer* anything, to advance himself and his brothers.

✝

the GREAT PALACE, A. D. 1028
AGED thirty-one

Romanus III Argyrus has been Emperor of Rome for a little more than four hours. The coronation in the Cathedral of the Holy Wisdom, unendurably tedious, is at last over. He has been escorted back to the palace through a mob of dutifully cheering courtiers. The Patriarch has gone back to his palace and Zoe has withdrawn, thank God, to her steaming pots of stink. Already the garlands are being taken down, the rose petals swept away. Dozens of high-ranking officials are waiting to speak to their new Emperor, but he has insisted on being taken straight to his bedchamber where he can rest his old bones. His neck and shoulders ache from the weight of the tiara, his legs are trembling. Still ahead of him is a night of celebration which he would do anything to escape from. He collapses into a deep chair. He orders everyone from the room, except for one man.

"Christ knows I didn't want this, John. Not at my age. Constantine threatened to blind me if I didn't take the crown and marry his fucking daughter. Blind me! Seventy years old, married to a good woman for fifty years. I'm half in the grave already and the stupid man wants me to get an heir on her? And then he promptly dies—may he burn in Hell—and here we are."

John kneels down, unlaces the red Imperial shoes, eases them off the feet with their yellowed toenails, and massages the feet.

"Oh, Christ, that feels good," Romanus groans. What a treasure you are. Enough now. Draw up a chair, sit next to me, we have things to discuss. You've waited a long time for your reward, John. God knows, you've earned it a thousand times over."

"My reward is to serve you, Majesty."

"Balls! I've used you in ways I wasn't always proud of, and you've never complained. Now I need you more than ever. All these others, the Grand Chamberlain, the Logothete, the generals, the eunuchs of the bedchamber—they were Basil's and Constantine's men. You are *my* man. I'm placing you in charge of the Orphanage of Saint Paul."

"Orphans? I care nothing for them."

"You think I do? John, a fortune in money flows into the orphanage from the Church coffers and from the treasury—you know how big the place is—and you will have the spending of it, accountable to no one. Keep what you like for yourself; I know your tastes are simple. And the rest you will spend on spies, young men that you mold yourself, as I molded you, who can be everywhere, overhear every conversation. Slit a throat, if need be. In rank, you'll be a *Protospatharios*, equal to Eustathius the Logothete. In fact, you'll have more real power than he ever dreamed of. Do this for me, John."

"Majesty." John covers the old man's hand with kisses.

Romanus pats his head. "I knew you would. Now go away and let me rest for a bit."

John, the Guardian of Orphans, slips quietly out the door.

✝

JOHN'S VILLA ON THE GOLDEN HORN, HOLY THURSDAY, A. D. 1034 AGED THIRTY-SEVEN

They have just returned from morning Mass in the small chapel on this, the day that celebrates Our Lord's Last Supper. They arrange themselves on chairs in John's dining room. It's a chilly April, with a wind blowing from the north that whips up waves on the water and rattles the shutters. The servants have been sent away. The doors and windows are shut tight. The business they have to discuss on this holy day is quite definitely unholy. In fact, it is sacrilege: the assassination of God's regent of Earth. The murder of Romanus III.

Brother George, three years younger than John, twists his emerald ring round and round on his finger, stands up, paces, sits again. Brother Constantine, two years younger than George, holds his belly, grimaces, and suppresses a belch. He is a martyr to his digestion. Brother Michael, the baby of the family, half the age of the others, cocky and self-assured, is humming to himself. Like their brother John, Constantine and George are eunuchs; physically, the three of them, soft-skinned and hairless, resemble each other like peas in a pod. Their father had a monomania for castration, convinced it would make the family's fortune and, so far, it seems, he was right, though he didn't live to see it. He was stabbed to death in a brawl with a man he'd tried to cheat with clipped coins. This was soon after Michael was born and was, no doubt, the only thing that saved him from his older brothers' fate.

John, as always, is impassive, his plump hands resting on his black-clad thighs as motionless as two slabs of pork. His eyes are pouched, he always looks like he hasn't slept. And, indeed, it is whispered that he never sleeps but prowls the city at night, looking for traitors. His upper lip is curled in a perpetual sneer. No one knows what he is thinking; no one is allowed to see the anger that seethes inside him, the anger of a wounded child. It is his habit to speak very slowly, forcing his listeners to hang on each word, and he growls in an unnaturally low register, not like the reedy piping of his eunuch brothers or Michael's unpredictable, adolescent squawk.

"If you ask me—" Constantine begins.

"I'm not asking you." John cuts him off. And Constantine shuts his mouth. "Everything has been arranged. Poison hasn't worked, I suppose the old man takes a universal antidote. Anyway, I'm not prepared to wait any longer." What John doesn't say is that he is already worried about Michael's health.

"Zoe's frantic to have him dead," Michael smirks. "It's practically all she talks about when we're alone." Michael has been sleeping with her for nearly a year now. "The stupid cow," he adds.

"Show some respect, little brother," John warns. "You're going to be living with her for a long time."

"Christ, I hope not. Old enough to be my grandmother. It's like fucking an overstuffed cushion—and she *wants* it all the time. I tell you, I've had just about enough, I don't know how long I can keep it up."

"You'd better 'keep it up'," George emphasizes the words while he raises his middle finger.

"And just what do you know about satisfying a woman?" Michael shoots back. This is the one thing that he has over them, and he is never shy about throwing it in their faces. He knows they're ashamed of being half-men, even John. Especially John. George is half out of his chair, his soft hand balled in a fist.

"Stop it!" John orders and forces him down with his eyes. "Little brother has the prick, I have the brain. And you two will do as you're told unless you want to find yourselves back in Paphlagonia selling meat on a skewer in the village square. Now attend to me. The old man will go to his bath at midday today as he always does. Four of my men will be waiting for him."

For six years John has trained a cadre of orphans to do his dirty work. It had been the Emperor's own idea. The irony appeals to John. Not that John takes any particular pleasure in murdering his benefactor, he feels no rancor towards Romanus. This is simply a question of the family's survival. Romanus is bound to die soon and if Zoe doesn't marry Michael then the family will have no position, no influence with whoever takes his place. They have too many enemies. If John doesn't act soon, it will be back to the gutter with all of them.

"What about the Varangians?" Constantine asks.

"There will be none on duty. I've arranged it with the Commandant.

"How much is that costing us?"

Idiot, John thinks, and ignores him. "By that time, we will be in our yacht standing off Boukoleon Harbor. If anything goes wrong Stephen's ships will take us to safety." Stephen is their brother-in-law, Maria's husband, and, thanks to John, Admiral of the Fleet. A profoundly stupid man, but loyal. "I've arranged for a signal to be given from the window when Romanus is dead. Then Michael, you will go straight to Zoe, she'll be in the Daphne, and stay with her. Kiss her, call her 'wife'. Make it good. She cannot be permitted to back out now. Bring her to see the body. She should look distraught, and so should you. But don't stay long, and don't answer any questions. George will go to the old man's office, take charge of his papers, and seal the place off." George holds the post, also thanks to John, of Master of the Wardrobe, second in rank only to the Grand Chamberlain. No one will question him. "Constantine will issue a proclamation in Zoe's name summoning the court to the palace on Friday. The wedding and coronation must take place immediately. We can't give anyone time to think. Surprise is everything. I will deal with the Patriarch."

"Has he been told?" Constantine asks.

"It would hardly do to tell him yet, would it? Christ on the cross, must I think for everyone?"

"And what if he balks?" Michael says.

"Fifty pounds of gold will change his mind." John pours himself a goblet of wine and drains it at a gulp. He drinks constantly. People say he is more to be feared drunk than sober. He sets the goblet down carefully. "Time to go."

11

I AM FOUND OUT
[*Odd resumes his narrative*]

The night following the banquet found me once again in Apgar's taverna, half-hoping I'd see 'Andreas', but the Armenian said he hadn't seen the boy since that trouble with the sailor. I decided to wait around a while. As the hour grew late and I was just getting ready to give up and leave, in she walked, carrying her game board under her arm. She saw me and ducked her head with a quick smile. I nodded back. Apgar beamed and brought her a cup of wine, and there was a quick exchange of Greek between the two of them with a glance in my direction. Andreas opened the board and set out the black and white counters. She looked at me and cocked an eyebrow. I felt my heart beat faster. That face of hers that hovered disturbingly between male and female fascinated me.

I brought my jug of wine over to the table and sat down. "My name is Churillo. What do you call this game of yours?"

"We call it *tavli*, sir." She used the Greek word that means 'tables'.

"Will you teach me to play? I hope you won't separate me from all my silver."

"That is up to you, sir." Her voice was husky—a maid trying to sound like a man. "We each throw two dice and the object is to move your fifteen men around the board and be the first to remove them all. It seems easy, but there are dangers and traps to be avoided. Land on the wrong triangle and you can be sent back to where you started. You almost always have several possible moves, but only one of them is best."

"Where did you learn to play?"

"My father taught me. He learned it in the East as a young man."

"He was a merchant? A soldier?"

Her lips tightened just a little. "A seeker of knowledge, a physician."

"I'd like to meet him."

She ignored this and handed me the dice cup. "A silver penny a game? You can go first."

And so we played for a while. I watched her more than I watched the board. She had a space between her front teeth and, while she considered a move, she would touch the tip of her tongue to it. Her eyebrows would draw together in concentration and she would tap a foot nervously.

I lost steadily, while Andreas explained carefully why every move I made was not the best. Finally, she said, "Sir, if you keep looking in my eyes instead of at the board you will never learn a thing."

"In that case, I give up," I laughed. "This is too hard for my thick head. You'd best take someone else's silver."

"Very well."

But there were no other takers this evening. After a moment, I said, "Shall we try somewhere else? I'll walk with you. It's a dark night."

Without meeting my eyes, she closed the board and stood up. "Not necessary."

But I followed her out the door. "Who are you, girl?" I touched her arm and turned her toward me.

"What do you mean? Let me go." She tried to pull away, but I held her. "I'm not a girl." She looked at me with angry eyes.

"I know the feel of a woman when I touch her. I also know that a boy doesn't sit with his knees together. What sort of game are you really playing here? I promise to keep your secret. You're a brave child."

"I'm no child. I'm eighteen and can take care of myself."

I doubted she was even that old. "Eighteen and not married?"

"What is that to you? I have no dowry, so that's an end of it. And if your next question is going to be do I have a lover the answer is no. I haven't time for such things."

"But your parents let you go out and mix with men like this? In my country that wouldn't be unusual, but here? I thought Greeks all locked their daughters up at night."

She shrugged. "My mother wouldn't have allowed it but she is dead.

And as for my father—well, he has much to occupy him at night. And whatever he doesn't like, he prefers not to see. The fact is we need the money."

"Is it only for the money?"

Now she smiled. "It's more than that. It's the battle of wits. It's getting one over on men."

"Not all men like being beaten—like the one who attacked you the other night."

"It doesn't happen often. I'm careful not to win too much."

"Tell me your name."

"Why?"

"No reason."

She hesitated. "It's Selene."

"Very pretty. Is that some saint?"

"I was named for the goddess of the Moon."

"Do you worship her?"

She looked at me from under long lashes. "That would be against the law."

She wasn't pretty, really. But there was intelligence in those large, dark eyes. And there was something about her that reminded me of little Ainikki, whom I had loved for so brief a time in Finland. But that child of the forest and this child of the streets would have nothing in common, except their courage, and maybe something more: an aura of magic that clung to both of them. While we talked, we strolled along the quay in the shadow of the sea wall; it was quiet on the water. A quarter-moon hung low over the Galata side.

"You said your father was a physician? But not a rich one. Surely, you can't make enough gambling to support the two of you? Do you have another trade?"

"I was once apprenticed to a silk weaving factory. I spoiled a piece of cloth, the matron beat me. I never went back."

"Good for you. And your father?"

"He takes patients sometimes. But he has little time for that. His life is devoted to the work."

"What work is that?"

Our shoulders had been almost touching but now she pulled away. "I've said too much. I don't know you."

"Then I will introduce myself. I am Churillo Igorevich, the envoy of Grand Prince Yaroslav of Kiev." I swept off my cap and made her a little bow.

"Rus! My God, you are a fierce, barbaric people."

I'd only meant to impress the girl, not terrify her. "Look," I said quickly, "I'm quite harmless, really. And I'm lonely here. I've been in the city two weeks and haven't yet been invited into a Greek home. I'd like to meet your father. I'll gladly bring a contribution for dinner."

"What? No, I'm sorry, it's impossible."

"But why?"

But she was already heading away from me down the street. The moon—her goddess—took that moment to disappear behind a rack of cloud plunging us into utter darkness. And I was left angry, baffled, and cursing the Greeks.

Then things got worse

✝

Two days passed uneventfully and then Psellus paid me a visit. Not the smiling, talkative young man of our last conversation. He was tight-lipped, frowning, and he avoided my eyes. All he would say was that the Logothete demanded my presence. What alarmed me most was that he brought two Khazar archers with him, as though he expected me to make a run for it.

There were more armed guards in Eustathius's office and the man himself was no longer the genial elf that I had first met amid his butterfly collection. He was pacing the room, and I noticed for the first time that he had a clubbed foot with a special shoe to cover it. He searched me with cold eyes. "Who the hell are you?" Before I could open my mouth, he went on: "I wondered why Yaroslav would send a new ambassador instead of Oleg Bogdanovich, who has been coming here for years. And someone so young, at that. Foreign intelligence is our specialty here. I know people who are familiar with Yaroslav's court. We know the names of all his boyars and 'Churillo Igorevich' isn't one of them. It has taken me a few days to confirm with our contacts that you are not who you claim to be. Who are you really and why are you here? What is this charade about?"

The first thought that flashed through my mind was of Ingigerd and how naïve she was, how little she really understood of how things worked here. To think that we could get away with this farce for more than a few days. By now, of course, I should have been standing over Harald's cold corpse; but I wasn't, and now I never would. The one bright spot, if you could call it that, was imagining how Inge was going to wriggle out of this one when her husband was informed of the deceit that had been practiced in his name. Perhaps this time she really had overstepped herself.

The Logothete's eyes searched me. "We don't like being fooled. I'll ask you one more time before I have my men beat it out of you. Why are you here?"

For a desperate moment, I ran through one possible lie after another. And then, with a feeling of indescribable relief, I decided to tell the truth. How I had been sent here as Princess Ingigerd's agent, not to negotiate the marriage of her daughter, but to murder the Varangian Guardsman, Harald Sigurdsson, whom she hated for reasons too complicated to explain. "And I had reasons of my own for killing him," I added.

"Harald who? Psellus, fetch down the Varangian muster book, it's on the high shelf behind you." Eustathius spent a minute turning the pages of the enormous volume. "Is this him?" He looked up. "Half-brother to the late King Olaf of Norway. Arrived here three years ago. Fine military record, important mission to Jerusalem, promoted to captain of a bandon, good officer by all accounts. The kind of man we like to see in the Guard. This is outrageous. I tell you right now, Churillo, or whatever your name is, you will make no move against this officer, or I will have you executed on the spot. The fact that a barbarian princess hates him for personal reasons is no concern of mine. I'm writing to Yaroslav at once. And I will order the Rus merchants here to cut ties with you; they'll be out of our city in a few days anyway, thank God."

"And what about me, sir?"

"What about you? You are entirely dispensable, Churillo Igor— Dammit, man, what is your name anyway?"

I told him, and tried to explain that I had pretty well given up the idea of killing Harald, but he cut me off. "For someone who is here under false colors, you seem to be very interested in us. Young Psellus has told me about your long conversation after the banquet. I fear he may have said more than he should. Exactly why do you want to know all this—how the government works, who does what? Don't bother answering, the question is moot now. You no longer have any reason to be here, so I'm afraid your curiosity about our affairs will have to go unsatisfied. You will, of course, move out of the hostel at once. If you want to remain in our city, you do so on your own. You know ships? You might be able to find work around the water front, caulking, sail-mending, something of the sort. Or, I would suggest the army, but we're not recruiting at the moment."

"The Varangians?" I ventured in a murmur.

"What? Out of the question. They don't take just anyone."

"Office of Barbarians? I speak three languages."

"Ridiculous."

Well, that was that then. No place to live. My subsidy, which Stavko had been doling out, would stop at once. I owned nothing but the expensive clothes on my back. How would I live? Where would I go? Obviously, not back to Kiev. I had no ship, no crew, no friends. My beautiful fantasy of rising to wealth and power in Golden Miklagard lay shattered in pieces. My long, tortuous journey from the ruins of my Iceland home had ended here in abject failure. Perhaps I should hang myself.

With tears in my eyes—I'm not ashamed to admit it—I stumbled out the door and made my way across the palace grounds. As I came in sight of the polo field, I heard the bray of trumpets and the tramp of feet. A raven banner fluttered in the wind. The Varangians were on parade. In spite of myself, I stopped for a minute to look.

"Tangle-Hair, over here!" came a voice I recognized.

12

i BECOME A SPY

"Gorm!" I called out in reply. Glum's brother, my one friend among the Varangians, trotted over to me. He was carrying his two-handled axe on his shoulder and his scarlet shield slung on his back.

"How goes it, friend Odd?"

"Not so well."

"Oh?" He looked genuinely sorry. "Well, this should cheer you up. We're on parade today, put on a real show for our Roman masters. Stand over here, you'll see everything."

The polo ground, situated in the middle of the palace grounds, was a wide field, bordered by a palisade. Once earlier, I had seen a team of Khazar horse archers playing against another cavalry regiment, thundering up and down on their ponies, swinging long mallets. But today the space was filled with infantry, both Varangians and other palace regiments—the Manglabitai, the Kandidatoi, the Noumeri and Teichistai—all fitted out in their bronze corselets and plumed helmets and uniforms or white, red and blue—marshalled rank by rank, performing their exercises.

On every side banners flew—one of them, the dragon-headed standard of the Varangians with its long streaming tail. Harald could be seen, and heard, some distance away bawling orders at his bandon as they charged, swung their axes, wheeled, and charged again. His men were the best-looking troops on the field, no question. Senior army officers stood on the reviewing stand along one side, applauding them. It *was* a sight to stir the heart. How I wished I were one of them, with the haft of an axe in my hand, charging, shouting, feeling the blood pounding in my head. Odin! It had been too long, too long. Suddenly, my cares came rushing back. No more for me the warrior's life. I remembered with a pang how years before I had watched Harald marshal Yaroslav's druzhina for our expedition against the Pechenegs. I was his skald then, his second in command. But now, landless, shipless, friendless, who would take me on? I turned to go.

"Tangle-Hair, stop, damn it." Harald waved a long arm at me. "Gorm said you were here. We'll talk, don't go away."

Well, what else did I have to do? I stayed and watched for a half hour more and was rewarded by an interesting sight: Harald in an angry shouting match with another Varangian. This man was old, his white whiskers spread over an enormous belly, and he limped on a crutch. His clothes were very fine and he wore a golden torque around his fat neck. I remembered Stavko had told me that the Commandant of the Guard was one Sveinn Gudleifsson, a gouty old fellow who enjoyed his pampered life in the city and was apt to resent an ambitious young upstart like Harald. It seemed likely that this was him. It wasn't clear what their quarrel was about, but both of them were red in the face. It took three or four other Varangians to pull them apart. Soon after, the parade disbanded and Sveinn stumped off.

I made my way over toward Harald, where he stood surrounded by his men. I pulled him aside and, before he could say anything, began the speech I'd been rehearsing for the past few minutes. "You said the other day that you had an idea how I can help you. You'd better tell me now for in another day I will be gone from here. I've been exposed and banned from the palace. The only bright spot in the whole mess is the embarrassment this is going to cause Inge. You should appreciate that. Yelisaveta's yours for the taking. But if you have anything for me, say it now."

"Walk with me, Tangle-Hair." We made our way to the Brazen Gate, the imposing complex of gates and guardhouses that forms the ceremonial entranceway to the Great Palace. "The Fourth Bandon is on guard duty this week," he said. "We have our quarters here with a private office for the captain, which is me. We'll take lunch there."

He sat facing me over a basket of bread and cheese and a bottle of wine. "I've neglected you. I'm sorry. I've been busy. I thought we had more time."

"Time for what?"

He frowned for a moment in thought and stroked his long moustaches. Every time I saw him he looked less like the overgrown boy—the 'unnatural weed'—that I remembered from Gardariki. "Let's get one thing clear, Tangle-Hair. I will need to trust you absolutely. I could ask you swear an oath on some saint's relic but we both know that would be pointless in your case. No, you must become my skald again, my poet, my advisor, my go-between. No need for you to be a Varangian, this is a personal bond, it's nothing to do with the regiment. I once gave you an arm ring. D'you remember?"

How well I did! Seven, almost eight, years ago. We sat in Jarl Rognvald's hall in Aldeigjuborg. Harald with his mentor, Dag, and all their men. I alone, estranged from my crew. Harald, only sixteen, had fled from Norway and was on his way to Novgorod to enlist under Yaroslav and plot to regain his brother Olaf's throne. Dag urged me to join them, to help him control this bumptious young prince. And I agreed. We spent the night drinking and swapping lines of poetry and, at the end of it, Harald gave me an arm ring, sliding it from the tip of his sword to the tip of mine in the old viking fashion.

"What's become of it?" he asked.

"I threw it away."

He coughed and looked away. "Yes, well, maybe you had reason, let's not go into that again. But we'll start fresh. Things will be different this time, you'll see."

"What is it that you need me for so badly? You said something about my speaking Greek for you. They have interpreters in the Office of Barbarians, why don't you send for one of them?"

"Because I prefer them not to know my business."

"Well, who are you talking to?"

He shook his head. "First the ring. And, as long as you're my man, Tangle-Hair," he spoke slowly, underlining each word, "you have nothing to fear from Halldor or Bolli or anyone else. Do you understand me?" Without waiting for a reply, he went out into the day room and ordered in half-a-dozen of his men, who were lounging there. In their presence we went through the ceremony, with all the high-flown words about honor and good faith and the bond between warlord and skald. And all I could think of was that other time: the heat of the wine, the warriors banging their sword hilts on the tables, and the rush of hope, promise, and honor between two young men in love with poetry and adventure.

There was none of that now. Now there was only cold calculation. I was no longer being paid to kill Harald and had, frankly, lost the urge. Too much else was crowding in on my mind. Not that we would ever be friends, but possibly we could work together for our mutual advantage. If not, I could always leave. Harald took a ring from his arm, a heavy silver one with twisting serpents around it, and I put it on. The onlookers murmured their congratulations without much enthusiasm, except for Gorm who gave me a bone-crushing squeeze on my sore shoulder.

"Have they thrown you out of the ambassadors' hostel?" Harald asked me when we were alone again. "Stay here, if you like."

"Thanks, but maybe we shouldn't be seen together too much."

"You're right, as usual. But be here when I need you. Here," he pushed a bag of coins toward me. "If you're not on Inge's payroll anymore then you will be on mine. Mind you, I'm not as rich as she is—not yet. Find yourself someplace to live. I'm told there are nice properties out by the ring wall in the Lycos valley. Open country—have you been out there?— very pretty. Have a bit of a garden, buy a horse. We're country boys, you and I, Odd, not like these citified Greeks."

I emptied the coins into my purse. "Thanks, I'll have a look round. When will you need me?"

"Tomorrow night if I can arrange things."

"And can I ask now who I'm translating for?"

"All in good time, my friend." He grinned and would say no more.

✝

The Orphanage of Saint Paul, which stood on the acropolis north of the palace, consisted of several old brick buildings and a church, arranged around a courtyard and surrounded by a fence. The courtyard was littered with untidy piles of lumber and stone; there was an untended garden where a little grass struggled to survive. Inside, it stank of cabbage and despair. It was past sundown when Harald and I arrived, both of us wearing dark cloaks and hoods. I felt faintly ridiculous; we'd probably attract more attention than otherwise costumed like this, but it appealed to Harald. We were met at the entrance by a lank-haired, pinch-faced young man with a patch over one eye and a missing front tooth. He said his name was Loucas and informed us that he was the Senior Orphan.

"I'm an orphan myself," I said, trying to banter with him.

He didn't smile. Holding up a lantern, he led us into the heart of this unhappy place. If I was expecting to see those well-scrubbed children in their chorister frocks, I was disappointed. We passed boys and girls on their knees with pails and brushes, dormitory rooms without doors in which the bedding was gray and tattered, and walked through one large room where boys sat on the floor amid coils of old rope, picking oakum out of the strands with tarry fingers and another where girls sat at looms peering at their work by the feeble light of a few smoky candles. Nowhere did we hear conversation, much less singing. Loucas spoke only once, when we passed a series of cells with bars on the doors. "Some of the children need correction," he said.

He brought us finally to the office of the Guardian of Orphans. There were two men inside, seated at a bare table. One was John, dressed as always in his monk's habit; the other, I learned, was his brother-in-law Stephen. I had heard a little about Stephen—none of it encouraging. The man had started out a caulker in the shipyards, had been lucky enough to marry into John's family, and now rejoiced in the title of Admiral of the Fleet, although the general opinion was that he was incapable of commanding a fleet of walnut shells in a bathtub. But it was he who had led the squadron that carried masons and architects to Jerusalem the previous year and got to know Harald, who was escorting them. Stephen was no genius but he had a sharp eye for ambition and greed—qualities worth cultivating—and mentioned Harald to John.

Stephen stood when we entered. John did not. He motioned us to chairs, sent Loucas out of the room and told Stephen, as if he were just some servant, to pour wine for us. I waved my glass away, thinking that I might need a clear head for whatever tonight's business was. I was not wrong. John leaned forward on his elbows and squinted at me. His eyes were hard as sling bullets, under heavy lids the color of bruises.

"Where have I seen you before?"

"At the banquet," I answered. "I enjoyed the singing. I hope the Emperor has recovered."

He slapped the table so hard we all jumped. He glared at Harald. "*This* is who you bring me?" He said this in Greek, of course, and it was clear right from the start that Harald was lost. "My skald," he began, "my—" he searched for the word—"my *poietes*, poet."

"Spy, you mean," John snarled. "The so-called ambassador from Gardariki. And the first day he's here he has a private meeting with *Zoe*. Why?" He turned his gaze on me. "You speak Greek, man? You'd better start talking."

Harald stared hard at me. He wasn't getting much of this but he knew there was a problem. To him, in rapid Norse, I explained that she had chatted with me about nothing, given me a bottle of perfume, and that was the end of it. To John I said the same and added that as an ambassador I was supposed to talk to Roman officials, and I assumed that the Empress of Rome could speak with whomever she liked.

"You assumed wrong," John shot back. "You will have gathered that the Empress is quite distracted in her wits—strange fancies, religious enthusiasms, this perfume business…" He attempted a smile of sympathy, which on him was merely grotesque. "You will not see her again."

"I haven't been invited, sir."

"And as for you being an ambassador, that appears to be no longer the case, Churillo, or whatever you call yourself."

"Odd Thorvaldsson. You know a lot about me."

"I know everything about you. That is my job. You came here to arrange a marriage for the Rus princess, the one Harald here fancies, which is why I have vetoed it." Turning to Harald, he said, "You don't consider this fellow an enemy?" I translated this. Harald replied that he held my life in his hands and I damn well knew it. I smiled at John and said, "We've been dear friends for years."

John returned his gaze to me. "The first moment I have reason to suspect your loyalty, don't doubt that I will protect myself. I know what you barbarians think of men like me. I warn you, in my case you would be quite wrong. I am not a soft man at all."

"I think it's time you explained to me what this is all about." I tried my best to look imposing.

"All right, let's see if you can follow this. Our young Emperor, my dear brother, Christ help him, is sicker than anyone realizes. It is vital that another member of my family occupies the throne when he dies. The only possible choice is my nephew, Stephen and Maria's son, who is little more than a child—"

"But a good lad," Stephen interrupted. "A bit wild, but he'll outgrow it." Stephen spoke in the same rough, uncultured accent that I did. Not the elegant Greek John used.

Ignoring his brother-in-law, the Guardian of Orphans continued. "We have already persuaded Zoe to adopt the boy as her son. But that isn't good enough. Her supporters—the Logothete among others—will try to marry her off to someone—someone who isn't one of *us*. That cannot be allowed to happen. What we need, what I need, is control of the Varangians. With their support I can do whatever I want. Unfortunately, the present Commandant is not a friend of ours. He goes back to Basil's day, he's loyal to the Macedonian dynasty, to Zoe, and I can't remove him. Not yet, anyway."

"That surprises me. You are the Emperor's brother."

He smiled sourly at me. "Sveinn Gudleifsson has survived at this court for thirty years. He may be old and crippled with gout but he's shrewd, tough, rich, and well-connected. He married into one of our leading families and so has his daughter. A lot of people owe him favors. We can't move against him openly without creating an uproar and the Emperor wants no part of that."

I translated this for Harald.

"The gouty old fool hates me," Harald sneered. "Picked a quarrel with me on parade today."

"That is because I went around him to get you appointed to the Guard," John replied. "Try deferring to him, he'll come around. I know diplomacy is not your strong point, Harald. Maybe you should take pointers from the 'ambassador' here."

While I translated this—selectively—I thought back to Dag Ringsson. He was a diplomat who had smoothed the way for young Harald at Yaroslav' court until Harald got tired of taking his advice and threw him over. How long, I wondered, would I last in the same role?

"Now," John resumed, "Harald here is a popular man, he is on his way up, the men will follow him. When the moment comes, he will assume command of the Guard—we will take care of Sveinn—and with their help we will put Zoe out of her misery once and for all and my nephew will become Emperor Michael the Fifth. This much has been worked out between Harald Sigurdsson and me, but slowly, laboriously. I doubt he understands half what we say to him. When the time comes, communication must be swift, clear, and secure. There must be no misunderstandings, no mixed signals. For obvious reasons we can't use interpreters from the Office of Barbarians. That is where you come in, my friend."

While I translated, Harald was looking morose and tugging at his long moustaches. "Tell the ballsless wonder that he needs to get me another promotion. It isn't just Sveinn. There are too many in the Guard who outrank me."

I put this into diplomatic Greek, but I suspect that John understood more of it than he let on.

"Tell the big, shaggy beast," he replied smoothly, "that it is too soon for that." John was taking a chance; what if I translated his words exactly? But he seemed to know that I wouldn't. I was beginning to feel like the only child in a bad marriage. It was obvious they disliked each other. And I didn't like either of them. I could feel the tension rising. The strain of translating—and not quite translating—was giving me a headache. "What we need," John mused, "is a nice war, a chance for Harald to shine and for Sveinn to be politely put out to pasture."

This was encouraging. What Norseman doesn't long for a war? I asked if there was one in the offing.

"Perhaps sooner than anyone thinks," he answered.

The conversation went on a while longer until Harald stood up suddenly. "Enough for one night. When will we meet again?"

"Oh, not for some time," John replied. "Eustathius has his spies, too. We can't be careless."

Out in the street again, Harald turned to me. "So you saw Zoe? You didn't tell me that. She invited me to her stink-works too when I first came here. She asked me for a lock of my golden hair. I told her I'd give it in exchange for a lock of her hair—the hair between her legs. Hah! Never heard a word from her after that. Old meat doesn't appeal to me. Of course, Tangle-Hair, you feel differently about old meat, don't you?" He let out a harsh laugh. I had no love for Zoe, who I hardly knew, nor for Ingigerd, whom I knew too well. Nevertheless, his sneer angered me. "Like old times again, eh, me and you, eh? But this time we really are on the same side, Tangle-Hair, aren't we?"

At that moment I wanted to hit him. Instead, I asked him if he was afraid of John. The idea seemed to astonish him. "Afraid of that capon!" he laughed out loud. "Of course not. Why should I fear *him*?"

Possibly because you lack imagination, was what I wanted to say, but didn't.

I smiled instead and told him goodnight.

✝

I had not succeeded that day in finding a country house to rent. After traipsing all over the fields and orchards that lay within the outer walls, I ended up back in the city, in a little street a few blocks off the Triumphal Way that was given over to ironmongers and cheap clothing stores. I moved my few belongings out of the hostel and packed Piotr off to Stavko, to his great delight. I put down five *nomismata* for two clean rooms on the third floor of a tenement and bought a strong lock for my door. I felt better being in the heart of things anyway than stuck out in the country. What a city boy I'd become!

Now, as I made my way along the darkened streets from the orphanage, lit only by a fitful moon, I pondered what an evil situation I was in. These men would abandon me the minute I ceased being useful to them. I already knew too many of their secrets to be safe. I'd trusted Harald once; I wouldn't make that mistake again. And what did all their scheming come to? To persecute a defenseless, possibly mad, old woman and put some young incompetent on the throne of a great empire. Should I care? To my surprise I found that I did. Still, I might have gone along with them for a time, except for what happened next. I heard footsteps behind me. I pulled my knife from my boot and quickened my pace. The footsteps stayed with me, turning the corner when I turned. I looked over my shoulder and saw a dark figure flatten itself against the wall of a building. I walked on, turned another corner, stepped into an alley, and waited. I heard the footsteps stop, then come on again. As my pursuer passed me, I stepped out, took him by the throat with one hand and pressed the point of my knife under his rib.

"Don't, sir!" I recognized the face with its eye patch. Loucas, the orphan.

"Why are you following me?"

"Orders. Guardian wants to know where you live." He twisted in my grip.

"Why?"

But he clamped his mouth shut.

"As one orphan to another, Loucas, if I ever catch you sneaking up behind me again, I'll kill you." I threw him to the ground and kicked him in the face. He let out a yelp, scrambled up and ran off into the night.

I think until that moment I hadn't quite decided whose side I was on. I doubled back, aiming toward the great arches of the aqueduct that loomed out of the dark, and followed it to the little street that I remembered. Once or twice along the way, I faltered and nearly changed my mind. This was a very dangerous game I was about to play—I needed no one to tell me that. But the more I thought about John and Harald the angrier I got. And, I suppose, I've never been one to weigh my choices prudently. I found the house I was seeking and pounded on the nail-studded door until someone stirred within. A small peep hole opened, a candle flame lit up an eye that peered at me.

"It's me. Let me in."

The door creaked open and there stood Psellus in his nightshirt and cap. He had a heavy candlestick in his fist. Behind him, I glimpsed two frightened women, clutching each other.

"Churil—" he started. "Odd!"

"We have to talk."

13

FRIENDSHIP AND A WARNING

He pulled me inside and locked the door. "It's all right, mother," he told the older woman, "go back to your room. You too, Phyllida."

I caught a glimpse of the mother as she and her daughter turned and fled up the stairs: a gaunt face with big, staring eyes; a black snood wrapped around her head and chin and a tattered robe cinched with a rope.

"Forgive me, Psellus, but—"

"What do you want here?"

And so I told him all that had passed between Harald, John, and me. Constantine Psellus was an excitable young man at the best of times. Now he flung himself around the room, rubbing his stubbly head with both hands and exclaiming "Dear God!" and "Incredible!" and "The Logothete must be told at once!" Finally he calmed down enough to ask me what I planned to do. I hardly knew myself, but told him that I very much wanted to talk to Eustathius and to be useful to them if I could.

"Useful? Why? What are we to you?" He looked at me with narrow eyes.

Why indeed? Because Harald and John were odious? Because I felt sorry for Zoe? Because I still, somehow, imagined a life for myself here—a life, maybe, with Selene, if I ever found her again? I don't think I made much sense. Finally, Psellus said, "You'll sleep here tonight and stay indoors tomorrow. God knows who may be lurking out there, watching for you. I will speak to the Logothete in the morning and then come back."

"I'm upsetting your household."

"Never mind. My mother—well—spends most of her time on her knees, praying. You won't see her. Cook will get you something to eat." And with that, he showed me to a small upstairs room, tossed some bedding at me, and bade me sleep well. Needless to say, I didn't sleep at all. I doubt he did either.

I spent a long, dull day in his house until, after sundown, Psellus returned with Eustathius in a closed carriage, the two of them rushing in through the door as though they expected the Guardian of Orphans to spring out at them from behind a shrubbery. This made a deep impression on me. If this man Eustathius, a powerful official in his own right, was so afraid of John and his spies that he must sneak into Psellus's house like a thief in the night, then truly I was facing something far more dangerous than even I had imagined—and I have a lively imagination.

Dinner was served to us by an elderly servant and for the next hour the Logothete interrogated me in his precise and careful way, making me go over my story again and again, dredging up every detail I could remember of what John and Harald had said. He wanted to know what sort of man Harald was. Here I was eloquent as I'd given that subject much thought over the years.

I repeated what Dag Ringsson had told me once about Harald's childhood: the 'unnatural weed' who by the age of thirteen was taller than most grown men and expected to play a man's part before he was ready; the sense of grievance against his half-brother, King Olaf, whose father came of nobler stock; the endless boasting that covered the gnawing fear that no one regarded him as well as he deserved; the ease with which he cast off friends who no longer served his purpose; the quite genuine talent for leading men in battle.

"You describe a very dangerous man," Eustathius summed up, smiling bleakly, when I had finished. "And you said you were sent here to kill him? I wish you had succeeded."

"That isn't what you said to me yesterday, sir," I reminded him.

"That was yesterday."

"He still could," Psellus offered.

"Out of the question. It would enrage the Varangians, it would frighten John—and John frightened is not something I care to contemplate."

"Well, at least," Psellus said, "we must warn the Commandant."

Again Eustathius shook his head. "Sveinn Gudleifsson drinks too much and talks too much. We can't have him charging about like a mad bull."

Psellus, having run out of ideas, lapsed into silence. Eustathius realized at once that the boy's pride was hurt and he lay a reassuring hand on his knee. "Thank you, Costas"—he called him by the familiar form of his first name: there was something of the father and son about these two—"we will hit upon the right plan." He turned an appraising eye on me. "You want to be useful to us?"

I nodded.

"Then you will continue to be Harald's man. Whatever you learn of his plans you will report to Psellus here, never directly to me. As long as the Emperor lives there is nothing we can do but, at the instant of his death, we must be ready. God forbid that young delinquent, Stephen's son, whom they browbeat Zoe into adopting, should ever come to the throne. Now, John wants his own Varangian? It occurs to me that I want *my* own Varangian. I don't know them well, not my job to. What if you were to join the Guard, Odd Thorvaldsson?"

My heart leapt. "Could it be arranged?"

"Yes, but not in haste. Nothing must seem forced. John is hoping for a war in which Harald can shine. Are you a warrior, too? I hope you are, because war is coming." He drained his glass and stood up. "I'm expected home. I'm a man of regular habits. Nothing I do, nothing you do, must seem out of the ordinary. Odd, I will escort you back to your apartment. The less Costas's family see of you the better. From now on, you and he will meet at a fixed hour, one day a week, always in a different place. Work out the details between you. From time to time he will have money for you, a retainer, as it were. Don't spend it ostentatiously. I gather he has already become your mentor, of a sort. You couldn't ask for a better one."

✝

Then began for me a time of alternating dullness, anxiety, and excitement. During the days, time hung heavy on my hands, with nothing to occupy myself beyond fishing in the Horn from a rowboat I bought for myself, or taking long rides out in the country on a hired horse, or exploring more of the city to the point where I could say without boasting that I knew every monument and church, every corner and byway of it.

I stayed away from Apgar's. Though I hardly knew her, I longed to see Selene again and I found myself thinking of her all the time. But I was ashamed to seem to be lying in wait for her.

Of course, there were repercussions to my knocking down John's orphan, Loucas. Harald summoned me the very next day.

"I've heard from John. He's so angry he's ready to abandon our plan altogether."

"I don't like being followed."

"It's what they do here," he shrugged.

"Anyone who follows me again, I'll kill him."

"You always had a bad temper, Tangle-Hair. An inconvenient thing, temper." He paused for a long moment. "All right, it won't happen again. But I have a right to know where I can find you."

"You only had to ask." I told him where my rooms were.

After that, from time to time, he commanded my presence to drink with him and his men in the barracks, to tell tales and recite poems, as a skald is supposed to do. (Stories involving Gorm's brother Glum, the berserker and werewolf, were always popular.) But these occasions were never carefree, though I did my best to pretend. I could never forget for a moment that I was playing a double game. One slip, one careless word in Harald's hearing could mean my death. Halldor and Bolli continued to act towards me like a couple of mastiffs who would tear my throat out if Harald should decide to let go of their leashes. At least, there were, for the time being, no more nocturnal visits to the orphanage.

But it was those weekly meetings with Psellus that I relished. I had to assume I was still being watched, although I couldn't catch anyone at it. Any urchin in the street could be one of John's orphans for all I knew. As instructed by the Logothete, we had arranged a series of meeting places: at the foot of the clock tower in the Augusteum, in front of the Church of the Holy Wisdom, at the harbor of Boukoleon, at the cistern of Aspar, and so on. And we always met an hour after dark. From there we would stroll until we found a place to sit and talk without attracting attention. After a couple of weeks, when I had nothing new to report, Psellus seemed disappointed. The excitement was wearing off. But, in place of this, we discovered that we had much in common and, strange as it may seem for two such different creatures as we, a friendship began to grow up between us.

Psellus was glad to spend as much time away from his gloomy home as possible. He gradually unbent and told me something of himself: how his younger sister, a beautiful and intelligent girl, had died of fever and his mother had gone insane with grief, cutting off her hair and tying it to the casket and, ever since, had lived like a nun in her own home, dragging beggars in off the street to wash their sores, and so forth.

"I lack her piety," he said, shaking his head. "I wish I had it but I don't."

His father had left the family altogether and entered a monastery. Psellus, rarely saw him. (I was right in guessing that Eustathius was more a father to him than his own father.) An uncle now was head of the family, while everyone waited impatiently for young Psellus to make his fortune in government service. "I will open my heart to you," he said one evening. "I love the work, of course, but it's a lonely life. Every man in the bureau is a competitor, a rival for advancement and honor. We all hide our true feelings behind a smiling mask—a skill that you will need to practice, by the way—but it leaves no room for friendship.

In return, I told him my history: how my half-mad father had taught me poetry and rune lore; how my family had been slaughtered in a blood feud and I driven from Iceland to seek my fortune as a viking. How my crew and I sailed and looted from Lapland to Gardariki, battled crashing storms at sea, were enslaved by a witch and how we escaped. He was endlessly fascinated by all this, especially when I recited bits of the old heroic lays and tried to translate them into Greek for him.

"But it's pure Homer!" he gazed at me open-mouthed.

"Who?"

And so began my education.

"Our greatest poet," Psellus exclaimed. "Centuries ago he sang tales of the heroes who battled under the walls of Troy for the love of a beautiful woman. He told of the voyages of Odysseus and the monsters and giants and witches he outwitted—in this very part of the world that we now inhabit. It's the sum and substance of our education. I was raised on it. And now I feel—how can I express it?—I feel like I'm sitting across the table from Odysseus himself. To us, they're only words on a page. You have actually *lived* it. Extraordinary." And he began to recite, *Menin aeide thea Peleiadeo Achileos ... Sing, goddess, of the wrath of Achilles son of Peleus ...* Greek, but a dialect strange and musical with many unfamiliar words, the syllables rolling off his tongue, the cadences marching as if to a drumbeat. And I, in my turn, was enthralled. Those long-dead Greeks—Achilles and Hector and the rest—could just as well have been Northmen. I felt as though I knew them, what drove them, what delighted them or shamed them.

From then on, I wanted nothing but to hear tales of those ancient Greek vikings and match them to my own. And Psellus would sometimes shake his head and wonder aloud, "What does it mean to call you a 'barbarian', Odd Tangle-Hair? Homer's heroes were no more nor less barbaric than you."

One night, inevitably, the subject turned to women. "I'm engaged to be married," Psellus confided in me, "but the girl is only twelve and it will be two more years before we become man and wife. I've only met her twice and scarcely know her. I'm a man of fiery passions, Tangle-Hair, though I may not seem it. It's hard to be patient. And what about you?"

I told him about my brief encounters with the mysterious Selene and how I despaired of winning her confidence.

"Life is full of coincidences," Psellus laughed. "If it's the same girl, then I know the family. We own a small silk works, you know. Now that my father has taken holy orders, my uncle runs it. He was an acquaintance of this girl's father, if it is her—a man named Melampus. His wife had worked for us as a weaver and, after she died, my uncle hired the daughter to stitch brocade. It didn't last long, she didn't care for the work. I don't know her personally or Melampus, though I've heard my uncle say the man will come to a bad end someday. One can admire the ancients and their priceless knowledge—I do myself—but you must be discreet about it. Melampus is said to be a magician and a devotee of the old gods and these are things that could get him burned for a heretic if he isn't careful."

"He sounds like my father. Do you know where they live?"

"No, but I can probably find out."

One morning during this time, I was loafing along the shore of the Horn on the Saint Mamas side, when I saw the Rus boats loading up for their voyage back to Gardariki. After a stay of three weeks, the vessels were laden with great amphorae of Greek wine, bales of spices, coffles of slaves, bolts of linen and silk. I pressed through the crowd and found Stavko. He greeted me with a scowl.

"Churillo, you left hostel. Then I don't know where to find you. So, tell me, what is happening with you?"

"I'm not Churillo anymore. I haven't killed Harald, and I won't. It's simply impossible. You can tell Ingigerd that."

He looked at me long and reproachfully. "Our money?"

"Is mostly spent, I'm afraid. I'm staying on here for a bit. I'll get by." More than that he didn't need to know.

Stavko shrugged. "Princess will not stop, you know. Will send someone else—to kill Harald *and* you, if you're still here. You were nice fellow, Odd Tangle-Hair. I liked you."

And, with those words, he turned back to his slaves.

14

Che Alchemist

Late afternoon on a wet July day. With my heart in my throat, I knocked upon the door and listened to the rattle of bolts and chains unfastening. The door opened to reveal the figure of an old man, very tall, with a cadaverous face. His eyes were deep-set, his brows dark and springing, his nose like an eagle's beak. His white beard hung to his waist and tufts of white hair stuck out from under a black velvet cap. He was shabbily dressed, the sleeves of his gown out at the elbows. He had the complexion of someone who rarely ventured out of doors.

"Doctor Melampus?"

Psellus had consulted his uncle and told me how to find the house of Selene's father. "But what good will it do?" he asked me. "You can't just walk in uninvited."

"I'll invent an illness. Ask for some physic, an amulet. Say your uncle recommended him."

"And then what?"

"I'll think of something."

Even with directions it had taken me an hour on horseback to find the place. It lay far out on the Mese, past the Church of the Holy Apostles, where the city begins to give way to countryside. It was one of a sprawl of old houses, hardly enough of them to call a village, once handsome but now fallen into disrepair. The tiled roofs were gap-toothed, the plastered walls peeling, and, after a day of steady rain, the alleys between the houses were narrow tracks, ankle-deep in mud where chickens pecked and naked children splashed in puddles.

I had knocked on several doors before finding the right one. Meanwhile, I rehearsed one improbable speech after another that I would make to Selene if she were at home. I'd happened to be in the neighborhood when I started feeling sick. Or, I longed to make the acquaintance of her illustrious father. Or, I was thinking of buying a house in the area and wanted to meet my neighbors. Anything but the truth—that I longed to see *her*, that I couldn't understand why she had run away from me, that I was ashamed to waylay her in the taverna again and didn't know what else to do.

"Come in, sir." His voice rumbled deep in his chest. He led me into a large, dark room, sparsely furnished but clean. Was she there? I took in the room with a swift glance. But the only other occupant I could see was a little monkey in a yellow silk jacket that sat atop a wooden chest of drawers, nibbling a lettuce leaf. It looked up and blinked at me. Now what should I do? A medley of smells assaulted my nostrils: some of them cooking oil and cabbage, others acrid, metallic, unnamable. The windows were shut and barred, the room was hot. I thought of Zoe's perfumery and kept myself from wrinkling my nose in disgust.

The old man eyed me warily. "I don't get many visitors from outside the neighborhood. Who sent you to me?" I named Psellus's uncle and he nodded. "And how may I help you, sir?"

"I'm, er, suffering from dizziness, doctor." I improvised. "From headache, vomiting."

"Ah. It could be *mati*—the evil eye. Have you recently crossed paths with someone who envies you?"

"Doctor, I think I can honestly say that there is no one in the world who envies me."

"Then you're a lucky man."

"Or a most unlucky one."

He offered a quick smile at this. "I will examine you. Please remove your tunic and shirt and lie down over there." He indicated a cot with a threadbare coverlet on it. When I had arranged myself, he studied me for a moment, placed his index finger in my navel, and frowned.

His hands were large, with big knuckles and knotted blue veins, and they shook with a tremor he seemingly couldn't control. "As I thought," he said, "no pulse. Your navel is wandering."

"My navel? But it's right here."

"The invisible navel, sir. When it wanders, the body is loosened. This is a very dangerous condition. Have you drunk cold water while you were sweating? Did you eat cucumbers while you were overheated? Have you lifted anything heavy?"

What a fool's errand I'd come on! Selene wasn't here, and how long could I keep this up? I should leave before I thoroughly embarrassed myself.

"There are various treatments," he continued, "let us begin with this." He produced a vial of some clear liquid that smelled strongly of onions, sprinkled drops of it on my stomach, and began to mutter a spell.

"Doctor, perhaps, after all—" I tried to sit up.

"Hold still," he commanded.

And then the door opened and in she walked, with her game box under her arm. She tossed her wet cloak in a corner. She was dressed as I had seen her before, in loose-fitting tunic and trousers that showed nothing of her figure. "Father, I—oh, I'm sorry." She glanced at me as I struggled into my shirt—then looked again. "Churillo? What are you doing here? Is that your horse?"

"Selene, what a surprise!"

"Get out."

Get out? Nothing more than that? I'd never flattered myself I was good-looking but what could she have against me?

Melampus looked from one of us to the other. "You know each other?"

"We've met," she said. "At a taverna."

He looked at me sternly. "Your aren't sick, are you, sir? It's my daughter you came to see, not me. You wouldn't be the first young man to do so. But you have imposed on me sir. You have come here under false pretenses. I will ask you to leave now."

What a disaster! What came out of my mouth then was none of the things I had planned to say. "I wanted to meet you, Melampus," I blurted in a rush of words. "My father was a magician and a believer in the old gods, like yourself." It was what Psellus had told me about him.

There was a very long silence during which the old man leaned close over me. "And why do you tell me this? Who are you?"

"My name is Odd Thorvaldsson," I replied, "called Tangle-Hair, a visitor to your city from Ultima Thule."

"Liar!" Selene cried. You gave me a different name. You're a police spy. Get out. We're good Christians here, we've done nothing wrong. Please. My father is an old man, harmless—" She ran to him and put her arms around him, to shield him from me.

But he put up his hand to silence her. "Thule? I've heard of that distant land. Fascinating. I never overlook an opportunity to learn some new thing. I believe you mean us no harm."

"Father—"

"It's all right, my dear. It's time for our evening meal, sir. Will you join us?"

In the kitchen that adjoined the sitting room, a shapeless old woman in a black dress and headscarf stirred a pot on the hearth. We sat on stools around a table that had one leg shorter than the others. The only light came from a couple of tallow candles in wooden candlesticks that smoked and guttered in the draft. The monkey, whose name was Ramesses, followed us in and hopped up beside Selene, like one of the family. She fed it from her hand. Melampus smiled apologetically. "I know that you Northerners are great meat eaters, but I'm afraid we have none to offer."

We dipped our spoons into a mess of gruel and boiled vegetables and washed it down with watered vinegar, the beverage of the poor. "Delicious," I lied.

"But the Guardian of the House," he said, "feeds on better stuff." I followed the doctor's gaze to the floor, where, to my astonishment, an enormous snake glided out from under the table and darted its tongue into a saucer of milk. Meanwhile, Selene ate steadily, without looking up or speaking. Melampus returned his attention from the snake to me. "And what about you, sir? Do you still worship the gods of your father?"

"It's a debt I owe my dead ones," I answered, casting my eyes down. "It gets harder the farther I travel. Odin seems very far away."

"Odin!" he cried. "Then I know your god, I know him well. He has many names. The Egyptians call him Thoth, the Latins call him Mercury. But his true name is Hermes the Thrice-Great, the son of Zeus, the greatest benefactor of mankind—poet, trickster, the sender of dreams, the guide of souls, the inventor of writing, the Supreme Magician. The middle day of the week bears his name, and the planet that lies nearest the Sun. He is the father of alchemy. Quicksilver is his metal, that precious stuff without which—"

Selene's face was suddenly alive; she shot her father a frightened look and then me. "My father is a trusting man, too trusting."

"Eh, daughter?" He touched his napkin to his mouth. "Well, perhaps I do go on too much. But I would like to meet this young man's father. What we might teach each other!"

"That cannot be," I said. "The Christmen killed him."

He bent his brows and looked solemn. "That is a tragedy, indeed. But you mustn't hate them for it, you know. Christ too was a magician, a very great one. There is room for all."

"They don't think so."

"But we know better, don't we? We few." He gazed away into the distance. "I was born in Alexandria in Egypt, once the glory of the Greek world, now a city of the Saracens. My father was a physician and I followed in his footsteps. But medicine did not altogether satisfy me. I longed for a deeper knowledge of the cosmos. The Saracens are not the barbarians that the Christians say they are. They prize Greek learning and have preserved it, even books that run contrary to their own teachings. I sought out these books of alchemy and divination and especially books that exposed the errors of the Christians and exalted Thrice-Great Hermes, Zosimus, Porphyry, Julian, and others. I found not only the books but a handful of men and women in out-of-the-way places who still read and understood them, and these became my teachers. My father grew frightened, he urged me to give up these pursuits, but I would not, and eventually I left home. After that, I lived in many places—Antioch, Athens, Thessaloniki—and everywhere I went I gathered knowledge of the secret truths. At last I came to this city and here I have lived for thirty years, devoting myself to the Great Work, to forging 'the stone of the Ancients', the transformative catalyst that turns base metal into gold."

His speech astonished me and thrilled me. *Odin is Hermes? Cells of secret worshipers? Gold from lead?* I was dumbfounded. It was as if a door had just opened into another world. Could this strange, kindly man be a new father to me? How I longed for one!

But again, Selene broke in, with a hard, challenging look at me. "Thor— whatever your name is, you are learning much about us but we know nothing about you. Who are you? What brings you here? What keeps you here? What do you do here besides hang about the tavernas? I'm afraid of you. What trouble might you bring down on our heads. I beg you, please leave us alone."

And she was right, of course. What could I tell them? That I came here to murder a man, then took an oath to serve him, but was now betraying him? That I was, more or less, a police spy? That, beyond that, I had no business here and no idea what to do next?

While I mumbled and stammered, Melampus said, "No, daughter, you are wrong. There is no danger here, I would know it if there were. I don't feel the 'Bad Hour' hovering near, I don't hear the *Stringlos* cry. My young friend, my daughter worries too much about me. Since my dear wife's spirit ascended to the stars we only have each other." He pushed back his stool. "If you will excuse me now. It is obvious that you came here to see Selene. Whether we are to continue this interesting conversation another time, I leave to her, she is the mistress of the house. And I—I have a night's work ahead of me. It goes best when the moon is rising. I'll say good night, then." He kissed Selene on the forehead—it was plain that he adored her—and with that, he left us, entering another room by a low door. As it opened, all those metallic and sulfurous odors came rushing out.

I searched for something to say. "Selene, your father doesn't seem like a man who's greedy for gold."

This only seemed to anger her more. "It's not greed. It's a spiritual quest. The quest for perfection. The alchemist must be pure, without guile, without greed. That is my father."

"And he can really make gold?"

She allowed herself a bitter smile. "If he could, would we be living like this? But some of our neighbors think he has made gold; people have broken in to look for it, and so we bolt our door and bar our windows."

"But is it even possible?"

"Why not? A seed becomes a flower, what a man puts into a woman becomes a baby. So why may not a tiny seed of gold reproduce itself infinitely? Base metal *wants* to become gold, just as a baby wants to be born. The alchemist is merely the midwife."

"You believe it?"

"I have to believe it. I love him."

"And in the meantime you support him by gambling in the taverns."

"I prefer it to begging or street-walking."

"There are girls your age who are servants, cooks—"

"I'm not much good at taking orders.

"Marriage?"

"I told you once already, I have no dowry."

Why was I badgering her like this? It wasn't what I'd meant to do.

"You want to know about me? Listen, then," she said. "My mother died two years ago when I was sixteen. She had earned most of the money we lived on. Now there was nothing, no food in the house. My father is a brilliant man but—impractical. I had beautiful, thick hair down to my waist. Without asking him, I went and sold it. When he saw my cropped head, he wept. But I looked in the glass and liked what I saw. I could pass as a boy, and a boy can do whatever he pleases. I went to the tavernas. I like the life."

"But how long can you go on being 'Andreas'? Sooner or later you'll be found out, or get badly hurt."

She shrugged, looked away.

"And you can live on your winnings?"

"My father earns a little also, selling amulets, purifying houses after childbirth, casting horoscopes, curing impotence and binding curses, scaring away the Nereids. People come to him when the priest fails them. But all his clients are as poor as we are. You must pay him for your visit, you know—six *folles*."

"But I will! In fact, I think the onion juice in my navel is doing me a world of good already."

"Don't make fun," she said—but she was smiling as she said it. The first real smile I had seen from her. And what a smile! Sweet and mischievous all at once. It softened the sharp angles of her face, it rose from her wide mouth to her large black eyes. In the instant before it vanished it revealed a different Selene—one who could laugh, could tease. I had not seen that Selene before. My heart leapt up.

On an impulse, I went and fetched her game box from the sitting room, opened it and set out the black and white counters in their triangles. I brought out a handful of silver from my purse and tossed it on the table. "Please allow me to lose to you again."

She pushed the coins aside with an angry gesture. "What do you imagine you're buying with this?"

"An hour's relief from loneliness, Selene. Grant me that much and then I'll leave."

Her expression gentled, the smile crept back. "You're a hopeless player. I don't steal."

"All right. Your father invited me to visit again, Selene. May I?" I held my breath.

She touched a counter with her fingertips as though contemplating her next move. "If you like," she said quietly.

I touched her fingertip with mine and she didn't pull away. "You'd better leave now," she said. "Our neighbors will be asking themselves what you're doing here so long."

I galloped my horse back to the city, singing out loud and drawing curious looks from passersby. I didn't care. I was in love. A thousand plans whirled around in my brain. I must talk to Psellus. He would teach me how to court her like a civilized gentleman and not a rude barbarian.

That day was the beginning for me of greater joy than I had ever known—and, at the end, greater sorrow. But I won't—can't— speak of that now.

15

İ TAKE A WİFE

The next month was a happy time. I saw Selene often. While the city baked in August heat, I spent most days and evenings in the countryside at her house. Old Melampus would sit in his cramped laboratory off the kitchen, grinding, pouring, heating, cooling, fermenting, distilling, tending his little domed furnace, which he called an *athanor*. He watched, with infinite patience, the beads of quicksilver slide along the glass tubing of his *alembic*, or he sat hunched over the pages of great musty volumes, dense with indecipherable diagrams and curious script. During these times he and I would talk of the gods, theirs and mine, and exclaim over their similarities—Odin and Hermes, Zeus and Thor, Aphrodite and Freya, Titans and Trolls, Nereids and Elves. The tortured ravings of my father that had frightened me so as a child now took on the luster of ancient, deep and universal wisdom. I would never doubt again. Selene would tease us for being a pair of dull old men, but she always had something to say that brightened the conversation. And she smiled at me and let our hands touch. I brought food and wine with me and we three would make a pleasant meal together.

There were other magicians and alchemists too who visited from time to time, a half dozen or so. The men, shaggy and solemn as ancient trees, the women, plump and matronly. I was impressed by their dignified manners and the lively intelligence in their eyes. They came and went stealthily, always after sundown, and they muttered darkly about the police and about monks at the nearby monastery, whose violence they feared. They were wary of me at first, but took me on trust as Melampus's friend. Their talk was over my head, but what struck me was their patient optimism. Always, the goal was just beyond reach, but they would reach it one day, they *would*, with just a little more of this, a refining of that...

I noticed that most of them suffered from the same tremors in their hands as Melampus did. "It is the quicksilver," he told me one night as we sat watching the apparatus bubble. "I don't allow Selene to touch it, nor must you."

"But if it does you harm—?"

"Nature does not give up her secrets without exacting a price. The seeker must be willing to pay it. My dear wife..." Suddenly tears filled his eyes and the life seemed to go out of him, his chin sank to his chest.

"It killed her?" I murmured.

"We don't know that," Selene said firmly. "Come, Odd, leave him alone now. When he's like this he wants to be alone." She kissed the top of his head and drew me away into the sitting room.

She and I often sat together while Melampus worked. He knew it was her I had come to see and he would shoo me out of the laboratory and close the door. We played tables for pennies until I got good enough to win an occasional game. We talked of this and that, of magic and healing, about which she knew a great deal. I told her about my home, my adventures at sea—the bits I was proud of, anyway. About Finland and my escape from Louhi the Witch. I mentioned Ainikki, who sacrificed her life to save us. That brought a sharp look from Selene.

"Was she pretty?"

"All young girls are pretty. Why?"

"Did you love her?"

"Selene, darling, that was long ago. I was young. Anyway, we barely knew each other."

"I wish I were brave."

"But you are."

"Not brave enough, not for the world you come from."

"You're my world."

She looked away. "You mustn't say that, Odd." She changed the subject. "And so you've come here to enlist in the Emperor's Guards and live on savings until you can join?" (That was what I had told them finally, only that.) "And you've been in the Great Palace? Tell me what it's like."

"Splendid beyond anything you can imagine. I'll take you there one day." (And one day she would see it—though hardly in the way I expected. But I will tell that in its place.)

✝

On a morning when the breeze from the sea was fresh, we went sailing in my little boat. Selene changed her boy's clothes for a pretty dress and red stockings. She had never sailed before. I gave her the tiller stick to hold, and she laughed and whooped as we shot along, and nearly capsized us. Ramesses, her monkey, squeaked and covered his eyes with his hands. I tied up along the coast a few miles beyond the great fortification wall, where there was nothing around but fields and woods, and we spread out a picnic lunch in the shade of a plane tree.

"I want to marry you."

"You'd regret it," she answered frowning. "I won't be confined to the women's quarters, treated like a servant, like a brood mare. My mother didn't live like that and I won't."

"My mother died swinging a battle ax, splitting the heads of our enemies. No one ever confined her."

"Barbarian!"

"Proud of it," I smiled.

"And if I wanted to keep gambling in the tavernas?"

"You wouldn't have to, I have money enough."

"But if I wanted to?"

"I would worry about you."

"But you wouldn't try to stop me?"

"No."

"We'd fight. You'd come to hate me."

"Never."

And suddenly she was in my arms and we rolled together in the long grass. She ran her hands up under my shirt but drew them back shocked when she felt the welts of the slaver's lash and the X branded on my shoulder. "My God, what you've suffered!" She filled her hands with my hair and drew me to her breast, pressed her lean, strong body against mine. Her tears wet my flesh.

"It's nothing. Long in the past."

"Odd, I've been around rough men, not much scares me. But the world you come from? I don't know if I could live with that."

I put my finger to her lips. What could I say? Someday I would ask her to go back with me to that world of ice and blood.

We made love then, fast and hard. Her naked body was thinner than I even imagined. I felt her ribs, the bumps on her spine. I was almost afraid I'd break something. But I knew too the strength in that frail-looking body. And afterwards, when our hearts were still again, we lay on our backs and watched the clouds, like sailing ships, drift across the sky.

"You're my first," she said. "I'm not very good at it. You still want me?"

I squeezed her hand and we were quiet for a while.

"What are you thinking?" she asked.

"Just that in the olden times, before the White Christ came to Iceland, a bridegroom would open the tomb of an ancestor, take the sword from it, and throw it at his bride's feet. I have no old sword to give you."

She wrinkled her nose. "What a blood-thirsty people you are! Never mind, we will invent our own ceremony."

Ramesses jumped up on her chest; she dipped a bit of bread in olive oil and put it between his lips.

"You treat him like a baby," I said.

"I hope our babies are better-looking."

"Then you should have picked a handsomer husband."

She lay her head on my chest. "I love you, Odd Tangle-Hair. It frightens me how much I love you."

If I had died that day, I would have died content.

†

It was Freya's Day, named for our goddess of love, whom the Greeks call Aphrodite. The wedding celebration spilled out into the alley, Melampus's house being too small to contain all the guests.

Of course, we should have been more cautious.

The alchemists and magicians came. And the neighbors and their children, scrubbed and wearing their best clothes: Christians, all of these, and yet they respected Melampus as a physician who charged them little for his cures; and they had loved his wife, who helped deliver their babies and foretold their futures. Even the local priest came to wish us well: a fat, comfortable man who took his religion lightly and never refused a drink or a bite of food. He mumbled a few words over us to make our union 'official' and we didn't object. Finally my friend Psellus came, bringing me the gift of a fine manuscript of Homer (only that bookish man would have thought of such a thing.) He showed great interest in Melampus's apparatus and books and asked if he might visit again and learn more of his experiments. He exchanged some words with Selene and found her charming.

During the previous two weeks I had bought a house in the neighborhood with the money Harald had given me; four rooms built around a small courtyard. It was even more ruinous than Melampus's, but I had ambitious plans to repair it. I kept the old widow I bought it from as a housekeeper, though she was deaf and half-blind. I had two gold rings made for Selene and me and I had brought in casks of mead and a great deal of food for the wedding feast. Melampus's cook, Maria, who was some sort of distant cousin, pinned a bunch of daisies to her shapeless black dress and was thrilled to have such fine ingredients to work with. She and the neighbor women toiled over the hearth, baking bread and pastries, stirring pots of lamb stew, and roasting fowls. I had paid Melampus a bride-price of fifty ounces of silver for his daughter and asked for no dowry in return except her mother's best dress and jewelry. She stood proudly in them now.

A little marble statue of a naked Aphrodite, about as high as my knee and so old that it had lost most of its paint and gilding, was set up on a makeshift altar in the sitting room; we stood before her and poured a libation of mead and asked her blessing on us; then Selene gave me a sip of the golden liquid to seal our union. I made the sign of Thor's hammer over the cup to consecrate it. We wore wreaths of flowers on our heads. Everyone cheered. Melampus laughed and wept all at once. Outside, we danced to the music of flutes and tambourines. I did my hopping Icelandic step while Selene whirled around and clapped her hands until we fell in each other's arms, laughing. The neighbors, who had never tasted mead before, got thoroughly drunk and everyone wanted to shake my hand and kiss my bride.

As evening fell, the torches were lit. One old magician was offering to cast my horoscope and I was explaining, as best I could over the uproar, that I didn't know what month I was born in…and just then I caught a fleeting glimpse of someone—a slim figure in dark clothing— hovering at the edge of the crowd. He could have been a neighbor, I didn't know them all by sight, or just a passerby attracted by the noise of revelry. But somehow I didn't think so. When I looked again, he was gone. But now a procession was forming up to escort Selene and me (and Ramesses) to our new home, and I put it out of my mind. Carrying torches and singing and shouting lewd remarks, as the custom is, the guests led us to our bedroom. We shut the door on them, and I kissed Selene.

"I'm pregnant," she told me later as we lay in bed. "I hope you're happy, I am. I love you."

"You know so soon?"

"I sprinkled drops of water into a bowl of oil and saw it. I'm not as light-shadowed as my mother but I do see things. You will have a son. He'll be a magician like my father and yours—a great one, I'm sure of it. All the true believers will pay homage to his wisdom and power. Perhaps he'll even make gold. We'll move to the city and live in a fine house. Wouldn't that be nice? Are you pleased?" When I didn't answer, she raised herself on an elbow and looked at me. "Odd darling, what is it?"

"Nothing at all." I kissed her again. "Of course, I'm pleased."

But there were troubling thoughts stirring deep inside me. Selene imagined us spending our lives in this city, growing old with our children and grandchildren around us. But I had sworn an oath to return to Iceland one day to avenge my dead ones and reclaim my home. That thought had lived with me over all these years and all those thousands of leagues that I had travelled since the night when I crouched trembling in the thicket of reeds at the edge of Rangriver and watched the embers of my burning house whirl up into the midnight sky. Could I put that aside now? Did I belong here among these Greeks? Odd Thorvaldsson, the outsider, the barbarian? As much as I might dress like them, eat like them, speak like them, could I ever *be* one of them?

Selene was almost instantly asleep. But I lay awake long, listening to her gentle breathing and aching with love for her and our unborn son. And my heart torn with doubt.

✝

"Congratulations on your marriage, Odd Thorvaldsson," The Guardian of Orphans twisted his lips into a hideous imitation of a smile. "What a surprise for all of us."

"And didn't think to invite me," Harald frowned. "I call that unfriendly, Tangle-Hair."

I stood in John's office, facing the two of them and trying to put a bold expression on my face. The air crackled with tension. I was in danger and I knew it. I had been rudely hauled out of my bed early in the morning after my wedding night by none other than Halldor and Bolli with a summons from Harald. They didn't put a hand on me, barely spoke, but the threat was plain. I went quietly, leaving Selene standing in the doorway and looking scared. They were on horseback but they made me walk between them all the way back to the city. I was expecting to be taken to the barracks, but instead they'd brought me to the orphanage.

Besides John and Harald, the other person in the room was the orphan, Loucas, still with a bruise on his cheek where I had kicked him that night when I caught him following me. It had been him, I realized now, whom I'd glimpsed in the crowd at my wedding. I grabbed him by his shirtfront and snarled in his face, "I said if you followed me again I'd kill you—" I shoved him hard against the wall.

John, speaking low, almost without moving his lips, said, "You will take your hand off Loucas or you will not leave here alive." I let him go. With a nod from John, he scurried out the door, shooting me a look of pure hate as he brushed past me.

"Why does he follow me?"

"Because I tell him to. We lost track of you for a while after you left your lodging in the city. But Loucas doesn't give up easily. It happens he saw you in a wine shop conversing with a certain junior clerk in the Logothete's office by the name of—" he glanced at a paper lying on his desk—"yes, Constantine Psellus. So, we've taken to following this fellow—it wasn't hard to learn who he is. His movements are painfully regular: home to office, office to home—but with a foray once a week to unfamiliar parts of town— to meet with you. We thought that was curious. Possibly some reason to hide? And imagine where he led us yesterday: your wedding party. And such guests! Heretics and pagans thick as flies on a dung heap. And who exactly is your bride's father?

Don't bother answering, we'll soon find out. I smell the odor of treason on you—on all of you. I swear it'll cost you your necks."

I reckoned I may as well take the wolf by the ears. I turned to Harald, whose brows were contracted in an effort to follow the conversation, and told him in rapid Norse what John had just said. "I'm your man, Harald Sigurdsson. Nobody can touch me or my family without your leave. Where do you stand?" I had only one ally in this room, at most. If Harald abandoned me then I was a dead man.

"What is this person to you," he demanded, "this Constantine what's-his-name"?

"It's quite harmless, Harald. He was assigned to me when I first arrived. Since then he's been helping me improve my Greek—the better to serve you. We talk about poetry as a matter of fact. It's what skalds do. I'll recite some for you one night, you'll like it."

But John's eyes bored into me; he shook his head slowly from side to side. "If it's as innocent as you say, then why the elaborate secrecy?"

"So as not to put him wrong with his boss. It seems the Logothete warned him away from me when I fell out of favor with the court at Kiev."

John chewed on this for a very long moment while I held my breath. Then he shrugged and let it go.

I translated this exchange for Harald, who shot back, "What have you told this fellow about *us*, damn you?"

"Not a thing. And if you don't believe me you can look for a new translator or start working on your Greek." One thing I've learned in life is when you're trapped, get angry. I started to pull his ring off my arm.

"Hold on!" His complexion was dangerously red, and he rose half out of his chair. "If you're fishing from both sides of the stream like you did back in Novgorod…"

"What I have learned from Psellus," I broke in quickly, "is that Eustathius the Logothete wants to send Zoe into hiding for her protection. No one's to know about it." Psellus had never said anything of the sort, but it came to me in a moment of desperate inspiration: I had to throw them something. If there were consequences to this false intelligence, well that was a problem for another day. I repeated it in Greek for John's benefit.

"I knew it!" John exclaimed, slapping the table. "The sly bastard. So, this Psellus talks to you about the Logothete's business, does he?"

"Well, just occasionally." *Back up a little; don't promise too much.*

"And if you encouraged him, he might tell more?"

"It's possible. The fellow likes to brag when he's drunk too much wine."

"So there might be a point in your meeting with him again." John leaned back in his chair. He made a temple of his fingers and rested his hairless chin on them.

"If you say so, Guardian."

I translated all this for Harald, who was lost again.

"Goddammit, Tangle-Hair, why does everything with you have to be so fucking complicated?"

"Life is complicated, Harald. I want it understood: no more following me or my friends, and *no one* is to approach my family. Do I have your word on it?" He stared at me long and hard before giving a curt nod of his head.

"From now on," he said, "I want to see more of you at the barracks and less of you anywhere else. Bring your wife if you like."

"I'll do that. She's a gambler, you know. She'll win the shirt off you."

At that Harald laughed out loud. "Will she, by God! Well, then we'll get on. Ha, ha."

Now it was John's turn to look lost; he drummed his fingers on the desktop. "What's the big oaf laughing at? What'd you say?"

"Oh, nothing. Just a private joke." *Let him wonder.* Any way that I could drive a wedge between those two was all to the good. "And now, if you have no further use for me this morning, gentlemen, you've taken me from my wedding breakfast. And—oh—as long as I'm here, Harald, I need more money." *Attack, always attack.*

Outside the orphanage, I found Halldor and Bolli had gone. I leaned against a wall and tried to take deep breaths. Sweat trickled down my sides. This had been too close. From now on, I must be doubly careful. And I must get word to Psellus, too.

I soon had more reason to be frightened. Not finding Selene at home, I went down the lane to her father's house. Everything was in turmoil: furniture overturned, glassware smashed in the laboratory, its precious contents puddled on the floor. And Melampus, sitting in the midst of it with his head in his hands. Selene was in a fury. "Police were here! Looking for heathen books, they said. Thank god, a neighbor warned us when he saw them coming; we just had time to hide some things in a hole under the bed and hang a crucifix on the wall. They slapped him, shoved him, my father. We've never had anything like this before. And meanwhile where were you, Odd? What were those men doing with you?"

"Darling, I'm sorry—I don't know what—listen to me…"

"No, you listen." She raised a white-knuckled fist to my face. "My father imagined a strong young man like you would protect us. Instead, you've brought your troubles to our doorstep. Now, either you tell me exactly who you are and what you're doing here or we're finished. And it's not that I don't love you, Odd. I do love you— too much—but you must tell me the truth, no more lies." Tears trembled on her eyelids.

Melampus stirred himself. "Daughter, don't talk so to your husband. Odd doesn't have to—"

"No," I said. "She's right. I do."

I told them everything.

16

FROM BARBARIAN TO GREEK

Thor's Day; four days after my meeting with John and Harald.

The setting sun at my back cast a red glow on the bronze statue of Theodosius atop his column as I made my way toward our meeting place. While I walked, I stole glances at every face that passed me, stretched my ears to catch the sound of footfalls at my back. That dirty-faced youth unloading a cart across the road? That girl walking carefully with a water jug on her shoulder? Were they orphans? Were they watching me? I could never go to a rendezvous with Psellus again without that itching feeling that unseen eyes were on me. Seeing me approach, he fell into step behind me and we walked in silence up one street and down another until we turned a corner and came to a little wine shop off a quiet alley. We took a table in the corner from where we could see the door. This was our invariable routine, although we chose a different place every time from a prearranged list. We sat close together and spoke in low voices.

"They've been following you. Followed you to my wedding."

"What?" He nearly knocked the stool over, leaping up.

"Sit!" I hissed, and gripped him by the wrist. He gave me a stricken look. Among Psellus's many fine qualities, physical bravery was not one. In a few words, I described the police raid on Melampus's house and my interrogation by Harald and John.

He writhed on his stool. "We must stop meeting."

"That would look worse. I think I persuaded them that you're doing no more than teaching me Greek."

"You think?"

"And I said that you're indiscreet, you talk about the Logothete, let things drop that you shouldn't. That got their attention."

"What things?"

"I made up some nonsense about smuggling Zoe out of the palace for her protection. If I'd had more time to think—"

"Oh, Christ!" He dropped his face into his hands. "John has doubled the guard on her. No one can get in to see her now without being searched right down to their skin—and the guards aren't gentle."

"Well, I'm sorry to have made things worse for her. But the point is John will be looking for more tidbits like that. Do you understand? We can tell him anything Eustathius wants him to believe."

"Disinformation?" He peered between his fingers, then smiled. "Tangle-Hair, you must have some Greek blood in you somewhere; you're revealing a genuine talent for duplicity."

I returned his smile and poured both of us some more to drink. "What else is happening in the palace?"

"The Emperor's in Thessaloniki, praying at the shrine of the Holy Martyr Demetrios for a cure for his falling sickness and his dropsy—which are getting worse by the day."

"And in his absence John is in charge?"

He nodded.

"And what about your boss? What *can* he do? Does he have any power at all?

"It's a delicate situation. Eustathius is an old and trusted retainer, and very good at what he does—foreign affairs, diplomacy, intelligence. John can't move openly against him, Michael wouldn't allow it. For all his family feeling, the Emperor doesn't entirely trust his brothers. But for the moment, John has the upper hand."

"What might change that?"

"War. In a war the Logothete is indispensable."

"It sounds to me like war might solve a lot of problems."

This brought a chuckle. "We don't relish war the way you barbarians do. We do everything we can to avoid it. We pay bribes, hand out titles, crawl when we have to."

"Then you're not the men Homer sings about." And so saying, I unwrapped the copy of the *Iliad* he had given me and opened it on the table between us.

We spent the next hour happily lost in poetry.

✝

Over the next months my life settled into a pleasant routine. Winter came on with weeks of rain and muffling fog, punctuated by crashing storms on the Bosporus and swirling snowstorms. And then it was spring again. During all this time, I had no more trouble with the police, nor any more orphans spying on me—or none that I caught anyway. When I wasn't patching my leaky roof or planting cabbages and onions in my garden, I was at Melampus's house, helping him to restore his laboratory, which the police had wrecked. I felt for the dear old man; he'd been badly shaken; it seemed that spark of optimism had been extinguished in him. The other alchemists were afraid to visit anymore and he felt terribly alone despite all that Selene and I could do to cheer him up. He aged visibly that winter, and his tremor grew worse.

But my wife flourished. The baby growing in her absorbed all her thoughts. She happily admitted to becoming a person she never imagined she would be. As her breasts and belly swelled, the sharp planes of her face softened, and she grew her hair out. She soon stopped going to the tavernas to gamble. This was her choice; we didn't argue about it. Instead, we spent our evenings reading aloud (I now owned four books besides my Homer), or entertaining the neighbors. I told stories—the ones my father had taught me long ago--and became a favorite of the neighborhood children.

To be a 'proper wife', Selene pestered our housekeeper Chloris to teach her to spin wool, though the old woman's eyesight was so bad she could hardly see her hands in front of her face. But Selene, alas, had no talent in this direction. It ended with her flinging the distaff and its tangled threads across the room with a curse. She was much better at decorating the cradle and other furniture I built, covering everything with beautifully painted wild flowers. She also loved to milk our goats and tend the garden. And she was an enthusiastic cook. She and Chloris spent hours together in our big kitchen, consuming olive oil and spices at a rate

I wouldn't have believed. After so many years of poverty, Selene developed an appetite that would have done credit to a Norseman. And I, between idleness and her cooking, felt my belt getting too tight.

I continued my weekly meetings with Psellus. I had nothing much to report about John and Harald except that Harald was getting impatient for a new promotion or a new command but that John kept putting him off, saying the moment wasn't right yet. On one occasion, Harald flew into a rage and started smashing things in John's office. He could be terrifying when he was like that. It was the first time I ever saw fear in John's eyes. After that, they seldom spoke.

Psellus, too, had little to report. The Emperor was still in Thessaloniki and Zoe confined to her quarters. Almost no one got in to see her. The unspoken question on everyone's mind was how much longer it would be until Michael died and what would happen then. The palace seemed frozen in a kind of suspended animation as though a spell had been cast over it.

I spent more time at the Varangian barracks, as Harald had ordered me to. His restlessness and ill temper seemed to have infected them all, but there were some pleasant times, too, when I could divert him with poetry, which he loved. I had translated some of Homer's scenes—the anger of Achilles, battles on the plain of Troy, the adventures of Odysseus. The Emperor's Wineskins were astonished to learn that the despised Greeks had once been as manly as themselves.

Sometimes I brought Selene along—with her game board. I was anxious about her in that crowd, but I shouldn't have been; she knew how to handle herself. She spoke Greek with the other soldiers' women and began to pick up a smattering of Norse too. I was proud of her. Halldor and Bolli ignored her although I don't think she noticed. But Gorm pounced on her like a big, friendly dog. He knew how to play the game (who would have thought?) and even beat her a few times, which made them friends. She was fascinated to learn that his brother, my old shipmate, had been a werewolf berserker. Lycanthropy was a subject she knew something about.

✝

With the coming of spring, the Rus trading fleet arrived. Had it been a whole year since I had sailed in on it? It didn't seem possible. Of course, I was curious. I went down to the quayside to see if I could find Stavko. But the slaver was not very interested in talking to me. All I could get out of him was that Yelisaveta was still unmarried at the shockingly old age of twenty, that Inge was said to be ailing, and that Yaroslav was, well, Yaroslav—vague, indecisive, and dithering. What I really wanted to know was whether another assassin had been sent along to do the job I had failed to do. But this Stavko couldn't, or wouldn't, say. He tore away from me in a flurry of swinging braids and flying spittle. I let him go. When I reported this to Harald, he shot me a triumphant grin, showing all his big teeth. Princess Yelisaveta was still his! And would stay his until he went back to scoop her up and take her to Norway. The possibility of another assassin bothered him not at all. If there was one, we never saw him.

✝

On the last day in May, our baby was born. Selene leaned back in the birthing chair, her hair sticking damply to her cheek, and smiled at me. "I promised you a son."

I kissed her forehead. "How are you?"

"Tired. Happy."

We named him Gunnar Hermius Oddsson. Gunnar after my dead brother and Hermius in honor of the god we worshipped—Odin by another name. I held him, red-faced and bawling, in my arms and swore that I would be a better father to him than my poor, mad father had ever been to me. Whether he grew up to be magician or warrior, I would do everything in my power to make his life a happy one.

Melampus came to purify the house from the pollution of childbirth, and he hung an amulet of great power, a carved amethyst on a silver chain, around the baby's neck and murmured words over him. Seeing his grandson, revived that spark of joy in the old man that had been so long dormant. His only sorrow, he said, was that his dear wife couldn't have lived to see this happy day. He and his daughter both shed a tear for her, and then Selene, who was worn out from a long labor, put little Gunnar to her breast (there would never be a wet-nurse in our house) and soon was asleep.

Melampus and the neighbors and I stayed up late into the night drinking. When I finally went to bed, I lay thinking about all that had happened to me in the space of a year. I lived almost entirely as a Greek now. Except on my occasional visits to the Varangian barracks, it was the only language I spoke. I had Greek friends, read Greek books. My son would be as much Greek as anything else, and that was all right. It was possible to believe that I was a barbarian no more.

But my mind is such that permanent happiness is alien to it. I'd named my son for my brother, and how had he died? Holding his guts in with both hands, gushing blood onto the floor of our burning house while our enemies, Strife-Hrut and Snorri—Halldor's father—and their henchmen howled around us. Could I, I asked myself for the thousandth time, ever let that memory go?

But my private concerns were suddenly overshadowed by greater events. One morning, just a week after my son was born, John the Guardian of Orphans collapsed in the bedroom of his mansion on the Horn, clutching his belly, sweating, vomiting, shitting, and screaming that he had been poisoned.

17

A BARBARIAN
ONCE MORE

The bedroom stank with the sour reek of vomit and shit, of sweat and fear. It was mid-afternoon, an hour after a messenger had arrived at the Varangian barracks with an order for Harald to go at once to John's mansion on the Horn and to bring me along to translate. Now, as Harald and I were ushered inside, the family turned and stared at us.

"What are these barbarians doing here?" John's sister, Maria, crouched beside his couch. Her voice was shrill. She put a red-nailed hand to her red mouth. The tension in the room was like a live thing. You saw it at once in the strained faces, in the way one paced, another drank in nervous gulps, and yet another twisted a ring round and round. *If John were to die ... Never mind the Emperor, this man held them all in his hand.*

The guards who met us at the front door had given us menacing looks. Tough-looking men with swords in their belts—not regular soldiers, but orphans, I guessed, who had grown too old for the orphanage and showed a talent for thuggery.

"Stupid woman!" answered her husband, Stephen, Admiral of the Fleet. "I sent for them, of course. Someone had to do *something.*" Stephen was a blunt-faced, broad-shouldered bullock of a man. He and Maria and her brothers, Constantine and George, were the only ones in the room besides John and one terrified servant girl.

"They're here, John, the Varangians," Constantine murmured in his brother's ear. The Guardian of Orphans groaned, struggled up on an elbow, opened his mouth, and spewed copiously on himself. He looked like he might die at any moment: his face bloodless, his eyes half closed, his nightshirt and pillow dark with sweat.

"The basin, idiot," Maria snarled at the girl, who was too late getting it under the master's chin. "A towel!" With a groan, John rolled over on his belly and drew his knees up to his chest.

"How long has he been like this?" I asked.

"Since this morning," said Constantine. "Almost at once after the doctor gave him his purgative."

"Could be an accident."

"He's been poisoned!" Stephen was red faced and shouting. "And we know who did it." The others nodded. No doubt of that in anyone's mind.

"Where's this doctor, then?" said Harald.

Stephen left and came back a minute later dragging the man by his shirt front; his hands were tied behind his back. "Zeno," he said.

The doctor was a sharp-nosed little man in his fifties with receding hair and a concave chest. Stephen let go of him and he sank to his knees, blubbering. "Take him to the Noumera prison," Stephen instructed Harald, as I translated. "Do whatever you have to, get the whole story out of him, he didn't act alone, we want them all. Arrest anyone he names. Here, Constantine's written out a warrant for you. We want only your own men involved in this, you understand? And send some of them to Zoe's quarters. No one is to go in or out. Tell her nothing. We've sent a courier to the Emperor in Thessaloniki. He'll deal with her when he gets here."

"Why don't I just torture him here?" Harald asked with a wolfish smile. This was work he liked.

"Good God, not here. What d'you think, this is a prison? We can't have screaming here, we have neighbors."

I felt sure somehow that the neighbors would plug their ears with wax and claim to have heard nothing at all.

"Now get him out of here," Stephen ordered.

From the bed, John grunted what must have been a word of encouragement.

✝

The Baths of Zeuxippos, near the hippodrome, had been built centuries ago when every citizen of Constantinople felt it was his privilege to bathe daily in surroundings fit for a king. In time, the Greeks started taking fewer baths, caring more for the purity of their souls than for the cleanliness of their bodies, and the building was converted to other uses—a silk works; a prison, the Noumera. Traces of its old splendor remained in the mosaics, the great empty basins that had once held hot and cold water, and the high vaulted ceilings that had echoed with the happy shouts of bathers. The only shouts heard now were not happy ones. We descended with our prisoner into the dank substructure, to the furnace rooms that were now fitted out as cells and torture chambers. A prisoner could scream his head off down here and never be heard out in the street. Our men took over the place, pushing aside the warders who ordinarily ran it.

Halldor and Bolli hung the little doctor up by his wrists from chains suspended from the ceiling, so that his toes barely scraped the floor. They ripped off his clothes, leaving him as naked as a plucked fowl: sickly white goose flesh, a patch of hair, a shriveled cock. Harald caressed a short whip of braided wire and circled the prisoner. Then he struck with the speed of a striking snake, cutting him across the buttocks, drawing a line of blood. "Why did you poison the Guardian of Orphans?" I translated, trying to make my voice as harsh as Harald's. Tears streamed down Zeno's cheeks. He hadn't, he swore it by the Holy Virgin. Harald circled. He cut him across the face, laying his cheek open. "Who put you up to it? Who gave you the poison? Was it the Empress? What did she pay you?" It went on and on like this—Harald striking out and shouting his questions in Norse, me shouting them in Greek and trying to translate the man's denials, which were nearly unintelligible, until finally there was no part of Zeno's body that wasn't cut and bleeding, and he fainted.

I am no stranger to pain. I've seen friends tortured, I've *been* tortured. And, like any fighter, I've caused my share of pain. But this turned my stomach, I felt the bile come up in my throat. Yet I dared not flinch. I must be as hard and cruel as the others because I had the feeling that Harald and his men were watching *me* as much as the prisoner; that *I* was being tested.

"You all right, Tangle-Hair?" Harald said to me at one point. "You look a little green."

"Don't worry about me."

Bolli threw a pail of water in the doctor's face and Harald started in on him again—this time pulling off pieces of flesh with hot pincers. And, yes, finally Zeno broke and told us, between sobs and cries, what we wanted to know. A eunuch named Moucopeles, the majordomo of the Daphne palace, had mixed arsenic in a dose of buckthorn for the Guardian's bowels; Zoe's eunuch Sgouritzes had given Zeno the stuff and promised him twenty pounds of gold if John died.

That night a dozen of us, with our swords drawn, burst into Zoe's apartment in the Daphne. The Empress was just preparing for bed. Her eunuchs and women ran around shrieking and Zoe shrieked louder than any, cursing us like a fishwife. She threw a chamber pot at Harald's head. He slapped her and ripped her nightgown half off. Her eye met mine for an instant; she must have recognized me. "Help me, young man, I beg you," she cried. I couldn't answer her.

"Where is Sgouritzes?" Harald yelled. She spat at him.

Then we ransacked her chambers, pulling down drapes, overturning chests, and on into the perfume factory, where the cauldrons bubbled. We turned them over too and smashed all the bottles, leaving a lake of the smelly stuff ankle-deep on the floor. Eventually, we found Sgouritzes under a bed—that parchment-skinned, dignified old man who had first brought me to Zoe's chamber. He recognized me, too, and shot me a pleading look. I scowled at him.

The old fellow was tough as a hunk of dried venison. He withstood the torture for three days and nights—everything Harald, who was beside himself with fury, could do to him. He died, admitting nothing. It was another day after that before we found Moucopeles. He was stopped as he tried to leave the palace disguised as a serving woman. A fat, soft man with oiled hair, he lasted only a few minutes before he told us everything—how Zoe had put them all up to it, promising them promotions and riches. When Harald was satisfied he'd gotten the full story, he cut the ears and noses off Moukoupeles and Zeno and, on Stephen's orders, had them tied to the tails of mules and driven out of the city—not such an uncommon sight; it attracted little attention.

Five days passed in this way. Five days in which I lived in the Varangian barracks when I wasn't in the torture cells. Five days during which I don't think I washed or changed my clothes. Five nights that I drank myself into a stupor, trying to get the screams out of my head, the smell of burning flesh out of my nostrils. And listened to a drunken Harald boast and gloat.

Meanwhile, Stephen and Constantine traveled back and forth between us and John, carrying reports and orders. By now the Emperor had arrived by ship from Thessaloniki. I didn't see him, but people said he looked half-dead. Zoe was a prisoner in her apartment, more closely confined than ever. John had relieved the Varangians of the duty of guarding her and sent in women and eunuchs of his own household. A bulletin was issued by Constantine that the Guardian of Orphans was suffering from nothing worse than a slight fever and would soon be up and about again.

And as for me? Two thoughts tormented me. How to get word to Selene, who had no idea where I was and how to contact Psellus and, through him, the Logothete, to warn him of the danger Zoe was in. Somewhere around the second or third day, I think, I sent Gorm with a note for Selene assuring her I was all right and that I'd be home soon. But there was nothing else I dared tell her. As for Psellus, I couldn't keep our usual rendezvous because Harald wouldn't let me out of his sight. I didn't know what to do.

And then overnight everything changed: Zoe was forgotten, John, who was still ailing, was pushed into the background. We heard the news from Stephen, who couldn't decide whether he was more delighted by it or alarmed: the Emperor had decided that this was the moment to reconquer Sicily from the Saracens. Eustathius, the Logothete, had much to do with this, I suspect. As Psellus had explained to me, a war would place him at the center of affairs, it would distract Michael from palace intrigues, it would get two of John's principal allies—Stephen the admiral and Harald the Varangian—out of the country on military service, possibly for years. It would buy time for Zoe's faction. And—who knew?—it might even succeed in regaining the rich island of Sicily for the empire.

"Go back and tell John," said Harald, gripping Stephen by the shoulders and bellowing in his face, "that he must get the Emperor to appoint me commander of the Varangian contingent. Either he does that or we're quits. You understand me? Tell him."

We waited an anxious day for Stephen to return. Harald paced, flung himself from one end of the barrack room to other, downed gallons of wine, and cursed. And at last, towards evening, Stephen returned.

"Captain," he hailed him. "You will take five hundred Varangians to

Sicily, serving under your old commander George Maniakes. Sveinn, the Commandant, pleads his age and his gout and has requested to stay in the city with the remaining hundred to guard the Emperor."

John had done it! He didn't like the idea of losing Harald but he was smart enough not to thwart him in this.

Harald leapt onto a table and pranced from foot to foot in a fine frenzy, shouted his battle cry, and shook his fists in the air. And his voice was answered by all the men in the bandon, pounding each other on the back, shouting "Harald, Harald!" Within minutes word had spread all over the barracks and men of the other banda streamed in (except for the hundred who weren't lucky enough to be going), all laughing and cheering and calling Harald's name. "At last!" They slapped each other's backs. "At last, out of this stinking city. Out of this tomb of a palace. To fight, to loot, to kill, to take women. At last!"

"Tangle-Hair," Harald threw an arm around me. "You're coming too as my skald. You'll praise my victories, give me your counsel. Like the old days when we fought the Pechenegs, eh? What a pair we were! And you'll make your fortune, come back rich, join the Guard, be one of us..."

"Odd?"

Who spoke? A woman's voice? Heads looked up. I turned to see—

Selene, wrapped in a traveling cloak, stood in the doorway; her face was wet with tears; she held little Gunnar in her arms.

"Selene, what are you—?"

"Do you forget us so soon?"

I took her elbow and steered her out into the corridor where we could hear ourselves talk.

"Selene, you're still *lechona*." Among the Greeks, a woman who has borne a child, a *lechona*, must not leave her house for thirty days; it is a rule never broken.

"I don't care. Where have you been, Odd? You look terrible."

"I sent Gorm with a message for you."

"He told me nothing except that you were here. What have you been doing?"

"I can't talk about it, I'm sorry."

"What can't you talk about? Is it something shameful? Have you been with a woman?"

"Of course not." I reached out to touch her arm but she pulled away.

The baby squirmed in her arms and began to whimper. "Selene, don't question me. Go home. I'll come when I can."

"Don't shout at me." She began crying again, and the baby began wailing, too.

I hadn't meant to shout. It was only that all those bad feelings, the anger and revulsion that I'd been holding in, had to find a way out. I felt myself suddenly becoming my own father—angry, sullen, violent. I turned away to get myself under control.

"Tangle-Hair, damn you," came Harald's voice, thick with drink, from the barrack room. "What are you doing out there in the hall? Come back, bring your woman."

"Look, we can't talk here," I said in a low voice, "it's a madhouse. I'm taking you to Psellus's. I'll try to explain things there. I need to talk to him too. Come now, dry your eyes. Here, give me the baby… I'm taking Selene home," I called through the door. "Be back soon."

Without a word, Selene followed me down the steps and out through the gate. There we found Chloris, our housekeeper, waiting in the pony cart. I took the reins and we drove in silence to Psellus's. I took a roundabout route and looked behind me often to make sure we weren't followed. It was dark by the time we got there. Psellus answered the door, still in his street shoes and his court costume. His smile died on his lips when he saw our scowling faces.

"Can Selene spend the night here? It's too late for her to go home."

"Of course, she can. What is it? What's happened? Here, come in, sit down. Let me pour you some wine. Give me the baby, babies love me." He laid Gunnar on his knee, who waved his little fists and burbled.

Then, in a few words, I told them about John. "You want to know what I've been doing, Selene? I've been watching men tortured. No, not watching, *helping*. Because it's my *job*." I couldn't keep the bitterness out of my voice. I could feel her shrink back in her chair, could read the loathing on her face.

"Poisoned!" said Psellus. "We guessed as much. Poor Zoe, did she really? They confessed to it? Moucopeles was involved? The foolish man. I only wish they'd succeeded. Things will be very bad for her now. Odd, you must talk to Eustathius tonight. I'll send my servant to bring him here, as we did before." He turned to Selene. "My dear, don't be angry with him. Sometimes we men have to do things we don't like. You must try and understand."

"I haven't told all," I said. "The Varangians are being sent to fight in Sicily. I'm going with them."

"Then you really must talk to the Logothete," said Psellus. He handed the baby to Chloris, who had taken a chair in the corner, and went off to look for his servant.

"To Sicily? Leaving us?" cried Selene. "Just like that? How can you?"

"Because it's what I *do*, damn it. I am a warrior, a *thegn*, as we say in our language—I can't translate it for you. I've done nothing but fight since I killed my first man at sixteen. I don't know any other trade. An Icelandic woman would understand, would cheer me on, drink to my victories and, if I died in a distant land, bear it without a tear."

"I thought you were no longer a barbarian."

"I thought so, too. We were both wrong. Listen to me, I love you Selene, and I love Gunnar, more than I have words to say, but you have to trust that I know what I'm doing. Harald rewards me for being his skald, the Greeks reward me for spying on him. None of this is what I came here to do, but here I am and how else are we to survive? Unless, of course, you go back to gambling in the tavernas or your father learns how to make gold."

"Don't ridicule him."

"Selene!"

She swung her fist at me—I grabbed her arm and bent it back.

"You're hurting me."

"Then act like a wife."

"I told you I wouldn't be a good one."

"Look, come with me, other officers bring their women."

"And leave father behind? You see how he is. How will he live without me?"

"I see. Then you've chosen."

We stared at each other in wordless anger.

Psellus reappeared and behind him was his mother, as always gliding like a silent ghost in her own house. "I've sent a man for Eustathius," he said. "I expect him soon. Selene, my dear, you must excuse us, this is men's business, the less you know of it the better. Go with my mother, she's made up beds for you and your servant. She'll stay up with you until you sleep. Tomorrow I'll take you home."

Selene allowed herself to be led away. And my heart was too sore, my feelings too raw, to find a word of goodbye.

It was the last time I would see her for two years.

Soon afterward, the Logothete limped in on his clubbed foot. "You've taken me away from my dinner guests. I hope you have a good reason."

I repeated to him everything I knew about John's poisoning.

"How lucky we are to have you, Odd Thorvaldsson." He clapped me on the shoulder. "So in a crisis John turns to Harald and his Varangians, as we expected he would. And he'll do it again. I don't like this Harald of yours."

"We can always hope he never comes back from Sicily," Psellus offered.

"We can do more than hope. You're going with him, Odd? Accidents can happen on a campaign, can't they?"

"I can't promise you that, sir."

"No, of course not. Still, you can keep an eye on him for us. By God, never was a war more opportune than this! The Emperor is completely taken up with it. I've been meeting with him every day, going over reports from my agents, planning our diplomatic moves. Zoe is far from his thoughts, which means that, for the moment, she's safe. And now the decision to invade has been made, we're not going to waste a moment. The home fleet—as many ships as are seaworthy—will sail the day after tomorrow with the Household Cavalry and your Varangians aboard. General Maniakes will pick up other troops and supplies at the depots on the Thracian coast and in Italy. Let us pray that Stephen doesn't manage to drown them all. The man's an idiot, a pygmy who fancies himself a Hercules, but I'm glad to see him leaving the city. John must be feeling pretty naked now without Stephen or Harald to shield him—may the man rot! And, as for you, Odd, I've told you already that I want you to be *my* Varangian someday. But first you must do military service with us, gain a reputation, impress Maniakes, fill your purse with gold. Make the most of it, my boy. I'm sure your new wife will be proud of you."

At that, Psellus shot him a warning look.

✝

The first rays of the dawning sun streamed through the windows of the Golden Banquet Hall. Under its high, octagonal dome a council of war was gathered. I had not slept all night, torn between love, anger, and remorse, no longer sure of what I felt for Selene, or she for me. But I was here as Harald's skald and translator and so I forced my tired brain to work. The fleet would sail in a few hours' time and we were already in our armor. Harald had outfitted me with a Varangian hauberk and weapons, white leggings and red cloak. Most of the Guardsmen accepted this without comment but Halldor, who was now appointed his standard bearer, and Bolli looked as though they would choke on their tongues.

We sat at the head table with the Emperor, his brother Constantine, the Logothete, Stephen, and General George Maniakes, whom I was seeing for the first time. At other tables sat the ships' captains and the colonels of the Household Cavalry regiments. Servants passed among us with quiet efficiency carrying platters of boiled meat and jugs of watered wine.

Everyone tried not to notice Michael's sad condition. The once handsome young face and athletic figure that had fluttered Zoe's heart were now grotesquely swollen by the dropsy, which, in addition to his epilepsy, was ravaging him. He moved like a man of sixty, not thirty. He was apparently too weak to support the weight of his crown and jewels and wore only a light cotton robe with a shawl around his shoulders. He spoke little and it seemed a struggle for him just to follow what was being said.

It was our *strategos autokrator*, our commanding general, who was the cynosure of all eyes. George Maniakes had ridden all night from his Anatolian estate to be here and still had the dust of travel on his gilded corselet. He seemed to fill the whole room. He was as big as a troll, easily as tall as Harald and bigger in the chest, with a pockmarked face, deep set eyes, a large nose, black hair, and a beard that jutted straight from his face like the prow of a warship. His only expression was a scowl. According to Harald (who, as I have said, served under him in Syria) he was a Turk by birth who had started life as a camp waiter—a fact that, far from concealing, he boasted of. He had risen to command armies by sheer force of personality and an explosive temper that made strong men quail. Behind him stood the captain of his bodyguard of Khazar archers, a man called Moses the Hawk, armed with scimitar, bow, and quiver, his hair in two long braids, his caftan hanging to his boot tops.

Maniakes noticed Harald at once and called out in a booming voice that could be heard to the back of the hall. "Eh, what's this? Where is

Sveinn Gudleifsson, then, the Commandant of the Guard?" They surveyed each other in mutual dislike. "You're taking his place, Harald Sigurdsson? By Christ, you've risen mighty damn fast in the ranks. You must have a powerful patron."

Of course, Harald did have a powerful patron, but this was not a fact to be acknowledged. Before I could finish translating Maniakes's words, Stephen leapt in, praising Harald's youth and vigor and deprecating poor old Sveinn, who could barely get around anymore. The admiral never knew when to shut up. Finding himself being listened to (which almost never happened), he took the opportunity to ask for our prayers for poor brother John, who would be with us today if not for his untimely bout of fever. This was greeted with fervent murmurs of assent from everyone except Maniakes, who belched loudly.

Hereupon, the Logothete stood up and, with a bow to the Emperor, called us to order. His eye swept over us. When his glance fell momentarily on me, you would not have guessed we had ever met before. He spoke with his characteristic quiet precision. "Forgive me, gentlemen, but time is short and there is much to discuss. As everyone here is aware, the Saracens invaded Sicily from Africa two centuries ago. First Palermo fell, then Messina and Taormina and Syracuse and all the other Greek cities. The Emirs of Palermo have grown rich and powerful off the fat of this island that once sent its grain and fruits to us. The eastern half of Sicily is still Greek in language and religion but in another generation it will not be, unless we make a stand now. It was the intention of the Great Basil to reconquer it, but he died and Constantine, his successor, abandoned the project. In my opinion, we have only one more chance to rescue our people from annihilation. Fortunately, the Saracens are deeply riven by factions—Arab against Berber, old settlers against newer ones, one religious sect against another—and some of them are willing to ally themselves with us.

"The present Emir of Palermo, Al-Hasan Ibn Yusuf, is supported by an army of six thousand Arabs newly arrived from Africa under the command of Abdallah, the son of the Caliph of Kairouan. But there are still loyal adherents of the former Emir, Al-Hasan's brother, a friend of ours, who was overthrown and killed two years ago. In addition there are the Lombards of Apulia. For the moment, young Duke Gaimar of Capua supports us. Time is crucial, gentlemen. We must strike while we still have any allies left." His words were greeted with somber silence. "I turn the floor over now," he concluded, "to our general."

Maniakes was clearly in a foul mood, or should I say a worse mood than usual because he was never in a good one. His face was like a thundercloud. It was folly to rush off half-prepared like this he growled. He needed more time, more men, more ships or he would not vouch for the outcome.

But he knew he had lost that argument already. He would lay out his plans for us. He had brought a map with him and unrolled it on the table, shoving plates and goblets onto the floor with a sweep of his arm. All of us at the head table huddled around it, and my eyes widened as he smoothed it flat for I had never seen such a thing in my life—a picture of the land as a bird might see it! Rivers, mountains, cities, all inscribed on it. How was it possible? Not for the first—or last—time I felt like an ignorant fool.

"Your Majesty," he addressed himself to Michael, ignoring everyone else, "let no one tell you that this campaign will be either easy or short. The Saracens have built strongholds all over the island. They are resourceful and fanatical fighters, as we have learned to our cost many times. As for our allies, I don't give a donkey's hind end for 'em, they'll all desert us when it suits them. But I will enlist Lombards at Salerno and make a landing at Messina. I will drive the enemy out of Rametta, which must be done to secure our rear, and then fight my way down the east coast, city by city," he stabbed each one with a thick forefinger, "until I reach Syracuse, which I will lay siege to. The fleet will sail parallel to us, to resupply us and take off wounded. Simple, straightforward, and—"

"And cowardly!" All heads jerked around. Need I say that this was Harald? "Translate," he barked at me, for I had hesitated a moment.

I searched my vocabulary for something that came closer to 'cautious' than 'cowardly.'

Harald struck the map with his fist. "If Palermo is the head, then chop off the head— wherever the filthy place is."

I translated.

There was a general intake of breath around the room.

Maniakes's jaw muscles bulged. Violence flickered in his eyes.

Moses the Hawk's hand moved to his sword hilt.

The Emperor looked as though he would faint.

Stephen smirked.

"Harald Sigurdsson," the Logothete spoke rapidly, spreading his hands wide. "If only we could understand your words as you speak them. I'm sure this young man who interprets for you has made some mistake. With your permission, Majesty—" he turned to Michael—"I will call the meeting adjourned. I believe the patriarch is waiting for us in the cathedral. Prayer will do us all good."

The man was a diplomat.

And pray we did (although I to a different god than theirs.) Under the Holy Wisdom's stupendous dome, choruses chanted, incense billowed, icons and gospel books were paraded, platoons of clergy performed their offices, and Patriarch Alexius asked for God's blessing on us and death to the Infidel.

Then, to the booming of gongs, we marched down to the Harbor of Boukoleon.

This harbor, on the Propontis at the foot of the Great Palace, is named for a large and striking bronze sculpture of a bull (*bous*) and a lion (*leon*) locked together in a death struggle, the one biting, the other goring. Harald and Maniakes? It struck me as a bad omen.

Now the waterfront echoed with the blare of trumpets, the shouts of sergeants and the bosuns' whistles, the tramp of thousands of feet going up the gangways, the rattle of yardarms coming down and of anchor chains hauled up, the whinnying of cavalry horses and the braying of pack mules hanging in their canvas slings in the holds of the transports, the rumble of carts loaded with water casks and sacks of hard biscuit and dried fish, with bales of fodder, with sheaves of arrows and bundles of lances, and with strongboxes full of gold and silver coin with which to pay our troops and our mercenary allies. Everywhere banners floated and snapped in the wind, gold and silver crucifixes atop their tall standards caught the light of the rising sun. The great triangular sails of the warships luffed and filled, clouds of incense from the priests' censers drifted over us. Thousands of rowers took their places at the benches, flexed their shoulders, and spat in their hands. Here, the encumbering armor of the heavy cavalry, carefully wrapped against the salt air, was carried aboard and stowed; and there, barrels of Greek fire, concocted in secret in the arsenal of Mangana, were rolled—very carefully—up the gangways. Constantinople hadn't seen a spectacle like this since the days of the great

Basil Bulgar-Slayer. There were forty great warships, which the Greeks call dromons, their decks bristling with catapults and bronze fire siphons. The dromons were accompanied by two hundred and twenty transports carrying fifteen thousand troops, mostly heavy lancers and swift-galloping Khazar archers plus another ten thousand sailors and rowers—free men, these, not slaves—and the Varangians, mailed and helmeted, with their axes on their shoulders.

The whole city had turned out to see us, crowding the parapet of the sea wall, spilling down onto the quay despite the efforts of soldiers to keep them back. And from the palace that rose tier on tier beyond the wall? Did the Empress Zoe, frightened, disheveled, half-mad, peer down on us from one of those curtained windows? What would become of her? Did they execute empresses in this country?

I stood, waiting for the order to board the *Pantocrator*, the admiral's flagship. It was a magnificent vessel with two lateen sails of purple silk bearing golden eagles, and a hundred oars in two banks of fifty. The admiral's pennant bearing the image of crossed fire-siphons flew from the masthead.

I searched the crowd for Selene's face. Since returning from Psellus's house, I had been constantly at Harald's side. Surely, I thought, she would put aside her anger and come to see me off. Instead, here came Melampus, with Psellus trotting beside him. The old man embraced me, with tears in his eyes.

"Forgive her, Odd, she's a willful girl, heaven knows. I could have ordered her to come but I've never ordered her to do anything in her life. She's used to having her own way. But she's crying her eyes out. She does love you. She's a good girl, Odd."

"I know she is. I love her. But whether we can have a life together is her choice to make. I must be the man I am."

"You have a precious child together, never forget that."

"One who won't know me by the time I come back—if I come back."

"That's in the hands of the gods. I've sacrificed and prayed to Hermes, he'll protect you. I've brought you this, put it on." He held in the palm of his hand a small onyx carved with mystical symbols and attached to a silver chain. I hung it round my neck. "Be brave now. Eh? Listen to me, an unwarlike old fool like me, telling *you* that." He forced a little laugh.

We embraced again. Perhaps I should have resented Melampus

for having a greater claim on his daughter's affections than I did. But I couldn't. Instead a great feeling of tenderness for him swept over me.

"And Odd," Psellus broke in, "I have the Logothete's promise that your family will be provided for while you're away, it's the least we can do. I shall make it my personal responsibility."

"Thank you, my friend."

"Here, I've brought you a present, read it when you have time." He handed me a slim volume wrapped in oil paper.

"More poetry?"

"Hardly. It's a military handbook, The *Strategikon*, written by the Emperor Maurice nearly five hundred years ago. Advice on marshalling an army, conducting a campaign; filled with tricks and stratagems for every contingency. Written by a soldier for soldiers. The Greek isn't hard."

"Friend Psellus, I'm not going to command an army."

"You never know," he smiled. Keep it to yourself—and take good care of it, it's my own copy."

"I didn't think warfare was one of your interests."

"No subject is alien to me," he said loftily. "And one more thing, Odd. Step away with me—excuse us, Melampus." We pushed our way through the crowd to the sea wall and stood in its shadow. He spoke in a voice just loud enough to be heard over the general uproar. "The Logothete would like your views on the campaign, Odd—the sort of things that aren't mentioned in official dispatches—personalities, ambitions, private agendas, whatever you think we might want to know."

"Harald, you mean."

"But not only him. George Maniakes wouldn't be the first rough soldier to aim at the throne—and gain it."

"He might be better than the invalid we've got."

"That's not for us to decide. Now, we have agents on the ground, in Messina, Catania, Syracuse, perhaps elsewhere, I don't know. From time to time, one of them will approach you and ask you to write something for us—not to go in the official pouch, we have other methods. He'll give you papyrus and a pen, I don't imagine those items are easy to find in a camp. And if you want to include letters to Selene, I will see that she gets them and that her letters get to you."

"My handwriting isn't much."

"It will suffice. Can you do this for us?"

"Of course."

"Just don't get caught."

"Tangle-Hair!" Harald bellowed at me from the deck of the *Pantokrator*. He was standing next to Maniakes, two angry giants back to back, towering over lesser men. I had better be on hand to translate—or not, as the case required. I turned and ran up the gangway.

"Cast off," ordered Stephen, trying hard to sound as though he deserved to command this splendid fleet. *Cast off, cast off.* The cry was echoed down the line.

Rowers grunted, oars rose and dipped and churned the sea. Once out of the harbor, the breeze caught us and bellied our sails. The wind sang in the rigging. It had been a long time since I'd stood in the prow of a warship—and never one like this. The power of it! I felt it surge with each stroke of the oars, felt the sting of sea spray in my face. It was thrilling to have a deck under me again. We heeled over and shot ahead—over the *wine dark sea*, as Homer would have said it, bound for an island that Odysseus knew well. Would I be gone from home as long as he? Would my *Penelope* be faithful? Would my son someday come searching for me? I turned my face to the wind and tried to put those thoughts away.

Their leader was a villainous-looking character with a squint in one eye.

PART TWO
SICILY
1038-1040

18

I GO TO WAR

The Norns do us both good and evil, they measure out our portions of victory and defeat, of joy and pain, and no man can see the end. In the soil of far-off Sicily grew the seeds of my fate—of the Empire's fate—and only the Norns knew it.

Driven by the strong summer winds that blow out of the north, we crossed the Propontis, passed through the Hellespont, under the eyes of the forts that dot its slopes, and out into the blue Aegean. Here we hopped, like frogs in a pond, from island to island—Lesbos, Chios, Andros, and others I never learned the names of—making our way west. The poor inhabitants of these islands were never glad to see us; we ate everything in sight, drank their wells dry, and left nothing behind but the litter of a great mob of men and animals.

The Greeks are skillful sailors, but not as brave as us Northmen. They never spend whole weeks in the open sea the way we do but beach their ships every night and build a camp on the shore. With a fleet as big as ours this was the work of half a day, every day. And so, despite the fact that we were in such haste to meet the enemy, our progress was slow. I was impressed by the discipline and order of this great host, watching them build their camps, each one with its palisade and ditch and tents arranged in even rows. They reminded me of ants in an anthill, all scurrying here and there, everyone knowing his place and his duties. I was impressed too with the cleanliness of the camps. Maniakes insisted that latrines be dug at a distance, that food scraps be buried or burned, that drinking water be purified with wine or vinegar. He would say that the killing of a fly or mosquito was as meritorious a deed as the killing of an Unbeliever. But even despite these precautions, fever and dysentery were never far from us.

But, as I say, all this took up a great deal of time. A fleet of Viking raiders would have struck swiftly and been away before anyone knew we were there. The Saracens had plenty of time to know we were coming and make their preparations. Our fleet spread out over a league of water and could be seen a long way off.

I have already said a little about these war galleys that they call dromons. During long days at sea I was able to study every detail of them with a sailor's eye. The *Pantokrator* was half again the length of my old ship, the *Sea Viper*, and deeper-hulled, although not much broader in the beam. She had a hundred oars to the *Viper's* thirty, and two masts with triangular sails that could be angled back and forth so as to sail nearer the wind than any Norse dragon ship can do. She had a crew of a hundred and fifty rowers, about fifty deck hands and artillerymen, half a dozen officers, and a complement of marines, made up of Harald's bandon and the Khazars of Maniakes's bodyguard.

Maniakes kept his crews busy. Although, with the wind behind us, there was little need for rowing, the oarsmen were drilled every day. Their backs were broad and sun-blackened, their muscles like knotted ropes, their hands as hard as horn. They were Thracians, Dalmatians, Greeks and Arabs. They were free men who served willingly because they ate better aboard ship than they would have done at home. At a signal, they would rush to the benches, run out the oars, which are thirty feet long and weigh a hundred pounds each, and pull together with perfect precision to the beat of a mallet. After a dash at top speed, which they could keep up only for a few minutes, they would sink back, panting like spent dogs, and drink deep from the water pails, which they kept beside them.

The helmsman is the most important member of the crew. Years before, I had learned to steer my ship under the eye of Stig No-One's-Son, my teacher in all things. But, where a Viking ship has one steering oar, the dromon has two, operated in tandem by one man. I watched for hours as our helmsman pushed one tiller forward while pulling the other back, putting the ship through tight maneuvers, until I thought that, just possibly, I could do it myself.

But what intrigued me most were the fire-breathing siphons. Our ship mounted two of them on the castle amidships and one in the prow. The composition of the 'Greek fire' they shot out was a deep secret—said to have been whispered by an angel of God into the ear of the first Emperor. Maniakes was not willing to waste much of it on practice, but a few times he had the gunners fire short bursts. These men wore thick leather aprons and gauntlets soaked in vinegar and, on their heads, leather hoods with eyeholes. They were arrogant men, proud of their deadly skill. I watched how they heated the fuel in bronze tanks below decks—tricky work as too much heat and the tank might explode—and how two men worked a big pump which sent the hot fuel up through a flexible leather hose to the barrel with its gaping lion's mouth. Here a match was lit and, when the gunner squeezed a lever, a stream of the fuel shot out and ignited. Under maximum pressure a tongue of fire could leap thirty feet or more, and it burned even on the water. We had catapults too—big crossbows on swivel frames that shot arrows a great distance—as well as ballistae that hurled stones, but it was the roar of those siphons that kept our enemies at bay. Only these made the Imperial Fleet master of the sea.

Except when he was overseeing our drills, Maniakes was seldom seen on deck or in camp. I think I know the reason for this. He believed that a commander inspires his men not through love but through fear, and the commander is feared most who is seen least. Whenever we mentioned his name, it was in a whisper, as though he could hear us wherever he was. Even Harald felt it, though he wouldn't admit it. Stephen, our so-called admiral, on the other hand, was always strutting about, issuing orders that had to be quietly countermanded by his officers, until the whole fleet despised him for a fool.

There was little for us Varangians to do during the long days at sea. (I say 'us' Varangians for I now thought of myself as one.) We watched the sailors with interest but never bore a hand in their tasks. We slept, we gambled, we talked about women. Gorm asked me about Selene, but when he saw it pained me he stopped. I read my *Odyssey*, translating it aloud to the men, until I came to the part where the hero and his crew passed the whirlpool Charybdis and the six-headed monster Scylla, which lived in the Strait of Messina—exactly where we were headed. Then Harald made me stop because the men were getting nervous. (I think Homer made it all up anyway because we never saw any such things when we got there.)

At the end of our first week at sea, we came to a city called Athens and docked in the harbor of Piraeus. This city, I've heard tell, was once a great and famous place but it is now mostly deserted and filled with ruins. We had three days' liberty here. Maniakes had a camp built as usual outside the walls, but Harald defied him and turned us loose in the town. We probably did as much damage as an invading army. At the end, most of the men had to be carried aboard ship because they were too drunk to walk. But I mention this because one evening while we were there I was summoned to Maniakes's tent. Moses the Hawk, the Captain of his bodyguard, found me in a taverna where I was drinking with Gorm and four Icelanders, who were my mess mates. In broken Greek he ordered me to come with him. I was just drunk enough to be tempted to refuse, but I thought better of it. I followed him out the door with my heart beating fast.

The general's tent was in the center of the camp, a huge affair of white silk, flying his banner from its top. A dozen Khazar bowmen squatted on their heels around the entrance. They leapt to attention when Moses approached. Inside, the furnishings were very plain: an ordinary soldier's camp bed, a couple of big trunks, a table littered with papers, an armchair and some stools. In one corner stood a framework with the general's armor, sword and shield hung on it. A couple of servants lurked in the background. Maniakes had a book open in front of him as Moses and I ducked under the tent flap. He looked up and waved me to a chair. "You know what this is?" he growled in his rumbling bass. It was an accusation, not a question. He held the book up for me to see. "*The Strategikon* of Maurice. You have a copy and have been seen reading it. I want to know why."

I'd only peeked at it a few times when I thought I was alone. *Was I again being watched?* He thrust his head forward and starred at me hard. "There is only one general in this army—me. What use is this book to you?"

"No use, sir. It was a present."

"You're quite a reader, I understand. Your Greek is good. Are you translating this for Harald? Is that it? The big Norwegian 'prince', as he calls himself, aspires to learn tactics? Strategy? Order of battle?" He emphasized each word with a sneer.

I shook my head. "Harald isn't interested in books. And you, sir, should not treat him as a rival. He's a brave warrior, his men are devoted to him."

"So you say. Then what about you? You're a queer bird. Who are you, anyway? What are you to Harald?"

"I have the honor to be his skald, to carry his messages and sing his praises."

"His praises!" Maniakes slapped the table and shouted in a voice like thunder. "His own mouth is so full of them I wonder he needs you."

I had nothing to say to this.

"And you translate for him. Why doesn't the prince bother to learn our language?"

"Maybe he doesn't plan to be here long."

"And you do?"

"In my case it was involuntary." I explained how I had learned Greek as a slave.

He gave me a long appraising look. "I was a slave once. Slavery can do one of two things to a man, break him or toughen him. Which did it do to you?" He went on without waiting for me to answer. "How did you come to know Harald?"

"We served together in Gardariki, in the druzhina, the elite regiment, of Grand Prince Yaroslav of the Rus." As I spoke these words, I happened to glance at Moses, who was standing at attention behind the general's chair. The fellow had a face that might have been carved from mahogany. His cheekbones were high, his lips thin, and his eyes slightly slanted. I'd never seen him change expression. Now those eyes narrowed for an instant with a look that might have been surprise. Or might have been hatred.

Again, Maniakes gave me a searching look. "And now you serve him faithfully?"

"Of course." *Did I hesitate for half a heartbeat? Did my color change? I felt naked before those piercing eyes.*

"You're not stupid. So many men are. I may have a use for you— what's your name?"

"Odd Tangle-Hair. It's hard to serve two masters, sir."

"But sometimes unavoidable, yes? Well, since you're his translator, translate this for him. He had better be careful if he doesn't want to be sent back to Constantinople because I will brook no more of his insolence. Tell him so."

"I will, sir."

The general leaned back in his chair, touched the book with his fingers. "So what have you learned from Emperor Maurice's handbook, eh? I myself have studied it from boyhood."

"I haven't read much of it," I answered. "One of his maxims sticks in my mind: *It is better to have an army of deer commanded by a lion than an army of lions commanded by a deer.*"

"Hah! Yes, by Christ," he laughed suddenly, showing yellow teeth. His laugh sounded like the bark of a big dog. "I know that line. And I am the lion in this army. Go back and tell Harald that in case there's any doubt in his mind. You can go now, I have a meeting with my captains. And keep reading, young man. Maybe it'll make a general of you too. Moses, take our friend back to whatever hell-hole you found him in."

We walked together through the camp, where the men sat around their campfires making their evening meal, past the horse lines where the big, shaggy-footed chargers of the heavy cavalry and the nimble ponies of the Khazar archers stood side by side. I'd seen these Khazars—Moses among them—at their drill, galloping with the reins in their teeth, loosing arrows at wooden stakes, seldom missing.

"You're Rus?" Moses spoke in a gravelly voice, hardly moving his lips. It took me a moment to realize he was speaking Slavonic.

"I'm an Icelander, why do you ask?"

"Khazars hate the Rus."

I laughed. "I'm not fond of them myself. Why do you hate them?"

Moses was a man who chewed his words slowly and spat them out one at a time. I will give here in brief form what I learned of his story on our walk back to Piraeus and at other times when we talked. He came from a place called Tmutorakan on the Sea of Azov. His full name was Moses ben Manasseh and, like all his people, he was a Jew. They had once been a great people, he boasted. From Atil, their capital on the Volga, they'd ruled over a hundred cities. The trade of the Rus, the Arabs, the Greeks, even the far-off Chinese passed through their hands. Their khagan lived in a walled castle and was served by four thousand slaves. Though they were Jews, they welcomed Mohammedans and Christians to their city and treated everyone alike. This ended some sixty years ago when Prince Svyatoslav of Kiev (Yaroslav's grandfather) destroyed Atil and scattered the people. Only a rump state remained now in the Crimea, where Moses hailed from. I had seen Atil when I voyaged to the East with Yngvar's expedition; it was a desolate ruin now, inhabited only by ghosts and wolves. but I did not say this to Moses.

He was born the son of a rabbi—what they call their priests—and was trained to follow in his father's footsteps. But he preferred riding and hunting to studying books of religion. He rebelled, and his father drove him out with curses. After that, he became a wandering mercenary. He served for some years in the army of the Caliph of Cairo. There he learned to speak passable Arabic and learned the valuable skill of pigeon handling. Finally he washed up in Byzantium where he joined the Khazar regiment of the Household Cavalry. He served under Maniakes in the East and, one day, saved him from being trampled by a runaway horse. From that day on, he and a dozen of his men became the general's bodyguard. A good life, he said, but a lonely one. His spare time he devoted to training pigeons, which the Greeks, like all armies, use for carrying messages.

"You've no family?" I asked him.

"I'm a Jew, though not a pious one. I must take a Jewish wife."

"Constantinople is full of Jews."

He spat in the dirt. "Shopkeepers' daughters. Their fathers hide them away when they see bloody-handed men like me coming. Soon there will be no more Khazars. My generation will be the last." There was no mistaking the bitterness in his voice.

We continued on in silence for a while, then I asked, "What do you think of our general? You must know him pretty well by now. In my country there are creatures we call trolls. Huge, brutish, dangerous, but stupid. We teach our children to fear them."

This seemed to amuse Moses. He allowed himself a fleeting smile. "A troll? Maybe. But stupid? No, by no means stupid. There isn't another commander in the army with his ability."

"I believe it. To rise from a waiter to a general. Extraordinary. Would you say that his ambition reaches even farther?"

Moses stopped and looked hard at me. "What are you asking?"

"An idle question, nothing more."

"Some questions are better left unasked."

"Of course." We had reached the door of the taverna now. "Stay and have a drink with me, friend Moses."

He hesitated. "The general wants me back."

"Another time then?"

"If you like." He was a hard man to read—yet, I thought that perhaps I'd made a useful connection.

He turned and made his way back down the lane, his bow-case and quiver swinging from one hip, his saber from the other. A time would come when I would be very glad I had made the acquaintance of Moses the Hawk.

✝

In the weeks that followed, we rounded the Peloponnese, sailed up the west coast of Greece to the island of Corfu, stood across to the heel of Italy, and down the coast to Reggio di Calabria, one of the last remaining Imperial outposts in the peninsula. Two miles across the strait from Reggio lay Sicily and the city of Messina. We expected to find a Saracen fleet prepared to challenge us but, to our surprise, our scouts reported that there were no ships in sight, so we sailed across.

Our ships crowded the waterfront, the crews were confined to the harbor, while the army, as always, built its camp on high ground outside the walls, and this time the Varangians were strictly ordered to stay in it—there would be no more of the riotous drunkenness that had made a wreck of Piraeus. Although Maniakes forbade looting under pain of death, still most of the Arab population fled the town, clogging the roads with their carts and donkeys, heaped high with whatever they could carry away. Stephen and Harald crowed over this 'victory', which was, of course, no victory at all, but Maniakes looked grim and muttered that it was all too easy. It was decided the next day to leave the bulk of our force in Messina under Stephen's command while Maniakes would lead ten dromons and an equal number of empty transports up the Tyrrhenian coast to Salerno, to collect the Lombard mercenaries we had been promised.

Salerno is a pretty town of whitewashed walls and red roof tiles that rises up on terraces from the water's edge. Duke Gaimar, a handsome youth barely out of his teens but very much in charge, entertained us for three days in his castle while his warriors streamed in from the countryside. It was obvious at once that these men were not happy to be leaving their homes and expected to get little out of it. They grumbled and gave us angry looks. In command of them was that same clever,

Greek-speaking Lombard named Arduin whom I'd last seen a year ago as an ambassador in Constantinople. We gave each other a friendly greeting now.

A band of Norman knights and their squires arrived as well. Unlike the Lombards, these men looked tough and eager for adventure. They wore their hair close-cropped, shaved their chins and carried long shields that tapered to a point. They were led by a pair of brothers, William and Drogo de Hauteville. William was powerfully built and could (and often did) bend a horseshoe with his bare hands. They were Norsemen, like ourselves, they said, whose ancestors had settled on the coast of Francia, but they no longer spoke our tongue except for a few words learned from their grandfathers. There being too little opportunity for plunder in their own country, they had come south to seek their fortune. Harald affected to scorn them as no better than robbers, but I had the feeling that these were tough men, prickly of their honor, and would need to be handled carefully. Not that anyone asked my opinion.

During these days, we swam in the warm Tyrrhenian sea and lay out naked on the white sand beach. It was as close to paradise as I've ever been. When it was time to set sail again, I was loath to leave it.

We were two days out of Salerno heading south, the sea choppy, the wind blowing across our bow out of the west, giving little purchase for our sails. It was work for the rowers, and, though they rowed in shifts of fifty, they were all tired. As evening approached, the question was debated whether to put in to shore, if we could find a sheltered bay along this rocky coast, or press on to Messina. We figured we were three, maybe four hours away. Harald was for stopping but Maniakes wanted to push on, even though it meant sailing in the dark. Enemy scouts were hunting for us—a fishing boat had followed us all morning and then disappeared out to sea. We'd be defenseless if their fleet caught us on a beach. The two of them went head to head over it. Their voices could be heard all over the ship. Maniakes, of course, had the last word and Harald stamped off to the foc'sle in a black mood.

Just then the lookout atop the foremast shouted, "Sail off the starboard quarter." We ran to the railing to look. Coming out of the blood-red setting sun, five—eight—twelve galleys sped toward us over the water. In another moment we could hear the rumble of their war drums and the cries of their warriors.

"Coming from the Liparis," Maniakes growled. "Their rowers are fresh. They knew exactly where we'd be."

Harald frowned and said nothing.

Our little fleet was strung out in a long line behind us. Maniakes sent up colored smoke signals ordering the ships to close up fast, but this would take time—more time than we had. Three Saracen ships in the lead recognized the admiral's purple flag flying from our mast and headed straight for us. If they could cut us off and surround us, they would decapitate our army at a single blow.

"Clear for action, strike the sails, every hand to his post, serve out pikes and swords!" Officers barking orders, men swarming everywhere, oars run out. Harald shouting at his men, "On with your armor, be quick!" Moses running back to where Maniakes stood beside the helmsman to hold his shield over him. Saracen arrows and sling stones already humming through the air, searching for his big carcass, the Khazars returning fire with their little, powerful bows. Atop the castle and in the prow, the gunners unlimbering their fire tubes, the pump-men below deck stroking the pumps to build up pressure, waiting for the command to fire, the enemy not near enough yet for the flaming jets to reach them. Rocks from Saracen catapults striking, bouncing along our deck, sending wicked splinters flying. One ricocheted off the mast and struck me on the thigh. Men dropping, heads bleeding. Rowers on the upper tier, with little to protect them, rolling off the benches—shoulders, throats transfixed with arrows. An arrow buried itself in the deck an inch from my foot, another glanced off my helmet. One enemy ship almost abreast of us now, its fighters leaping up and down, waving their sabers, their archers marking us. Three others not far behind. Maniakes shouting, "Hard right rudder," and the helmsman working his twin tillers so that we swung sharply around to face them prow to prow. Harald bawling at us, "Into the foc'sle, prepare to board."

"Siphons ready—fire!" cried the gunnery officer. But three of the gunners atop the castle were already struck down by missiles. There was one siphon in the prow where we huddled with our shields over our heads. The gunner, right beside me, screamed and rolled away, the feathered end of an arrow protruding from his leather mask. I tossed down my shield and took his place—no thought, no act of will, only instinct. "Pump, pump!" I shouted to the men crouching below the half-deck at my feet. I squeezed the firing lever, as I'd seen it done. Again and again, as I swiveled the tube. With a roar, jets of orange flame, brighter than the sun and hotter than Hel, arced from the muzzle, raking the enemy's deck. The sulfurous stench was like the volcano of my homeland, the fiery mouth of Hekla. Along the deck men shrieked and cowered, tore at their flaming clothes, threw themselves into the sea, where they kept burning until they were only blackened cinders. Then, with a shudder and groan our two hulls ran together.

"Varangians up!" cried Harald. He leapt onto their smoking deck, whirling his ax over his head, and we went screaming after him. Thrusting, hacking, slipping on the scorched and bloody planks, kicking bodies out of our way. I took a saber cut on my right arm but hardly felt it. I ran one man through the body, smashed my shield into another's face and lopped off his leg with a backhanded slash of my blade.

We cleared their deck. Saracen warriors flung themselves over the side to escape us. Their captain and helmsman lay dead. We'd taken a fine prize. Where puddles of Greek fire still burned on the deck, we threw cloaks over them and stamped them out. Below decks, the rowers chained to their benches, were shrieking with fear, pleading for their lives. Unlike our oarsmen, these were slaves, most of them Italians, judging from the few intelligible words I could catch. They'd row for us with a will. But we had no time to congratulate ourselves; two other ships were bearing down on us, and there were more behind them. And only two of our ships, with another bandon of Varangians and some of the Normans aboard, were close enough now to engage them.

Maniakes hailed us, "Harald, break off, get to Messina, bring help."

But Harald looked about him, puzzled. "In this? How do we steer this great beast?" Like the Greek ships, it had twin steering oars lashed together; no Norseman had ever handled a ship like this.

"I can try." I ran back to the stern and grasped the two tillers in my hands. "Tell the rowers to back water."

Harald shouted the command down into the hold—in Norse, of course—but they knew what they had to do.

Though blood ran down my wounded arm, I worked the tillers carefully, one forward and one back with hardly any effort, feeling the great ship respond like a spirited horse to the tug of the reins. We rowed away, leaving behind us the stink of sulfur hanging over the water.

Our oarsmen were pulling for their lives, for freedom from their masters, and we soon left our pursuers behind. Night fell, leaving us all alone in the sea with only a quarter moon and a handful of stars to show us the black outline of the land. I steered as close to shore as I thought was safe. We fought the wind all the way and made slow headway. At last, with dawn lightening in the eastern sky, we saw the roofs of Reggio and then, across the strait, Messina.

Harald marched straight to Stephen's tent, shouldered his guards aside, and hauled him out of bed. "Make ready to sail," he ordered.

But no, Stephen wailed. It was too dangerous. Who knew how big an enemy fleet was lurking out there, waiting to pounce?

Harald shook the man like a terrier shaking a rat. And this was, remember, the brother-in-law of his patron, John, the most powerful man in the empire (assuming he was still alive). To Harald's credit, at that moment, he didn't care.

We roused one of the camp doctors to patch up my sword cut and, an hour later, twenty dromons sailed out of Messina. We found our ships scattered up and down the coast, wherever they had gone aground. We had lost a dromon and three transports sunk or captured by the Saracens before darkness forced them to break off the fight. We had suffered many wounded, one of them Moses, who took an arrow in the arm. The bodies of the dead, or the nearly dead, were already drifting toward shore. Of the enemy, we shackled the ones who looked like they might be worth ransoming and left the rest for the crows. Our Lombard allies were threatening to go home until Maniakes hit one of them in the head with his fist and laid him out cold. The Normans, who kept to themselves, looked thoughtful, but said nothing.

Varangians crowded around me, many of them men I hardly knew but suddenly they all seemed to know me. They had either seen or heard the story of what I'd done. Where did I learn to steer a galley like that, they asked, and how did it feel to fire that devilish weapon?

How did it feel? In the heat of battle I'd felt powerful, like a god, like Zeus hurling thunderbolts. But afterwards I felt differently. I've seen people burn before—my mother, my brother—I decided that I never wanted to touch that weapon again. It's the way Greeks fight, not the way a man fights. But I kept these thoughts to myself. Maniakes came up and gripped my hand in his huge paw—as eloquent a gesture of praise as a mouthful or words might have been from any other man.

But I saw Harald looking at me sideways. I knew that look. I murmured something inconsequential and turned away. I was a skald. My job was to praise, not to be praised. I was already composing in my head an ode for Harald—wolf-crammer, feeder of ravens—in fine, thumping Norse, with every kenning for battle and slaughter I could devise. This was my job, what Harald wanted and needed from me, and he would have it.

✝

Since we were forbidden by Maniakes to go into the city except in small numbers, an impromptu market soon sprang up outside our camp, where baskets of olives and almonds, grapes, apricots, and lemons filled the stalls and the merchants hawked silk scarves and brass bowls. On the second morning after our return from Salerno I was wandering among their tents and awnings, sampling the wares and wondering what to spend my money on, when an old woman approached me. She was a Greek, short and stout, olive-skinned, with a black mole on her forehead.

"You are the one called Odd?"

"How do you know me?"

"There is a present for you from a friend."

"What friend?"

"Just come." She pulled me under the flap of her little tent. Inside was a table heaped with ornate wooden chests. She held one out to me, a shallow box, about a foot square, with a carved walnut lid. She lifted the lid, then closed it again quickly. "Bring it back tomorrow, say you want to change it for a different one."

The Logothete! The box contained sheets of papyrus, a reed pen, a small bottle of ink. I was stunned. I'd only half believed Psellus when he said that their agents would find me in Sicily. The webs these Greeks wove astonished me.

With the box under my arm, I walked away until I found a quiet spot in a grove of fig trees, a quarter mile from the camp. I sat with my back against the rough bark, the box on my lap for a writing desk, and dipped my pen in the ink. My first secret report to the Logothete could be completed in a few lines: Stephen a coward, the Lombards unwilling allies, Maniakes and Harald in a shouting match: all the things that our general might not care to include in his official dispatches. Quickly done.

But Selene? My hand hesitated. The Greeks know how to express themselves in flowery language, but we Icelanders are not brought up that way; we're a close-mouthed race who keep our feelings to ourselves. I missed her terribly. I tried to imagine her, sitting in her chair with Gunnar at her breast, reading my letter—with what feelings? What could I say to my angry wife? She already hated that I was here; what could I say that would make her hate it less? I wrote a word, scratched it out, wrote another. My heart failed me. I sat for a long time, writing nothing.

19
SELENE'S TALE
JULY, 1038

Selene lays down the sheet of papyrus, covered with Odd's crabbed, slanted handwriting. She shifts little Gunnar to the other breast, and erases a tear with the back of her hand. Her face is white. "He says he's been in a battle," she says to her father. "Has he been hurt? He wouldn't tell me if he were. I have dreams, they frighten me."

Melampus reaches out a palsied hand to stroke her hair. She has moved back to her father's house to look after the old man—he has grown suddenly so weak—and because she can't bear to stay alone in the house that she and Odd shared. "Dreams often go by opposites, my dear, you know that. If anything were wrong we would know. *I* would know, I would see it." She looks pleadingly at Psellus, who has brought the letter and stayed to take the midday meal with them. "He's all right, then?"

He gives her a cheerful smile. "You have my word on it. Not only that, Odd's the hero of the day. We've had a dispatch from Maniakes, praising him. Fought off the Infidels practically singlehanded, rescued the fleet. It seems he's made quite an impression, your husband. So you're not to worry."

"But that was weeks ago. Where are they now?"

Patience. We'll have more news soon, I'm sure. Now, then, I must be on my way. You'll want to write him, won't you? I'll come back for your letter tomorrow."

"My friend, we're putting you to too much trouble."

"Not a bit, Melampus, it's my pleasure. The information Odd's sent us—well, one mustn't talk, but it's of use, believe me. Now, one of these days when I have more time I want to talk with you about your alchemical experiments. Fascinating stuff."

"I hardly do any—" Melampus starts to answer, but falls silent and looks away. Lately, he seems to lack the strength for the all night vigils, watching the red cinnabar steam and bubble, exuding beads of precious mercury. And when he tries to pour in the acids, his hands shake so that he spills them. Someone will make gold one day, of that he has never doubted, but it won't be him. He knows that now.

Psellus lets himself out. They hear him mount his horse and ride away.

"May I, my dear?" Melampus takes up the letter and scans it quickly. He loves you, he misses you and the baby. He regrets the hard words. And so do you—you'll tell him so. He needs to hear that." He takes her chin in his hand.

Selene nods and weeps. Her tears fall on Gunnar's curls, as black and tangled now as Odd's. If only she could hold that head to her breast. Then the two of them, father and daughter, sit silent for a time, wrapped in their own thoughts.

The sound of horse's hooves on the cobbles outside, the jingle of harness. A rap at the door. Is it Psellus coming back for something? Selene wipes her face while Melampus goes to the door and opens it. It is a stranger, a man in his forties, with blond hair and beard, expensively dressed in a brown silk robe shot with silver threads, on his finger a ring with a sapphire the size of a pigeon's egg. Behind him, an open carriage, a servant holding the horses' heads. In the carriage the figure of a young girl swaddled in a blanket so that only her small pale face peeks out. "You are Doctor Melampus?" The voice is deep, the accent educated. "My name is Alypius. A friend sent me, I hope you can help us."

20
∩EARLY CAUGHT
[*Odd resumes his narrative*]

Nearly two months went by before I received more letters or had another chance to write. It was now late summer of 1038 and I was in Catania, which we had just liberated four days earlier after a long siege. This time, as I was poking around the marketplace, an elderly priest sidled up to me with elaborate stealth, glancing this way and that, and introduced himself in a loud whisper as Father Macarius. I was beginning to feel like a marked man, the way these agents of the Logothete were able to spot me. With much rolling of his eyes, he motioned me toward his little church. It was dark and cool inside, a relief from the noonday sun.

The Christmen of Sicily have fallen on hard times since the Saracen conquest. Most of their priests fled to southern Italy, taking with them anything of value that the Infidels didn't steal first. This church had only wooden candlesticks in place of silver ones, its icon screen was broken, its altar cloth replaced by a piece of sacking. But Father Macarius did what he could to fight back—sending information to the Logothete whenever he could. His son owned a boat, he said, and that was but the first in a tenuous chain of links, some by sea, some by land, that stretched from Catania to Constantinople.

Before he would hand over my letters, though, he made me light a candle and pray with him. I knew all about these rituals from the daily devotions of the army. I did my best to contain my impatience as he droned through the liturgy. At last, he handed me a big book with a worn leather cover—again with many nervous glances, although we were quite alone in the church. I opened it to find that a hole had been carved in the pages and in it was a travel-stained packet of letters. One letter, a single sheet of fine parchment, was folded in half and fastened with the gold seal of the Office of Barbarians. The other letter, written on three pages of tattered papyrus, was sealed with wax and the imprint of a crescent moon. Selene's stamp. My heart beat fast. Father Macarius offered to read them to me and was astonished when I told him I could read and write. Taking the letters, a sheaf of blank papyrus, and pen and ink, I went out into the little churchyard, where the light was better, and sat down on the low stone wall that encircled the grounds. I should have had more sense. I tore open Selene's letter. Out of it fell a curl of black hair. My son's! I read through it hastily, then set it aside. I would deal with the Logothete first; he didn't rouse the turmoil of emotion in me that my wife did.

We—your friend Psellus and I—hope this finds you well [I read]...your last letter very interesting... spend more time with Maniakes if you can ... how well do you know him? What is his plan? He tells us almost nothing... How are he and Harald getting along now?

Sir [I wrote], *Maniakes must have written to you about our great victory at Rometta, so I needn't go into detail about that...*

After the sea battle, our army had marched up to Rometta, which is the fortress that commands the pass linking Messina with the road to Palermo. There we won a great victory over the Emir. The Saracen army made a spectacular sight, with its huge green banners and masses of roaring kettle drums, and ululating priests whipping their men into a frenzy. Still, it was our cavalry that swept the field—rank after rank of steel-clad lancers, charging knee to knee. Nothing could withstand them. And at their head rode Maniakes himself, mounted on a huge black stallion, carrying aloft the banner of Saint George. The Varangians and other infantry were held in reserve and never got into the fight—which made Harald furious.

After the battle, [I continued] *the army cheered the general. But then, he spoiled everything. He was not happy with the way one lancer regiment, the Athanatoi, had conducted themselves; they had nearly let their flank be turned. So he called their commander out, a well-born and popular officer, and beat him nearly to death with his fists. The men watched this in deep silence. A general who can't control himself is a danger to everyone. He'll lay hands on the wrong man one day. The Varangians are angry, the Lombards were never enthusiastic, the Normans are unhappy about not getting enough of the spoils—it's all they care about. And now he attacks his own officers.*

Following our victory, we headed south down the coast (although Harald again argued against this strategy), captured Taormina and now Catania, and we will soon march on Syracuse. How long that city will hold out I have no idea. We are already suffering greatly from short supplies and from the heat.

Pounding heat, blinding heat, crushing heat.

There is a wind they call the sirocco that blows day and night like the blast from a potter's kiln, spinning the dust up in whirlwinds. It had followed us all the way from Messina. It was especially hard on us Northerners. Mile after weary mile I trudged under a molten sun with my shield slung on my back and my helmet as hot as a cooking pot, the haft of my ax slick in my hand and my eyes fixed on the shimmering horizon. Heat rose from the road in waves. The dust choked us even though we wore kerchiefs over our faces. Varangians fainted dead away, keeled over in mid-step, and had to be carried to the side of the road and dashed with water. Stragglers were picked off by marauding gangs of peasants and stripped of their arms, their shirts, their trousers, their boots.

And we were already short of provisions, even with the fleet to revictual us. By the time we entered Catania, there was little left in the town to eat. Children in the streets begged us for food but we had nothing to spare them. All around us, the Saracens were burning crops, poisoning wells, staking dead animals in the streams upriver. Everywhere was the smell of blood, of death. Burning houses, corpses of men and horses swollen to bursting in the sun. The roads were choked with refugees—Saracen and Christian alike—fleeing their villages. We took from them whatever we could lay hands on. We broke into the wine cellars of Greek houses and drank ourselves senseless. Of course, women were raped—though not by us Varangians, not after Harald hanged two Guardsmen for doing that.

Taormina held out for two weeks—and paid a heavy price. The defenders were massacred, their women and children loaded aboard the ships to be taken off and sold.

Here in Catania, after holding out for a month, the defenders have been allowed to leave under flag of truce because Maniakes is anxious to get on to Syracuse. Harald violently denounced this—he actually accused Maniakes of taking a bribe from the Saracen commander to let them go. There was a shouting match; these are becoming daily occurrences, with me, as always, in the middle. Arduin the Lombard and William the Norman watch these explosions of temper with worried eyes. They didn't sign on for a campaign so rancorous and divided. The camp now is very tense. Harald keeps us billeted apart. The chief of Maniakes's bodyguard—a man called Moses the Hawk, who I've gotten friendly with—tells me that the general spends hours in his tent, brooding about Harald and cursing him, especially when he's drunk, which he now is most nights. I'll write again from Syracuse, if your agent there can find me. Farewell.

I folded these pages—I'd filled two sheets, front and back—and turned back to Selene's letter.

My darling, Gunnar has taken his first steps. He looks more like you every day... I tell him how brave you are ... we both miss you ... Father sends you his love. He's sitting here now... He's been feeling poorly, I worry about him. But he has a new patient. A man brought his daughter to us today, a sweet little girl. Father thinks she has the falling sickness, he's already planning how to treat her. Well, it will give him something to do and extra money for us, the man looks rich and is willing to pay ... Please write again soon. I dream of you. Sometimes my dreams frighten me ... I love you ...

I lay down the pages and sat with my pen in hand, trying to think what to say. My heart was full but, just as before, the words came hard. In the midst of all this blood and misery and death, what could I say that wouldn't frighten her or revolt her? My own mother never turned a hair, listening to my father boast of the slaughter he'd done on his enemies. Selene was a brave girl in her way, but she wasn't one of us. Should I say that the war would be over soon? I doubted it would. That I was amassing booty? I was, but *how* I was doing it, she would rather not know. That I was well and healthy? Not always. Like most of us, I had suffered bouts of fever in this pestilential country. (When the chills and vomiting came, the only cure was opium dissolved in a cup of goat's milk and wine. That put me in a wonderful stupor that lasted for hours. My only fear was that I would grow to like the stuff too well.) Instead, I would describe the countryside and the people, as if I were spinning a travel yarn to a child.

When I look up from where I'm sitting I can see a great, smoking volcano, capped and streaked with snow, that fills the whole western horizon. It is called Aetna and I reckon it is three times the size of the volcano I was born under. It has followed us for miles as we march south. Vapors rise from it in a hundred places and the peasants say that the forge of the blacksmith god Hephaestus lies beneath it. I can believe it. It reminds me of home.

The people here have short legs and wide shoulders and hands twice the normal size. Saracens, Christians, and Jews all live side by side. The women wear veils—not only the Saracen women but the others as well. And the women carry all their wealth on their bodies—headdresses, necklaces and bracelets made of old coins. Some of the Saracens are a people called Berbers; they dress all in blue, and the dye comes off on their skin…

And so I went on for another page, cudgeling my brain for anything that might possibly interest Selene and her father. And when I was finished, I was dissatisfied. There was so much I hadn't, *couldn't*, tell her.

I'm sorry to hear your father is unwell. When I have more time I will write a letter just to him. I miss you all. Kiss Gunnar for me.

I put down my pen and was just re-reading what I'd written when I saw out of the corner of my eye Halldor and Bolli—always inseparable—striding toward the churchyard. They were looking at me. How much had they seen? I could not explain these letters—even the one to my wife—without letting slip that I had some private means of delivering them. And that would be fatal. Maniakes would cut my ears and nose off. So, probably would Harald. I was a spy—even if what I had to say was of little importance. No one would defend me.

I dropped the pen and ink bottle at my feet, stood up slowly, pretending not to see them, and walked back into the church. Father Macarius started to smile, and then changed his expression when he saw my face.

"Burn these. Now!"

"What? All? Why?"

"Quickly, hold them to the candle."

"But parchment won't burn."

The Logothete's letter—the most damning of all.

"Well, hide it, do something, quickly."

I steadied my breathing, turned and sauntered out the door, forcing myself not to look around and thinking furiously what I would say.

"What're *you* doing in church, Thorvaldsson? Not praying, I think. Not a devil-worshipper like you." Halldor stood squarely in front of me, his legs planted wide apart, his hand on the hilt of his sword. Bolli, meanwhile, was watching the churchyard.

"You've been here a long time, we passed you earlier. Reading something? Tell me what."

"None of your business, friend."

"Really? I think I'll just go in and have a look round. Get out of my way."

It would take minutes to burn or hide those sheets. It would be better to provoke Halldor to fight me here in the street. Bolli had come over and was standing behind his brother-in-law's shoulder, looking nervous. "Bolli," I smiled evilly, "why don't you take your handsome boyfriend off to some dark tavern where you can stroke his cock. We all know he uses you like a woman."

"I'll send you to Hell," Halldor screamed. He landed a blow with his fist that sent me staggering back against the door. Then his sword was out and the blade whistled past my head as I crouched and turned. I got my sword out just in time to parry his next cut. Steel rang on steel and everywhere in the little marketplace heads turned toward us. Now the two of them came at me together and I had no place to run.

"Hold!"

Gorm! He and half a dozen of his Swedish mates pushed toward us through the crowd. They threw their cloaks over our swords and pulled us apart. Halldor roared and struggled but they were too many for him. Bolli let himself be dragged away.

"Tangle-Hair," Gorm appealed to me with his broad, honest face. "You know you're not to fight with these men. Harald said."

"It wasn't me who started it."

"I think we must take this to Harald."

Anything to get them away from this church. "By all means," I answered.

Harald glowered at us, pacing up and down in his tent. Halldor was so angry he could barely speak. Luckily, that has never been my problem.

"In a church?" Harald demanded. "Reading? Reading what?"

I gave him an easy smile. "I've put it about the market that I'm interested in texts of Greek poetry—you know me. And the priest had some pages he wanted to sell me. I looked them over, couldn't make sense of the stuff, and gave them back to him. Nothing more."

Halldor spat. "Don't let this pagan filth lie to you. Something's wrong here. I smell it. I'm going back to the church and shake that priest until his teeth rattle. I'll learn what this is about."

"You will *not*." Harald rounded on him. "These people happen to be on *our* side."

"But—"

"Let it go, Halldor. I *need* Odd."

"And you don't need me? Your standard-bearer? Thank you very much. I'll just collect what's owed me and take myself back to Iceland."

"Don't be ridiculous. I need both of you. Look, we cannot be fighting among ourselves. What other friends have we got? *Greeks*? I've told you once and I won't say it again. Do not draw steel against each other or, by God, I'll flay the lot of you. Now get out."

"Can I ask what that was about?" said Gorm, as we walked away together. "Those two hate you. I've overheard them talking you know. They won't be satisfied until they have your head on a stake, whatever Harald says. What were you doing in the church anyway? Haven't turned Christman, have you?"

"No," I smiled, "never that. I'll say something to you that Moses the Hawk said to me not long ago. Some questions are better left unasked."

"I wish my brother were here," he said out of the blue.

"Glum? So do I. He saved my life more than once. As you have just now. Thank you."

"Let's drink some wine," he said.

"Just what I was thinking, friend Gorm."

We went off arm in arm.

The next morning at dawn trumpets blew and the order was passed to fall in. We were leaving Catania, which had no more food in it to fill our bellies.

No one, friend or enemy, would read my letters now.

And they were the last I ever wrote.

21
SIEGE

Syracuse held out for eighteen months. By the time it surrendered, the city would be the haunt of dogs and vultures, its defenders few, sick, and starving, and our own army worn down to the point of mutiny. And I—I would be twenty-seven years old: ravaged by fever, my skin a map of battle scars, my feet nearly crippled, and my heart sore with longing. Abandoned. Angry. If the Logothete had agents in the city I never found them.

Maniakes had ordered a forced march from Catania, hoping to take Syracuse by surprise. We covered the thirty-seven miles that lay between them in two days. But the Saracens knew we were coming. The city was crammed with provisions and fighting men, and their commander, Ibn al-Thumnah, was a stubborn man. The city's ramparts stand thirty feet high on the landward side. In its wide harbor is a fortified island called Ortygia, connected to the city by a walled causeway which was the work of ancient kings, rich, proud men who made their city a jewel of the ancient world.

It was the job of our fleet to capture this island. Of course, Stephen failed at this, as he did at everything. Meanwhile, our catapults began to pound away at the walls and towers. This was work for specialists, and we Varangians were mere spectators. All day long, I listened to the creaks and groans, whoosh and snap of the great, long-armed trebuchets. I watched while boulders the size of wagons and great bundles of flaming pitch, baskets of scorpions and sacks of quicklime, arced toward the walls. The defenders hung out mats of woven hemp and sacks of grain husks to protect them, and answered our fire with their own catapults, launching showers of missiles, which sometimes pierced a man through the body or took off his head. We did some damage, breaking the teeth of the battlements, pulverizing the stone facing here and there to expose the brick core, but it wasn't enough. The walls stood firm. And before long, we ran out of boulders or anything else we could send at them. Then the trebuchets stood silent, like cranes at an abandoned building site. Maniakes began to pace and fume. His temper grew more savage every day.

He decided to order an assault with 'tortoises'. We had left six of these outside Catania because they were slow to move. Now it took us a week to take them apart, load them on carts, and reassemble them. And then they were too short for Syracuse's walls and needed extra stories added at the top. At last, one morning in the half-light before dawn, they rumbled toward a section of the wall, seeming to move by themselves, the men pushing them from inside. We Varangians, together with the Lombards and Normans, crouched behind the gangplanks at the top. Through a slit, I watched the enemy's fire arrows streak toward us. I felt the shock of stones strike us. I later learned they had begun tearing apart old buildings for ammunition. I felt the whole tower wobble and tip crazily as if it would go over with us, heard the squeal of wheels, the grunts of the pushers. I gave a wink and a nod to Gorm, who was beside me, tightened my grip on my spear, and sent up a prayer to Odin. Finally, I could forget everything, could lose myself, in the madness of battle.

The gangplank fell with a crash. We flung our spears and swarmed over the parapet, screaming our war cry and slashing right and left with our swords and axes. Harald was in the front, Halldor beside him, holding high our dragon-headed standard. "Varangians to me!" Harald yelled but his words were drowned by the answering roar of *Allahu akhbar.* from the Saracen fighters. They loosed a storm of arrows at us. Arrows in legs. Arrows in throats. Men went down, tumbled backward off the wall, falling screaming to the rocky ground below. Al-Thumnah's elite guard faced us. Broad shouldered, with white turbans and gilded armor, they came at us, whirling their long straight swords around their heads. One of them struck me, cracked my shield with a blow, my arm numb with the shock. Step by step, he drove me back over the blood-slick stones, and suddenly

I was hanging in space, legs kicking in empty air, shield gone, sword gone, fingertips scrabbling at the parapet's edge, letting go, falling ...

Then a grip like iron had me by the wrist and pulled me up, as if I were as weightless as a rabbit. I looked into the face of the Norman giant, William de Hauteville. He covered me with his long shield while I scrambled to my feet. I snatched up a spear, used it with both hands and stabbed at two of the enemy until it shattered. Then I rushed in under another man's guard, grappled him around the waist, tripped him with a wrestler's move, went down on top of him, got my dagger in under his jaw, the blood spurting up over my hand. I took his sword from him—a magnificent weapon, finer steel than ours—and turned to fight another. But now the sun was coming up over the bay, pouring into our eyes, the heat beginning to tell on us. We had hoped to clear the rampart of defenders and race down the inner steps to open one of the postern gates. But we were too few.

"Back, back!" someone shouted. We retreated, trying to carry our wounded, as many as we could. The gangplanks went up, the 'tortoises' began to move away, all of them shaggy with arrows, their cowhide covers smoldering, the stink of it in our throats. A shout of victory went up from the wall, *Allahu akhbar*, again and again. The kettle drums roared.

Later, when Harald mustered us, some ninety men had been killed or crippled from our whole force of five hundred, twenty-three from the Fourth Bandon alone. Halldor took a sword cut across his handsome face, which spoiled his appearance and did nothing for his mood. All of us were battered and bleeding one way or another. Three of the 'tortoises' were a total loss and there was not enough big timber in the neighborhood to build more.

After this, we settled down for a long siege. We scoured the countryside for food and firewood, finding not enough of either. Autumn came. Winter bore down on us with heavy rains and sickness in the camp. We grew thin. Wounds would not heal. Then summer and another winter. It was only a question now of who would break first. The defenders launched sorties against us, which we beat back, with heavy losses on both sides. Eventually, these came less and less often. And we assaulted the walls again, with ladders, but could never get a foothold.

The passage of time could be marked by the deterioration of our kit. Shields were battered into uselessness; sword blades nicked and bent, sharpened and re-sharpened until the steel wore away; helmets dented and hammered back into shape; the leather backing of our hauberks rotted away from sweat; our red tunics and cloaks patched and faded. Everything we owned had to be replaced from army stores, so that at the end we looked more like Greek soldiers than Varangians. Harald took the opportunity to adopt a cavalry officer's long surcoat made of overlapping gilded bronze plaques. Its skirt being nearly as long as a girl's dress, the men dubbed it 'Emma'. "Does pretty Emma keep you warm at night?" they joked.

By the time a year had passed we had lost nearly half our men to wounds or disease. We buried them in wide trenches, and remembered them with stories—this one's word-wit, that one's fine head of hair. Men whose wives and parents back in Snaefellsness and Laxdaela, in Varmaland and Uppsala, in Aland and Jutland would wait and wonder and never know what became of them, and eventually set up rune stones: *Thorir, or Ermund, or Bodolf fared east in Grikland and fed the crows there.*

By mutual agreement between Maniakes and Harald, who couldn't bear the sight of each other, we Varangians continued to bivouac apart from the rest of the army. The Lombards and Normans joined us, leaving the Greeks to themselves. Although I was still not officially a Guardsman, everyone—except for Halldor and Bolli—seemed to have forgotten that I wasn't. And because of the closeness of camp life and the brotherhood of battle, a bond grew up between me and these men that never could have happened back in Constantinople. There were a few Icelanders in every bandon and most of them were willing to be my friends, whatever my religion. Halldor, being a great chieftain's son, tried to lord it over them and wasn't, in fact, very popular.

The days crept by. We devoted much time to sports. Harald insisted that we keep fit, and he took the lead in wrestling and running and lifting rocks. Every bandon had its champions, and rivalry was fierce. The nights we passed around our campfires, faces flushed with firelight and wine, drinking, telling stories (mine were always in demand), and, like soldiers everywhere, complaining. Harald took the lead in this, too. Did that brute, Maniakes, that ex-*waiter*, know his business? Harald spat the man's name, always with a sneer on his face and a hard edge to his voice. He never missed an opportunity to mention Maniakes's low birth in comparison to his own, the half-brother of a king. The saintly Olaf was always in Harald's mouth. We stifled yawns listening to him repeat, for the hundredth time, the shining tale of Stiklestad, how at the age of fifteen he had stood over his brother's corpse, beating back the heathen rebels; how he had escaped and made his way to Gardariki; how he wooed and won the Rus prince's beautiful daughter whom he would marry and carry home to Norway one of these days, and damnation to her wicked mother. All of this I knew well—too well—and none of it was quite the way I remembered it. But I held my tongue.

The Normans, William and Drogo, would listen to him, though they only understood a little of our language. One constant visitor, however, picked up our speech with amazing quickness. This was Arduin the Lombard, the henchman of Duke Gaimar of Salerno. He was a man of about thirty-five with a long beard, after the fashion of his people, and shrewd, intelligent eyes. And, unique among his fellows, he had been educated in Greek and spoke it fluently. His manners were thoroughly Greek, too. No one would have guessed he was a barbarian. He knew something of poetry and appreciated my telling of Homeric tales, contributing details himself. But most of all he listened to Harald and would question him about laws and taxes and such things. Here is a man, I thought, who aims to be a king in his own country someday. We spoke Greek to each other, and I helped him with his Norse. We got on well, and I have always been sorry that we ended as enemies. I blame Maniakes for that, too.

Like the other men, I acquired a woman. Her name was Demetra. Camp women had followed us all the way from Messina. They cooked our food, washed our clothes, guarded our belongings, polished our armor, collected herbs for the stewpot and leaves and roots for healing—all for a few coins and protection from rape and beatings. I wanted a woman to sleep with, but one who would remind me as little as possible of Selene, who was so lithe and quick. Demetra was typical Sicilian: olive-skinned, heavy-breasted and thick-ankled, short and sturdy with a round, smiling face and a deep laugh. She went barefoot in every weather—her feet were black, the toes splayed, the soles tough as shoe leather. She could march as well as a man, carried a donkey's load of stuff on her back, and never complained. The fellow she was with when I met her was hitting her for some reason. I shoved him away and put my hand on the hilt of my sword. She turned a questioning eye on me. I gave her a silver coin, which she tested with her teeth, and then smiled.

She was older than I and, in a certain way, more a mother than a mistress. She had had a husband who'd died of something or other, and children, too, though she never spoke of them. We spoke very little, in fact, as I could barely understand her dialect, but she knew how to cook rice and onions with a scrawny chicken or a hare or some other meat that I didn't care to examine too closely. She would bathe my face and cradle me whenever my fever returned, and at night she would pick lice from my hair and then comb it and oil it. It was between her muscular thighs that I fathered a child, a baby girl, who was born that winter and lived only a few months. Demetra buried it and never said a word. Once another woman came and offered herself to me and Demetra broke her nose.

I shared a tent with five other men and their women. Some evenings we would just lie by the embers of our fire, while rain drummed on the canvas, and brag about how we would spend our loot if we ever got the chance. At sunset and sunrise, the Infidels' call to prayer carried to us from the city. Life went on there, too, though grimmer every day. The wind carried the smell of rotting flesh. It was plain that the inhabitants were starving to death faster than they could be buried.

We entertained ourselves as best we could with lizard races and scorpion fights and such things. And sometimes musicians would gather in the nearby villages to celebrate some saint's day or a wedding and afterwards come through our camp, hoping to make a few coins. They played the *zambogna*, the skin of a whole goat, tied at neck and feet, with pipes attached. It made a wild, shrieking sound and Demetra loved it, dancing and snapping her fingers. But Gorm grimaced at the sound and paid them just to go away.

One evening a Greek cavalry trooper came around with a 'tables' board, hoping no doubt to win some money from us ignorant Northmen. I played him and cleaned him out. But the sudden flood of memory, of Selene touching the tip of her tongue to the space between her teeth when she studied a move, was almost unbearable. That night I dreamed of her. I was chasing her down endless streets in a vast city, she, always ahead of me, and just when I was about to touch her she would vanish and reappear streets away.

Nothing could distract me from thoughts of her. I tried to imagine her life. What was she doing? Who was she with? How did she fill her days? And I longed to see my son. What did he look like at one, at one-

and-a-half, at two? I tried to notice children around the camp who might be his age, children with black, curly hair, just to have something to fasten my imagination on. And where, *where* was this promised agent of the Logothete who would bring me her letters and take mine to her? If he was trapped in the city, why weren't there others? The woman at Messina, the priest in Catania?

Christmas came and then Epiphany of the year six thousand five hundred forty-eight from the Creation (one thousand and forty, as we would call it), though we celebrated with little joy. It was a cold and misty morning and Maniakes ordered the whole army and most of the ships' crews out on parade while the priests went among them, hearing confessions and giving communion. I pleaded fever, which was not a lie, and stayed in my tent with Demetra, drinking wine with a pellet of opium in it, gnawing a pig's knuckle, and thinking of home. Why was I forgotten so completely? Why had Psellus, my old friend, broken his promise?

I drifted into a drugged sleep, thinking about him.

22

PSELLUS'S TALE

The Throne of Solomon, borne on the breath of angels, descends slowly from the height of the ceiling and comes to rest upon its podium between the roaring golden lions. The blast of the organ, which masks the whirring of its mechanism, dies away.

"Constantine Psellus, elevated to the rank of *Protospatharios* and Senator, approach the throne." The Master of Ceremonies taps his gilded staff on the marble floor and at once another thundering chord from the water organ reverberates through the vast hall. January the sixth, the Day of Epiphany, the day on which bureaucratic promotions are announced.

Psellus adjusts the new crimson cloak that hangs from his shoulder, touches the new ceremonial sword at his side, and advances through the throng of courtiers. They part to make way for him. Hundreds of curious faces watch him. Most of them don't know him, but he knows them; he's made it his business to. In a few of those faces he reads envy. He doesn't mind. He expects, intends, to make them envious.

He casts a quick glance up to the gallery where spectators hang over the railing. Somewhere up there are his mother and father in their black robes, released from their monastic cells for this special day. And dear Olympia—fifteen years old, four months now his adoring bride and already pregnant with their first child; and her well-to-do parents, delighted to have this ambitious young man for a son-in-law.

Passing down the aisle, he catches the Logothete's eye and his quick, encouraging smile. *Only twenty-two years old,* Psellus reflects with a rush of satisfaction, *and I am now his Chief of Staff, First Secretary of the Office of Barbarians, with a fine new house, and a salary of seventy-two gold solidi a year, and much more than that under the guise of 'gifts' that a senior bureaucrat is entitled to collect. No one in memory has come so far so fast.* And then he considers again, *If only we lived in happier times.*

He kneels at the foot of the throne where Michael and Zoe sit side by side, swathed in their brocaded wraps like a pair of elegant corpses. Michael sick unto death; Zoe, a prisoner in her chambers, paraded only on these few occasions in the year.

Then the Emperor leans forward stiffly—as he will do dozens more times throughout this long day—to kiss the honoree's head, to fasten the collar of office around his neck, and hand him the ivory plaque inscribed with his name and title. It is all Psellus can do to suppress a shudder: those bloodless lips, those eyes swollen nearly shut with the dropsy, the breath—well, try not to breathe... He rises and steps backward from the throne, feeling the weight of the collar on his neck. Applause from the spectators. It is all just a piece of theater, in which they are simultaneously actors and audience. But where would the empire be without theater?

✝

"A toast?" The Logothete extends his wine glass and clinks rims with Psellus. "To your bright future."

"I owe it all to you, sir."

"Nonsense, my boy, not at all. Your public speeches, the matter so learned, the expression so apt. The Emperor is charmed by your eloquence—especially in one so young."

Psellus lowers his eyes modestly, but it's true. He has labored hard over them—models of explication on a dozen different subjects; they are, if he says so himself, brilliant.

They are sitting together in Eustathius's private dining room, the small one at the back of the house, to which only particular guests are invited. A beautifully appointed room, where part of the Logothete's butterfly collection hangs on the walls. Psellus squeezes his eyes, under their heavy brows, and passes a hand over his head. It's been a tiring day. The ceremony in the throne room, followed by the procession to the cathedral, where the Blues and Greens chanted their acclamations; then hours of standing through the liturgy as they venerated the right arm of John the Baptist in its jeweled sheath. Then the banquet. The last thing Psellus wants is more to eat, but this intimate late-night supper is a mark of favor and friendship not to be refused.

Eustathius dips a prawn in cumin-laced sauce, places it between his teeth, crunches it and sucks the meat. "Delicious. Try them, my chef's specialty."

Shellfish don't agree with Psellus, but dutifully he selects one and tastes it.

"Another toast," says Eustathius, refilling Psellus's glass. "Confusion to our enemies."

"Amen to that, sir."

The Logothete waves the servants away and lowers his voice. "The Guardian of Orphans, our ruler in all but name. That man, my God. The arrogance of a demi-god wedded to the soul of a bookkeeper. We're at war with him, I don't need to tell you that, and he is winning."

"Surely, your influence—"

"—is shrinking by the day. I'm not listened to anymore. It's the war of course. Sicily. Costing us a fortune and no end in sight. And John has used it as an excuse to invade *my* office, questioning *my* accounts, cutting *my* budget to the bone, doing everything he can to destroy the Department. 'No more field agents,' says John, 'we can't afford them, or the couriers. And who needs them anyway when my brother Stephen tells us everything we need to know?'" Eustathius drains his glass, pours himself another. He's getting drunk. There is nothing here that they haven't talked about many times before, but the old man can't leave it alone.

"And we learn nothing from Maniakes?" Psellus says.

"You've seen his dispatches. They say less and less. The man's in a funk, doesn't know what to do and won't admit it. All he does is ask for more troops, which we can't spare him. I've no idea how things really stand there and now I have no other ears to the ground."

"Odd Tangle-Hair, sir?"

"What? Oh, that young barbarian? Yes, I was sorry to lose touch with him. He did tell us one or two things that were useful. It's been what? Nearly two years now? I wonder if he's still alive. Probably not, there've been so many casualties."

"I liked him."

"I did too, but it never pays to become too attached to these mercenaries, you know. They live hard and die young." A dismissive shrug.

Psellus nods, yet he hopes that Odd is still alive. He invested a good deal of time in him. Odd was his project, the living proof of his theory that barbarians were educable. "Could we ask Maniakes about him?"

"Not without revealing that we even know the fellow, which we have no plausible excuse for. You can't enquire about your spy from the man you're spying on. One question leads to another. No, too risky. Best to let it go."

"We've been paying his wife a small subsidy."

"Yes, well, that's gone by the board. *Frivolous expenses*, you know. John again."

"I should look her up. I've neglected her. I invited her to my wedding but she didn't come. Something gives me the idea there's another man."

"Really? Well, not surprising."

They were silent for a while.

"I'm getting too old for the battle," the Logothete sighs. "I don't relish it anymore. I have a villa on Rhodes. I long to retire to it, doze in the sun, listen to the birds…"

He has aged lately. Thinner, frailer. Psellus was never close to his own father, but he feels a great love for this gentle man with his wry smile and kind eyes. He chose Psellus for advancement from an office-full of young aspirants, attracted by his passion for the work. Psellus isn't from a rich family; he *needs* to succeed.

"But you won't, will you, sir—retire?"

The Logothete reaches out a hand and touches him on the arm. "Don't look so alarmed. No, not yet. That's what John's hoping for. Cheer up now, this is a happy occasion, we'll weather the storm. And I expect great things from you. But you must be careful, make friends wherever you can, do favors—you can afford to now. You're too young yet to have enemies at court, John sees no threat in you, but that won't last. He will try to intimidate you, use you."

"He won't succeed, sir." Psellus dares not admit that the Guardian of Orphans scares him.

"I know he won't. Well—" Eustathius pushes the jug toward him. "More wine? Another prawn?"

23

CHE LAST MAN
IN CHE WORLD
[*Odd resumes his narrative*]

Soon after Epiphany, whether moved by the prayers of the priests, or maybe by his horoscope (for he was addicted to astrology), Maniakes seemed to regain a measure of his old energy. Moses told me that the general was studying his *Strategikon* with new attention, poring over it day and night, underlining passages, talking to himself about this or that stratagem and chuckling. Finally, one rainy day around the end of January, he called a meeting of his war council—the first in many months. He had given up his tent for a comfortable country house a mile from the city. So, while the rest of us slept on army cots or on the ground, our general was enjoying a soft down bed and other comforts. This did not endear him.

Besides Harald and me, there were Arduin the Lombard, William the Norman and his brother Drogo, Stephen of course, and several Greek officers of the Household Cavalry--in particular a very capable young man named Katakalon, who had risen to favor lately.

It amused me to study how this group arranged itself. No one smiled. There was no conversation. We slouched in chairs turned at angles so that we could avoid each other's eyes, avoid even accidentally touching one another. The room smelled of defeat and recrimination. Whatever our general had in mind, we sensed that this was his last throw of the dice. That if this failed we would soon have to give up the siege and sail away. The ships' bottoms were already starting to rot; they'd been in the water too long, and the crews were in shockingly bad condition.

"Tunnels!" shouted Maniakes. "Here, here, here, here and here." He stabbed at points along a sketch of the city's land wall.

"Five?" murmured Katakalon. "Those walls must be forty feet of solid stone at the base The labor of it, we haven't the men."

"No." Maniakes grinned and chuckled, disturbingly like a madman. "Only one of them has to punch all the way through, but the enemy won't know which one, d'you see?"

"And who will dig them?" said Arduin.

"Conscript the village men and boys. I'll put you in charge of that. If they aren't enough, your own men will dig. All they're good for."

"My men," Arduin answered curtly, did not come her to burrow like moles."

"You're men came her to obey orders," Maniakes snarled. "If you need more, take rowers from the ships."

"*My* rowers? Never." Stephen was on his feet, the muscles bulging in his arms—the arms of a man who'd started life as a ship's caulker, a common laborer.

Hate flashed in Maniakes's eyes. *If he hits him,* I thought, *we're all finished.*

"And who will fight their way through this tunnel?" This was Harald, in a low voice. Surprisingly, as everyone else got angrier, he got quieter. I translated.

"Why, the Emperor's Wineskins, of course." Maniakes turned on him with a smile that I didn't quite like. "Surely, Prince, you wouldn't allow anyone else to steal your glory? Your men didn't like the heights"— referring to the 'tortoises'—"maybe the depths suit you better?" It was a sneer and everyone knew it. "And your bandon will take the lead."

Well, what could Harald say to that?

As we left, Moses gave me a wink and a nod.

✝

We'd been four days digging under the wall between the North and South bastions. First, the great, bronze-sheathed battering rams cracking the hard stone, then the pick and shovel men widening the openings and shoring them with timber. Arrows, rocks, boiling water poured down on us from above had taken a toll.

"Sst! I hear something."

"What?" Harald was right behind me, bent nearly double in the low-roofed passage, fifteen feet beneath the wall. Behind him, Halldor, Gorm, the others.

"I don't know. Pass the word up to the diggers, tell 'em to stop."

I didn't like it in here. The damp smell of raw earth; the smoky, unbreathable air; the cramps in my legs and shoulders. And a palpable sense of dread. I knew where that came from: it invaded my dreams at night. Pohjola. The Copper Mountain. Where Old Louhi had buried her lover and sat raving and drooling over his corpse, and I, foolishly, had followed the wizard Vainamoinen down into its depths that stank of magic like a rotten egg. That memory would never leave me.

"What is it now? What the hell's the problem?" Halldor's voice, surly.

But what was coming at us wasn't magic. It was worse.

Suddenly, the tunnel ahead filled with the smoke of burning straw, and out of the smoke hurtled a humming whirlwind of black and yellow bodies. In our mouths, in our eyes, crawling on our arms and legs, so thick we could barely see. And stinging and stinging and stinging.

"Run, in Christ's name!" shouted Harald, his voice shrill with fear.

The tunnel was so narrow two men could barely stand side by side. We trampled each other, clawed at each other to get away. No use. We huddled, motionless, helpless while the hornets stung us everywhere they could reach.

I've been in a lot of battles. I've never, before or since, heard grown men wail and scream like this.

Finally, our mates dragged us out and beat off the last of the insects. I was told later that Saracens are masters of the science of counter-mining. That they placed overturned metal bowls along the base of the wall, that magnified the sound of our digging, and they dug their own tunnel to intersect ours. As we straggled away from the wall—without our weapons; we'd dropped most of them in our frenzy to escape—there was laughter from above. And not only from above. There were catcalls from the Greeks too. And some even ran up to us, flapping their arms and making buzzing noises with their lips. The high-and-mighty Varangian Guard: lumpy, swollen, sore, tears running down our cheeks. Our humiliation was complete. Total. And enjoyed by all. It was then, I think, that we began to truly hate our enemy.

That night Demetra and the other camp women collected plantain leaves, chewed them into a paste and daubed us with it. It helped a little.

After this debacle, Harald knew that he had to do something to restore our morale. He waited a week until the swellings on our faces and hands had mostly gone away and then he and I together rowed out in a small boat to where Stephen's flagship rode at anchor in the harbor. Harald was done taking orders from Maniakes; we were striking out on our own. He had decided to make the Varangians into his own private army. We would go where we wanted, when we wanted, and keep all the spoils for ourselves. The Greek fleet, in addition to its big dromons and transports, also had about twenty light, shallow-bottomed scout craft, hardly different in size from our Norse long ships. Stephen readily handed these over; nothing pleased him more than helping his barbarian friend while sticking his thumb in Maniakes's eye.

And so we set out to be vikings.

Day after day we rowed, sometimes one ship alone, sometimes several together, feeling our way south along the coast, all the way to the southernmost tip of the island; stopping wherever we spied a village or a town, or best of all, some rich country estate, surrounded by fields where the crops were starting. And we weren't particular who we attacked, Saracen or Greek. These were pirate raids pure and simple; anyone was our meat. We struck like lightning, and wherever we struck we left smoking ruins in our wake; and anything living, man or beast, that wasn't worth taking, we killed.

We were often gone for a week at a time and when we sailed back our boats were laden with jewelry and coin and captives to be ransomed, or sometimes only goats and chickens, because we were always hungry. It was the life I had once led; I loved it. The rest of the army gave us envious looks, but stayed out of our way. And Maniakes, who had gone back to sulking in his headquarters, ignored us.

It pains me to admit it but maybe this is the place to say how impressed I was with Harald. In spite of all his boasting and bullying, he was a brave warrior and a skilled tactician. He kept us in line, he settled quarrels, broke up scuffles that could turn deadly if they were allowed to. He was stern when he had to be (he hanged two Guardsmen for rape), but never savage like Maniakes. I learned a lot about handling men from watching Harald. He had the makings of a king, as would be proved hereafter—but for all that, I could not bring myself to like him. I'm not sure that anyone really *liked* Harald, even Halldor, who carried his standard and stood next to him in the battle line. Harald's self-love was so huge that he wanted only praise—and that constantly—not affection.

As proof of what I mean, take the stories about these raids in Sicily that Harald told in later years and that found their way into his *Saga*. For example, the one where he had the idea to burn down a town by tying sulfur to the tails of the swallows that nested in the eaves of the houses; or the one where he staged his own funeral and had his coffin carried through the town gate where we wedged it open and he leapt out, sword in hand. If only the truth were so amusing. Mere truth was never quite good enough for Harald. But then who am I, an old man now, penniless and alone in my ruined house, owning nothing but my memories, to criticize Harald the Ruthless, the late, great King of Norway?

It is of no matter for now I come to the part of my story that really is amazing. And whether you want to believe it or not is up to you. Sometimes I hardly believe it myself.

We had beached our ship at a little promontory called Punta del Cane and struck inward on foot, following a well-trodden path that must lead somewhere. There were only twelve of us from Harald's bandon, but we felt tough enough for anything we might meet. An hour's tramp brought us in sight of a very handsome country estate with a big central house, outbuildings, gardens, orchards, all surrounded by stands of poplar and cypress.

"Ah," Gorm breathed, balancing his ax. We would dine well tonight.

All at once, the dogs started barking, Harald yelled "Charge!" and we leapt the fence, crashed through the door, and rushed into the house. It was a Saracen house. They were just sitting down to dinner. Veiled women ran around shrieking. But twenty men, some young, some old, all armed with razor-sharp scimitars, stood facing us, ready to sell their lives. Their leader was a villainous-looking character with a squint in one eye. He was dressed in a long, loose gown of fine cotton and a turban, whose tail was drawn across the lower half of his face. We halted and stared at them. The man with the squint slashed the air with his scimitar and came toward us. This was more opposition than we usually encountered.

"Throw down your weapons," yelled Harald (in Norse, naturally, what else?) "and we'll spare your lives."

"Fuck your mother, half-troll," said the man with the squint. "Come and get 'em."

The funny thing was that he said it in perfect Icelandic.

That squint. That gravelly voice. No...

"Stranger," I said to him, "uncover your face for me."

We stared into each other's eyes.

"Tangle-Hair!"

24

TOO CLEVER BY HALF

"Stig?"

His ugly pockmarked face broke into a smile. "Well, it's a small world, as they say."

"But what are you doing here?"

Before he could answer me, the others crowded around us.

"You know this man?" asked Harald, incredulous.

"He was my shipmate, my friend, my—well, it's a long story."

Stig turned to his men and said something low and guttural. Their points dropped.

"What, no looting?" said Halldor, truculent. It was clearly a rich house. The walls were decorated with colorful tiles, the carpets expensive, pots of flowers and cages of plumed birds, copper plates chased with silver on ebony tables, the room itself spacious and surrounded by arched colonnades that led to gardens beyond. The stuff here could be worth a fortune.

"So what if he's some old friend of yours," Halldor kept on, "what's that to us? Probably a heathen like you. Let's just kill him and go."

The men looked at Harald, who, for a long moment seemed uncertain. Finally, he said, "I want to hear this man's story. Then we'll decide. Put away your swords."

Halldor spat in disgust, rammed his sword into its scabbard, and stalked away.

"Who's that charming fellow?" said Stig under his breath. I could see beads of sweat on his forehead.

"Would you believe Halldor, the son of Snorri-godi?"

"Hmpf. Should've guessed. Same sweet temper."

Of course, Stig had been with me at the Althing when Snorri, the most powerful chieftain in Iceland, had gotten my brother and me banished on a trumped-up charge of murder. And it was Stig who planned my escape after the house-burning, who taught me to sail and went a-viking with me. His eyes flicked back and forth between Halldor and me and he looked thoughtful. "I'm surprised one of you hasn't killed the other yet."

"We've tried," I said.

"And what wind blows you here, Tangle-Hair?"

"I could ask you the same."

"Well, if we aren't going to fight," Gorm broke in, "can we at least sit down?"

"Forgive me," said Stig, "where are my manners?" He addressed Harald. "I don't know your name, stranger, but the Prophet, peace be upon Him, tells us never to turn away a guest. My larder is poor but you and your men are welcome to share what you were about to steal."

I saw a flicker of a smile cross Harald's lips.

We sat on cushions, crowded around a huge steaming platter of saffron rice with bits of mutton, vegetables, dates, and olives. A servant poured scented water over our hands and Stig recited a prayer in that strange language and touched his beard (he had grown it very long and full and grey was starting in it). Following his example, we scooped up the food with our right hands. (Gorm, who was left-handed, tried to use that one, but Stig corrected him. The left hand is only for wiping your ass.) While we talked, a young girl, sitting in the corner, played tunes on a lute.

Stig peered at me. "You've aged some."

"So have you." I reckoned he was closer to fifty than forty now. It had been nearly ten years since we parted in Aldeigjuborg. That memory was still bitter. We had been friends. Stig had taught me everything I knew about sailing, and much else. Yet we had parted enemies thanks to my pigheadednes.

"The big Norwegian boy," said Stig, "the one who nearly sank us in the Neva because you wouldn't steer out of his way? I wonder where he is now?"

"You're sitting across from him. Allow me to introduce Harald Sigurdsson, a captain in the Greek Emperor's Guard. I'm his skald."

Stig looked off into the distance, as was his way, and spoke to a point above my shoulder. "The Norns have woven your fates together, you and he."

"I fear they have."

Then there were questions all around, everyone wanting to know our story, and Stig and I talked about Lapland and Finland and Norway, about storms and battles. It was pleasant to hear Stig confirm all this. I was afraid no one believed my stories. Sometimes I wondered myself if half of them were true.

Gorm leaned forward eagerly. "You knew Glum, my brother?"

Stig studied him. "Your brother? Yes, I see it in the face. I say, you're not a … a…?"

"Berserker? No."

"Well, I'm relieved to hear it. I liked your brother, good man in a fight, but he was, ah, unpredictable sometimes. Well, fancy us all being together like this."

Only one ingredient was lacking to our feast. "Stig, is there any wine, it's been a thirsty day."

"Ah, Tangle-Hair, a Believer may not drink wine."

There was some grumbling about this from our men, but Stig ignored them.

"Are you serious?

"Absolutely."

I gazed around the room. The beautiful latticework windows through which the setting sun shone, the costly furnishings, the hovering servants. "Stig, how…"

He took a sip of sherbet, dabbed at his beard and began his tale. "After I stopped you from ramming Harald here in the river—"

"And knocked me down."

"Yes, well you were having one of your fits, weren't you? That was an evil day. I hope we're friends again now."

"With all my heart, Stig. How I've missed you!"

"Anyway, a few days later I heard you had fallen ill and were like to die. I went up to Jarl Rognvald's hall to, well, to try to make things right between us, but Einar Tree-Foot turned me away, saying you were feverish and out of your head and weren't to be vexed. The way that old man watched over you, like a mother with a sick child. And then the next thing we heard you'd recovered and gone up to Novgorod.

"We wintered over, me and the lads, and when spring came, we sailed out in the Viper to raid in the Baltic. But we got little for our efforts and by the end of that summer we decided to split up and sell the ship. I thought about going back to Nidaros, to Bergthora. But I felt ashamed to go back poorer than I left, just to sit about in the inn and grow fat on her larder. It's no life for a man. I thought of going back to Iceland, too. You remember old Hoskuld promised me a reward just for keeping you and his grandson out of trouble—as if I could.

"But there was still so much of the world I hadn't seen. So I signed on to pull an oar in a Danish merchantman bound for Spain. We prospered at first and I loved the life, until we were captured by an Arab pirate off the coast of Tunisia. I was sold as a slave and, after changing hands a few times, found myself here in Sicily in the household of my master, Youssef ben Aziz, a man of wealth and importance. In time, I learned to speak the language, though it's fearsome hard, helped him in his business—I'm shrewd that way, you know—and earned my freedom. He died two years ago, leaving behind three widows and two married daughters, but no sons. Well, I and the principal wife got along so well that I turned Muslim and married her—she's older than me but so was the Prophet's first wife, blessings on her. And then I married the other two as well. And now I control a considerable property, both estates and merchant ships. These handsome young men"—he indicated the two sitting closest to him—"are my sons-in-law, Jafar and Othman. The rest are my retainers. I feed many from my table."

"I heartily congratulate you on your good fortune, Stig, though I never thought of you as a family man, or a religious one."

"Times change, young Tangle-Hair, and we change with them. When I worked for your uncle Hoskuld Long-Jaws I was a Christman—to outward appearances anyway; now I'm a follower of the Prophet, peace be upon Him.

"I've heard there's a certain operation involved? On your thing?"

"There is, and it's damned uncomfortable, but one recovers."

"Three wives! I'd like to meet the women who could live with you," I laughed. "I swear no Iceland woman could."

"Ah, but these are gentle as doves. None of your Icelandic Valkyries for me. Never had any luck with them anyhow, poor landless ruffian that I was." He clapped his hands and presently five shapeless figures emerged from the adjoining room. They were dressed in garments that covered them head to heel and they peered at us through tiny eye-slits. Their fingers and toes were stained with henna and they wore massive silver rings on their wrists and ankles.

"Fatimah, Safiya, and Jumayah," said Stig, "are my wives. "Aisha and Halima are my step-daughters." They inclined their heads to us. Stig spoke a few low words to them, and they left us.

"And you've never missed home, Stig?"

"What, that stinking, barren, icebound rock, when I can live here and pick fruit off the trees? Where I bathe and wear clean clothes every day? Sprinkle myself with rosewater—"

"Rosewater? Stig!" I think at that moment my jaw actually dropped open, the idea was so ludicrous.

"And you know what they call me here? Musa Ibn Abihi al-Qabih. That is, Musa No-One's Son, the Ugly. Just what they called me back there."

"And people take you for a Saracen born?"

"No, of course not, not with my accent. I don't pretend to be other than what I am, but converts are dear to Allah."

After dessert, which was iced sherbet and sugared almonds, Stig leaned back, screwed his eyes up at the ceiling, and said: "I am a man of peace now. I try to take no part in wars. But I am informed of your affairs; the siege isn't going well, is it? Now, I'm no particular friend of the Greeks, but as for our present Emir, I shit on his head. Two years ago he invaded our island, overthrew the old Emir, and slaughtered half a dozen relatives of my former master, who had been the old man's ally. And ever since, he's kept the island in turmoil, which is bad for business. I swore I would have my vengeance on him, and now I think I see the way to do it."

"What are you leading up to?" I asked warily.

"If I could help your side to defeat him, would my estate be safe from pillaging? Would there be a bag or two of gold in it for me? Of course, what I have in mind is risky—for me and especially for you, Tangle-Hair, but you've never been afraid of a little danger since that day we stole Strife-Hrut's ship." He rolled his eyes and smiled at the memory of that great occasion, the start of our viking career.

"Danger to me? You'd better say what you mean."

"Better yet, let us explain it to your general Maniakes and see what he says. Is there one among you who speaks his language?"

"I do."

"You, Odd? Well, why am I not surprised? Clever lad. Let's go then."

Less than four hours later we were sitting in Maniakes's headquarters: Stig, Harald and me, Halldor and a few of the other Varangians, and Moses the Hawk. It hadn't been easy to persuade the general to this meeting. He was always half-drunk by this time of evening and in a surly mood. If it was anyone but me I think he would have refused, but for some reason, which I never understood, he liked me.

We spoke in a jumble of languages: Norse between me, Stig and Harald. Greek between me and Maniakes. Slavonic between me and Moses. Arabic between Moses (who, you will recall, had once served in the Caliph's army) and Stig. To make the story easier to follow, I will omit references to all the cross-translating that went on.

"I have business contacts in Palermo," Stig said, "who tell me that fresh troops have arrived from Africa and more are expected. Everyone's ships, including mine, have been commandeered to transport them. The Emir has sailed with the vanguard from Palermo and landed at Santo Stefano. He's marching inland now with the idea of skirting the southern slopes of Aetna and taking you in the rear. Right now he is mustering at Mistretta, not so very far from here, while he waits for the new levies to arrive."

"Mistretta? How do you know all this?" Harald broke in. "I'm suspicious of a man who seems to know too much."

"Stig's a man who knows things," I said, "he always has been. Don't ask how."

Maniakes leaned forward and cocked an eyebrow. "Go on."

"Now, wouldn't it help," said Stig, "if you could be sure when he will march and by what route, so that you can head him off as far west of Syracuse as possible, ambush him if you're clever. In fact, what you really want to do is tempt him to march before he's ready. For example, if you could persuade him that your army is getting ready to give up and go home, that if he strikes at once he'll catch you disorganized and unprepared. If we could just get him to take the bait."

"And how do you propose to do that?"

"The oldest trick there is. A deserter from your army. One of your mercenaries, who has run away to escape punishment, say, and whom I apprehended lurking about my estate. Loyal Mohammedan that I am, I take him to the Emir because he claims to know something important."

Maniakes eyes lit up. "By God, a ploy right out of Maurice's *Strategikon*. And who do you suggest to play the part?"

Stig slid his eyes toward me—that same probing look he had turned on me once before, when I was lying, burned and brain sick, in Uncle Hoskuld's hall. The look that said, *What are you made of, boy? What are you game for?*

"Stig, you bastard, no."

Then Harald jumped in. "I forbid it. Anyone can play deserter, it doesn't have to be my skald. I need him more than you. I'll not let his life be thrown away on a hare-brained scheme like this."

But Stig said mildly, looking at none of us in particular, "I would trust no one but Tangle-Hair with this mission. He has more wits than any other six men I know."

"I agree," Maniakes said. "It's Odd or no one. I don't know that I can trust you—you seem to me too clever by half—but if you mean to betray us then it's only fair that your friend should pay with his life."

My head swung back from one to the other. There was a lump the size of a fist in my throat. As I translated Maniakes's words for Stig, I felt like I was signing my own death sentence. I was about to protest again when Halldor, with an evil glint in his eye, said, "I agree. Odd should go—unless he's afraid."

I think that decided me. I *would* go, damn it, and I would come back alive just to spite Halldor.

Harald glared at all of us, but held his tongue.

"There's a flaw in this plan, though," Maniakes went on. "Getting into the Emir's camp is one thing, but how do you propose to get word out? How will I know when the Emir starts his march and what route he is taking?"

We looked at each other. And then, to everyone's surprise, Moses spoke up. And when he had finished, Maniakes gave one of his rare grins and said, "Pigeons, by God." And Stig caught my eye and we shared a smile, too. I knew what we were both thinking: One-Eyed Odin's two talking ravens, *Huginn and Muninn*—Thought and Memory—who flew far and wide gathering news and reporting it back to him.

"Now hear me, Moses," Maniakes said, laying his hand on the Khazar's shoulder. "Just as Harald doesn't want to lose Odd, I wouldn't like to lose you. But it's the only way. You'll pose as this man Stig's Jewish doctor—most of the doctors hereabouts are Jews, and they have little love for the Greeks—and a pigeon handler as well, which you are. Now it can't appear that Stig and Odd are of the same nation, that would raise suspicions."

"I will go back to being Churillo Igorevich," I said, "one of the Rus Varangians. The 'Jewish doctor' here speaks my language, that's why he's coming with us."

"Excellent." Maniakes raised his wine cup and took a long pull. "Here's to success. You'll leave tomorrow, which, in case you'd forgotten, happens to be Easter Sunday, the luckiest day in the year for a Christian. God will surely give us his blessing."

I had forgotten. I could never keep these holidays straight without being reminded. And Stig and Moses certainly didn't care. But if it gave Maniakes courage, then all the better.

I only wish it had been my lucky day.

25

AMONG THE SARACENS

We traveled for five days, following a track that wound into the high country along the valley of the Simeto, swollen with spring rain. It was all rocky hillsides and steep, bramble-choked gullies, gnarled olive trees, acacia, and cactus. The air was cool and smelled of wild thyme and heather—if I had been in a mood to appreciate it. We were a small cavalcade of seven. Stig and his two sons-in-law rode horses. Moses was mounted on a fine white mule. He had changed his cavalry uniform for a simple long-sleeved robe and a high felt cap and, instead of his bow and saber, he had a physician's kit slung over one shoulder. The two servants who attended us rode mules as well. And I—the deserter, the prisoner, my face dirtied, my clothing torn, a cut carefully administered to my forehead—was tied to the bony rump of a spavined donkey, like the rest of the baggage. We would pass travelers on the way just often enough, Stig said, that I must keep up this pretense all day long. Only at night, when we camped out under the stars, could I be freed to stretch my legs and rub some feeling into my backside.

The sons-in-law, Jafar and Othman, handsome, lively young men, kept up a constant chatter in Arabic—about me, I'm sure—and stole glances at me when they thought I wasn't looking. Stig and I spent our nights in conversation. I had nine years of history to recount: my affair with Princess Ingigerd, betrayal by Harald, escape, enslavement, return to Kiev, my mission to murder Harald.

"And why didn't you?" Stig gazed at a distant tree.

"I'm still asking myself that."

"I think one day you'll wish you had."

And Stig, as usual, was right.

He and the other Mohammedans in the group prayed five times a day. *La ilaha illa'lah Muhammadun rasul Allah.* I, dirty, sore, and full of doubts as the days stretched on, prayed many more times than that—to Odin, to Thor, and, yes, even to the White Christ, to get me out of this alive. What an idiot I was! And when thunder muttered in the hills, I prayed even harder.

Around evening of the fifth day, just as I was beginning to think that Stig really had no idea where he was taking us, we broke through a line of trees and found ourselves a bowshot away from the Saracen pickets.

Stig spoke a few words to a sentry, who frowned and shook his head. But a few coins changed hands and we were led through the camp to the Emir's pavilion. The camp was a big one, laid out in concentric rings of tents. Everywhere green and black banners, splashed with indecipherable writing, flew from tall flagpoles. Though I kept my eyes cast down, like the humble creature I was supposed to be, I managed to see enough and what I saw worried me. This was a powerful force, very strong in cavalry, not only mounted on horses but on those long-necked, hump-backed beasts that I had heard of but never seen before. The Emir's army was a jumble of nations—Arabs, Berbers, Turks, Kurds, and Negroes, each in their distinctive costume. And from what I could tell they were well-disciplined and well-armed.

The pavilion of the Emir, Abdallah ben al-Muizz, son of the Caliph of Africa, beloved of Allah, was a vast, sky-blue canopy, strewn with carpets of red and pink. Brass lamps in filigree-work hung from its peak and cast moving shadows on the silken walls. As we filed inside, Stig struck me across the back with his riding whip and forced me to my knees. *You bastard, you're enjoying this*, I thought.

Flanked by his Negro guards, who were naked to the waist and armed with golden maces, the Emir Abdallah sat cross-legged on a divan. He wore a white burnoose and a head cloth secured with bands of black and silver thread. His ivory-hilted scimitar and his shield lay beside him. But this dreaded conqueror was, in actual fact, an unprepossessing young man, soft-skinned, pudgy, drowsy-eyed, and giving off a scent that reminded me of Zoe's perfumery. I began to think better of our chances. At his side, however, stood a lean, hook-nosed man with a white beard. His head supported an immense turban of silk, looped with strands of pearls and adorned with a ruby pin and a spray of egret feathers. The Grand Vizier, as I was to learn.

Stig and the others knelt and touched their foreheads to the ground. "*Bism'illah, ar-rahmani, ar-rahim*," Stig addressed the Emir—In the name of God, the Merciful, the Compassionate. (Of course, I didn't understand any of this jabber; I can only repeat what they told me later.) "I am called Musa Ibn Abihi, your servant, Sidi." His hand swept backwards. "And these are my sons-in-law, and this other man is my physician, a Jew, a clever man who speaks many tongues, and the one who cringes at your feet is my prisoner, a Rus mercenary, he says, from Kiev. I eat your salt, Sidi, and I have come to do you a service. First, please be gracious enough to receive these poor gifts from me."

Along with his religion, Stig had acquired a quite surprising gift for speechifying. We had brought an expensive Koran bound in Morocco leather, a huge carved tusk from an animal called an *oliphant* (an African beast that uses its nose as a hand, or so Stig claimed), and six snow-white, plump-breasted pigeons, each with a silver capsule the size of my thumb tied to its leg. We had carried them in their coop all this way on donkey back. They belonged to Moses, who fed and watered them and talked softly to them every day. They got far better treatment on our journey than I did. But they were crucial to our plan.

These treasures were carried in and laid out for inspection.

"More birds?" the Emir sniffed. "Already have a flock of carrier pigeons. Don't need any more. Maybe I'll just let these fly and give my falcons some exercise. Heh? What d'you think, Grand Vizier?"

The huge turban inclined. "As you command, Sidi."

I saw a look of fear flash between Stig and Moses and, before more could be said, Stig launched into the story we had prepared, explaining that I was a deserter from the army of the Unbelievers (may God damn them), that he had caught in the act of stealing a chicken from his farm, that I was willing to trade valuable intelligence to save my wretched life, and that he had wasted not a single moment to bring me here. "Speak now, tell the Emir what you told me." Stig commanded, not neglecting to shove me with his foot.

"We're all hungry and sick and fed up," I whined, speaking in Slavonic and pausing to sniffle and wipe my nose on my sleeve, while Moses translated my words into Arabic. "Men deserting every day, we can't stick it any longer. Everyone's drunk, no one stands guard duty, the Lombards and Normans are mutinous. The general's given up, ships' bottoms are rotting, he's got to leave soon ..." And so on and so forth, throwing in every detail I could contrive (and some of them weren't so far from the truth, either.)

When I finally ran out of things to say, Stig took over again. "Sidi, heed this man. Though he is a filthy, uncircumcised swine-eater, he is telling the truth, I know it for a fact. If you were to march on Syracuse at once, even with a small force of picked men, the Polytheists would beg for mercy, the cursed Maniakes would grovel in the dust at your feet, the city would be saved, and you would end your jihad with a ringing victory. Think of it."

The Emir smiled. But it was the Turban who spoke. "Who are you, Musa. Not Arab, nor Berber from your speech? Where do you come from? And why do you make this long journey with gifts and information? No one does such a thing unless he seeks a favor in return."

Though I couldn't understand a word he said, I didn't care for the Vizier's expression. But Stig had his answer ready. He was a *ferenghi*, a convert, a Believer who enjoyed all the blessings of Allah—that is, up until the present war. But now he was a poor man, his lands overrun, his business interfered with, and, worst of all, members of his wife's family trapped in Syracuse, starving to death. And so he begged, he *implored* the Emir in the name of Merciful God to move swiftly to relieve the city.

"What's that?" The Emir's eyes narrowed in anger. He jumped down from the divan and slapped Stig full in the face with his soft palm. "You think to bribe me, you selfish dog, into doing my duty? You think only *your* relatives are starving? You think I don't intend to raise the siege? I am not ready yet, these things require time, money, planning. My father the Caliph is already raising fresh levies of *mujahedeen* to send me." The Emir now noticed Jafar and Othman. "Your sons-in-law, you say? They look fit for service. Grand Vizier, get them equipped and put them in the infantry. Let *them* fight to rescue their relatives."

"As you command, Sidi.

The boys looked terrified. Stig tried to speak but a warning look from Moses silenced him. He bowed his head in submission.

"And," said the Emir, "how do we know that anything this deserter says is true? A deserter will say anything to save his life."

"Indeed, Sidi," the Turban nodded. "Torture may allow us to make sure."

"You mean Musa here?" the Emir looked hesitant. "But God forbid we should torture a Believer."

"Of course, Sidi. The physician then?"

"No, God forbid we should torture a Jew. You're a Jew yourself, Grand Vizier."

"Quite right, Sidi." His sharp eye fell on me. Crouching on the floor, I tried to make myself as small as possible. Moses spoke up now, rapidly in a language that was neither Slavonic nor Arabic. The Grand Vizier answered him in the same tongue, with an unmistakable warning in his voice. Moses shrugged and looked away.

"This one, then," said the Emir. "The *falaqa* is most effective, I think? We'll let Turan work on him. See if he sticks to his story when his feet are tickled."

"As you command, Sidi. Here?"

"No, not here, I don't care to hear screams. Not in my nature. Take him to one of the supply tents—out of earshot. Report to me later."

The Grand Vizier bowed. He signaled to two of the Negro guards, who yanked me to my feet and half-dragged, half-carried me from the tent, one on each arm, with a strength I couldn't resist, though I writhed and struggled. Moses followed a few steps behind.

In the supply tent, they threw me on my back, pulled off my shoes and tied my feet together with a bowstring. One of them brought over a stool and lifted my legs onto it. A minute later a fat man, heavy-jowled and thick-armed, ducked under the flap. He looked at me and shook his jowls. "Get the feet higher," he told the guards, "how you expect me to work like this?" The accent was Turkish.

"What are you doing?" I cried. "I've told you everything."

The guards dragged over a big box and hoisted my legs over it so that my feet stuck straight up in the air.

"Better," said the Turk. He flexed a rod in his hands, about a yard long and thick as my thumb. He glanced at the Grand Vizier. "There's an art to this, you know. It is possible to cripple a man forever if one isn't careful. You want me to be careful?"

"If you can," the Vizier answered coolly. "We may need him later."

I have told in an earlier part of this saga how I questioned Zoe's servants while they were being beaten and burned, how I made my voice harsh and my eyes like stones while Harald did unspeakable things to them. Maybe there is a fate that comes round and pays us back for the ill we do. Moses now played my part—standing behind me so our eyes couldn't meet as the Grand Vizier barked questions and the torturer slashed with his rod at the arches of my feet.

The next hours were very long.

"What's your name?"

Slash.

"Churillo! Please—don't hit me again."

"What regiment are you in?"

Slash.

"Varangians."

"Why did you desert?"

Slash.

"Charged with rape."

"What is the strength of the Greek army?"

Slash.

"Eight thousand, I think—ten, I don't know."

"You don't know? Don't lie to me."

Slash.

"Not lying ... Ahhh."

"Why are you here?"

Slash.

"I told you ... please."

"You say the Lombards are disloyal? How do you know this?"

Slash.

"Someone said so. Please."

"Said so? Only hearsay?"

Slash.

"How many dromons are in the harbor?"

"About fifty-sixty."

"You can do better than that. How many?"

"I don't know."

Slash.

"Don't waste my time. Is there sickness in the camp?"

Slash.

"Yes, yes, a lot."

"Could you draw us a map of the Greek camp, showing the sentry posts, Maniakes's tent, if we let you live?"

"Yes, I will, I can do that."

"Who are you really?"

"I told you."

"Tell me again."

Slash.

And so it went, until I couldn't speak for the pain. The Vizier sighed. "There's no more to be gotten from him. Throw him in the corner. Give him a little water."

"Untie his feet?" asked one of the guards.

"Why not? He's not going anywhere on those. And you, Doctor"—he gestured to Moses—"come with me. We'll find a place for those handsome birds of yours. Much too valuable to feed to the falcons."

They left me there, curled on my side, my throat raw with screaming, the blood pounding in my feet, sending pains like lightning bolts up my legs. *And here,* I thought to myself, *I will lie until I die, and for what? Damn you, Stig.*

The last thing I saw before I lost consciousness was the face of my wife.

26

SELENE'S TALE
FEBRUARY, 1040

The cart jolts along the frozen track from the city, rattling her teeth with every bounce. Selene shivers and hugs her cloak tighter to her chest. The little pony cart gives no protection from this wind, an icy gale that blows down from the Golden Horn and whirls snowflakes around her so thick she can hardly see. Her eyes stream with tears. *From the wind? From humiliation? Anger? All.*

Her mare lowers its head to the wind and struggles on, as cold as she is, poor beast. When at last they reach her father's house, it turns in at the path and heads for the shed, needing no word from her. It whinnies and there is an answering whinny. Alypius's pair. *He* is here again. Now she sees his big covered carriage with its gilded doors and velvet curtains pulled up beside the house. The liveried coachman emerges from the shed and runs toward her.

"Let me help you down, Miss. You must be half frozen." *Miss. As though she were a mere girl without a husband.* "I'll see your animal is rubbed down and fed. We've brought a bushel of good fodder with us this time."

"Thank you, Paulus." She doesn't like accepting these favors. There have been too many of them.

Alypius meets her at the door and draws her inside, putting his big hands around hers and rubbing them. A handsome man of middle age, his hair blond with gray starting in it, a comfortable paunch, florid face, expensive clothes. "Horrid weather to be out in. What were you thinking,

Selene? Why didn't you ask to use my coach and driver? Melampus tells me you went to see some petty bureaucrat? I hope you found him, at least."

The room is stifling, braziers smoking in every corner of it. The charcoal another gift from Alypius. Well, they need it, don't they? In spite of the heat, her father lies in his bed, wrapped in blankets up to his chin. He lifts an eyebrow at her. *Was Psellus there? What did he say you?*

"No," she answers both of them. "It seems the man has moved house lately. I went to the palace but no one there would tell me anything."

"Shocking," says Alypius in his loud baritone. "Can't say I'm surprised. These high and mighty officials. But why didn't you ask me to go with you? I'm not without influence, you know." *She knows. He says so often enough.* "Anyway, sit and have something warm to drink. Your father and I have had a jolly time, talking about demons and spirits and such. I always enjoy our conversations." *Does he, really?* Alypius claps his hands. "Martha, bring your mistress a warm posset." *He orders their servant around as though he were in his own house.* "Come, take that off, it's wet." He removes her cloak for her, leaving his hands on her shoulders a moment too long. "Still no news of your husband, then?" *Have they no secrets at all from this man?* She has little to say to Alypius, but her father … the old man, so trusting, so guileless.

She goes to the bed and kisses his forehead, the skin dry and yellow as parchment. He never leaves his bed anymore, the tremors are too violent for him to stand, and he has no more breath in him. The vapors of mercury—the precious stuff of Hermes, the key that he hoped would let him perfect nature, turn base metal into gold, maybe even bestow immortality—they are killing him instead. He smiles at her wanly, "When spring comes, my dear, the sailing season. I'm sure …" He pats her hand.

When spring comes. They always say this. But Odd has been gone for two springs now. It has been a year-and-a-half since his one letter arrived from Messina. It has been eight months since the money stopped arriving from the Logothete's office, money they depended on to survive—or would, if it weren't for Alypius. "When spring comes," she and her father tell each other, each pretending, for the other's sake, to believe it. And meanwhile not a word from Psellus. He has abandoned them, or maybe is just embarrassed to have nothing for them. And she has been too proud to ask, until finally Melampus pleaded with her to go and speak to him, and she couldn't refuse any more because her father will soon be dead. They both know it. So she went, carrying a bundle of the letters they have written to Odd over these months, written and saved with no way to send them—and failed to find Psellus. And now what?

Myrinna, Alypius's eight-year-old daughter, has been playing in the corner with little Gunnar and the monkey. She runs up to Selene and takes her hands. "Didn't you bring me anything from the city, Auntie?" *When did she become this girl's 'auntie'?*

"I'm sorry, no, dear. How are you feeling today?" Myrinna is thin, with mouse-colored hair and skin you can almost see through.

One always has to ask how Myrinna is feeling. She has a variety of complaints. Her father brought her to their door back in the summer of 'thirty-eight, not long after Odd had sailed away. A widower with a sick child, needing to consult a doctor. He was, he told them, an architect and builder, of good family, doing very well for himself. He had a house in the city that was much too big for him, he said, and an olive orchard he had recently bought in their neighborhood. Melampus had been recommended by a mutual acquaintance—both as physician and as delver into the mysteries of the cosmos. Since then, his daughter seems never to get much better or much worse, but Alypius continues to bring her, once a month, sometimes more, sometimes less. Once there was an unexplained hiatus of several months and then he reappeared. He always pays Melampus's fee as if this were a real consultation, although it is obvious that the old man is past curing anyone. And he always brings food and charcoal. Unobtrusively, not with any great display. But there it is. And there are more intimate gifts for her—an amethyst bracelet, a topaz ring. These she has tried to refuse, but he won't allow it. You don't argue with Alypius. And what, Selene asks herself, will he demand in return? He has done nothing so far but *look* at her. But she feels herself go rigid when she knows his eyes are on her.

Now Gunnar runs up to her, clutching Ramesses in his little yellow coat. The children have been feeding him chestnuts. She lifts boy and beast in the air and spins them around. Odd once laughed that if they had a baby it would resemble the monkey. She smiles to think of it. What a handsome boy he is now! Sturdy legs and strong arms, straight black brows and long lashes, and his head a mass of unruly black curls. 'Tangle-Hair', she calls him sometimes.

Tangle-Hair. Is he alive or dead? Happy or sad? Alone or with a woman? Has he forgotten them entirely? At night, when Gunnar crawls up beside her in the bed, she lies awake for hours, stroking his hair and thinking. What would she do if Odd were to walk in the door at that moment? Throw herself in his arms, or spit in his eye? Sometimes she feels one way and sometimes the other. It wearies her to think of it.

And when Alypius, as he too often does, delivers his thoughts on the subject of barbarians, his face pulled into a sympathetic frown, his voice insinuating—"Can't trust those fellows, all of 'em the same, irresponsible, care about nothing but their bellies and their balls, pardon my bluntness"—then she excuses herself and goes into the bedroom and fights back her tears.

✝

march

She has tried again to see Psellus, and this time has gone into the palace and wandered the corridors until someone shows her to the Logothete's suite of offices. But Psellus isn't there. She waits in an anteroom for hours, watching men come and go, catching at scraps of whispered conversation. An elderly usher takes pity on her, gives her a cup of water and a sympathetic smile. Should she have brought money for a bribe? That's how things are done here. But she has none.

She is about to go when suddenly Psellus bustles through the door, dictating a letter to a secretary who trails behind him. She catches at his sleeve as he passes by. He is startled. At first, he seems not to recognize her. Then he looks embarrassed, apologetic. "Selene, what a long time it's been! News of Odd? Alas, no. The siege drags on. Frustrating for all of us. Our communications with Sicily, well, they've rather broken down. But we haven't heard that he's *dead*. Always room to hope. Send someone to *find* him? I'm afraid that's not possible. The subsidy? I'm terribly sorry, these days we must all make sacrifices. I'd like to help, truly." He reaches into the purse at his belt and pulls out a few silver coins. "Afraid I haven't much on me, but, you know, whatever I—"

She hesitates an instant, then snatches them from his hand and flees.

"I'll send a man with …" Psellus starts to say, but she has already vanished down the crowded corridor.

At home again, she sits by her father's bed. Mercifully, Alypius isn't here and they can speak freely, father and daughter.

"If he offered you marriage, my dear?" She has to strain to make out his words, his voice is like a whisper of wind in tall grass.

"I *am* married, Father."

"But we must be practical, about money, you know. I never was. Forgive me."

"There's nothing to forgive." She kisses his hand, dropping a tear on it.

He goes on. "Alypius likes you … more than likes. I notice things, you know. Needs a woman in his house, Myrinna needs a mother, Gunnar a father. I loved Odd, too, but we must be realistic. I won't be here—"

"Stop now, please."

†

APRIL

"A carriage ride's just the thing," Alypius says. "Lovely weather out, everything blooming, we'll bundle him up, do the old fellow good, fresh air, take the young 'uns along too, where are they, outside?"

They thought Melampus was asleep. He'd had a very bad night, coughing, struggling to breathe, but finally dropped off around sunrise. Suddenly, he sits bolt upright in the bed. "Odd! It's Odd!"

She rushes to his side, puts her arm around his thin shoulders to hold him up. "What about Odd? What do you see?"

Because as the soul parts from the body it sees more clearly. Everyone, knows that.

"Darkness … pain, such pain … no hope …"

"Father, don't say so."

The old man's heart is fluttering like a bird's, his eyes fixed in a distant stare. What does he see?

"Selene, you … you …"

"Hush, dear." Then the eyes go blank. A thread of saliva runs from the corner of his mouth. His soul flies up to the stars, where Thrice-Great Hermes reigns and everything is gold.

She lays her head on his breast and lets her tears flow.

Alypius comes up behind her, touches her on the back. "Well," he says and clears his throat. "Very sad, very sad. I know he had his own notions about religion but I'll see he gets a proper Christian burial nonetheless. Can't be too careful in these matters. You leave everything to me."

27

ṪHE BAṪṪLE OF ṪROIṄA
[Odd resumes his narrative]

My feet were swollen to twice their normal size and were turning black. I was terrified I would lose them. Escape was impossible. I tried dragging myself along the floor of the supply tent on my elbows and stomach, but even that was too painful. Day after day I lay there, listening to the sounds of the camp—distant music, the whickering of horses, the throaty groan of the camels, the five wailing calls to prayer that punctuated the day. Guttural unintelligible voices, occasional laughter. I could see nothing but the alternation of light and shadow creeping across the narrow opening of the tent flap. Twice a day a guard brought some foul rice gruel and a cup of water. Once, the Grand Vizier stepped inside to look at me, said nothing, and left. I don't know how long this went on; a week? Maybe longer. And during all this time I saw nothing of Stig or Moses. Where were they? Had they left me here to die?

And then one morning I was wakened from my stupor by the noise and bustle of the camp breaking up. Officers shouting orders, tents coming down, protesting camels lurching to their feet, the clatter of arms. A couple of soldiers dragged me from my little prison, tossed me into the back of a donkey cart, and tied one of my arms to the side of it. Presently the Grand Vizier appeared with Moses at his side.

"Where are we going?" I asked, shocked by the croak of my voice; I hadn't heard it in days.

The Vizier answered and Moses translated. To Syracuse. The

astrologers, he said, had consulted their charts and promised a perfect alignment of the planets. The Emir's victory was assured. "And when we get there, you will draw us a plan of the siege lines and we will let you live—that is, if you still want to." He cast a glance at my feet. He walked away, leaving me alone with Moses.

Moses put out a hand and touched my shoulder lightly. "Odd Tangle-Hair, I come from a race of hard men. I've never seen anyone live through a beating like this and not break down."

"I did break down."

"You didn't. Otherwise we'd all be dead now. Anything you ever want from me, just ask."

"But we failed."

"Not yet. Those beautiful pigeons of mine? It seems last night someone left their cage open. They've all flown away."

"And they'll get back to Maniakes?"

"If there is a God."

"Where's Stig?"

"With his sons-in-law. The boys are scared witless, they weren't brought up to soldiering. He wants to see you, to apologize for—all this. But it wouldn't look right for him to show any more interest in you. Me either. I'd better go now. Try to hold out."

✝

The Emir's army, in a long straggling column, marched for four days across country from Mistretta. The jolting of the cart put me in constant pain, it was much worse than lying in the tent. On the fourth day we passed through a defile and debouched into a narrow valley overlooked by the village of Troina, high on its jutting peak.

I had been sleeping fitfully but awoke. It was late in the afternoon. The air was still. The cart I rode in, along with the rest of the baggage train, came to a halt near a stand of wild olive trees where a little stream ran by. While grooms and drivers were busy watering the animals, I gazed off into the distance. Something moving in one of those trees caught my eye—something white—a white pigeon. Fluttering its wings as it flew from one branch to another. Were they ours? Were they all sitting there placidly in a tree? Was all my suffering for nothing after all? "If there is a God," Moses said. Well, whose god? Not his, not any of mine. At that moment I gave up all hope. I think I cried aloud.

Then I wiped my eyes and looked again, up past the trees—and saw a flash of metal on the hill to the west. And then a line of lance points glittering in the setting sun! And then the whole ridge was dark with moving men, like a spreading shadow. There were no trumpet calls, no shouts or war cries. It was Maniakes, and he was following the rule in the *Strategikon* that says an army should advance in absolute silence until the last fifty yards. It is an unnerving sight, that silent advance. You can imagine with what feeling I watched it.

Our men were almost upon them before most of the Saracen camp realized what was happening. And then there was panic. Men, horses, camels running this way and that, colliding. Tents crashing down. Greek and Norman lancers charging, wheeling, thundering through the camp, riding down everything in their path, Maniakes on his great black warhorse brandishing the standard of Saint George. Khazars whooping, circling, loosing volley after volley of arrows. And the Varangians. The long-tailed dragon standard fluttering above them, Harald at their head, carving a bloody path with their axes, yelling their war cry. And then Stig and Moses were beside me, helping me down from the cart, one under each of my arms.

Arrows were flying so thick it was dangerous to stick your head up. The three of us crouched behind the cart until it was all over. Which wasn't long. The sun had barely set behind the hills when the fighting ended. We suffered almost no casualties, but the slaughter among the Saracens was great. The ground was carpeted with bodies.

I lay that night on a pile of silks and sheepskins in the Emir's gorgeous tent, now occupied by Maniakes and Harald. In both their faces I saw pain—pity, I suppose—when they looked at me.

Stig knelt by my feet, applying ointments and cold cloths for the swelling. A Greek doctor, Maniakes's personal physician, tried to interfere but Stig drove him away with a look. I remembered how Stig had treated my scorched feet with that same gentle, almost woman's touch all those years ago when I was a boy and had crawled through a hole in the wall from my burning house. But my wounds then had not been his fault. These were. I saw it in his eyes.

"Tangle-Hair, I—"

"Stop. None of that." I knew what he wanted to say. "I volunteered for this. There's no more to be said."

As news spread of what we had done and what I had suffered, the tent filled with Varangians eager to congratulate me. (Although Halldor and Bolli weren't among them.) "You must make up a poem about it, Tangle-Hair," said Gorm.

"No, I will compose a poem for my skald," said Harald. "A brave man shouldn't have to sing his own praises."

"And I," said Gorm, "will make you a pair of crutches. You'll have them tomorrow."

Maniakes pulled up a stool beside me. "When Syracuse falls, which it must soon now, you will find me generous, Odd Thorvaldsson. We owe you much."

✝

Two of the six pigeons, he said, had made it back to their roost with notes that Moses had written in minute handwriting, giving the date that the Emir started out and his route of march.

"I came at once with the cavalry, leaving most of our infantry behind, except for a hundred Varangians at Harald's insistence. We mounted them on spare horses."

"And our backsides!" laughed Gorm. None of the Varangians were experienced riders.

"Let him sleep now," said Stig. He mixed a pellet of opium in a cup of wine and held it to my lips. Before I closed my eyes, I'm sure I saw Stig, the Muslim abstainer, lift the jug to his own lips and take a long, grateful pull from it.

But the next morning brought bad news. Our men had spent the night stripping the dead and looking for survivors who might be worth enslaving. Stig went with them to search for his sons-in-law. One of the dead was Jafar, the younger of them, Stig's favorite, I think, with the broken end of a cavalry lance in his back. This was a hard blow, but Stig took it like an Icelander. He carried the young man's body in his arms to the tent and washed it, while he mouthed a silent prayer, whether to Allah or Odin, I still wonder. Then he and Moses dug a grave among the olive trees. He never shed a tear that I saw or mentioned Jafar's name again.

Worse news for us was that the Emir was nowhere to be found.

They did find the Grand Vizier, however, under a heap of bodies. His enormous turban was gone. One damasked sleeve was ripped at the shoulder and his right arm hung limp at his side. He and the Emir and a few others had tried to escape disguised as women. The Emir had gotten away but the Vizier's horse fell with him and he'd broken his shoulder.

They brought him to Maniakes for questioning. It was only necessary for Moses to rap the Vizier's foot with his riding whip and raise an eyebrow suggestively. His face turned the color of whey and he told us everything including that the Emir was headed back to Santo Stefano on the coast, where the transports were.

"Excellent," Maniakes crowed. "I left orders for Stephen to sail there with twenty dromons. He'll trap them in the harbor. We need another day here to rest the horses. We'll start after him tomorrow."

The Vizier was handed over to the Khazars to guard. The next morning he was found with his throat slit and his ears cut off. Moses never said he did it. He didn't have to. Maniakes must have suspected, but he didn't say anything either, at least not in my hearing. Some time later Moses presented me with two brown and shriveled scraps of hide, one with an earring in it; I kept them for a long time.

At dawn we mounted our horses. Maniakes had offered to send me back to Syracuse in as much comfort as possible together with the Emir's wives and the prisoners, but I refused. I wanted to see this through to the end. So I rode with my feet out of the stirrups and with Moses at my side to steady me.

Two days' ride brought us to the coast. There were no ships. Not the Emir's and not Stephen's. We had missed the Emir by a matter of hours, the townspeople told us. By now, he was on his way to Palermo. And where were our dromons?

They arrived later that day. And now a thing happened that had long consequences, not foreseen by anyone—least of all by General George Maniakes, the victor of Troina.

Stephen had hardly set foot on the dock before he began expostulating. The wind had been against him all the way, the waves too high in the strait. By Christ, he manned an oar himself. What more could he...? He never got to finish that sentence.

Understand that Stephen was no weakling. He'd grown up rough, laboring as a caulker in a shipyard. But Maniakes towered over him the way Mount Aetna towers over lesser peaks. And his anger was just as volcanic. Not for the first time—and, unfortunately not the last—our general lost his mind. "Fucking moron!" he roared.

One hammer blow in the face laid Stephen out. Blood streamed from his nose, he tried to stand, but Maniakes snatched up a length of ship's rope that was lying nearby and began to beat him with it. One stroke, another, and another—Stephen cried out and put up his arms to shield his head, looked desperately around. Dozens of us stood there watching this, our mouths open in astonishment. Because this was no hapless cavalry officer. Stephen was an incompetent and no one respected him, but he was the Emperor's *brother-in-law*. More important, he was *John's* brother-in-law.

He saw only one man in the crowd he could appeal to. Harald. Their ally. Stephen was the one who had recommended Harald for the Guard. This was no secret. Maniakes knew it, anyone who cared to know knew it. Stephen crawled to him while the blows continued to rain down on his back. He stretched out an arm, touched Harald's knee. I wish I had the power to describe the play of emotion in Harald's face at that moment, the swift calculation that flickered in his eyes.

Harald winced, turned from him and stalked away. Maniakes watched him go, then tossed the rope aside. Two of Stephen's petty officers helped him to his feet and up the gangway to his ship. The last we heard was a string of curses as he disappeared under the deck awning. The oars moved. The ship warped out.

Where was he going? What would his revenge be?

28

CALAPHATES'S TALE

He reaches a pudgy hand toward the plate and helps himself to another honey cake.

"Put that back, you greedy thing.—And don't give me that look." His mother Maria slaps his hand. "Look how he stuffs himself." She rolls her eyes, appeals to her brothers.

"Oh, let the boy have another one," Uncle Constantine smiles. "We want a happy boy today, we're going to ask much of him." He gives Calaphates a wink. The boy likes Uncle Constantine.

They are in the dining room in Uncle John's villa on the Horn. His mother has dragged him here this morning from their house in the city. And here is the whole family gathered together. And they are all looking at him. It makes him nervous. What has he done now? What is it all about? There's some secret here—the way they exchange glances and have sent all the servants out of the room. Calaphates is getting bored again. His eyes wander, he squirms in his chair. He scratches at a pimple on his chin, draws a spot of blood.

He doesn't understand much but he understands how important his uncles are: Uncle Constantine, rich and generous with his money, always buying him things and taking him places, playing the role of indulgent father in Stephen's absence; Uncle George, the Master of the Wardrobe, an important position with many duties; and Uncle John in his plain monk's robe, who claims to be nothing more than a humble guardian of orphans. (Calaphates was taken to see the orphanage once by his uncle; it gave him nightmares for a week).

All of them eunuchs. What would it feel like to be castrated? he wonders. He knows vaguely that their father did something to them when they were small to make them this way. He is fascinated by eunuchs. He has grown up among them, of course; the palace is filled with them, glossy skin, voices like flutes. Not like his skin, his honking voice. And all of them so very powerful. When he was a little boy he'd thought he might like to be one. Not any more, though. He has felt the stirrings of desire for a woman. He hasn't had one yet, but soon he will.

John seems to notice him for the first time. "Now, Calaphates, pay attention please." There is a parchment on the table between them, he pushes it toward the boy—edged with gilt, covered with writing in purple ink. "Read it, if you like, and then put your signature on it. Take your time."

They know he can hardly read. He feels all their eyes on him as he traces the words with his finger and moves his lips. His tutor has given up on him. And the other palace boys, the sons of high officials and officers, make fun of him, of his walk, his laugh, how bad he is at games, how sometimes, when he's nervous, he falls down in a faint. Though his given name is Michael, they call him *Calaphates*, Caulker, ridiculing his father's low birth; and now even his own family calls him by the nickname. He hates it.

"Adoption? The Empress Zoe?"

"Just sign it," says his mother. "You can do that much can't you?"

"It means," says Constantine coming to his aid, "that the Empress will adopt you as her son."

He screws up his eyes with the effort of thinking what this means. Then takes the pen that Uncle John presses into his hand and scrawls a large M followed by a few squiggles. "Must I call her Mum now?"

Maria pinches him hard on the cheek and hisses, "Just don't ever forget who your real mother is." Christ, he hates her, the witch. All red lips and nails, dead white skin and heavy jewelry so that she clanks when she walks. And never in his life a kind word for him.

"You do understand what this means?" Uncle John frowns at him. "You will have the title of Caesar and when Uncle Michael goes to heaven"—he crosses himself hastily and turns his eyes upward—"you will become our Emperor."

"But I don't want to be the Emperor. It's boring, you have to sit there for hours with nothing to do. People stare at you, I don't like it when people stare at me."

"But," Uncle Constantine cajoles, "you'd like to go up in the flying throne, wouldn't you? Up and down, as often as you please?"

"Is it really magic?"

"Of course, it is."

"And I could go up and down whenever?"

"As much as you like."

The boy is doubtful. "So what's the magic word, then?"

His uncle smiles. "*Abramasax.*"

"I want to try it now."

But Constantine pushes him back in his chair. "I'm just teasing you, boy. You'll learn the word when the time comes."

"Constantine, stop it." John shoots his brother a pained look. "Stop filling the boy's head with nonsense. He has little enough brain as it is."

Then Uncle George, who hasn't seemed to be paying attention at all, says, "Will the Empress agree to this?"

"She will," John answers. "I will have her signature on this tonight."

"And does the Emperor consent?"

"Naturally."

The Emperor. His other uncle—Michael the Fourth, the invisible presence in this room—who had been kind to him when he was little but now ignores him, too sick to care about anything except his own soul. They are already talking of their brother as though he were dead. And he, young Calaphates, will be Michael the Fifth? Why him? Why not Stephen, his father? Which reminds him … "When's my father coming home?" It has been two years. He has trouble remembering the man now, except that he had broad shoulders and rough hands and would take him sailing sometimes and didn't laugh at him.

There is a long moment of silence in the room. He sees their eyes dart back and forth. Then Uncle John says, "I've had a letter from your father recently, he's not with the fleet anymore, he's in Italy, he says he likes it there very much."

"Why isn't he with the fleet?"

"Never mind about that. I expect we'll be seeing him soon."

Calaphates sinks back in his chair and pouts. They're always telling him to mind his own business, that things he overhears aren't meant for his ears. But he isn't as stupid as they think he is. And when he does become Emperor, that will change. Oh yes, he'll show them who is master.

29

ZOE'S TALE

She looks up, startled, and there he is, a black apparition in the trembling lamplight, in her bedroom! without a knock on the door, without the warning sound of a footstep.

"Good evening, Zoe. They said you were in here. Do I find you ready for bed so soon? Well, I will only take a minute of your time."

John! For a moment she can't breathe, the blood beats in her temples, she clutches her dressing gown to her throat. "How dare you come here without invitation? I am the Empress."

"Of course you are, Zoe. May I?" He draws a chair up to her bedside. "You're looking very well." He takes hold of her hand and draws his fingernail along the back of it. The soft flesh yields and springs back. It feels like a cockroach is walking on her. It takes all her strength not to pull away. "Remarkable skin for a woman of your age. You never seem to grow old." His smile like curdled cream.

But she knows she is old. She knows it in her aching knees when she kneels to pray; knows it in the heaviness in her chest when she lies in bed at night unable to sleep; knows it in the quaver in her voice, which she is struggling now to control. She is old, but, by The Virgin of Pharos, she will outlive this mincing capon, this devil, if it takes every atom of her being.

"How have you been, Zoe? How do you spend your days?"

"Talking to Christ," she whispers.

"Really. You surprise me. I thought only saints did that."

"Tell me what you want and then go away."

"All right. We need you to become Calaphates's mother."

His mother! The child was pathetic, a half-wit, uneducated, undisciplined. He stole and lied. He'd had a succession of pets that all died mysteriously. Well, what could you expect from parents like Stephen and Maria? "He has a mother," she says.

John smiles again. "I believe Maria's willing to part with him. I've brought the necessary document."

"So he can succeed to the throne through me and keep you Paphlagonian scum in power?"

"Scum, is it? May I remind you, Zoe, that nobody forced you to marry our brother. You threw yourself at him—a mere boy. Disgusting, really. And your first husband? What should we say of him? Died opportunely? And now you regret it all? Too late, I'm afraid.

I will sign nothing. Get out."

"Poor Zoe, I can make your life much more unpleasant than it is. Try me. On the other hand, if you cooperate perhaps we could permit the perfume business again? You'd like that wouldn't you?"

Her perfumery has been idle—ever since the 'incident.' The vats empty, the fires extinguished, her assistants dismissed. Only the smell lingers faintly on, in the draperies, the carpets, the furniture.

"We could perhaps allow you a little more freedom?"

She had tried to poison him two years ago. He knew it, she knew he knew it. But there had been no formal accusation, no admission. It was a fact that neither of them could afford to acknowledge. Her servants had been tortured in secret and forced to confess. Loyal Sgouritzes, that dear old man, burned with irons. All her people had been sent away and replaced by John's picked guards. Her little dog had been found dead in the garden one morning—poisoned. Now, except on state occasions where she is led like a performing ape, to the audience hall, the hippodrome, the cathedral, she spends her days alone, without companions, without visitors. Her letters are opened, her every movement watched. She has thought of throwing herself on his mercy. But the man has no mercy.

"I don't believe my husband approves of this. I demand to see him."

"Your husband, Zoe, has recently returned to Thessaloniki to pray for a cure at the shrines. Didn't you know?" It is a sneer. Of course, she doesn't know. She knows nothing. "Now sign the fucking paper." Suddenly his hand is gripping her wrist with a strength she wouldn't have guessed. "Sign it and we can both go to bed."

She signs. What else can she do?

And, as silently as he appeared, John is gone.

After he has left, she goes to the little altar, where votive candles flicker in the dark. She lifts from it the little figurine wrapped in purple silk, lovingly unwraps it, holds it to her lips, kisses it, wets it with her tears. Her Christ. A luminous thing that is sometimes gold, and sometimes silver, and sometimes as red as blood. It speaks to her that way. And what it says to her now is "Be strong, Zoe. There will be another time. You won't always be the weak one."

30

AN END AT LAST

[Odd resumes his narrative]

We returned to Syracuse, where the siege was drawing near the end of its second year. But things were different now—we could taste victory. Our one worry was Stephen. We had heard no more from him, but no one was fool enough to think that business was over. Maniakes tried to pass it off with a joke, but I saw worry in his eyes. He knew he had taken a step too far.

I was hobbling about on one crutch now but I was still in pain and treating it with opium, which made my brain sluggish. Maniakes offered to send me back to Constantinople on the next ship with our other wounded. And I would have agreed—if it hadn't been for Harald. "You're my ears, Tangle-Hair," he pleaded, gripping my hand, "my mouth. Whether you can walk or not doesn't matter to me"—of course not, to *him*—"It won't be long now, and the reward will be great. I'll see you made a Varangian, one word from John is all it takes. Leave now and you lose everything."

Well, I reasoned (not thinking very clearly, you may say), the Logothete and Psellus have deserted me. Selene, too, for all I know. If I go back empty-handed now, I'm no better than a used-up cripple with no future. What can I do but stay with Harald? He's all I've got. Maniakes shook his head in wonderment when I told him my decision.

And, as Harald promised, it wasn't much longer. Syracuse fell in less than a month after our victory at Troina. Even though the Emir had slipped through our fingers, we had his tent, his banners, his wives, his money chests, his prize stallions, and numbers of his high-ranking chieftains. All these we paraded under the walls of the city. The defenders made one last desperate sortie. Their commander, Ibn al-Thumnah, led them in a charge against the part of our lines where the Normans were posted. And here happened one of those remarkable opportunities in battle that give a man lasting fame among his countrymen. The Norman William de Hauteville—the horseshoe bender, the equal of Maniakes and Harald in stature—challenged al-Thumnah to single combat. They were both mounted on big chargers, armored head to knee in ringmail hauberks, and carried shields and lances. They came together with a crash of steel on steel. The Saracen's horse was driven back on its haunches and threw its rider. With a shout of triumph, William leapt to the ground and swung at al-Thumnah's head with his sword, cracking it like an eggshell. And that is how William came by the nickname *Bras-de-Fer*, or Iron Arm. He sawed through the neck and held the head up while the Normans cheered themselves hoarse. A fine deed, a brilliant deed—if only it hadn't rankled in Maniakes, who felt that it should have been him holding up that head.

The Saracen defenders threw down their arms and marched out. They were starved, hollow-cheeked, dirty, some leaning on the arms of comrades, and were greeted by jeers and catcalls from our side but they held their heads high although they knew that chains and a life of slavery awaited them. They were brave men who had done their duty and more.

And we marched into a ravaged city, where the smell of death hung heavy. Syracuse was a city of staring eyes and swollen bellies and skeletal arms. The Arab population hid in their houses, but the Greeks met us with one continual wild cheer. They stretched their hands to heaven, brought out the holy icons and relics that had lain hidden for years and waved them in the air. Delirious throngs capered through the streets, dancing, banging on drums or old pots or anything. Church bells rang. Flocks of carrion birds and clouds of blowflies, affrighted by the racket, rose up indignantly from their banquet of flesh.

Maniakes wanted to spare the city any more suffering, but Harald demanded the right of pillage for his men. We raced through the Emir's palace in a frenzy of looting (I, too, as well as I could manage on my crutch). It was a sprawling place of arches and colonnades, latticed windows, fountains, and tiled courtyards. We broke into the harem, but found no one there save a few cowering eunuchs. The women seemingly had slipped out into the city crowd where they would be safe. After more searching, we found the treasure room. Sacks of gold dinars and silver dirhams, ropes of pearls, baskets of gems, bales of silk. Harald had it all carried out under guard. For a few heady days we imagined ourselves as rich as kings.

Aside from the palace, Maniakes would allow no pillaging by our troops. But it was a harder thing to keep the Greek population from taking revenge on their Saracen neighbors. Shops were looted, a mosque was burned, each dawn revealed a fresh crop of bodies strangled or stabbed.

During those next days, as order was restored, I explored this city that we had shed so much blood to capture. Once it must have been one of the great cities of the world. Wherever you looked you saw the ruins of what ancient kings had built—temples to their gods, theaters, stadiums, baths. Those ancient pagans all vanished now, leaving it to the followers of Mohammed and Christ to fight over the remains like two dogs tearing at the carcass of a noble steed.

Wandering about with Gorm one day, I found the library. The entrance was heaped with trash and bricks where part of the cornice had fallen, but it was unguarded so we made our way inside. Long, dim corridors seemed to stretch for miles, lined with books and scrolls. I stood astonished. I touched a volume, thumbed the dust off the binding and read the title. It was an author I'd never heard of. I felt very small here. In ten lifetimes, I could not absorb so much learning, and that made me think of Melampus and of Psellus. And that made my heart throb with something between sorrow and anger. Gorm was complaining that the dust made him sneeze, and so we left.

Maniakes's first job was to get food into the city, care for the injured, and bury the dead to avoid pestilence. This took a week. Then it was time to celebrate our triumph. He paraded all the men and the ships' crews and, after interminable prayers of thanksgiving to God and various saints, he distributed the spoils. Alas, what had seemed like a fortune beyond imagining when it was all heaped up in one room, now looked less when it was spread out to be divided among ten thousand men. One-third of the spoils by custom must be set aside for the Emperor. Maniakes took a full fourth for himself.

Harald was given a sizeable sum to divide among the Emperor's Wineskins, a share of which went to me as his skald (another large share went to Halldor, his standard-bearer.) I was also given a handsome sum by the general personally from his share as a reward for my exploit. So were Stig and Moses. Putting it all together, I wasn't as rich as I had hoped, but I reckoned I had enough to afford a comfortable house in the city with a few servants. I had no complaints.

But here our general made his second fatal mistake. From the shrinking pile of booty, he intended to give most to his Greeks and short-change the allies. William the Norman, who had slain al-Thumnah single-handedly, felt insulted by his small share—a bag of silver and some not-very-attractive women. And so did Arduin, that clever, Greek-speaking Lombard noble. He had demanded, among much else, a fine Arabian stallion as a prize but Maniakes stupidly insisted that he give it up. Arduin argued with him. What happened then may be hard to believe but I saw it with my own eyes. Maniakes knocked him down, kicked him and ripped his shirt off him. Beating up Stephen was one thing—no one respected him. But Arduin? The man was well-liked and had hundreds of Lombard and Norman warriors at his back. I thought we would have to fight them then and there, but our cavalry moved in quickly and pushed them back.

That very day, eight hundred Lombards and Normans, angry and embittered, boarded ship and sailed back to Italy. We watched them go in silence. Too late, Maniakes seemed to realize what he had done. And his remedy? To send the Varangians after them, to occupy Reggio and stiffen the small Greek force that was holding Calabria and Apulia. I believe Maniakes was looking for an excuse to rid himself of *all* these troublesome barbarians, including us, and this was it.

I had thought I was on the point of going home. Now the prospect of more endless months of campaigning stretched before me. Again Harald urged me to stick with him, and again I yielded.

I made my goodbyes.

"Demetra, could you live with Infidels?"

"Don't mind as long as I'm fed," she answered.

"Then I pass you on to my friend Musa, who has a fine house and will give you light work to do."

"I will miss you. You were a good fellow, as barbarians go." She managed to squeeze out a tear.

"Stig, a long life and many sons."

"The same to you, Tangle-Hair. And I pray that when you finally get home you'll find everything as you would wish."

"Thank you, Stig. We may meet again. Who knows?"

"Inshallah," as we say, "God willing."

But we didn't. I never saw him again.

I gripped arms with Moses. "Someday back in Constantinople, my friend."

And he and I would meet again, though the circumstances were bitter. He deserved a better master than Maniakes.

✝

The next months I will pass over quickly for they brought us no joy or profit. We had hardly established ourselves in Reggio when word came that Maniakes had been arrested and taken back to Constantinople to face a charge of treason. This was Stephen's doing, of course. He had been hiding out all the while at the court of Duke Gaimar of Salerno. He now returned to Sicily as its governor—and with astonishing speed managed to lose Syracuse and every place else that we had fought so hard for. (We were told that he died of a fever in the course of this debacle.) Within a year the island fell once more to the Saracens, and we never got it back.

Meanwhile we had our hands full in Italy. The Lombards and Normans, our former allies, were now our enemies and, fighting on their own ground, they were formidable. One after another, the Apennine hill towns went over to them thanks to Arduin's powers of persuasion. A new Greek commander—another incompetent appointed by John—arrived to save the situation. His army, including our men, suffered a disaster at the River Olivento. We were driven back by the Norman horse, led by William, into the rushing waters and hundreds were drowned. I was in that battle. By now, I could bear the pain in my feet and I was ashamed to lurk behind in the tents. One who almost drowned was Gorm. He had taken a deep spear thrust in his side and was weak with loss of blood. I barely managed to drag him to shore. But many other friends of mine died. Halldor and Bolli, I'm sorry to say, came out of it unscathed. Harald was so angry and humiliated I feared he would take his own life. He'd never been beaten like this before. Two more defeats followed this, and by high summer of the year one thousand and forty all Southern Italy had gone over to the Lombards.

But this was when our fortunes changed, Harald's and mine. One rainy morning a ship with purple sails, flying the Emperor's pennant, sailed into the harbor of Otranto, where we were bivouacked. A Varangian officer stepped ashore—one of those Varangians who had been left behind to guard the palace. He found Harald brooding in his tent, and with a happy smile saluted him as the new Commandant of the Varangian Guard. His orders were to return with his men to the city at once.

This was not as great a surprise as you might think. Harald—seeing that there was no glory to be had in Italy—had sent a message to John, worded in Greek by me, demanding to be recalled and promoted. Of course, the Guard already had a Commandant—old, fat, gouty Sveinn Gudleifsson—a man with many friends at court. How convenient that Sveinn had just died.

We shouted, we sang, we celebrated all day long.

Harald insisted that we have all new clothes and arms, for we were a shabby, battle-stained bunch and he was ashamed to lead us back to Constantinople looking as we did. He paid for it all out of his own pocket like the prince he was. This occupied a few days. But, at last, we bade goodbye to our sullen Greek comrades and boarded our ships. Not as many ships as we had come out in, though. Half our number had given their bodies to the crows in this wretched country.

What a joy it was to leave. But, as we made our way slowly back across the Aegean, battling contrary winds all the way, I slept badly and felt a nameless dread growing in me. What was I going home to?

"Take me to my husband." For a moment, her voice was firm, commanding, a queen's voice.

PART THREE
CONSTANTINOPLE
1040-1043

31

RETURNED FROM THE DEAD

JULY, AD 1040

Our ships sailed into Boukoleon harbor on a brilliant morning, just as the rising sun struck fire from the gilded domes of the Great Palace. Harald had sent a small boat ahead to announce our arrival, and a platoon of Varangians was drawn up on the quay to welcome us. They had brought wagons to take our baggage, and especially our money chests, straight to the barracks. Word of our approach had spread fast and already a noisy crowd of palace officials, dock workers, and passers-by had gathered. I searched their faces. No Selene. No Psellus.

Led by Harald and Halldor carrying the dragon standard, we shouldered our axes and marched down the gangway in perfect order. Then order dissolved as we mingled with old comrades, slapping backs and pumping arms. Some men kissed the ground.

"Tangle-Hair," shouted Harald over the uproar, "I'm going to the orphanage to meet with John and his brothers. I'll need you."

"I'm going to look for my wife," I said over my shoulder and, handing my ax and shield to Gorm, walked away from him.

The sun was near its zenith by the time I had rented a horse and ridden out along the Mese to the little cluster of houses near the Gate of Charisios. The day was turning hot and I sweated in my armor. The yard was unkempt, our little garden overgrown with weeds. There was no answer to my knock. One or two neighbors stopped to gawk at me in my mail shirt and helmet and scarlet cloak; none of them came near. I pushed open the door and found myself in an empty room that smelled of mildew, the chairs tipped up against the table. In one corner, Gunnar's baby cradle, the one I had carved for him, sat covered with dust. *Of course, she's at her father's.* I ran the short distance to Melampus's house. But here too was only dust. The sitting room, the laboratory, deserted.

"It's me," I called. "Melampus, Selene?" No answer. And then, as I was turning in bafflement to leave, I heard the chattering of a monkey coming from the kitchen. Ramesses in his tattered yellow coat. He scampered out and leapt into my arms. A moment later, Martha, Melampus's old housekeeper, peered at me from the doorway.

"Master Odd! Is it you? Oh, sir, it is good to see you." Tears started in her eyes. "The doctor? He died in April, God bless his soul. Selene? Gone with that man, Alypius. Her and Gunnar. I am sorry, master, I begged her not to, but she wouldn't listen. It's the money, you see. After the doctor died, we hadn't any, not a brass penny, except what she got from that man. The poor girl had no choice. They left me here—he said he had a houseful of servants and I was too old and useless. And Ramesses? He said he couldn't abide the filthy beast. Oh, how little Gunnar cried at that. I thought his little heart'd break. Mistress left me with a few coins and said she'd come back, but she hasn't, and they're all gone now. So here we've stayed on our own these three months with not a bite to eat but what a kind neighbor can spare."

I was carrying a small parcel—a bracelet and cameo brooch for my wife and a book for Melampus—it fell to the floor unnoticed.

"Who is this man? Where does he live?"

"A rich man, an architect, handsome enough, smooth ways about him. Lives in the city, but where? They never said. Oh, I am that sorry, master Odd."

I pressed some silver into her hand. "Live on this until I come back."

I leapt on my mount and kicked it savagely to a gallop. *Somewhere in this vast city is my wife. Psellus will know. He cuts off her money, passes her onto some rich friend of his. He knows where they are. I'll beat it out of him.*

But when I pounded on Psellus's door—it was evening now—a strange man's face appeared, fear in his eyes. "Doesn't live here anymore ... sold this place, oh, months ago. Where? No idea. Don't murder us, sir, I beg you."

I backed away, stumbling out into the shadowed street. A scream rose in my throat. I didn't mean to, but I opened my mouth and let it out—the howl of an animal, long and high and piercing. All along the street shutters opened and then banged shut.

After that, I scarcely knew where I went. I came to a tavern where I drank a jug of wine, and then another. Finally, I threw down some coins and stumbled out. I was too drunk to ride the horse. I left it tied up. Eventually, I found my way to the Varangian barracks and managed the stairs to the second landing—the Fourth Bandon's quarters. Harald was still up, drinking with some of the men. He eyed me coldly.

"Goddammit, Tangle-Hair, where the hell have you been all day? I had a meeting with John. Wanted to talk about Italy and about me being Commandant, but that's about as much as I could understand. We had to put it off to tomorrow. You can't *do* this to me."

I simply stood speechless, feeling all their eyes on me. One of them was Halldor, and I thought I saw a look in his eye that I would remember later—like a man suddenly struck by an idea. "Go to bed," Harald said, "you look like shit. We'll talk in the morning."

But long before Harald was awake, I was gone. To the palace. I hadn't slept all night, and I was past caring if John's spies saw me talking to Psellus, that little traitor.

I burst into his office—oh, what a splendid one he had now—shoved the doorkeeper aside and went straight for him. "Tell me where she is."

"Tangle—!"

His eyes bulged, I had him by the throat, pinned against the wall. Two guards ran in with their swords drawn.

"No, don't hurt him," he croaked, "leave us, it's—it's all right." They looked doubtful but backed out. "Odd, let me go—please." I took a step back. Psellus rubbed his throat, red and white from my fingers. "Sit down, for God's sake. We thought you were dead."

"So it seems. Where's this man you gave my wife to?"

"I don't know what you're talking about, I swear to you. No, don't touch your sword, please. Calm yourself, let us talk. It … it's good to see you." He shut his office door, smoothed his clothing, and with a shaking hand poured wine into two goblets. "Here—and please sit down. There, that's better."

I sank into a chair, suddenly overcome with weariness, and accepted the proffered goblet from this man who had betrayed me. It is my failing, that I don't kill the people who have wronged me. There is some weakness in me. I'm not my father's son. Black Thorvald would have cut his heart out and roasted it.

"Selene's gone?" he said.

"With your rich friend Alypius. Why did you cut off her money? Why have there been no letters from her for *two years*?"

"I don't know any Alypius. And as for the money, that's a bitter tale." He told me in a few words how the Guardian of Orphans had cut their budget, got rid of their couriers, was now behaving like Emperor in all but name, with Michael sick in Thessaloniki.

"But you've done well for yourself." I glanced around his spacious office. "New house, too, I gather."

He gave an apologetic smile and a small shrug. "Odd, how can I help you?"

"Where do I find this man? Rich, an architect. That's all I know."

"First of all, there are laws against murder in this city. You do know that, don't you? Second of all, I don't know who he is, but I can probably find out. The rich are few enough even in this great metropolis, and there can't be so many architects. I venture I'll know someone who knows someone who knows him. It may take a while. Patience isn't one of your virtues, but try. In the meantime we have serious matters to discuss with the Logothete."

"I have nothing to discuss with the Logothete. I don't need him. Here's a piece of information you can have for free. Harald is about to be named Commandant of the Guard and I'm to be a Varangian. All thanks to John, not the Logothete."

Psellus sank back in his chair and sighed. "Understand this, Odd. John has the whip hand now, but that can't last. There will be a turning point soon—very soon. When it comes, you need to be on the right side."

"Thank you, but from now on I'll decide for myself which is the right side. All I want now is my wife back."

Psellus shook his head. "You aren't the same man who sailed away two years ago. I liked that man better. What have you been through?"

"What do you know about war outside the pages of Homer? Believe me, my friend, it is much nastier than that. Much crueler. And not heroic at all. That's what I've been through."

He waved this aside. "I will tell the Logothete that you're back, he'll be relieved. We need you with us, Odd. None of this was his fault, believe me. We'll be in touch with you. And I will find your wife for you, count on it. In the meantime, by all means stick close to Harald, translate for him and John—most important thing you can do for us."

I gave him a hard look, and left without saying another word.

✝

The Throne Room, One Week Later

On Harald's handsome face was a look of triumph, of exultation—the lips curved in a fierce smile, the head high, the eyes on fire—the look of a man who, after seven long years of waiting and plotting, has finally gotten his reward, finally clawed his way to that pinnacle of power that he had always lusted for. Standing at his elbow, John the Guardian of Orphans was smiling too, and for the same reason. These were now the two most powerful men in the empire.

John had organized this ceremony to create three hundred new Varangians, myself among them, to make up for our losses in the Sicilian campaign, and to appoint Harald as the new Commandant. Harald now held the exalted dignity of *protospatharios* and was given the added post of *manglabites*, with powers to arrest and imprison, even to have a ring of keys that unlocked the palace gates. Nothing was beyond his reach now— the salary, the bribes, the favors—a bottomless river of gold. Not bad for a man who could barely order a glass of wine in the native language. He stood in the middle of the great hall, resplendent in his scarlet costume and jeweled collar, drinking in the applause of the gathered functionaries, while we Varangians, ranged in a semi-circle around the throne, clashed our axes against our shields.

The organ thundered, the Master of Ceremonies called out our names, the golden lions roared and lashed their tails, the jeweled birds sang, the throne (whose mechanism still mystified me) rose and descended—but with one striking difference: sitting upon it was not the Emperor, but a pimply-faced boy, wearing a set of robes a size too big for him and a diadem that only his ears held up. Our new Caesar, we were informed by John—his nephew, and next in line to the throne, whenever God should see fit to take poor, ailing Michael up to heaven. Before a few weeks ago almost no one at court even knew who this young man was. But then John had organized an investiture ceremony at which, shockingly, the youth was made to sit on Zoe's lap.

Now, surrounded by guards and an immense throng of courtiers, the boy looked glassy-eyed. Was he thrilled by all this or simply terrified? Beside him, Zoe sat still as a statue, her eyes half-shut, revealing nothing.

Besides the Emperor's there was one other notable absence—George Maniakes. A name not to be uttered now. He was, in fact, not very far away, in a narrow, airless cell in the bowels of the palace. I wondered if he could feel the distant reverberation of the organ, hear the clashing of our shields, the shouted acclamations. Harald, who was his jailer now, had gone to see him that morning, and I, of course, went along to translate.

Harald held his lantern to the general's face. Maniakes threw his arm over his eyes and shrank away. After four months of captivity, the great man was nothing but bone, his cheeks hollow, his hair gray at the roots (I always suspected he dyed it). He wore leg irons and an iron band around his waist with a chain fastened to the wall. His clothes hung in rags from his great frame.

"Have you come to kill me?" The old thunderous voice was now a whisper.

"Not today."

"When?"

Harald shrugged. That wasn't up to him. Maniakes could be executed tomorrow, or he could lose his nose and ears and be banished to an island, or he could just be left to rot in this cell forever. John would decide.

But if this man should ever be uncaged, I wondered, *what violence was he not capable of? What retribution?*

Maniakes turned his face to me with a flicker of a smile. "Good to see you on your feet, Odd Tangle-Hair."

I nodded. "It's a pity to see you like this, General."

"Do you want a priest?" Harald asked him sharply.

Maniakes shook his head, no.

"Stephen's dead, you know."

"Good."

There was no more to say, really. We left him.

✝

The ceremony ended and the hall began to empty. You may wonder what thoughts were in my mind at that moment. *Someday*, I said to myself, *Harald will go back to Norway and again there will be room at the top. If Harald could reach so high, why not me? But did I want it badly enough to seize it with both hands, to lick some eunuch's ass for it, to kill for it? Stop it,* I told myself. *All that is too far away; for a while just be content with what you have.* But, of course, I wasn't content. My heart ached.

And then, as we were marching out, Psellus appeared at my side. I hadn't even known he was there. "Congratulations, Varangian. I've kept my promise." He came close and tucked a scrap of parchment in my belt. "The directions to Alypius's house. I wish you luck, I mean it. And in return I will want a favor from you one day."

Before I could answer, he had slipped away into the crowd.

32

NO SICKNESS IS WORSE

No sickness is worse for a man than to have no one to love him. Thus speaks Odin in *The Sayings of the High One.* I had been sick that way for too long.

I went straight from the palace, in full armor, with my shield on my back and my ax over my shoulder. I was a Varangian. In a city of unarmed men, I could go where I pleased and no one got in my way.

It was an elegant two-story house built around a garden in the fashionable Sphorakion quarter, near the Milion Arch. I hammered on the door with the butt of my ax. The door slave retreated before me, too frightened to speak. The foyer was marble-tiled with tapestries on the walls and expensive vases on little tables.

"Selene!"

A man came running down the circular stairway from the upper floor, pulling on a loose morning gown, his blond hair tousled, eyes puffy like someone who had just woken up, though it was almost noon. He knew instantly who I was.

"Where's my wife, Alypius?"

"I don't know who you mean, get out of my house."

Bold words, but I could smell his fear. I didn't say anything. I just lifted my ax.

"I'm not afraid of you. You come back after all this time? You threaten me? Selene doesn't want to see you. She's very happy here. I don't permit her to have visitors. She has everything she wants here. Now you will leave my house or I'll summon the police."

"I *am* the police." I leaned against one of the little tables and sent a large vase crashing to the floor. Now I could see sweat on his forehead.

And then she appeared—coming in from the garden, followed by my son and an older girl and a maid. Her face was white as milk. "Odd?" She put a hand out to the door jamb to steady herself. We just stared at each other. Seeing her again, I realized that my memory of her had grown faint, like a drawing blurred by water. Her cheeks were fuller, her hips a little wider, her hair was long now, not the boyish style she had kept before.

"He keeps you well," I said. She wore a sheer silk dress of dark green with silver threads, shoes sewn with tiny pearls, and on her arm a gold bracelet set with sapphires.

"Please, Odd, don't—"

I took a step toward her. "You really thought I wasn't coming home, to you, to our son?"

"I didn't know. No one would tell me anything. I did what I had to." Her eyes flashed, the words tumbled out—words that I think she had been rehearsing to herself for months. "I would have gone back to gambling in the taverns if I could still pass for a boy. How many times have you told me that the women of Iceland are strong and independent. Well, so am I, and you knew it when you married me. So I gave myself to a man. Don't tell me you didn't have women in Sicily, because I won't believe you. What are you going to do now, kill me? You've got your ax. Strike!" She thrust out her head.

The two children, goggle-eyed, hid behind the maid's skirt. I let the ax fall from my hand; the steel rang on the marble floor. "Selene, are you married to this man?"

Alypius, who had lost his voice, found it again. "Don't be stupid. A man like me doesn't marry people of her class. I wanted a companion, I was willing to play father to her boy. Look, maybe I've wronged you. I have money here, jewels, take what you like…"

I picked up my axe and took a step toward him. Alypius backed away, bumping into one of the little tables. Another vase gone. He held out his arms to ward me off. "All right, I'm not going to fight with a barbarian thug over some woman. Get out, the both of you."

In an instant, my wife was in my arms, crying, kissing me, begging my pardon.

(If ever anyone reads this saga of mine, I imagine he is smiling now, shaking his head. How impossibly perfect! Did it really happen this way or is it only a lonely old man's fantasy? No matter, I cherish it. What else have I but these memories to keep me warm at night?)

"Gunnar," Selene said, taking his small hand, "this is your father, your real father. We're all going home now."

He looked like he might cry.

"Ramesses is at home," I said, smiling at him. "He misses you." That made his eyes brighten. I put out my hand to touch his curly head. What a handsome boy he was! I thought my heart would burst.

"Take the brat and get out." Alypius snarled. "And I'll have that bracelet back, it cost me enough."

She pulled it off and flung it in his face.

"Myrinna, come and see us whenever you like—" Selene started to say, but Alypius grabbed the girl's arm and dragged her to him. "She will not."

✝

That night, after we made love, Selene studied my naked body, every inch, and cried over the scars on my feet. And we talked all night long.

"I wish you could have been here when my father died. He loved you."

"Take me to his grave tomorrow. I will pour a libation to his spirit."

And after a time she said in a small voice, "Are you going to stay now? Not leave us again?"

"I can't promise you. I'm a soldier, I go where I'm ordered to. But you must believe that I will always, always come back."

She lay in my arms, with her head against my chest. Toward dawn we fell asleep.

✝

Within a week we moved to a rented house not far from the Varangian barracks. Several of us came back from Sicily rich enough to live separately, away from the noise and crowding of the barracks.

Harald had no objection as long as we were on hand for daily drill in the parade ground and our rotation at sentry duty. He himself took over his predecessor's splendid mansion. Our house needed painting, repairs inside and out, and the attentions of a gardener. When we were ready to show it off, I invited Psellus and his wife to dinner. I wanted to keep his friendship, though I would make no promises to the Logothete.

And so I settled down with my family to what I expected would be a peaceful life.

33

HALLDOR'S TALE
ICELAND, JUNE, AD 1030

Snorri-godi, fat and bewhiskered, the most powerful chieftain in the Southern Quarter, champion of the Christian Church, pulls off his helmet and wipes a sleeve across his sweating brow. The embers of the house—Black Thorvald's house—still throw off a quivering heat. The smoke that hangs in the twilight air makes him wheeze. For a big man, he has weak lungs. He views the scene with satisfaction: the charred timber posts; the gaping roof where the sods have fallen in; the corpses of Thorvald's sons, Odd and Gunnar, and their womenfolk, lying in pools of black blood amid the wreckage, their clothes smoldering. A dozen of his own men dead, too—this was a costly victory, but still sweet. Around him, his henchmen brandish their weapons and do a dance, leaping and shouting. At last, he has destroyed his hated enemy, the heathen renegade, the sorcerer and all his brood. Surely, no one can have escaped this holocaust.

"Halldor, Bolli," he calls to his son and son-in-law. "Take some men, fill pails from the river and douse all this, then drag the bodies out. I want to see their faces before we leave." The two young men run to obey.

†

CONSTANTINOPLE. AUGUST, AD 1040

"Halldor, give it up, you'll never be as good as he is."

"I don't have to be as good as he is, Brother-in-law, I just have to be good enough."

"He said it took him years."

"Maybe I have more word-wit than he does. I'm not stupid."

"You're obsessed, is what you are." Bolli, scratches his head, exchanges a fretful look with Ulf, leans back in his chair, and watches his brother-in-law pace the floor of their new apartment. Sheets of papyrus scrawled with lists of Greek words cover every wall. On the table a lexicon lies open. Halldor goes back to his reciting. Philomena, a pretty, olive-skinned girl of fifteen, corrects his accent.

Halldor, who has despised Greeks for as long as he's lived here, is now surrounded by them. He has hired a Greek cook and a Greek man servant and his niece, with orders to speak Greek to him every spare hour of the day. These people have all worked for Varangians before and so know a little Norse. That helps.

"*Basileus*, Emperor. *Basilissa*, Empress. *Synomotes*, conspirator. *Prodotikos*, traitorous. *Pseustes*, liar. *Machomai*, I fight. *Phoneuo*, I kill..." These words, and so many others, and enough grammar to stitch them together—all this he will need to know when he replaces Odd Thorvaldsson as Harald's interpreter. The labor of months, but he has time now that the Emperor's Wineskins do nothing all day but stand sentry duty in the palace. Hours and hours with nothing to do but memorize.

Halldor stops pacing, pours himself some wine and hands the jug round to his brother-in-law and their slow-witted friend, Ulf. He sends the girl away for a while. "He tricked us, Bolli," he says. "You remember it. Somehow he got out of that house alive. And then years later he turns up here, and suddenly Harald can't do without him, heathen though he is. And now he's become a Varangian! Christ Almighty, I wish I'd killed him back in Catania, or a dozen other times when I had the chance. Now, I don't dare. But he's playing a double game with us, Bolli—I know it, I can smell it. He's not really one of us, with his Greek wife and Greek friends, he's no Norseman anymore. I've told Harald this time and again, and he knows I'm right. He only uses him because he's got no one else who speaks the damn language. Well, that will end one day. And then we'll just see what becomes of clever Odd Tangle-Hair."

34

ḣOLƆIᑎG OUR BREATꞰ
[*Odd resumes his narrative*]

My peaceful life at home was not fated to last long. Almost at once a rebellion broke out among the Bulgars—the result of John's overtaxing them. Led by two cousins, Deljan and Alusian, this horde of wild horsemen invaded northern Greece and got as far as Thessaloniki, where the Emperor was. And here an astonishing thing happened: Michael, ill as he was, announced his intention of leading his army in person against the enemy. He was now nearly paralyzed, his legs monstrously swollen and rotten with gangrene. The smallest movement was agony to him. His brothers, John and Constantine, begged him to spare himself. Nevertheless, he mounted his horse and organized the defense of the city.

I had no wish to go to war, but where the Emperor goes the Varangian Guard must follow. And so I soon found myself saying goodbye to Selene and my son once again. This time, though, I was determined not to lose contact with them. I hired couriers of my own to carry letters between us by sea or land, which they were able to do except during the worst months of winter.

I was away for nine months, from the summer of 1040 to the spring of 1041. I will say nothing about the campaign, which was a hard-fought one, except that it was a boon to my career. One of our columns, with the Emperor in the lead, was ambushed in the mountains of Macedonia. The Bulgar horsemen were showering us with arrows and, at that moment, Michael fainted and tumbled out of his saddle, but I was able to hold my shield over him while his grooms dragged him to safety. For this, he rewarded me with the command of the Second Bandon of the Guard, whose captain had been killed in the skirmish. Harald did not look pleased, but there was nothing he could do about it. I asked for Gorm to be my standard-bearer.

I should tell something here about the Guard. At full strength it numbered six hundred men divided into six banda. But it was largely a new Guard, of which we few Sicilian veterans were the hard core. The rest were either older men who had not served in Sicily and felt no connection to Harald or they were new recruits—Swedes, Rus, and a handful of Icelanders—who had been serving in the regular infantry, sometimes for years, while saving up their enrollment fee and waiting for an opening. The Second Bandon was made up mostly of these. Good fighters man for man, but not yet a tight unit. It was my job to make them into one. By the time we marched back in triumph to Constantinople, I had a hundred men who would follow me anywhere. If there was to be a showdown with Harald someday, I knew I could depend on them. Meanwhile, I continued to be his praise-singing skald and his translator whenever he needed me. I never suspected I had a rival for that job.

During the campaign, I ran into Moses now and then. No longer a bodyguard, he was serving in a regular regiment of the light cavalry. He asked about Maniakes and I told him.

"Will they ever let him go?" he asked.

"I doubt it."

Our triumphal procession was a spectacle like no other I have witnessed. We marched in through the great triple arches of the Golden Gate, topped with the gilded statues of Winged Victories. Cheering crowds lined the Mese, which was strewn with garlands, all the way to the Forum of Constantine. There the patriarch and the court gathered to meet us. Michael rode the whole way on a white horse, with a cavalryman either side of him to keep him steady. His fingers were swollen to the size of a man's wrists. The pain must have been unspeakable, but not a single groan escaped him. We proceeded from the Forum to the Cathedral of the Holy Wisdom for a service of thanksgiving and from there to the hippodrome, where our booty and prisoners were displayed. The rebel leader Deljan, minus his nose and eyes, was paraded on the back of an ass. The crowd went wild.

Afterward, there was the awarding of honors and spoils. Harald was given the exalted rank of *spatharokandidatos* to add to all his other dignities. All of us captains received bags of gold, collars, and swords. But, more important to me than any of that, Selene presented me with a baby daughter, Artemisia, named for her mother. A beautiful child.

Over the next months I watched my family grow. Gunnar was three years old now. I took him fishing, took him with me to the parade ground to watch the men drill, or to watch the polo matches where the cavalry regiments competed for prizes. I introduced him to Gorm, who grinned and tossed him in the air. And to Moses the Hawk, who shook his hand gravely and gave him his bow to hold. I always spoke Norse to him, told him stories about elves and trolls and gods—but not the frightening kind my father had told me. And sometimes I wondered how it might be if I took him to Iceland, to show him the wild, beautiful country of his ancestors. But no, I told myself. Not yet. Perhaps not ever. That thought made me sad. I would not speak of it to Selene.

Much of my time, though, was taken up with the duties of a Guards officer. I divided my days between home and barracks. I drilled and inspected my men every day, praising one man for his swordsmanship and another for his aim with a spear. I drank with them, swapped stories with them, welded them into a band of loyal brothers. Once a month, our bandon drew sentry duty in the palace. Michael held no audiences or banquets—he was far too ill for that—so at least we were spared the tedium of standing at attention during those interminable affairs. But we were called to attend wild beast hunts and occasional chariot races in the hippodrome to control the crowds who would get completely out of hand otherwise. And then on Sundays and feast days we accompanied Zoe and others of the Imperial family to the cathedral. These were the only occasions when the people saw their Empress and they knelt in silence as she passed by as though to a living saint. Not a reassuring sight for John, I imagined.

I must say more about this cathedral (which in Greek is called *Hagia Sophia*). It was a place soaked with magic. Each of the columns that supported the galleries was made of a different colored marble and each had healing powers when rubbed by a sick person. One cured kidney ailments, another headache, and so on. And attached to the great door by a ring was a silver tube which, if you put your lips to it, would suck the sickness out of your body.

I spent countless hours watching from the upper gallery the solemn rituals that were enacted below. I would be lying if I said that I wasn't swept up by the music and the incense, the color, the voices swelling under that huge dome, the priests in their jeweled robes, making their mystic gestures under the unblinking eyes of Christ Pantokrator—of course I was. But, as much as I had come to feel that this city was *my* city, still something, a single taut strand of a spider's web, attached me to my home, my past. As slender as that thread was, it had not snapped. It was still there and always would be. *I am still Black Thorvald's child,* I thought, *still Odin's child, even if I no longer know where he is or how to worship him.*

And one day, as I patrolled the upper gallery, it occurred to me that, just as this magic place has left its mark upon me, I might leave my mark on it. Looking around to make sure that no one was watching, I drew my dagger and scratched runes on the marble balustrade: *Odd Tangle-Hair an Icelander carved these runes.* And who knows? Maybe centuries from now some idle fellow, peering closely at a dark corner of the gallery will read them and will know that I existed.

When I wasn't on duty or with my family, I resumed my conversations with Psellus. We dined with him and his wife Olympia, a charming and intelligent young woman of sixteen, once a week, sometimes at our house, sometimes at theirs. Our talk ranged over many subjects—poetry, history, the mysterious workings of nature. But we steered clear of palace politics. Really, there wasn't much in that area to talk about. It was as if an unnatural calm had descended over everything; as though we were all holding our breath, waiting for Michael to die—which was taking a lot longer than anyone expected.

Harald was displaying his customary restlessness and irritability, already chafing under the dull routine of the capital. He had a succession of girls, beautiful ones, but none of them distracted him for long. He would get drunk and talk to me interminably about his love for the fair Yelisaveta, the poor princess locked away in Kiev. How she must be pining for him, waiting for him to swoop down and rescue her from her dragon of a mother. And soon, soon, he swore—banging his tankard on the table and spilling half his wine—he would do that. Take her by force, if need be, back to Norway to be his queen. By God, he would do it tomorrow!— except that he was raking in so much gold nowadays that he just couldn't afford to leave yet. He had, as I have described earlier, sent the girl love poems together with gifts of jewels to her father. Now he was ready to send another gift, a bag of choice pearls and other gems together with a letter to Yaroslav, which I had to write for him in Slavonic. It began with wishes for the health of the whole family, expressly including the lovely and gracious Grand Princess Ingigerd (I told him to put this in though it made him grind his teeth). It proudly announced his appointment as Commandant of the Varangian Guard. It described his triumphs in Sicily and boasted of his new wealth. It swore his undying love for Yelisaveta. And, without being precise, hinted that the time would not be long before he arrived to claim her hand in marriage. He entrusted this to a Rus Guardsman named Dmitry to deliver. The trading fleet from Kiev had arrived in the spring as usual and was now ready to depart. I'd gone down to look them over, wondering if I would see Stavko again, but he wasn't there. One of the traders told me he had drowned in the Dnieper a year ago when his boat capsized in the rapids. Anyway, Dmitry would sail with them, in the guise of a merchant. I wished him luck, and meant it. The sooner Harald left us, the happier I would be.

35

TWO SISTERS

Earthquakes and violent hailstorms shook the city during the five months that followed our return from the Bulgarian campaign. Comets were seen in the sky over Constantinople and other cities of the empire. Street corner soothsayers muttered darkly that all this portended some great evil. They were right.

On the eighth of December, in the middle of the night, I was roused from my bed and summoned by a messenger to a meeting at the palace. I told Selene to go back to sleep, pulled on my boots, wrapped a fur around me, and went out grumbling into the snowy night. What could possibly be so important? A Varangian met me at the gate and led me to the office of George, the Master of the Wardrobe, adjacent to the rooms where the Imperial regalia are stored. Besides the brothers George and Constantine, there was Harald and, to my surprise, Halldor. He had never come to one of these meetings before.

"Michael is dying," Constantine began without preamble. "John is with him—"

I cleared my throat to translate but Harald cut me off. "You just listen, Tangle-Hair. Halldor will translate for us tonight. It seems the fellow's been studying, I want to give him a chance. You'll help out if we need you."

He said it so casually, with a wave of the hand, in the slightly mocking tone that he always used when he was about to stick the knife in you.

Halldor meanwhile was grim-faced and serious, sitting on the edge of his chair, and not looking at me.

I forced a smile, but my stomach sank and my mind raced. *Halldor aims to replace me—he's turned Harald against me. He's been working at this for months, surely. And why have they brought me here at all? Just to frighten me, warn me, humiliate me?*

"Friend Halldor," I said, making my voice easy, "Greek is a riddling language, not easily mastered."

Halldor ignored this. Constantine looked back and forth between us, wondering why the room suddenly crackled with tension. He swallowed his bile and made a sour face: the stomach pains that plagued him were getting worse.

The conversation proceeded painfully. By the end of it Halldor was sweating. He stumbled over his grammar, stammered over his words; when he was met with uncomprehending looks from the Greeks, he shouted. I said nothing. But Harald gave him encouraging looks and seemed satisfied with his poor performance. The essential information did get conveyed—and it was dire.

"His Majesty," Constantine told us in a mournful voice, brushing an imaginary tear from the corner of his eye, "has withdrawn to his monastery of the Healing Saints to prepare his soul for its journey. He has laid aside his diadem, taken the tonsure, and put on the holy mantle of Christ, the robe of a simple monk. We begged him not to, but his thoughts now are fixed on God. John will stay with him until the end." George, who rarely spoke, sighed wheezily and shook his head. "And so," Constantine continued—and suddenly the tone changed: it was sharp, peremptory, businesslike—"and so we have brought the Caesar Calaphates to the palace, where we can produce him at a moment's notice. Nothing must be left to chance. We have enemies everywhere. You understand me, Commandant, your men must be ready. Call your captains together—but quietly, we want no panic. Starting tonight I want double guards on all the palace gates as well as the hippodrome, the Forums of Constantine and Arcadius, the houses of the senior officials and patriarch. And here"—he slid a paper toward us—"is a list of the people you are to..."

At the crucial moment Halldor went blank. *Syllambanein*, it seemed, was not a word he had learned. I waited. "Well?" Harald demanded finally, shooting me an angry look.

"To arrest," I murmured.

As the meeting ended, Constantine gave me my orders, ignoring Harald. "Your bandon will guard the throne at the coronation. I want someone there who *really* speaks our language." (Halldor winced at this.) "Zoe, of course, must be there: keep her away from everyone except the family. Oh, and give the Caesar your arm if he needs it, he sometimes faints."

I gave Harald an inquiring look.

"Be where I can reach you," he snapped. "And talk to no one."

I went home full of worry and told Selene everything.

We were still awake two hours later—there would be no more sleep for us that night—when a carriage drew up at our door and out stepped Psellus and his young wife, Olympia. We saw them often, but never at so late an hour.

"Odd, what in Christ's Name is going on? I've just come from the Logothete's..." Psellus started talking as they came through the door, propelled by a gust of icy wind. The words tumbled out of him. We pulled them inside and helped them off with their cloaks. Selene put her arms around Olympia, who was pale and trembling. "There are armed men outside Eustathius's house—not in uniform, but big men—Varangians, who else could it be? And no one's seen the Emperor for two days—or John either. You know something, don't you? Talk to me. Is Michael dead? What have they done with him?"

This was it, then. I'd seen this moment coming a long way off, like a distant sail on the horizon, and now suddenly here it was. Right on top of me. The moment when I would either obey my orders, like a loyal Guardsman, or join the Logothete's side. That offer had been made a long time ago and I had spurned it, resentful of how he had abandoned me in Sicily. I'd imagined my future lay with Harald. Well, that was over.

"Not dead yet," I said, "but soon. Sit down, both of you, there's a lot to tell." Old Chloris shuffled in from the servants' room; I told her to bring us hot wine and light the fires. "Eustathius is safe for the moment. I saw the list of people to be arrested, his name wasn't on it, or yours either, I'm happy to say."

"Whose then?"

"The Cerularius brothers, Dalassenus"—these were old senatorial families who might lay claim to the throne—"some others I didn't recognize. They'll be banished, or executed, as soon as Michael dies."

While I recited everything I knew, Psellus alternately sat, stood, paced, sat again, rubbed his forehead, wrapped his arms around himself and gripped his elbows, again went to pacing. I'd never seen him so agitated. He cast glances at Olympia, who looked like she was about to cry. Olympia was blond and plump, her manner was shy, but she was smart and had opinions on everything, though she uttered them in a little girl's voice. And she idolized Selene. Selene now held her hand tight.

"Calaphates is nothing but a vicious, ignorant lout," Psellus swore, "you must see that, Odd. With Sicily and Italy slipping away, the Bulgars still rebellious, the empire needs a strong man at the helm or it won't survive. Michael, for all his bad beginning, turned out to be a good Emperor. But this boy? Ask yourself, Odd, do you care who governs us? Who governs *you*? Or are you only a passing stranger, here to line your purse with gold and then move on? Someone like Harald. I hope we mean more to you than that?"

In that instant I made up my mind. "What can I do, Costas?"

"Eustathius and I have turned over every possibility. If there were only some way to get Zoe out of the palace and take her to the Emperor before he dies—to beg him to rescind the Caesar's nomination, give the power back to the Empress and a privy council of senior ministers."

"Why would he listen to her now when he's treated her as an enemy for years?"

Psellus threw up his hands in despair. "Why? Because he is face to face with his mortality. Because if he doesn't do the right thing now, he never will. He must know what Calaphates is like."

Suddenly Selene spoke up. "How would you get her out of the palace? Who's allowed in to see her?"

"As far as we know," Psellus replied, "only a few holy women who come to pray with her."

"Then, they're the ones to get her out. If you could forge a summons from the Emperor good enough to fool her guards, the nuns could deliver it and take her out."

Psellus waved the thought away. "Ask nuns to do that? Even if we knew who they were?"

"I didn't mean real nuns. I meant me and Olympia."

We all stared at her.

"You're not serious," I laughed. "You a nun? What would your father have thought about that?"

"I think he would've been delighted; magicians love deception."

"But you don't know anything about being a nun."

"I fooled you into thinking I was a boy. This wouldn't be any harder."

"No, it's too dangerous. If you were caught...? Think of our children."

She looked at me gravely. "I am thinking of them, Odd. This will be their country."

Then Psellus sputtered, "The idea's absurd. I couldn't possibly allow my wife to..."

"But she knows her way around the palace and I don't," Selene argued. "And don't nuns always travel in pairs?"

"No, I'm sorry—"

"I'll do it," said Olympia in a small voice. "Please, husband. My sister and one of my cousins are nuns. I can get habits for us." She gave him a hard look. "My dear, how often can a woman make a difference in this world? If there's any chance at all, you must let us go."

Psellus and I looked at each other helplessly.

✝

Che CENCH OF DECEMBER

The women's footsteps echoed along the empty corridors. It was the hour of lamp-lighting; except for servants and ushers and a few late-working officials, the Daphne was deserted.

After much debate, Psellus had decided that the scheme would work best under cover of dark. Selene and Olympia had spent all day trying on their black robes and veils and rehearsing what they would say when they were face to face with Zoe. Meanwhile, in the Logothete's office, Psellus was forging a letter from Michael, sealing it with a signet that resembled the Imperial one closely enough to fool the guards. As the hour drew near, the whole thing looked more and more hopeless. A thousand things could go wrong, and I was on the point of forbidding it. But Selene and Olympia were determined, and really, we had no better plan.

At the entrance to the Empress's suite, four women lounged on a bench. Tough and thick-bodied, with the look and accents of the street.

Matrons from the orphanage, they were now Zoe's warders, appointed by John. Selene held out the parchment to the one of them who seemed to be in charge. She broke the seal and squinted at the ornate script, tracing it with her finger. "You're new here, ain't you?"

"We're from the Convent of Holy Mary Pammakaristos," said Olympia softly, keeping her eyes cast down, the way a nun should. The Emperor is in the monastery nearby, they say he's close to death. He's sent for the Empress, to make his peace with her. We have a carriage waiting. Please, there isn't much time."

The warders exchanged puzzled looks, handed the parchment around, muttering among themselves. Finally, the one in charge said, "She's taken to living in the Purple Chamber lately. Dunno why, it's cold as a tomb in there."

"She likes it there," said another, "where her mum bore her, she says. Spends hours in there talking to herself. The old thing's soft in the head if you ask me."

"Follow me, then," said the first girl.

Porphyrogenneta: Born in the Purple Chamber. An empress born of an empress. Not all empresses were—but Zoe was. It was all she had left now, just that meaningless shred of dignity.

The walls of the big room were all of purple marble, and purple damask drapes hung over the windows. Zoe was in bed, huddled under a heap of furs in the frigid room, her head wrapped in a turban. She wasn't ready for sleep, she almost never slept anymore, but only the bed was warm enough. Her guards often forgot to bring coals for the braziers. A lamp on a bronze stand cast a pallid light—that and the candles on her little altar against the wall. The nuns knelt at her bedside. She eyed them suspiciously.

"I don't know you, do I? Who are you? Who sent you here?"

"Friends who love you, Empress," Olympia said. It had been decided that no names would be spoken. If Zoe were ever forced to talk, it would be death for all.

"What friends? I have no friends."

"Please, Empress, your husband is dying, we're taking you to him. You must plead with him to appoint yourself and a council of ministers to govern—not the Caesar. You understand? Not Calaphates. You must persuade him."

But Zoe shrank back under the covers. "You're lying, it's a trick.

Get out."—her voice rose to a screech—"I won't go anywhere with you. Guards—guards—!"

Olympia looked around in wild fear but Selene clapped her hand over Zoe's mouth and pushed her down on the pillows. Zoe thrashed and then lay still. For a moment, Selene was terrified that she had suffocated the old woman. "If I let you up, you won't scream?" She took her hand away. "Here," she said, "here's the document, read it."

Zoe gasped for air, her eyes big with fear. She clutched the parchment to her chest. "My husband wants to see me? Truly?" Such pleading in those old eyes. It was heartbreaking.

"Yes, Empress, he's asking for you."

A lie, but there was no other way. If they could just get Zoe as far as the monastery—well, and then what? All they could do was pray that Michael, in his final moments on earth, with his soul shriven, this man who owed her everything and had used her so cruelly, *would* be overcome by remorse, *would* heed her plea. That was the sum total of their plan. And, just maybe it would work.

Zoe, vain as always, dithered over what to wear, how to do her hair. Selene and Olympia flung warm clothes at her and urged her to hurry. Then she must pray. They all knelt in front of the altar. Olympia knew the words; Selene moved her lips. Then she must take her little statue of Christ and whisper to it. The minutes crept by. What if Michael were already dead? Why had they waited so long?

The female warders let them pass. They raced out into the night, down the snow-covered garden paths, under the looming shadows of buildings. At the Brazen Gate, where the doors had stood open an hour earlier, now a dozen Varangians barred the way. One of them approached. Ulf Ospaksson. He'd seen Selene on the parade ground and in the barracks a few times. Would he know her? She pulled her veil closer to her face. Olympia spoke to him—"The Emperor's order, we're bringing the Empress to see him"—and held out the parchment. Ulf called another Guardsman over with a lantern. Neither of them could read the Greek but they were persuaded by the look of the thing.

"This is her here?" Ulf gaped. "Really?" He lifted the edge of her hood and peered into her face. "Well, I'll be damned. It's no night to be out in, Empress."

"It's urgent," Olympia pleaded.

Ulf shrugged. "Go on with you, then. Goodnight, Sisters."

Four men pulled the great bronze gate open. The coach was waiting in the street, one of Psellus's servants at the reins. They had wanted their husbands to go with them, but no, Psellus said. Zoe knew him by sight, she might even remember Odd's face. If she were made to talk—too dangerous. It was snowing heavily now, the wheels left deep tracks as they made their way slowly up the embankment along the Horn toward the Blachernae Quarter.

"What shall I say to him?" Zoe asked them again and again. She was losing her nerve.

"God will give you the words, Empress," they assured her. "Trust in God."

The Monastery of Cosmas and Damien, the Healing Saints, built by Michael in a vain bid to win their favor, was a sprawling collection of buildings—a chapel, a rectory, an infirmary, a dormitory of cells—surrounded by a high stone wall. They stopped the coach before the nail-studded oaken door and helped Zoe down. The three of them stood together, freezing and pulling on the bell cord, for what seemed like minutes before a monk in hooded cassock opened the door a crack and held up his lamp.

Inside the refectory, the Guardian of Orphans confronted them. In his black cassock belted with a rope, only his smooth eunuch's cheeks distinguished him from the real monks, who were bearded to the waist; that, and the malice in his eyes. "Zoe! How in the name of God did you get here? Leave at once, or I warn you—"

"Take me to my husband." For a moment her voice was firm, commanding, a queen's voice; somewhere she was finding the strength. "Do as I say."

They weren't alone in the room. Three or four monks and their abbot looked on in dismay. And there were others too, not monks but several hard-looking young men in dark clothes. John's orphan thugs.

It was almost the hour of vespers and the monks were anxious to begin the service. "Surely, Guardian," the Abbot began, "the Emperor must..."

"*I* speak for the Emperor." John rounded on him. "Michael *hates* this woman. Now get her out of here, goddammit."

Zoe faltered and shrank back in the face of his fury, her little bit of courage seeped away.

"You heartless man!" Selene, eyes blazing, her hands balled into fists, stepped between them.

"What?" cried John. He came toward her, peering into her face. "You talk mighty bold for a nun. Who are you?"

"Only a humble Sister, Guardian,"

"Not humble enough. You need to learn meekness, Sister." He snatched the rope from around his waist and raised it to strike at her face. Olympia tried to pull her back but Selene didn't flinch. The rope struck hard across her head, ripping aside her cap and veil so that her long hair tumbled loose.

"You're no nuns. Who sent you?" John raised his hand for another blow...

"He's dead, God save his soul!" A young monk burst into the room.

"What?" John whirled around.

"The Emperor, sir ... in his cell, just this moment."

"Michael? My brother?" In John's eye something flickered for an instant that might have been genuine emotion. "I must see him. Abbot, don't let these women leave." John rushed from the room, leaving the monks and the orphans behind.

"Empress," the Abbott pushed them toward the door, "take your women and go. Quickly! You can do nothing here. Christ's love goes with you."

Monks and orphans pushed and shoved at each other while the women escaped. Outside, in the black night, they stumbled through the snow beyond the monastery gate, searching for the carriage. They couldn't see a foot in front of them.

"Where is he?" Olympia cried. "He can't have left us."

Then Zoe fell and couldn't get up. Selene ran back and struggled to pull the old woman to her feet just as the orphans shouldered the monks aside and burst through the refectory door.

"Selene," Olympia screamed, "Selene, hurry!"

A horse's whinny somewhere ahead. A dark shape moving slowly toward them.

"Petrus, help us."

The coachman jumped down from his box and ran to where Selene, on her knees in the snow, was trying to lift Zoe. The old woman looked half-dead. The orphans were almost upon them.

"Selene," Olympia cried again. "Leave her!"

But Petrus, who was a strong young man, hauled them both to their feet and dragged them to the coach, shoving Selene and Zoe inside just as the orphans grabbed at their cloaks.

He leapt onto the box and cracked his whip and the coach lurched forward. Inside the three women, wet and freezing, huddled together, Selene and Olympia with their arms around the sobbing Empress.

It was late at night when the coach returned, letting Selene off at our doorstep, then going on to take Olympia home. I'd been in a frenzy of worry all evening, cursing myself for letting her go. And when she told me how close they'd come to being captured—all I could do was hold her tight, speechless with relief.

"We failed," was all she could say at first. "I'm so sorry. I feel for Zoe, it took courage for her to face John—that man is a demon. And afterwards, coming back in the coach, I thought she would be angry at us for dragging her out on this hopeless venture, risking her dignity, her life even, but instead she thanked us, she kissed my hands and Olympia's. I want to help her, Odd."

"I know, I know," I told her. "It will come right in the end. And you'll have a story to tell our children. I'll write a poem about you, as I would for a warrior."

Chloris and I gave her warmed wine to drink and put her to bed. She smiled, and was almost instantly asleep.

And that, I thought, was the end of it.

Of course, I was wrong.

36

ᴅᴇᴀᴛʜ ᴏꜰ ᴀɴ ᴇᴍᴘᴇʀᴏʀ

The Emperor, so rumor told, had hobbled barefoot from his cell into the monastery chapel, leaning on two monks. He had refused to put on his red Imperial shoes and there were no other sandals that fit his swollen feet. But the effort was too much; gasping for breath, he was carried back and laid upon his straw pallet, where an hour or two later, he died. He had reigned eight years and seven months, most of that time as an invalid. He was only about thirty but he looked like an old man. As Psellus had recounted, he started badly, conniving at the murder of Zoe's first husband, and then turning against her, perhaps out of remorse, but he grew into the role of Emperor and, despite his failing health, he played his part with fortitude. He spoke no last words and he was buried without ceremony in the chapel, beside the altar.

Before putting Michael in the ground, one small precaution had to be observed. His signet ring must not fall into the wrong hands. But Michael's fingers were the size of sausages.

"Cut it off," said his loving brother John.

"What, the finger?" an incredulous monk replied.

"Yes, you idiot, the finger."

They would place that ring on the thumb of young Michael the Fifth Calaphates: because now nothing could keep that boy from the throne.

But three days would pass before that happened. Three days during which John stayed shut up in the Monastery of the Healing Saints, weeping—if one could believe it—at his brother's graveside. Three days in which rumors raced through the city and the churches filled with people praying for the Emperor's soul. Three days in which Varangians kicked in doors and dragged enemies of the Paphlagonian faction off to prison. In the palace, where I was stationed, fear was as suffocating as a fog at sea. Bureaucrats hid their papers, broke their signet seals, spoke in whispers. I don't know where the Logothete was, but I saw Psellus once, scurrying down a corridor. He avoided my eyes. We hadn't spoken since the night we planned the escapade with Zoe. My bandon and Bolli's were on alert day and night, patrolling the palace grounds, watching everyone who went in or out. I didn't go home for three days.

And then, at last, John returned. The scene was extraordinary. When the Guardian of Orphans passed the gate, his brothers and young Calaphates approached him with their hands outstretched, as if they were about to meet God himself. They gathered around him, smothering him with kisses. Calaphates even stretched out his right hand for his uncle to lean on. John announced the Emperor's death and then proclaimed in a loud voice that nothing now could be done without the consent of the Empress Zoe. And so off they went to the Purple Chamber. What happened there, I have heard from the lips of Zoe herself. The young Caesar flung himself at her feet, promising that he would be her slave. This was seconded by the uncles, who called down God's wrath if they were lying. They needed her, you see, to play her part, to issue a proclamation blessing the new Emperor and asking the people to return peacefully to their homes because by now large crowds had gathered in the streets. Was Zoe fooled by this? She later claimed they had bewitched her. Who can say? The fact is, she simply had no choice.

And that same day, the empire of the Romans gained a new ruler, His Holy Majesty Michael the Fifth, God's Vice-regent on Earth, the seventeen-year-old son of a ship's caulker, ignorant, untested, and to all appearances under the thumb of his Uncle John.

A Roman coronation is a spectacle worth seeing—although this one was hastily put together. Trumpeters, drummers, flute players, massed flags and standards. Calaphates rode a white horse from the palace to the great central door of the cathedral. Flanking him was my bandon of the Guards. Behind us marched units of the other household regiments and, following them, all the senior officials—at least those who weren't languishing in jail cells.

The choruses of the Blue and Green circus factions lined the way, chanting "*Axios, axios!*—Worthy, worthy!" to this boy who was worthy of nothing. And the common people of Constantinople cheered wildly, happy, I think, to see anyone take the throne without blood running in the streets.

Patriarch Alexius met the new emperor at the cathedral door and escorted him inside. He blessed the imperial cape and tiara and placed them on the boy. I never saw a priest less eager to perform his office—he hated these Paphlagonians. After that, a solemn Mass was performed, and then we marched back to the palace. Along the way, we Varangians halted and attempted to raise our new ruler up on a shield for all the people to see. It nearly ended in disaster. I and Gorm and two others had Calaphates at shoulder height when his eyeballs rolled up in his head and his knees buckled. Only my reaching up to grab his hand kept him from tumbling into the street.

The Emperor's first audience should have been held in the Golden Hall. But, no. Calaphates wanted desperately to soar up to the ceiling on the Throne of Solomon, and so we gathered instead in the Magnaura throne room. Zoe was brought in and made to sit next to her adopted son on the throne's broad seat. Incredibly, another throne was placed next to them for John. And there he sat, in his simple monk's robe, looking like he could scarcely keep from laughing. From where I stood, I could see his brothers Constantine and George standing farther back in the press of courtiers. They were not laughing.

Calaphates was a pale, gangly, pinch-faced, youth, unmuscular and awkward in his movements. This could have made him appealing in a way, except for the eyes which were cold as death. In a faltering voice, he attempted a speech from the throne and was heard to say, "... the Empress ... my mistress ... I am her servant ..." And he called John "my master." The voice trailed off in a whisper. Then, at a hurried signal from the Master of Ceremonies, all the court flattened themselves in obeisance and our new ruler got his heart's desire: the golden lions roared, the jeweled birds chirruped, and he and Zoe rose high above our heads.

The next morning things turned ugly between Harald and me. I was still on duty in the palace when he summoned me to his quarters. I brought Gorm along with me—some small voice warned me not to go in there alone. I found him and Halldor waiting for me. Harald waved me to a chair and ordered Gorm to wait outside. Gorm went as far as the doorway and stood there, filling it with his shoulders.

"John told me a curious story last night," Harald began, in a quiet voice that stirred the hairs on the back of my neck. "Halldor here translated it for me—his Greek's getting better, you know. It seems that two women posing as nuns spirited Zoe out of her quarters and took her to see the Emperor. Incredible, isn't it? Naturally, John had the warders flogged but the stupid women could tell him nothing. Nor could that fool Ulf, who was supposed to be guarding the gate. But one of John's orphans thought he heard one of the women call the other one 'Serena', or was it 'Selene'? Your wife's name." Suddenly his fist came down hard on the table. "What was your *wife* doing there?"

"My wife was at home with our children," I said, looking him straight in the eye.

"The Emperor's whereabouts was not common knowledge, Tangle-Hair. In fact, it was only mentioned at our meeting with Constantine and George. Now, Halldor here swears he didn't tell anyone. That leaves you."

"Hardly. The palace is a hotbed of rumors, probably a dozen people knew where Michael was."

"Funny, I don't believe you."

I saw Halldor's fist tighten on the pommel of his sword. I moved my hand towards mine and called to Gorm. If we were going to fight, it would be even odds. Harald and Halldor were on their feet. The four of us stood nose to nose for a long moment with no one speaking. Then Harald drew a deep breath and forced a smile.

"Now, now, there's no call for swordplay. The escapade came to nothing anyway. But I warn you, Tangle-Hair, we've come a long way together, and I wouldn't like things to end badly for you. I mean, with your head on a stake."

I kept my eyes on him and said nothing.

"You've gotten an exaggerated sense of your importance here, Tangle-Hair. You need to learn a lesson. I'm taking away your captaincy. I never approved of the appointment and there's no reason to prolong it now that the Emperor is dead. And"—he thrust his chin out at me—"you give me one more reason to suspect you, and you'll be out of the Guard and out of the city. You understand me?"

Gorm was usually the mildest of men, unless he was aroused. He was aroused now. He growled something deep in his throat and, for a thrilling instant, I heard an echo there of his brother Glum—the man-wolf.

Harald blinked.

"You remove Odd," Gorm said in his husky voice, "and the Second Bandon will mutiny. I will go to their rooms this minute and call them out. Odd has friends here."

"Bloody treason," Halldor snarled, and drew his sword half from its scabbard. But Harald stopped him. I could sense his thoughts: with a new Emperor only one day on the throne and the Guard overstretched to control the city, a mutiny was the last thing he could afford. And it would ruin his credit with John. He raised his hands in a gesture of peace.

"It's been a long few days, my friends. We're all a bit touchy, aren't we? Perhaps I was hasty. We'll let it pass."

Gorm and I left them to themselves and went off to have a drink together.

"Would the men have mutinied, Gorm?"

"Don't know," he shrugged his big shoulders. "Hope we don't find out. I'd be careful of Harald, though, if I were you."

"That, friend Gorm, is something I learned a long time ago."

That night I went home, kissed my children, and talked late into the night with Selene.

37

A SECRET REVEALED

JANUARY, 1042

It was evening and I had just come off guard duty. I had changed my uniform for a warm robe and fur hat and was walking down the promenade from the Magnaura to the Brazen Gate when I heard voices approaching and looked up to see our new Emperor coming in my direction. With him was a pretty young girl, one of the dancers who entertained at banquets, and an elderly official in court dress with a bunch of keys at his belt. I recognized this man by sight as the Papias, the majordomo of the palace, who was responsible for its maintenance and all its operations. Behind them walked a burly slave wearing a leather cap and a thick leather belt. They swept by me without a glance, and I thought I caught the word 'throne' as they passed through the tall, silver-shod doors and disappeared within.

Intrigued, I followed, and stole silently behind them, keeping to the shadows along the wall of the side aisle.

"Majesty, it is not a toy, not a plaything," the Papias protested. "It is the outward sign of your divinity. If the vulgar mob, or the barbarians, understood it, it would lose the power to awe."

"Do as you're told, man," the boy answered him curtly. "I want to show her. We'll go for a ride together, won't we, dear?" If the girl made any reply, it was too faint to hear.

The golden Throne of Solomon glowed dully on its podium in the light that sifted through the clerestory above. The two golden lions stood motionless on either side of it, their jaws open, their long tails upraised, and, in the tree, the jewel-eyed birds did not stir on their gilded branches. All was silence except for the echoing voices of the Emperor and the Papias. At the end of the hall a purple tapestry, embroidered with square-shouldered Roman eagles, hung from ceiling to floor and stretched across the whole width of the chamber, some forty paces. I had been here many times but had never been close enough to see that this curtain was, in fact, divided up the middle, just behind the throne. From even a few feet away you couldn't see the separation. The Papias held a fold of it aside now and they passed through into the darkness, their voices growing fainter.

What was back there? I'd gone too far to turn back now. It's the sort of fellow I am and just as I had once followed old Vainamoinen down into the depths of the Louhi's Copper Mountain, I waited a moment, drew a deep breath, and crept after them. Behind the curtain, I discovered a flight of a dozen stone steps leading downward. At the foot of them, the Papias lit a lamp, bringing the chamber and its contents to life. Two brass wheels, each as wide as my two arms outstretched, stood on stanchions with ropes around them as thick as ships' cables that ran into apertures in the floor. Next to these was an array of bellows similar to those of a dromon's fire siphon with handles for two men to work in tandem.

"Tell her, Papias, show her how it works," Calaphates commanded.

"But Majesty," the official protested again, "only a handful of people ever see this mystery. The men who operate it have their tongues removed..."

"Well, we won't remove her tongue, will we—her clever tongue that knows so many tricks," Calaphates laughed. "Go on, now, just as you explained it to me."

The Papias sighed. "Water and air make it all work, just water and air, but the force of it is immense when exerted on a single spot. The ancient scientists of Alexandria called it 'hydraulics' and we are the inheritors of their wisdom." In spite of the man's reluctance to speak, there was no mistaking the note of pride in his voice—pride in the genius of the Greeks. "When this wheel is turned," he tapped the nearer one, "it opens a sluice and water from the Reservoir of Aspar—you've seen it, Majesty, you know how vast it is—flows through pipes into a chamber far below us and the weight of it lifts the piston in its shaft. But great care is needed, the wheel must be turned only a little. Too much water and—well, there could be an accident.

"Now this piston is made from a single enormous tree trunk thirty feet tall, hollowed out with the two halves glued together and banded with brass. You see the tip of it here and the steel rod that projects from it through the slit in the curtain to the back of the throne. The throne itself is only slats of wood, gilded and jeweled, and not as heavy as it looks. To the audience watching in front, from a certain distance, in dim light, the throne appears to float in the air as the piston rises. Meanwhile, other slaves pump these bellows to deliver air to the lions, the birds, and the organ. That is where the sound comes from, like this." He puffed out his cheeks and whistled. "To lower the throne, you turn back the first wheel to close the sluice and turn the second one, again slowly, which allows the water to run out into the harbor. Now, the Caliph of Baghdad, it is said, has a similar ..."

From my hiding place, I listened with astonishment. From that first day when I saw the throne soar above my head I was convinced that some sort of machine worked it, that all their magic and mummery was only deception practiced by the Greeks upon us simpleminded barbarians. Still, I could never have imagined an apparatus like this. The labor of it! And all for mere show. On such fictions did this empire sustain itself. And it was a well-kept secret indeed. Even Psellus—my dear friend Psellus who taught me so much—had always evaded my questions about it.

"Thank you for your learned explanation, Papias," said Calaphates, cutting the man off. "Now we will ascend, my little friend and I."

"But Majesty..."

"Obey me, damn you!" the young Emperor, dragging the girl by the hand, turned and came back up the stairs and through the curtain. I only just had time to dodge ahead of them and crouch behind a pillar.

"Take us up now," he shouted.

Without the noise of the lions, the birds, and the organ to mask it, you could hear the mechanism groan. The throne rose, and rose. I peeped around the pillar and followed it with my eyes.

"Ooh!" the girl squealed, "make it go down, please, my head's spinning."

"You don't like it up here?"

"It scares me awful."

"And what if I did *this*?" Calaphates gripped her wrist, put a hand behind her back and shoved her to the edge of the seat. She shrieked and began to cry. He liked her fear, I could hear it in his voice. "You want down? Kiss me first." He pressed the girl's face to his while she squirmed and struggled.

This went on for a minute or more. I'd seen enough and was wondering how I could make my escape when suddenly doors at the end of the hall banged open and in marched the Guardian of Orphans, looking angrier than I'd ever seen him. "Tracked you down at last, you scamp. Come down at once. Who permitted this? I'll burn him alive."

"The Papias, Uncle—his idea, his fault…" Calaphates's voice cracked and faltered.

That functionary now appeared and sank to his knees before John. The throne began its descent. "I'll deal with you later, Papias," John snarled. "Calaphates, you had an appointment an hour ago with the Logothete and me to discuss the day's business. And instead I find you here? You have papers to sign. God knows, I don't ask you to *read* them. And then you're having dinner with your mother, both of your mothers. Have you forgotten that too? the Empress —we still need to conciliate that woman, the people love her, Christ only knows why. We can't keep her locked up all the time. Maria is trying to win her over, be her friend. You're expected to join them. Try to smile for a change."

"But I hate Zoe," Calaphates whined. "The way I have to call her 'Mistress' makes me feel like biting off my tongue and spitting it out. Why can't we just kill her, Uncle?"

"Because she is the only thing that keeps you on the throne. Will you ever understand this?"

"I can do whatever I like, I'm the Emperor. Uncle Constantine says so."

"My brother is a fatuous ass." The upper lip curled, the voice dripped with sarcasm. "Now come with me. The Papias will put the girl under arrest. Do you understand, Calaphates, that you've cost this child her life? Pity."

Calaphates, with his eyes downcast, slid from the throne and trotted behind his uncle, followed by the weeping girl, the wretched Papias, and the burly slave, who tongue-less, would never regale his friends with this escapade.

I waited 'til I could no longer hear their voices and slipped away. My brain buzzed with thought. I would keep my new knowledge to myself but I now had something to report to Psellus, for what it was worth. Calaphates was refusing to play his part as the Empress's dutiful son. There were cracks in the regime.

38

CONSTANTINE NOBILISSIMUS

FEBRUARY, 1042

Michael Calaphates and his favorite uncle, dressed in their hunting leathers, stretched their legs to the fire and drank hot spiced wine from golden cups. Calaphates was on his third or fourth, his young head beginning to spin. Constantine took small sips and swallowed almost nothing. Wine hurt his stomach anyway, but more than that he needed all his wits this evening. There was a reason why he had spent the past three days in the company of this childish, coldblooded, possibly crazed young man. He had invited him to spend a few days at his Thracian hunting lodge, just the two of them, nephew and uncle, roughing it in the bracing air, coursing after small game in the hills, like friends, like comrades.

Calaphates was a poor horseman and a worse shot but his uncle had carefully instructed the beaters and trackers. One of them dragged a half-dead fox from the jaws of the dogs, held it up by its ears, and offered it to Calaphates to dispatch. The boy giggled like a girl as he drove his javelin into its throat. Constantine applauded. "Well struck, Majesty! You've earned the brush."

Now Constantine refilled the boy's cup. "Do you like your new stallion, Majesty?" He had made the boy a present of a white Arabian as well as a pack of prize wolfhounds.

"'Course I do, Uncle. Thank you. And again, I ask you to call me 'Michael'."

"But Majesty, you are our Emperor, I honor that. It pains me to say that there are some in the palace—in our own family—who do not."

"Uncle John." Calaphates spat the words out.

Constantine offered a sad, sympathetic smile and spread his hands. "Drink up, now, Majesty, and then I'll have Cook bring in our dinner."

Calaphates drained his goblet, letting the wine run out his mouth and drip from the scant hairs on his chin. "I drink to you, Nobilissimus"—he slurred the esses—"to your new appointment."

"So kind, Majesty. I hope I shall be worthy. It's a heavy burden you lay on me."

Calaphates had just created Constantine Grand Domestic, that is, Commander-in-Chief, with the rank of nobilissimus, a dignity second only to the Emperor himself. It was of no concern to him that his uncle had never drawn a sword, never seen a battlefield. Until now, Constantine had held no position in the state. Now he commanded the army and navy.

Constantine refilled his nephew's goblet. He leaned closer to the boy and spoke in a low voice, although there was no one to overhear them but a single servant who loitered near the wall. "Majesty, you won't mind, I hope, if I give you a warning? Things are happening that disturb me. I feel I must speak. Your three cousins, the children of your father's sister—you hardly know them, none of us do—but they are ambitious young men and they are in the city now. John has brought them here and, behind your back, he entertains them, gives them money, encourages them to hope for—I'm not sure what—your crown, I fear?"

Calaphates swallowed hard, nearly choking. "Why?"

"Because he knows he can't control you anymore. You're grown up now, a real Emperor, a mind of your own. You don't need him now. But your uncle is used to being obeyed—by the sycophants who surround him, by those filthy orphans of his, and yes, even by us, his own flesh and blood."

As he spoke, the memory flashed through Constantine's mind of his childhood home: the wretched poverty, the brutal father who had crushed his sons' testicles in his hands, and John, who treated the younger children like his personal slaves, teaching them to steal pears from the neighbor's garden, even little Maria, and bring them to him. He would choose the best for himself and leave the spoiled ones for them.

"Those papers that he gives you to sign every day," Constantine went on. "Well, of course, you don't have time to read them all as carefully as you might. But one of them was nothing less than a grant of immunity for those young men if they should be discovered conspiring against Your Majesty. It's true. I have my spies too, you know, just as John has his."

"Uncle, what should I do? I'll have them killed, I don't care what I signed. We'll ride back to the city at once." Calaphates was on his feet, staring around him as if he expected to see assassins leap from the dark corners of the room.

"Now, now, now, Majesty, sit down, yes, take a breath, yes, that's better. It will be all right, you have me on your side. John's great mistake is that he gives no one else credit for brains. We can return to the city tomorrow if you like, although personally I'm enjoying myself here. But when we do, you will be careful to give nothing away to John, either by word or expression of your face. Can you do that Majesty? We must wait a while longer before we beard the lion in his den. We must sharpen our weapons."

"What d'you mean, Uncle?"

"I'm new in my command. I need to make sure of the loyalty of my senior officers."

"Good God, Uncle, you think it will come to civil war?"

"One must be prepared. You must trust me to know when the moment is right. Agreed? Excellent." He touched his nephew's knee and gave it a squeeze. "And now to dinner. I've worked up an appetite. How about you?"

The Emperor of the Romans replied with an uneasy smile.

✝

MARCH

It was Constantine who had invited them to the little family dinner in his apartment. John had accepted with an ill grace and was angry about something, that much was clear. The two brothers made an odd pair: both beardless, both middle-aged, but where John was big and solidly built, with a spreading paunch, Constantine was thin, almost cadaverous. And then there was their costume: John's, as always, a shabby monk's robe, Constantine's a gorgeous plumage of silks and furs.

Waiters removed the remains of the fish course. The talk had been desultory so far.

"I want a wife," said Calaphates, apropos of nothing.

"You're too young," John replied around a mouthful of food. He was drunk. He had become drunk at lunch, and now he was more drunk. "What d'you want with a wife anyway? Don't you force yourself on every female in the palace under the age of forty? I swear the boy's part goat." He licked his lips and smiled at his own joke, glancing around the table.

Calaphates threw his napkin down. "Do not call me 'boy', Uncle. I am the Emperor."

"Yes, and don't ever forget who made you one."

"Now, John," Constantine said mildly, "we could just put out feelers to the Bulgars, the Rus. Wasn't there some ambassador here a few years ago trying to shop Yaroslav's daughter?"

Calaphates grinned. "Just what I want—a wild barbarian girl. What do you think of that, Mother?"

But before Maria could answer, John thumped the table. "No wife. End of discussion." He reached for the decanter. As usual, he was drinking more than anyone else. Maria, who sat next to him, laid a hand on his arm. He threw it off.

Conversation flagged. Then George, who had said nothing so far, began a rambling monologue about the condition of the Imperial vestments and the price of silk. His voice trailed off when he realized no one was listening. The waiters carried in a steaming haunch of venison and began to carve.

Then Constantine, dabbing at his lips, said, "By the way, I've issued a contract for refurbishing the fleet and adding ten new warships. I've consulted with my captains, they're all for it. I'm sure you'll agree, Majesty?" He exchanged a look with Calaphates. This was the moment they had planned, the moment Constantine had waited all his life for.

"Absolutely, Uncle, quite so."

John's lip curled. "*Your* captains, brother? And who are you to decide this? You call yourself 'Grand Domestic'? It's a joke. I didn't approve this promotion of yours. Calaphates, you should have asked me first. My brother is wholly unqualified for the position. The fact is, the treasury cannot afford this expense. Out of the question. Next time, Constantine, ask me before you go consulting anyone."

Constantine carefully laid down his cutlery. "John, you've lorded it over us long enough. You are not our master. You are finished, Brother John."

Maria and George stopped chewing in mid-mouthful. Calaphates smiled at his plate.

"Now, brothers," Maria pleaded, "there is no cause for such talk. We're a family. If we don't stand united—why, well, we're lost, aren't we?" She glanced anxiously from one man to the other.

John stabbed a chunk of meat with his knife as though he were burying it in his brother's chest. The bloody juices spattered his hand. "A family, yes, and *I* am the head of it. *I* make the decisions, *I* do the thinking." He sawed off a piece and chewed it savagely.

"But Uncle John," said Calaphates with a smile, "doesn't that big, bulbous head of yours grow weary from so much thinking? What you need is a rest, Uncle—a long one. In a monastery, I think."

John's face contorted in a look of astonishment. "Listen to the boy's insolence. Constantine, I blame you for this. You think I don't know how you toady to him, all the gifts, all the winking behind my back? It's disgusting. Be careful, Brother, I fear we've raised a serpent in our bosom. This boy would gladly see us all destroyed, you as much as me."

"John, stop it." Maria was looking desperate. "He isn't a bad boy, not a serpent. If only Stephen were still alive to guide him."

"Maria, your husband couldn't guide his right hand to his asshole. I accept the blame for putting him in charge of the fleet but I won't make that mistake with little brother Constantine here."

She flared in anger. "You—you mind how you talk about Stephen. He had *balls* even if he hadn't a brain."

In an instant, the carefully learned city manners were stripped away and all that was left was a family of Paphlagonian peasants snarling at each other. There was a long moment of shocked silence—broken by a loud horse laugh from Calaphates. "Good for you, Mother!"

"Calaphates, excuse yourself from the table," John commanded. "This conversation has taken an ugly turn, not for your ears."

"Oh, no, Uncle. I'm enjoying myself. This is better than the pantomimes."

"Of course, His Majesty must stay," Constantine said, laying his hand on his nephew's shoulder. It is you who must leave, John. Leave now, leave at once!" Constantine's voice cracked in a shrill falsetto.

John struck out with his arm, sweeping everything off the table. Silver plates clattered to the floor, glassware smashed. He lurched to his feet, knocking over his bench. His cheeks—those immovable slabs of white fat—quivered with anger. They had never seen him like this. "I will leave. I will take myself away. And you'll see how the senators, the heads of bureaus, will follow me, how every man of sense in this city will follow me. And in a week, when you discover that you know nothing about governing the Empire, you will all be begging me to come back."

Maria wrung her hands; helpless tears made tracks in her face powder. George looked as if he had been smacked with a board. Constantine and Calaphates shared a secret look of triumph.

The waiters busied themselves cleaning up the mess on the floor. Except for one, who slipped out of the room unnoticed—one of the Logothete's spies.

And John was right. He boarded his yacht and sailed, not to his mansion on the Horn, but to Prusa, across the Propontis, far enough away to frighten them and bring them to their senses. And half the court did follow him, Maria and George among them. He reigned there like a king. A week passed. A week in which Constantine and his ships' captains and regimental commanders laid their plans, in which nobles and officials who hated John were sounded out, one of them being the Logothete. Then a letter was sent, stamped with the Imperial signet, begging John's pardon, asking him to return, assuring him that he would find everything just as he would wish.

So John came back. Constantine Nobilissimus and the Emperor stood together on the palace roof, a cold wind whipping their cloaks around them, looking down at the Great Harbor as the yacht sailed in.

"Give the signal, Majesty," Constantine murmured.

The yacht was almost at its mooring post. Calaphates raised his right arm. A warship darted out, came alongside and threw out grappling lines. Marines swarmed over the side. If you listened hard, you could hear the shouting. If you squinted into the morning sun, you could see John looking up to the palace, shaking his fist. You couldn't see the expression on his face. But you could imagine it.

The warship departed, taking the Guardian of Orphans to the monastery of Monobatae, on a small island in the sea, where, in due course, he was blinded.

Now Constantine ruled the family and the empire.

39

TEMPTED

Gone? Just like that?

The city was stunned. And, if the Guardian of Orphans could fall, then who was safe? Constantine's people ransacked John's offices in his home and in the palace, seizing his private papers—great stacks of them. It would be the labor of weeks to study them all for evidence incriminating his cronies, making note of his enemies, tracing embezzled funds, building a case against him. Meanwhile, there was tight-lipped fear. No one knew what would happen next. Certain people made haste to leave the city for long vacations. One of those was Eustathius, the Logothete.

The orphans did not fare well. Those who were old enough to have served John as thugs or spies were interrogated and then tossed out in the street to fend for themselves—no more free room and board at the State's expense. The younger ones were simply neglected. It wasn't long before they ran away or stayed to roam the orphanage like packs of feral dogs. Eventually a battalion of monks and nuns was sent in to restore order; but that was only weeks later.

Meanwhile, Calaphates moved swiftly against his cousins, the ones whom his uncle John was supposedly raising up against him. Two of the young men were barely in their twenties, the other just fourteen. Since John's banishment, they had been hiding in a house he had provided for them. Calaphates located them, with Constantine's help, and invited them to dinner, showing them every mark of courtesy and affability and sending them off with expensive presents.

The next morning he ordered them to be castrated.

And this odious task was assigned to the Varangians. Harald ordered me—as some kind of punishment or just to dirty my hands—to see it done. I refused. So did many others—even Halldor, to his credit. Finally, a group of the younger Guards was dispatched to do the deed. They were supposed to arrest the youths quietly and take them to Noumera prison. But the boys cried bloody murder and ran out of the house. Our men chased them down the street, ripped off their clothing and cut their balls off in broad daylight while they shrieked and appealed to passersby for help. It caused a panic in the neighborhood and it couldn't be kept quiet. The older two died at once; the boy lingered for a few days.

For us, this was a humiliating fiasco. The men were very angry when they heard about it. "We are the Emperor's Wineskins," they protested, "an honorable regiment, not common assassins." Harald, defending himself, made the mistake of openly blaming the Emperor. This was just what Calaphates had been waiting for.

He and his uncle distrusted us—they knew that Harald owed his promotion to John and had carried out his orders. But, while Constantine was canny enough to try and win Harald over, Calaphates simply detested us. And so he formed a new bodyguard for himself made up of young eunuchs whom he had purchased in the slave market some time previously. They were mostly Slavs, I think, but he called them his 'Scythians' after the name of some ancient tribe. He dressed them in outlandish costumes of checked jackets and boots and tall pointed hats, and equipped them with hatchets and bows.

One morning at dawn, heralds accompanied by these Scythians arrived at our barracks in Saint Mamas and at the Brazen Gate to announce that we were all relieved or our duties and confined to quarters until further notice. The charge was disloyalty. I happened to be at the barracks. So was Harald, sleeping off a night of drinking. It was a startling way to be awakened.

And it got worse.

Our men crowded into the dining hall, as many as could fit, others jammed the corridors and stairways. All of them shouting threats and curses—at the Greeks, at Harald. They didn't know who to be angry at, they just knew they were angry. Quite a few threatened to resign their commissions and go home—to Sweden, to Gardariki, or to Iceland (these included Halldor, Bolli, and Ulf, among others). Harald jumped up on a table and shouted back, but he was drowned out. He tried turning his back on them, he tried stamping and throwing things, and finally, when he could make himself heard above the din, he was reduced to begging them to just be patient awhile.

Later that morning, Harald called me to a private meeting. He was all conciliation.

"Tangle-Hair, we've had our differences, dammit, but that's all over now, isn't it? You're a clever fellow. I mean, you are my skald, it's your job to advise me. Halldor's loyal and all that, but not a quick thinker like you. It's all gone wrong. Not my fault. These fucking Greeks with no balls..."

I knew exactly what he was thinking. The Paphlagonians—the people he had invested his career in—were turning against each other, and against him. His position was crumbling, events had slipped out of his control, he suddenly felt himself isolated and he didn't know what to do. It showed in his face, in the way he paced furiously up and down the room, tugging at his long moustaches.

"Then why not pack it in, Harald?" I said. "Go to Kiev, collect Yelisaveta, go home to Norway, kick your half-brother off the throne, and claim your kingdom. Surely you're rich enough now? It's what you've been threatening to do for years—why wait any longer?"

"Oh, yes?" He stopped pacing, took a deep breath through his nostrils, and stared at me hard. "Maybe that's what you'd like me to do, heh? Make room for you? Is that it?"

"Harald, you asked—"

"Well, I won't. I'll leave when *I'm* ready. I won't be driven out." His fist was an inch from my face. It was hard not to flinch.

"All right, look, calm yourself. If you aren't going to run, then you have to fight. Calaphates is a fool, but Constantine is shrewd enough to know when he's gone too far and needs to pull back. We will guard our Greek masters whether they like it or not, and pay ourselves out of the treasury if we have to."

I never knew a man change moods as many times in a minute as Harald could. Now his face broke into a wolfish grin and he clapped me on the shoulder. "Yes, Tangle-Hair, right you are. We fight!"

Within the hour, Harald and I led three banda of Varangians into the palace. We took up our stations at the gates, in the throne room, at the door to the treasury, all the places we were accustomed to guard. The Scythians took one look at us, flung down their useless weapons, and fled. Calaphates fled, too, to his private apartment, and wasn't seen again for three days. Constantine approached us and tried to pretend that the whole thing was a mistake. He looked unwell and several times clutched his stomach and groaned. *He's frightened*, I thought. *He knows the mad dog has slipped its leash.*

Calaphates, having failed to rid himself of us, then struck out in a different direction. He declared war on the aristocracy. Dozens of arrest warrants were signed and Harald, who was determined to get back in favor, ordered us to carry them out. He and Constantine had a meeting.

I don't know exactly what was said; Halldor translated for him. But we found ourselves day after day dragging these men from their homes or stopping them at the harbor or the city gates as they tried to flee. We hunted for them in cellars and in closets. We pulled them from the arms of their wives. We found one crouched in a grain bin with a bushel basket over his head. Some of them fought us, most came meekly.

And then, to take their places in the Senate, Calaphates appointed anyone willing to pay handsomely for that cheapened honor. One of those, I learned, was my wife's seducer, Alypius.

✝

MONDAY, APRIL 12

Around midday, Psellus sent his carriage to our house with an urgent invitation to call upon him. Selene and I left the children with their nurse and came at once. He and Olympia met us at the door. He had deep circles under his eyes, and Olympia's pleasant face was pinched with fatigue. Plainly, neither of them was sleeping. Our wives embraced and kissed cheeks while Psellus drew me inside. This was the first time the four of us had been together since the Zoe escapade. The shadow of that sad night still hung over us, but it had made us closer comrades than ever.

We sat at the table in his large handsome dining room and ate from a platter of lamb and ham, leftovers from the family's Easter dinner of the night before.

"We live in terror, Odd. In the palace. No one speaks. We avoid each other's eyes. No one knows who'll be taken next. It might be me. I'm no aristocrat but, with Eustathius in poor health, I am the acting Logothete now. I've tried my best not to make enemies but I'm no partisan of Constantine's either. And it's you Varangians doing it—taking people away in the middle of the night. I know, I know, not your wish, but still…"

He jumped up from the table, went over to a chest by the wall, and returned holding a ringmail shirt that drooped from his hands to his knees. It would have been a good fit for someone twice his size. "I shall wear this from now on under my tunic. But it's *heavy*. I never imagined. How do you bear the weight of such a thing?"

"A tight belt helps," I said, trying not to laugh. "But this is nonsense. If someone comes at you with a spear, I suggest running away. A strong thrust will punch a hole in that thing anyway."

He looked sheepish. "It will? Well … well, I will carry a dagger on me." He let the shirt drop in a heap on the floor and sank wearily back in his chair. Olympia touched his hand and made a brave smile.

"It's all about Harald," I said. "He's made up his mind to win Constantine's favor just as he had John's. Whatever it takes. And in the end, he'll fail. They'll never trust him. They just haven't figured out how to get rid of him."

"But what about the Guard?" Psellus said. "Where is their loyalty? Everything may depend on that in case—" He didn't finish the thought. *In case of revolution.*

"There are six hundred of us, I can't vouch for all. Many of the new men don't care one way or another, but the older ones, the ones who go back to Basil's day, are for Zoe and against Calaphates. Some of them have come to me privately to say they are ashamed to be acting like police thugs. It hurts their pride and they're angry about it. Angry at Harald."

Psellus turned thoughtful eyes on me. "And you, Odd? If the men deserted Harald? The Logothete still wants to make you Commandant of the Guard, if he has it in his power. What would you say to that?"

"This comes from him?"

"It does. He'd tell you himself but he's keeping close to home. Surely you're tempted?"

I didn't answer for a minute. I tried to catch Selene's eye but she frowned and looked away. She hadn't spoken at all so far which was unusual for her. "In the end it may not matter much who heads the Guard," I said. "If we tried to remove Calaphates—that's what you're talking about, isn't it?—I don't know. In two-hundred years the Varangians have never overthrown an Emperor. It's a step that once taken can never be taken back. Besides we aren't the only troops in the city. There's the Household Cavalry, the mercenaries, the navy. And Constantine commands them all."

"But the officers, at any rate, come from aristocratic families, some of them—the very ones being persecuted."

"Yes, by us. Constantine is a clever man. Cleverer even than John was. And then there's the city populace to think of. Haven't you told me about riots years ago that almost reduced this place to ashes? Would we have to fight them?"

"No," Olympia said suddenly. "No, I don't think so." Psellus looked up in surprise. In fact, we all did. She was not a person who spoke much, though when she did, you knew there was a brain there. "Yesterday at Easter services in the cathedral, up in the women's gallery, while the priest and the chanters were droning on below—all our eyes were on Zoe. And the gallery was abuzz with murmurs about how ill she looks and how harshly she is being treated by that despicable Calaphates. There's great sympathy for her and anger at the Emperor and his uncle. And I think in any church you went to you would have heard the same."

"Well, yes, women—" Psellus began with a shrug.

"No, she's right," Selene jumped in. Don't underestimate us women."

In the end, we departed without me giving Psellus an answer to his question. While he went outside to summon his man to bring the carriage around, Selene and Olympia embraced for what seemed like a long time. I wondered if they were whispering something.

Late that afternoon, Selene and I rode our horses out to her village to visit Melampus's grave. It was the second anniversary of his death. The marker was just a simple stone but it was set in a pleasant grove of cypresses with a brook running by. We poured wine on the ground, sent up a prayer to Hermes-Odin, and then sat for a while on the grass enjoying the warm spring air.

"When I come here I feel his spirit nearby," Selene said. "It's a good feeling."

"That used to happen to me sometimes—my father. It seems a long time ago."

Selene took my face between her hands and looked into my eyes. "You do want it, don't you, command of the Guard?"

"It's too soon to think of that. Harald isn't—"

"Don't lie to me, dear heart, I know you do. And it frightens me."

"Why should it?"

"I don't know," she sighed. "To rise high is to fall far. Daggers will be drawn against you."

"That's been true all my life. I'm not afraid."

"Then be afraid for me. Odd, I'm the daughter of an alchemist and a fortune-teller. I was raised among magicians and astrologers and demonologists. We've always lived on the margin. Always made use of when needed, but still disreputable, mistrusted. Suddenly I'm to be thrust into the center? The wife of the Commandant? A lady of the court? I won't know what to do. I've never been ambitious for wealth, Odd. We have more money now than I ever dreamed of, more than *you* ever dreamed of. Maybe we've risen high enough. And what if someone strikes at you through me? What if you have to fight just to keep me from being hanged as a witch?"

"Hush now, Selene," I took her hands in mine. "That isn't going to happen. Look, Psellus doesn't think the worse of us for not being Christians. He admired your father."

"Psellus is a rare man, Odd. There aren't many like him. And even he is careful to live like a Christian, whatever he believes." She gazed moodily at the sky, where the setting sun reddened the clouds. "Sometimes as a girl, you know, I wished I had my mother's gift. I wish it now more than anything—to know what our future will be."

As she said these words I suddenly had the strangest feeling. I was seventeen years old again, lying half-dead of exhaustion and soul-sickness on the floor of a stinking hut in a Lapp village, where we had drifted in the fog. And the *noaidi*, their ancient seer, in some mysterious way, had traveled to the land of the dead to plead with the ghosts of my murdered family to leave off haunting me. And the little man, Nunna, who translated for him, was crouching beside me and saying, "...he has sent his spirit into the gray wolf, and into the albatross, and into the seal. Everywhere he has searched for the end of your fate, but it lies a great way from here and even he cannot see all the threads of it. He says that you will travel far and, for a time, will forget your home. But one day, he says, the time of your returning will come and when it does you will know it..."

"Odd?" Selene was shaking my shoulder.

"I'm sorry—what?"

"Where were you just now?"

"Nothing, it's nothing. A stray memory."

"Tell me."

But how could I tell her? And what did that old man really see? I pushed the thought away.

She leaned in and kissed me on the lips. "I'm sorry to lay my fears on you. You must do as you think best. I trust you. Tell me you love me."

I put my arms around her and we rolled together in the grass over and over, pulling our clothes loose, making love until our hearts were pounding.

Afterwards, we lay on our backs and watched the treetops bend in the evening breeze until it grew too dark to see. As we rode back to the city, a light rain fell.

40

REVOLT

On the Sunday after Easter, Calaphates appeared in a public procession along the Mese to the Church of the Holy Apostles. His path was strewn with carpets, purple hangings were draped from the windows, and the whole city turned out to cheer him. This show of enthusiasm was hardly spontaneous. The Emperor and his uncle knew they were in bad odor, what with the castrations and arrests, and this outpouring of love was carefully stage-managed by the circus factions. Nevertheless, Calaphates believed that he had the popular support now to take a drastic step—ridding himself of Zoe forever.

Later that day, I happened to be walking on the parapet overlooking Boukoleon harbor when there was a sudden commotion below: a gang of soldiers dragging a woman in nun's habit out the postern gate and down to the water's edge, where a launch was tied up—the woman raising her arms skyward, shrieking, "Great Basil, look down from heaven! Can you see what they're doing to me, your own blood?"—the sailors bundling her aboard and casting off—her screams drifting over the water until they faded away.

I couldn't see Calaphates, but Constantine was there with his personal bodyguard of sailors.

I ran down to see what it was. One of the sailors was a man I knew from Sicily.

"The Empress," he said. "The Emperor put her on trial in his private chambers only an hour ago, charged her with trying to poison him, banished her to the convent on Prinkipo." (This, I knew, was a tiny rock of an island not far off the coast.) "Hacked her hair off," he went on, "stripped her naked, dressed her in gray. She'll die there." He had tears in his eyes.

Then a moment later, here came Harald, Halldor, Bolli and Ulf, pounding up from the direction of the Brazen Gate. I told them what had happened. Harald shouldered his way through the crowd to where Constantine stood and began to protest, with Halldor stumbling over the Greek: Why were the Varangians left out of this? Eager to help—earned your trust—always ready to serve…

Constantine backed away from him, looking either annoyed or alarmed, I couldn't tell which. "Quite so, Commandant," he stammered, "no aspersion on your loyalty, no, no, gratified to hear it, didn't need your men for this, less display the better, you understand…" With a swish of his robe, he turned and hurried back through the gate, leaving Harald speechless.

That night I told Selene what I'd seen, but she already knew all about it, and she was furious. She'd had a note from Olympia that day. Olympia had gone to church and it was all that the women there were talking about. Selene, too, had gone out in the street to visit the shops, and heard angry talk everywhere. The city was abuzz with the news. If Calaphates thought he was going to get rid of Zoe without an uproar, he was a bigger fool than anyone thought.

"What will they do to her, Odd?" Selene demanded. "People disappear into those places and never come out again. They could strangle her there and no one would know. We risked our lives for her, and now this!"

I had to confess I didn't know what would happen. As long as Harald commanded the Varangians we would do nothing to rescue her. "We will see what tomorrow brings."

What tomorrow brought was beyond anyone's imagining.

✝

MONDAY, APRIL 19

The following morning, Harald marshalled the entire Guard at the Forum of Constantine to provide protection for the City Prefect, who was going to read out a message from the Emperor. Determined to make himself look indispensable, Harald had volunteered us for this, although the Prefect had guards of his own.

The Forum is a spacious oval in whose center is a towering column topped by a statue of Constantine the Great. Here vendors of clothing and food ply their trade. At this hour of the day it was jammed with people. A platform of planks had been set up at one end and our men formed a ring of shields around it. The Prefect, a corpulent man named Anastasius, a flunky of the regime, mounted and began to read from a scroll. He denounced not only the Empress for attempted poisoning (and maybe she had—who knows?) but named the Patriarch Alexius, too, as her accomplice. This traitorous cleric was being arrested at that very moment and would be dealt with—

A rock arced through the air and struck the Prefect on the forehead. He staggered and dropped his scroll.

"Let Calaphates's bones be broken!" came a voice from the crowd. "Give us back Zoe, our Mother!" came another, a woman's voice.

There must have been near a thousand people there. In an instant they had broken up the vendors' stalls and charged at us, swinging pieces of wood, brandishing hatchets, spades, knives—whatever came to hand. And we were jammed so close together we couldn't have used our weapons if we had wanted to. The mob drove us out of the Forum and back along the Mese toward the palace, a distance of a few hundred yards. From the rooftops that lined the avenue, people hurled furniture, emptied chamber pots and braziers of coals on our heads. The rattle of rocks bouncing off our shields made a noise like rolling thunder. A hot coal lodged between my neck and shoulder and burned me. We stumbled, we trampled each other's feet. The fat Prefect clutched his bleeding scalp and gasped for breath. From somewhere I heard Harald yelling, "Charge, charge them, you dogs!" But we could only crouch under our shields as missiles rained down on us, and retreat step by step.

Then, off to our right, above all the other din, we heard the reverberating boom of the great gong coming from the Cathedral of the Holy Wisdom. The patriarch's people had chased away the men sent to arrest him and he was sounding the alarm. Within minutes, the gongs of every church in the city rang out in reply. People poured out of their houses and streamed toward the cathedral and the palace—a moving, churning sea of humanity—artisans, shopkeepers, beggars, loungers, householders, rich and poor, young and old, men and women and even children all mixed together.

Carrying the Prefect and our injured comrades with us, we squeezed backwards through the triple portals of the Brazen Gate, thrusting with our swords to keep the mob at bay until we were all inside and could force the great doors shut. In the forecourt just within the gate, I caught sight of Psellus in a knot of officials. Dismay was written all over his face. There were *women* in this mob—and not just market women or prostitutes, but housewives decently clothed and coifed, and all of them shouting the name of Zoe and beating their breasts. To a Greek of Psellus's class, this was a deeply shocking sight. We looked at each other and the same thought occurred to both of us: where are our wives?

But we had no more time to think of that.

By now, rioting had broken out all across the city. Mobs were breaking into prisons and freeing the prisoners. Others attacked the houses of the Emperor's cronies and relatives, looting them and setting them afire. Soon we could see columns of smoke rising everywhere. One of these houses was Constantine's splendid new mansion just off the Mese. Constantine was a brave man for a eunuch, a fighter despite his poor physique and weak stomach. When the uprising started, he was at home with George and Maria and a gang of armed sailors. Somehow, they hacked their way through the crowd and got to the palace. Constantine looked grim, but his sister Maria's face—I got a glimpse of her as they passed us in the forecourt—was a mask of pure terror.

The question in all our minds now was the army and fleet. Constantine commanded them all and if he unleashed them on the city, there would be carnage. And yet it didn't happen. At every moment we expected the troops to step in and defend their Emperor, but they never did. Were their officers keeping them in barracks until they saw which way the wind was blowing? Had they ever really accepted the Emperor's uncle as their commander-in-chief?

As for Calaphates, he was cowering in his apartment. His uncle went straight there. We grounded our arms in the courtyard and waited. When Constantine returned, he saw me and motioned me to come with him and translate for Harald, who was standing nearby.

"Your men are a disgrace, you're a disgrace." his thin eunuch's voice trembled with anger. "Attack that rabble at once, Commandant. Give the order or I will do it myself."

Harald visibly flinched. He'd never been spoken to like this before. "Tangle-Hair," he turned to me. "Get your men ready, your bandon will lead the attack."

I wasn't Harald's favorite fighting captain; I just happened to be closest. It could have been any of us.

But it was me.

And at that moment I had to decide.

"No, Harald Sigurdsson," I said. "You've picked the wrong side. For Zoe!" I yelled at the top of my voice.

"Zoe!" my bandon roared back and clashed their axes on their shields. And then others picked it up. "Zoe, Zoe!" the cry echoed from a hundred throats: Varangians who despised these wretched Paphlagonians and who no longer trusted Harald.

"We're marching out. Swords sheathed," I ordered, "spears and axes reversed."

We pushed open the gates and, crying the name of 'Zoe', we streamed out into the roiling crowd. There was fear on their faces until they understood that we weren't attacking them. And then they swallowed us up, embracing us, reaching out their hands to touch us. If they'd had flowers in their hands instead of bricks and clubs, they would have pelted us with them.

What I tell now I only learned later from Psellus and others who were left inside the palace. Harald, who was in a snarling fury, demanded to be put in charge of the defense of the palace with the handful of Varangians who had stayed with him. Constantine agreed. He was willing to make a fight of it. Then, unexpectedly, Calaphates himself arrived in their midst, clutching his mother's hand.

"Damn you, Uncle, for sending Zoe away," he whined.

"Me! You gave the order, Majesty."

"Fools, both of you," said Maria. "Get the wretched woman back."

So they sent another launch to Prinkipo Island to chase the first one. Hours went by while the mob milled outside the gates, chanting Zoe's name. It was past midday when the launch returned with the Empress. She stepped ashore inside a cordon of marines. People who saw her say she looked exhausted, confused, frightened. Constantine threw a jeweled robe over her grey cassock and shoved a diadem on her head, hoping to cover the few tufts of chopped hair that were all that remained of her golden curls.

There is a circular staircase that connects the Daphne wing to the Imperial viewing stand in the hippodrome. Constantine, Calaphates, and Harald rushed her up this way, and at the same time, they ordered the stadium doors to be opened, and the crowd flowed in—a hundred thousand of them, me and my Varangians among them. Calaphates pushed Zoe forward to the railing and he and his uncle made a great show of bowing before her and kissing her hands. But there were no smiles on the sea of upturned faces below them. As long as the Paphlagonians were with her, the people knew that Zoe was not a free woman. Constantine tried to make himself heard above the jeers and catcalls, while rocks and arrows flew dangerously close. At last, they gave up and retreated back down the stairway to the palace.

Then an unexpected thing happened. From some voice in the crowd— no one ever knew whose—rose the cry, "Theodora!" And soon everyone was chanting it. "Theodora, Theodora, fetch Theodora!"

Who?

✝

It seems that Zoe had a younger sister. They had hated each other since childhood, and Zoe had forced Theodora to take the veil and retire to a convent on the Bosporus (this was back in the reign of Romanus, when Zoe had the power to do such things.) The unfortunate woman had never been seen since. Neither Calaphates nor his uncle knew of her existence. But, nun or not, Theodora was of the blood. She was technically an Empress.

Within the hour she was fetched—literally dragged against her will—from the Petrion Convent. Draped in a purple robe, she was carried bodily through the streets to the cathedral. I and my men marched in behind her. If the Varangians' duty is to defend the Throne, I decided, then our place was with her, at least for the time being. Alexius the Patriarch stood before the great golden altar to receive her. In a ringing voice he proclaimed Michael Calaphates deposed and Theodora joint Empress, together with her sister Zoe. The furious old lady received the crown while a vast concourse of people cheered her.

I approached and knelt before her. She was a tall, angular woman with a scrawny neck, an unusually small head, and a beak like a bird. Her expression was severe; she was plainly frightened, but doing her best not to show it.

"We are your Guards, Majesty. Command us."

"Where, then, is Harald the Commandant?" Alexius asked.

"In the palace defending Calaphates."

"Then he is no longer Commandant. You are. What is your name?"

I told him.

He turned to Theodora. "Empress, order it so. You will need these men."

My men hurrahed—a sound that echoed around the vast chamber—and some of them lifted me on their shoulders. At that moment, I heard Selene call my name from the back of the nave. The crowd parted to let her and Olympia through. Her face was dirty, her clothing disarrayed, but her face was shining, exultant. The women of Constantinople had just helped topple a government.

She threw her arms around me and kissed me while my men cheered and laughed.

It was a grand moment. But the battle was not over yet. Calaphates still held the palace. And Zoe had no idea that she was condemned to share her throne with the woman she had wronged.

41

A Pitiful Ending

This was a delicate moment: we now had no legitimate Emperor but *two* Empresses. To grasp the strangeness of the situation, you must understand that the cathedral, the palace, and the hippodrome, are part of one whole—side by side and linked together by passageways. Theodora and Zoe were only a few hundred yards apart but, for the moment, they inhabited different worlds, each in ignorance of the other. Add this to the fact that Harald still commanded some Varangians in the palace and had no idea that I had been named Commandant in his place by Theodora. My next step should have been to march with my men, escorting Theodora from the cathedral to the palace and take charge there.

Two things got in the way.

First, Theodora steadfastly refused to leave the cathedral while the battle was still in doubt. Second and more serious, we were unexpectedly attacked by a force of Greek soldiers under an excellent officer named Katakalon, who had just returned from Sicily, sailing into the harbor under cover of darkness. Katakalon sized up the situation and decided it was his duty to defend his Emperor. He led his men into the palace and they took up positions on the walls and roofs. Meanwhile, on our side, the good people of Constantinople were dancing in the streets and drinking themselves senseless, thinking they had won the day. Now, all at once, the balance of power had shifted in Calaphates's favor.

Selene shot me a frightened look. If we lost now, I was a dead man.

Calaphates and his uncle—not to mention Harald—would make my last few minutes on earth very unpleasant.

I ordered the gong to be sounded again and readied my men for battle. From the forecourt of the cathedral we could look up and see torches moving along the battlements and hear the shouts of the soldiers.

Leaving Selene behind, I led my bandon back to the Forum of Constantine. I had to bring some order to the mob out there and organize an attack on the palace to begin at dawn. Half a dozen men came up to me and announced themselves leaders of the revolt and willing to take my orders. None of them looked very soldierly but they would have to do.

†

CUESDAY, APRIL 20

During the night, more citizens streamed in to join us. As dawn broke over the city we started our attack, a three-pronged assault through the hippodrome, the polo field, and the Brazen Gate. I led this force because I expected to find Harald there.

That day was one of the bloodiest in the city's blood-soaked history. Katakalon's men fired volleys of arrows from the towers and windows. Our side brought ladders up to the walls and fought them hand to hand. The battle swayed back and forth all day and late into the night with citizens without armor or proper weapons flinging themselves against well-drilled spearmen. And yet, these shopkeepers and tailors and bakers and stable boys fought desperately and didn't give way. It was later said that we lost three thousand dead or wounded.

At the Brazen Gate, I commandeered a heavy wagon, we loaded it with bricks and cobblestones, and crashed it against the center portal four or five times until the hinges cracked and it fell in. Then I and my bandon poured into the domed hall that lies between the gates and the guardhouse.

We found only a few Varangians, but no Harald. "They're in the throne room," cried one of them when I applied the edge of my sword to this throat. "Harald, the Emperor, his uncle, some sailors, a few of our men, Halldor, some others—don't kill me."

I shoved him aside and raced out into the courtyard, with Gorm beside me, carrying my standard, and the rest at my heels. We burst through the Magnaura's silvered doors and found the Emperor and his retinue all huddled at the far end of that huge hall, at the foot of the throne. Calaphates and Constantine cringed behind a knot of their sailor guards. But Harald, flanked by Halldor and Bolli, came toward me with his ax in his fist.

"You little traitor," he snarled, "I should have killed you five years ago. First you were Ingigerd's dog and now you're Zoe's? What is it about you and old women, Tangle-Hair? Well, come and let me carve you meat from bone, little dog. Either that or slink away."

"Harald Sigurdsson," I answered, keeping my voice steady, "tell your men to throw down their weapons. I am the Commandant now. Take whoever wants to follow you and sail away. It's time for you to go."

"Make me!" He yelled his war cry and charged.

And might have killed me.

But Gorm thrust the long pole of our standard between his legs and tripped him as he rushed past. Harald flew forward—that great bulk—and landed head first on the stone floor. He lay there like a felled tree, senseless. I lifted my ax to strike him.

"Hold, Tangle-Hair," cried one of his Norwegians. "God forbid you slay the brother of Saint Olaf! Let him live, if it's God's will. Let us take him away."

"You are the Commandant," said another. "Don't begin by killing one of us for the sake of these Greeks."

Slowly, I lowered my ax. They were right. Harald dead would be a blot against my name and the regiment's. No Varangian had ever killed another. But then what to do with him? A wild idea flashed through my mind. Who can say where such inspirations come from?

"Gorm," I cried, "help me lift him. You others stand clear of the throne."

With me at Harald's head and Gorm at his feet, we half carried and half dragged him up the steps of the podium and dumped him on the sacred Throne of Solomon. He sprawled there, glassy eyed. There was a gasp from the onlookers, Greeks and Varangians both. Gorm shot me an astonished look. What was I thinking?

Before anyone could make a move to stop me, I darted behind the throne, through the divided curtain and down the steps, and—just as

I had seen it done—took the big wheel, the one that opens the sluice, in my hands and spun it as fast and as far as it would go. I heard the groan of machinery far below, felt the vibration of water surging beneath my feet, and saw the great piston shake itself and then, with a whoosh, shoot upward--not with stately grace but like a bolt shot from a bow, shuddering to a stop just short of the ceiling. I went back and peered through the curtain. Every face was tilted upwards. The Greeks were dumbstruck, shocked to silence by this sacrilege. My only thought had been to keep Harald out of my way until we'd secured the palace. I hadn't meant to humiliate him. But my Varangians, first a few and then more and more, began to point and laugh—because Harald was conscious now, gripping the arms of the throne with white knuckles, his eyes wide, his mouth twisted in a silent scream, twenty-five feet in the air with no way to get down and plainly scared out of his wits.

I ran back to the front and joined my men. They made way for me as though I were a sorcerer or a god, the possessor of some undreamed of, inexplicable magic. Harald must have thought so too.

"Prince," I cupped my hands and shouted up to him, "you've always wanted to sit on a throne, how does it feel?" There was more laughter from my men.

He found his voice and answered me with a string of curses. "I'll have your balls for this, Tangle-Hair! All of you, goddamn you, I'll kill you all! Let me down!" Spittle flew from his lips, he writhed on the seat, twisting this way and that, looking wildly around him.

"I'll let you down when I have your promise to leave Miklagard forever. Meanwhile, enjoy the view. Now everyone out," I ordered. We still have work to do."

It must have looked a long way down to Harald but rage and desperation gave him courage. With a cry he flung himself from the throne. I crouched ready to meet his attack. But his legs buckled and he rolled on the floor, clutching his right knee, gasping with pain.

Halldor, Bolli and Ulf ran up to help him.

"Get him out of here," I said, "and don't let me see his face again. As for the boy Emperor—" I began.

It was then I noticed that Calaphates and his uncle had slipped away in the confusion.

†

WEDNESDAY, APRIL 21

In the morning, Katakalon came out under a flag of truce to parlay with us. I had known him slightly in Sicily and knew he was a good soldier. He informed us that Calaphates and his Uncle Constantine had fled by boat, dressed in monk's clothes, to the monastery of Studion, which lies on the coast where the outer ring wall comes down to the sea. There was nothing more for his soldiers to defend. We let them march out with their standards and weapons.

I led my men into the palace, where a haggard Psellus greeted me. His first words were of Olympia. I told him she and Selene were safe in the cathedral with—guess who?—a sister of Zoe's who was now co-Empress.

"But this is a disaster," he moaned. "Zoe would rather see a stable boy share her throne than Theodora."

The city mob, which had been disciplined during the battle, went completely out of control once it was over. Neither I nor any force on earth could stop them from racing through the grounds and buildings, looting and smashing; there were just too many of them. I set my men to defend Zoe's apartments in the Daphne, as well as the Magnaura with its throne room, and the treasury, and let the rest go.

Hours later, when a semblance of order was finally restored, the Patriarch came over from the cathedral, escorting Theodora. Selene and Olympia were in the crowd that followed them. Zoe received them in the throne room and, contrary to Psellus's worst fears, she embraced her sister and they exchanged dry-lipped kisses. And so these two elderly ladies—Theodora who had lived fifteen years as a virtual prisoner in a convent, and Zoe the one who had put her there—sat stiffly side by side on the Throne of Solomon while the Patriarch smiled beatifically and we all shouted, "Many years, many years!" Though, in truth, it seemed unlikely that they had many years left between them.

While this touching ceremony was being enacted, the mob was surging along the Mese toward the monastery where Calaphates and his uncle had taken sanctuary. One of my men burst into the throne room with the news. The people would certainly tear them apart. Psellus, who, as acting Logothete, was the most senior official there, and I with him, approached the throne and asked for orders. Should we try to rescue them? Arrest them? There was a long moment of silence. Zoe said nothing. Then Theodora in a clear high voice, said "Blind them."

Psellus and I could hardly hide our astonishment. We would have expected this from Zoe, who had every reason to hate these men. But from Theodora, who had never laid eyes on them? I think she must have feared that Zoe, if left to herself, would weaken and put Calaphates back on the throne rather than allow her despised sister to rule with her. But Theodora, once there, was not going to leave. Plainly, this elderly nun was a woman to be reckoned with. Zoe gave her a long, hard look, then nodded agreement.

Psellus and I, with a detachment of my men, set off down the Mese, a distance of about a mile, to Studion. That sprawling collection of buildings on the water's edge is one of the largest and richest monasteries in all Anatolia. At its center is the church Saint John the Baptist. By the time we reached it, the mob was howling around the place, while hundreds of monks, clearly terrified, did their best to bar the doors. We pushed them aside and entered the chapel.

Calaphates and Constantine, in monk's cassocks, their heads shorn, clung to the pillars of the altar. They recognized Psellus and thought they saw a spark of sympathy in his mild young face. What they got instead was a stern lecture—Psellus at his most schoolteacherish. He actually shook his finger at them. What had Zoe ever done to them that they should have mistreated her so shamefully? What right had they to mercy?

"What could I do?" Constantine pleaded. "I knew nothing about the plot against her. The Emperor is headstrong. If I had tried to restrain him it would have cost me my life."

Psellus brushed this obvious lie aside.

Calaphates, his face streaked with tears, moaned, "I was wrong, sir, but I've paid my penalty, haven't I? Punish me no more." A bad boy begging not to be whipped. "What are these soldiers doing here? Send them away, they frighten me."

I looked to Psellus to take the lead. "We can't do it here," he said, "not in this holy place. Take them outside."

Constantine, seeing that there was no hope, came without a struggle. As for Calaphates, I had to pry his hands from the altar and carry him, screaming and blubbering out of the church. Outside, the mob jeered and mocked him. We took them a little ways back up the Mese, the crowd following behind us. Psellus cast his eye about and said, "This is far enough. We'll do it here."

There was a sidewalk vendor of what the Greeks call *souvlaki*, chunks of lamb turning on spits over a bed of coals. Psellus went over to the man. "Take the meat off one of those spits and heat the point of it."

Psellus handed the cool end of the spit to me, wrapped in a rag. "Do it," he said, "before the iron cools."

Blinding was nothing unusual to Psellus. It is what these Greeks do to enemies of the State. People say we Norsemen are cruel, barbarous and savage, and I will not deny it. But it takes a Greek to think of this. Even as mild a soul as Psellus, could order it without a qualm.

My stomach clenched. "Isn't banishment enough?"

"A blind man can never sit upon the Throne of Solomon. Do it, Odd. Harald wouldn't hesitate."

"I'm not Harald."

"You are the Commandant. You wanted the job. Did you think it would always be pleasant? Now, do it."

This was the first time I ever saw Psellus angry. I took the spit from his hand.

"Take me first," said Constantine. "Make the people stand back and you will see how bravely I bear my calamity."

"Someone tie him down," Psellus ordered, but Constantine waved him away. "If you see me flinch, you can *nail* me down." He got down on his knees and then stretched out on his back, taking care that his legs were decently covered. I plunged the spit into his eyes, first one, then the other. The flesh melted and hissed. It's a sound you never forget.

Calaphates shrieked all the louder. His screams could be heard all the way to the palace. "Mother, help me!"

I don't know which mother he was calling on, Maria or Zoe, but neither could help him now. This poor, ignorant, thoughtlessly wicked child. At the end, it was impossible not to pity him. It took four men to hold him down. The bile rose in my throat. The crowd fell silent. Some people crossed themselves. He had sat on the throne for only four months, but still he was an Emperor.

He and his uncle would live out their lives—not many years for either of them—on the charity of the Church. Years afterward, I happened to learn that Harald, boasting of his days in Miklagard, took credit for this blinding—as if anyone should want bragging rights for such an atrocity.

✝

THURSDAY, APRIL 22

Psellus paid a visit to my office in the guardhouse of the Brazen Gate to tell me that old Eustathius, the Logothete, had died during the night. "I was with him. His last words were, 'I've lived long enough to see the end of these Paphlagonians.'"

"And you're the Logothete now? Congratulations. It's a big job—embassies, espionage, the public post, the Office of Barbarians."

"I shall do my best. And you, Odd—you seem comfortably installed as Commandant. What are you working at?" He peered at the papers that covered my desk. "What is that scrawl?"

"Names written in runic," I answered. "I'm going over the enlistment rolls that Harald kept. There are men listed here who I know for a fact died in Sicily and he was still drawing their salaries from the treasury, with John's knowledge, of course

Psellus shook his head. "And Harald is—?"

"Dead, I hope. Or else licking his wounds somewhere. Halldor, Bolli and a few others have disappeared too."

"That doesn't worry you?"

"I've too much to think about at the moment."

"The vicissitudes of life," Psellus exclaimed. "You know this morning we caught Maria and George at the harbor, trying to buy passage on a merchant ship to the Black Sea. She was wearing four purple silk gowns and a sable cape—in April. And had a chest of golden plates and spoons and knives so heavy it took two men to lift it. We took it all away from her. Quite a scene—cursing, screaming, scratching. Well, what can you expect from peasants." He smiled wearily. "I hope I never see another three days like these as long as I live. Olympia talks of nothing else but how the women passed the word in church, how they gathered, marched. She was out in that mob. She could've been killed. I'm still trembling. I scolded her but she won't listen. What is happening to our women? How will we keep them at home again after this? I suppose Selene is the same?"

I smiled. "Selene has never been content to stay home."

"And now two women on the throne. How will it end?"

"We were lucky. If the army—"

"Ah, that. Cost us a fortune in bribes, you know, to keep them out of it."

"You had something to do with that?"

"I played a part," he answered modestly. "It was only Katakalon, just arrived from Sicily, whom we couldn't negotiate with. But there's more to it than that. We also made them a promise. Not one I'm happy with, but we had no choice. Perhaps you can guess."

I looked a question.

"Have you forgotten the name of George Maniakes? Their old commander? The terror of the Saracens?"

"And all this time in prison."

"No more. A free man now. And, I fear, a bitter, dangerous and unpredictable one."

42

ᏟᎻᎬ ᏢᎬᎡᏌᎷᎬᎡᎩ ᎪᏳᎪᎥᏁ

Now that the 'Paphlagonian scum' were gone, the Empress Zoe lost no time in restarting her perfumery. Once again the copper cauldrons bubbled in the big, high-ceilinged room next to her bedchamber, and the heavy aroma of attar and aloes and sandalwood seeped into every corner of the Daphne palace. The first guests whom she invited to visit her there were Selene and Olympia.

It was nearly five months since the mad escapade when they had disguised themselves as nuns and smuggled Zoe out of the palace to make a last appeal to her dying husband. What a disaster that had been, and Zoe might have resented it but instead she conceived an almost pathetic affection for these two brave young women. They were now her favorites among the court ladies, her 'daughters', as she was wont to say.

Psellus took a cynical view of this: Zoe understood where power lay. Selene was the wife of the new Commandant of the Varangians and Olympia the wife of the new Logothete. Zoe needed our loyalty, and the way to that, in her mind, was through our wives.

But Selene had a different view, and I think she was right. The sad woman, who all her life had been terrorized and imprisoned, neglected by her father, deprived of the chance for motherhood, and abused by one husband after another, had an enormous need to unburden herself now, to defend and explain herself, and—yes—to mother someone.

'Wear light and comfortable clothing,' the invitation read. It was quickly apparent why. (I recount the scene now from what Selene and Olympia told us afterward.) The two friends were brought to the door by a young eunuch. Both were both nervous. Until that day they had met the Empress only at receptions or banquets where they were among a mob of court ladies. This was the first time they would be in a room alone with her. Of course, they knew all about the notorious perfumery from their husbands, and they weren't looking forward to it. Selene whispered a silent prayer to Thrice-Great Hermes and touched the amulet that hung between her breasts under the thin fabric of her dress. She and Olympia exchanged a quick smile to give each other courage. The door opened, letting out a rush of pungent, torrid air. Selene swallowed hard.

"My dears, such a pleasure to see you," Zoe burbled, as the two women were ushered inside. She was dressed in a plain linen shift that clung damply to her rounded figure, her sleeves were rolled up to the elbows, and a scarf confined her grey-blond curls. Her face, still preternaturally smooth, was glowing. "You come at a critical moment, I shall want your advice. We're mixing a new skin lotion, my own recipe."

"Your Majesty is very kind to invite us," said Selene.

"Majesty? Oh, no, no, my dear." Zoe seized her by the hands. "After what we have been through together! We are equals here. You may call me 'ma'am'—*kyria*—as you would your own elderly aunts. You know, I'm old enough to be one, though no one would guess it." She touched her buttery cheek and smiled archly. "And when we're among ourselves we will use the familiar *esu*. Come along, now."

She led them to a vat in which some white and viscous liquid bubbled gently. A sweaty female slave clad in an apron stirred it with a long-handled paddle. Elsewhere in the room other women and men stirred other kettles, while along the farther wall still others worked at a long bench, filling and stoppering glass flasks. "Rub a little on your palms," Zoe urged. "Tell me your opinion truthfully now." Obediently, the women dipped their fingertips in, rubbed them together, sniffed.

"Lovely," Olympia exclaimed.

"I've never felt anything like it," said Selene—which was the truth because none of this stuff was to her taste. Her young skin needed no lotions, and she rarely wore scent.

For the next hour Zoe led them in turn from cauldron to seething cauldron while she recited in exquisite detail the ingredients of this and that potion. "Spikenard … myrrh …" A sudden crash of breaking glass interrupted her in mid-word. A clumsy slave had dropped a whole tray of flasks and a puddle of perfumed ooze spread over the floor in one corner of the room.

"Dolt!" Zoe shrieked, "Idiot!" She struck the woman across the face with the back of her beringged hand, leaving a red welt. "I'll have you whipped. Clean this up!" The unfortunate woman fell to her knees and began to mop with the hem of her dress, while others ran for pails and rags. Selene and Olympia exchanged tense glances while their host was distracted.

Zoe returned to them, composing her face with an effort. "You see what I have to contend with? That monster John killed all my old staff, or drove them away, and now I must begin all over again with these unskilled people. It's hard, very hard."

Suddenly Selene felt as though she were going to faint—the heat, the smell, and maybe the fact that she was newly pregnant with our third child. She tottered and grasped Olympia's hand to steady herself. "Oh," cried Zoe, full of consternation, touching her pale cheek with moist fingers, "forgive me. You ladies want a cold drink, don't you, and something to eat. I've kept us here too long. We'll go out into my little dining room."

They sat around a small table, sipping chilled white wine and eating pastry stuffed with dates and nuts. The heat and the smell followed them even here, but compared to the mixing room it was bearable. *When*, Selene wondered to herself, *did those unfortunate slaves get to rest and sip a cool drink?*

"You see why I told you to wear light clothing, my dears," said Zoe. "I always do, when I can. I hate court costume, so heavy, so confining, I'm sure you agree with me. And don't ever swaddle your children the way I was, wrapped in brocade so stiff I couldn't move. I've hated it all my life. But, of course, one can't always choose for oneself."

The two women murmured agreement. *No*, thought Selene, *this was a woman who had had very few choices in her life, and none of them good. What if she had tried to poison John, or her first husband, as rumor had it. Could you really blame her?*

"I hope your children are well?" Zoe continued amiably, pouring herself another glass of wine. "They say there's fever in the countryside, I do worry. And your husbands? Fitting well into their new positions? Both

so young, but so capable. Thank God for them. Psellus's wise counsel and Odd's martial valor. Where would we be without our Guardsmen and their brave captain, whom we had not known above a month ago?"

Did the woman not realize, Selene wondered, *that she had met Odd five years ago when he came to them posing as the ambassador of Rus? Or again, when he and Harald and the others ransacked these very apartments and arrested her servants on John's orders? Did she really not know that this was her husband? Or was it something else—the convenient amnesia of a ruler who has survived a revolution?*

"The Varangians are devoted to your dynasty, ma'am," Selene replied fervently, "and my husband will lay down his life for you."

Zoe smiled sweetly, then raised a quizzical eyebrow. "Selene, my dear, we've known Olympia's family for years, of course—very prominent in the city. But you are a mystery to me. Where do you come from? Who are your people? How did you meet your husband? I know you'll pardon my curiosity…"

This was the question she had hoped would not be asked, but there it was. *Lie now,* she told herself, *and you'll go on lying forever.* She looked at Zoe levelly. "I met my husband in a taverna where I supported my family by gambling. We come from the countryside, out on the Mese beyond the Church of the Holy Apostles. My mother was a healer, a midwife, and had some skill in reading the future. Some unkind people called her a witch. My father was a physician, a man who sought to penetrate the mysteries of the cosmos, a student of alchemy. He spent his life trying to turn base metal into gold—without success, I'm afraid."

Olympia shot her friend a panicked look. To be interested in alchemy in a theoretical way was one thing, many people were, but to actually practice it —that smacked of paganism.

Zoe's smile congealed. There was a long moment's silence.

And then Zoe leaned back and let out a full-throated laugh. "Alchemy! But it's exactly what we do here. Mixing, heating, distilling, purifying, all to turn something base into something perfect of its kind. It's a noble pursuit. It's how I worship God. I'm sure it was the same with your father."

Selene let her breath out slowly. "He was a very religious man."

"Then I am sorry not to have known him. More wine, my dear?"

They sat together for another hour, while Zoe drank glass after glass of wine and gave voice to a rambling monologue. "Let me speak to you as a mother, I feel that I am—yours especially, Selene, since you have none. We women are weak, we must use all our wiles, all our weapons. I've learned that lesson in a long and unhappy life." She dabbed at her eyes with a corner of her napkin.

And what about her sister Theodora's long and unhappy life, Selene thought, in that nunnery to which the young Zoe had condemned her? No mention of her.

"It's only faith in Christ that has sustained me through the dark times," Zoe went on. She crossed herself and her eyes turned momentarily upward. "He and I talk, you know. One day I will show you my own little Christ, he tells me things, warns me of danger by changing his color. It's the truth, you'll see. But the dark, dangerous days are over, aren't they? Now, at last, I look forward to a little happiness, to finding a true man who will love me—dare I hope for it? I'm not so old yet, am I? Still desirable? But it's lonely here at best, you know. I would rather have been some tradesman's wife, living in honest poverty, than Empress of Rome. I envy you your freedom, Selene. Gambling in the taverns—what an exciting life you've led."

Selene, in spite of herself, felt a growing sympathy for this vain, eccentric, vulnerable woman. Still, she would never be at ease in her company. She had seen that flash of rage, of cruelty. *Never forget, she warned herself, that this is a woman with the power of life and death over us all.*

"And now, my dears," said Zoe, setting down her glass and snapping her fingers for the servant, "I will let you go home to your husbands. I must take my bath and then I have other business to attend to. The Empire doesn't run itself, you know."

As they departed, she planted a motherly kiss on their foreheads and gave them each a basket filled with bottles of scent and lotion. "You'll visit me again, of course. We women have so much to talk about."

They had arrived in mid-morning and it was now it was well past noon. Outside the gate, before they mounted their carriages, the two friends embraced. They hardly knew what to think about this strange morning. Were the dark days over? For Zoe, for the Empire, for their husbands, for themselves?

43

Che General Returns

On the eleventh of May, less than two weeks after those terrible three days of revolution, Constantinople put on its gayest clothes to celebrate the founding of the city by Saint Constantine the Great. One of their most joyous festivals, it is a day of parades and street dancing, of chariot races and wild beast fights in the hippodrome, of neighbor visiting neighbor, of Emperors—or now Empresses—showering the crowd with coins. Both inside the palace and out, people seemed determined to honor the day with a gaiety that was almost desperate, to banish the past with its horrors, and sink themselves in enjoyment of the present with a collective sigh of relief.

For the occasion I organized an exhibition in the hippodrome of my Varangians going through their military exercises and dueling with ax and sword—not to the death, of course, as those old Romans used to do, but still exciting enough—and the crowd loved it. We were the heroes of the day. I stood in the Imperial box with the other luminaries of the court and drank in the cheers. At my side was Selene, beautifully gowned and coifed, and Gunnar, four years old, dressed in a scarlet tunic and cloak, standing at attention with his face drawn into a stern expression, just like a Guardsman. My heart swelled to see him. What a warrior he would be someday.

I wondered, though, who all the cheering was really for. Was this outpouring of love more for Zoe or for Theodora? Was some of it for me, who had led this same crowd in battle to retake the palace? Or was it for Maniakes, the hero of Sicily, unjustly abused by the hated Paphlagonians, and now standing among us, gaunt and grey-faced, but with his flashing black eyes undimmed by his ordeal?

Let me back up a bit. To quote Psellus, for the first time in our lives we saw the transformation of the women's quarters into an Emperor's council chamber. Zoe and her sister liked to hold court in the Golden Hall, not far from there. Neither of these old ladies was interested in riding the flying throne in the Magnaura, which Theodora complained gave her a nosebleed. Each of them sat on her own throne, but Theodora's was placed slightly behind Zoe's. Every morning save Sunday the chamber was crowded with courtiers, senators, officials high and low, and hordes of petitioners. There were lawsuits to be settled, questions of public interest, audiences with foreign ambassadors, and so forth. Officials—sometimes Psellus, sometimes another—did most of the talking, but the Empresses would occasionally ask a question or offer a comment.

Needless to say, each Empress had her faction, her throng of sycophants and favor-seekers. Zoe, of course, had grown up in the charged atmosphere of the court, heavy with intrigue, jealousy, and smooth-tongued flattery. From babyhood it was the air she breathed. To Theodora this was all absolutely new. But she was learning.

Psellus was in Zoe's faction, but I knew he was already regretting it. He fretted constantly about her recklessness with money, her lavishing of huge gifts on all and sundry. She had always been this way, except when her husbands had barred the treasury door to her. Now there was no holding her back. I found it hard to complain because I was one of those who greatly benefitted. Selene and I found ourselves rich beyond imagining. I, the poor Icelandic farm boy, who had once gazed wonderingly at a worn silver coin given to me by my brother, who got it from some merchant captain. It was a coin stamped with a man's gaunt, bearded face and inscribed with strange letters. "From far-off Miklagard," my brother had said, "wherever that is." Well, I had lost that coin years ago but never the memory of it. Now I had chests full of them. We hardly knew what to spend it all on.

But if I was rich, Harald—if he was still alive—was rich no longer. Just a few days after Constantine's blinding, one of his people confessed to knowing that a huge stash of gold, siphoned from the treasury by the Paphlagonians and Harald together, was hidden somewhere on Constantine's property. I had him dragged from his monk's cell and questioned him myself. And what a sad spectacle he was—halting, trembling, his sightless eyes bound with oozing bandages. It took little persuading to get the truth out of him. In a cistern in back of his house we found five thousand, three hundred pounds of gold. Enough to supply even Zoe's mad generosity for a very long time.

He confessed that John and he had siphoned it from the treasury over many years.

"Did anyone else know about this?" I asked him.

"Harald found out somehow. He claimed it was as much his as ours and he treated it as his own. What could we do?"

"And he spent it?"

"He helped himself from time to time. What he spent it on I don't know. Women, I suppose, like all you barbarians."

I said nothing to anyone about Harald's part in this massive theft. I only had Constantine's word for it and what was the point anyway? It would only bring more dishonor on the Guard. But news of the discovery couldn't be kept secret, and it was soon known all over the palace and then the city.

I have already mentioned Maniakes. For two years he had languished, chained to the wall in a tiny cell that stank of piss beneath the palace. Ignored, forgotten, his estates confiscated, his wife and children dispossessed. Harald and I had visited him once, you will recall, after our return from Italy. After that, I never saw him again. If Harald did, I didn't know about it. But now, by order of Zoe, he was a free man. At the very first morning levee that Zoe and Theodora presided over, he was brought into the hall. They had dressed him in decent clothes, but they hung on his frame like rags on a scarecrow. His fleshless face was disfigured with sores. He was bent at the waist after two years in a cell where he could not stand up straight, and he walked with a strange gait, lifting his feet high at each step as though he could not adjust to the absence of the heavy shackles that had weighted them down. I hardly recognized in him the man I remembered. There was dead silence in the hall as he shambled forward. The mob of perfumed and elegant courtiers shrank from him as from a plague victim. No one spoke until Theodora half rose from her throne and let out a cry of "Holy Mary, who is this poor creature?"

Zoe flashed her most beautiful smile. Indeed, there was something childish and embarrassing in the way she had arranged this 'surprise'. She addressed him in a loud, clear voice. "General, you have been shamefully abused. Know that your enemies are destroyed and now your country needs you. We pray God that your health has not been broken because it is Our wish that you lead an army to Italy with all possible dispatch, punish the rebellious Lombards and Normans, restore Imperial rule to the country, and govern it with the rank of *Catepano*."

Then she ordered an attendant to fetch the general's military cloak and his sword. She stepped down from her throne, hung the sword belt over his shoulder, and pinned the cloak with her own hands.

The courtiers, on cue, cheered long and loud, myself among them.

Maniakes blinked, almost like a man waking from a dream. He pulled his face into that scowl of authority that I remembered so well, and replied in a husky voice that he would sail within the month and wreak God's own vengeance upon the empire's foes.

Uppermost in Zoe's mind, I think, was not so much the condition of Italy but the necessity of getting Katakalon's soldiers out of the city. They had fought on the losing side in the revolt, gained nothing from it, and were growing more unruly by the day. I, thank God, would not be going. As Commandant my place was here with the Empresses. But the Varangians would send a contingent. I would have to think of who I wanted to command it.

Two weeks later, while ships and troops were still being readied, who should knock on my office door but Halldor.

I eyed him sternly. "You've been off duty without leave, you and Bolli. I can sack you for that."

There was nothing hang-dog in his manner. "In that case, Odd Thorvaldsson, we'll be on our way back to Iceland, won't we, to our families and farms." (He didn't have to add: "Which is more than *you've* got to go home to.")

"What do you want, Halldor? Make it quick, I'm busy."

"I come with a message from Harald."

"Harald! Where is he?"

"Ah, he has a small place out in the fields, a bolt hole for just such times as this. You don't need to know where. He wants to make a bargain with you."

"Harald and I have nothing to bargain about."

"He wants to go with the army to Italy. He wants a command."

"To command Varangians? You're joking. I'm saving that plum for a friend, not an enemy. Many are begging me for it. Why should I give it to Harald?"

"Because you know he can stand up to Maniakes."

"Meaning what?"

"You don't trust that Greek, do you? He's an angry man, an ambitious one."

"So is Harald."

"Precisely. So let them watch each other. Wouldn't you rather know where Harald is than have him on the loose, up to who knows what? Let Harald do what he does best, wage war. Let him recoup a little of his honor and his fortune, and then you'll see no more of him. You have his word on that. And it would be a gesture of reconciliation that the whole Guard would be glad of. Harald still has friends, you know. And his only crime was to defend his Emperor, which he was sworn to do."

"Not quite. He also stole a great deal of gold—which we have found."

"I know nothing about that, and if he did so what? Stealing's what they all do here, you know that."

"Maniakes would have to agree," I said, "and why would he? They didn't get along."

"The general needs a victory. He knows Harald's worth on the battlefield. You have no one else who even comes close."

I searched for reasons to refuse. "Zoe could forbid it."

Halldor smiled. "I'm sure you can talk the old lady around."

"Is Harald fit for service? How is his knee?"

"He's mending. Be fit as a fiddle soon."

"You and Bolli would go with him?"

"Wouldn't that please you? Bolli, as it happens, is ill. I would go."

I was silent for a long moment. In spite of myself, I could see some sense in what Halldor proposed. "Harald must ask me in person and swear an oath of loyalty," I answered finally.

"Done," Halldor replied and moved toward the door. There he paused and turned back. "How did you do it—the throne?"

"Ah," I winked at him, "let that be my secret."

Once again, dromons and transports filled Boukoleon Harbor. It wasn't only Katakalon's force that was being sent back, but all the Household Cavalry regiments and all the mercenaries as well. Anatolia was emptied of soldiers. Again Maniakes and Harald, both in splendid armor, stood on the deck of their flagship, looming over everyone else by a head. Around Maniakes stood his old Khazar bodyguard, one of them my friend, Moses the Hawk. And Harald now commanded three hundred Varangians.

He had come to see me at the barracks in St. Mamas, causing quite a stir among the men as he limped along the corridor, leaning heavily on Halldor's shoulder. He was pale and clearly in pain; not quite as mended as his friend had promised. Some Varangians turned away from him, but others came forward to greet him with sympathetic looks. A few even cheered. He ignored all alike and made straight for me, where I sat in the dining hall, finishing my dinner.

I nodded him to a chair. "You look like you need to sit."

"I'll stand."

"As you like."

"What oath do you want from me?"

I had given this a good deal of thought and talked it over with Gorm and some of the others I trusted. I'd sent word to Zoe and met with Maniakes. "That you will serve at my pleasure. That you will obey Maniakes's orders in all things. You will take only as much loot as someone of your rank is entitled to, and when the campaign is over you will depart from the Empire and never come back." It was like drawing up a contract—a thing we Icelanders are good at. I hoped I hadn't left him some loophole.

"And who shall I swear this by?"

"By whatever you hold dear."

"On the body of Saint Olaf, then."

His half-brother? Whom I always suspected him of hating? But I didn't quibble. "All right. In a loud voice then, in front of these men. (There were a dozen or so gathered round us.)

And he swore.

"You'll take the first, third and sixth banda, I told him."

"Not the fourth?" That was his old bandon, the men who had stood by him during the revolt."

"Not them."

He shrugged. "You've come far in this world, Tangle-Hair. Mind it doesn't go to your head."

"Harald, there's a word the Greeks use: *hubris*. It means the pride that goes before a fall."

"Learn that from your little friend, Psellus?"

"Maybe. And I just mention it because it's something we ought both keep in mind."

"I'll work on it. Are we finished here?"

"Report to the general tomorrow. There's lots to do. And Harald—good luck."

"A man makes his own luck," he shot back. And with that he was gone.

Psellus and I observed them now from the top of the wall.

"This is a terrible mistake." Psellus regarded me gravely. "We haven't done the diplomatic preparation, we have no allies there, and no spies. I'm sending one of my agents along incognito to keep me informed, but I have no one who speaks the Lombard tongue. And Maniakes isn't the best man for the job. How long will it be before he flogs another officer? And as for you giving Harald the command of half the Guard? Forgive me for saying so, Odd, but I think you've lost your mind."

"You worry too much, Logothete. Just pity the poor Italians. They don't know what they're in for with those two trolls competing to slaughter them."

He frowned. "If only they go no farther than that."

44

WHERE IS HARALD?

On the eleventh of June in the six thousand five hundred and fiftieth year from the Creation of the World (in other words, AD 1042), the Empress Zoe, now sixty-four years old, and beginning to show her age with a slight tremor of the head and hands, was married for the third time. Not, however, by Patriarch Alexius, since third marriages are forbidden by the Church; he assigned one of his priests to perform the rite while he discreetly looked the other way. But later that day, in the Cathedral of the Holy Wisdom, Alexius anointed Zoe's new husband, Constantine Monomachus, Emperor of the Romans, the ninth of that name. Much satisfaction, not to say relief, was felt by us all.

The feeling was strong that, after a month's rule by the two old ladies, a man's hand was needed at the helm. Theodora had no objection and Zoe was thrilled. She consulted her circle of advisors, which now included Psellus and myself, and we drew up a list of candidates. The first one begged off. The second was poisoned by his wife. The third was Monomachus, and he was good enough, or prudent enough, to accept the offer.

He was everything Zoe's girlish heart could desire: rich, good-looking, though well into middle age, charming, sophisticated and fun-loving. He had been exiled to the island of Lesbos by Michael IV, for what reason I don't know, and was living there comfortably with his mistress when the Imperial yacht came to fetch him. We Varangians formed a guard of honor to welcome him and an ecstatic crowd cheered him on his way to the palace, where his bride awaited. The wedding and the coronation were splendid affairs. The Greeks know how to do these things properly.

But if we hoped that this man would be a restraining influence on Zoe or curb her wild spending, we were much mistaken. Instead, he indulged the two Empresses in all their luxurious habits and money continued to flow out of the treasury like a river of molten gold. But this was the least of the empire's problems: a disaster was looming both for the State and for me and the people I loved most. The comet that we saw that month in the night sky above the city should have been a warning. But, between the picnics and the boating parties and the hunting parties and the theater and the races, we were all having too much fun to notice.

You might have thought that Monomachus would leave his mistress behind on Lesbos. Not so. Her name was Sclerena and, while not beautiful, she was every bit as charming and witty as he was. They had been together for years, he was devoted to her and had no intention of giving her up. He persuaded Zoe to invite her to the city and before long she had moved into the palace and was sharing his bed again. She was actually given a throne, just a little less ornate than Zoe's or Theodora's, and the title of Augusta. Surely, there has never been such a bizarre arrangement at any other court in Europe. We now had an Emperor, two Empresses, and a royal mistress, who was virtually an Empress. And the strangest thing is that they all got along so well. Whatever Zoe privately felt about it, she kept to herself. I imagine she was happy just not to be terrorized any more. That at least was my wife's opinion: Selene found the whole thing vastly amusing.

It wasn't amusing for long.

During the next three months, while we savored the high life of the Capital, George Maniakes was prosecuting the war in Italy. The general's dispatches were full of news of victories won by himself and Harald (although Harald got scant mention). Psellus's private agent confirmed this in his own dispatches but added gruesome details. Before Maniakes's arrival, the Lombards and Normans had inflicted crushing defeats on our forces and had occupied strongholds all over the South, leaving us only Messina. But Maniakes waged war against them with a ferocity that was remembered there for generations. He smashed his way back and forth across Apulia leaving a trail of smoking ruins and mutilated bodies in his wake. Men and women, monks and nuns, old and young, no one was spared. He hanged them, beheaded them, even buried them alive.

Not pretty, but effective. The general was well on his way to reconquering the whole of southern Italy and already making plans for the invasion of Sicily. If only he could have been left alone to finish the job.

But Fate would not have it so.

The charming Sclerena had a brother, Romanus Sclerus, who was the opposite of charming. He was an arrogant man, a bully, and one who never forgave a wrong. He and Maniakes owned neighboring estates in Anatolia and had been feuding for years. Maniakes had once nearly beaten him to death—as, we know, Maniakes had a bad habit of beating people he shouldn't. Sclerus now took advantage of the general's absence to pillage his estate and even, it was said, seduce his wife.

Then he took a step too far. He got his sister to ask the Emperor to recall Maniakes. The general had been recalled once before and spent the next two years in a prison cell. He was not likely to make that mistake again. Psellus and I and the other senior officials begged Monomachus not to do this. But he would deny nothing to Sclerena. In August, an officer was sent out to relieve Maniakes of his command. Some weeks later Psellus received a frantic dispatch from his agent who reported that the general had seized this man, stuffed his mouth and nose with horse dung, and tortured him to death.

And then proclaimed himself Emperor. His troops, Greek and Varangian alike, raised him on a shield and cheered until they were hoarse. He was now preparing to march on Constantinople.

I knew Maniakes well enough that I think I was the only man at court who wasn't astonished by this.

We had sent him off with almost the whole army, including all four regiments of the Household Cavalry. He commanded some twenty-thousand men, battle-hardened and victorious. We could muster only my three-hundred Varangians and some companies of light infantry from Thrace and the islands, a few thousand at most. The response of the palace to the news of Maniakes's revolt was panic. Recriminations. Blame-shifting. And some very bad decisions. Sclerus should have been arrested. Instead, he was rewarded. A note should have been sent to Maniakes offering him just about anything he wanted short of the throne itself. No note was sent. For my part, I kept wondering what Harald had to do with all this. I had sent him out to be a counterweight to Maniakes. Had I been so mistaken?

Another message from Psellus's agent came close on the heels of the last one. Maniakes had ferried his army across the Adriatic from Brindisi to Dyrrachium, first performing a human sacrifice, it was said, to calm the waves. Here Macedonian and Serbian rebels were flocking to his standard. Any day now he would set out along the Via Egnatia—the road that leads straight across northern Greece to the gates of Constantinople.

In this crisis, some competent officer should have been appointed to command us. Instead, the general's cloak was draped over the soft and scented shoulders of one Pergamenus, a eunuch of Zoe's. In vain, I pleaded with Zoe and the Emperor to make a different choice. The man was so fat and ill-conditioned that he had to be carried everywhere in a palanquin supported by eight groaning slaves. He spoke with a lisp, his hair dripped oil, he wore earrings in both ears and a jeweled collar under his quivering chins; his cheeks were, of course, as smooth as a baby's. He had never commanded an army, although he boasted that he had read all the military manuals. He came to Zoe as a wedding present from Sclerena. And this was the man they were sending out against George Maniakes, the Terror of the Lombards. He vowed he would bring that "damned rebel" back to Constantinople in chains. I was to be second in command.

I was so angry I couldn't speak. Psellus was in despair.

On the last day of August we mustered our small force. The royal family came out to see us off at the triple-arched Golden Gate in the city's towering ring wall. Here the Via Egnatia begins. I was taking all my men save a few old veterans who weren't up to the march. Gorm carried my standard. What of Harald? the men asked me. Would they have to fight their own comrades again? And what could I tell them?

Pergamenus had himself carried among the troops, gesturing to them with a fat, be-ringed hand. The cheering was half-hearted at best. We faced weeks of forced marching through some of the roughest country in Europe. Our supplies were scant, we hadn't enough mules or wagons to carry more, we would have to live off the land, and that land yielded little. With luck we would find the enemy. With luck we would defeat him. With luck we would get home before snow trapped us in the high mountain passes. Luck was everything.

Selene and the children came to see me off. We both put on brave faces for the children's sake. I kissed little Artemisia, tousled Gunnar's curly head and promised to bring him back some souvenir. He begged to come with me. "You must take care of your mother," I told him. "You are the man now."

✝

The Via Egnatia, which runs all the way from Thrace to the Adriatic, was built by those Romans of olden days with a skill that no one today can match. Following the Aegean coast as far as Thessaloniki, the going is easy. From there, the road turns inland and climbs into the mountains of Macedonia. This was territory I knew well—as did Harald—because we had been here a year before when Michael campaigned against the Bulgars.

After three weeks of marching fifteen or twenty miles a day, we were worn out, hungry and cold. Every night a few more of the mercenaries slipped away. As we neared the little town of Ostrovo, tucked away in its mountain fastness some hundred miles beyond Thessaloniki, I began to wonder if we had somehow missed the enemy altogether. We had no cavalry scouts for reconnoitering, the locals were sullen and close-mouthed and told us nothing. If we did meet Maniakes somewhere on this road, we would blunder into him without warning.

Which is exactly what happened.

There had been a crashing rainstorm the night before and after that a thick fog had filled the valley so that we did not see their campfires until morning. Except for Pergamenus, who slept in his palanquin, we had all slept out on the bare ground that night because the baggage with the tents had not kept up with us. We were soaked to the bone and had nothing for our breakfast except soggy biscuit and a little goat cheese.

When the sun was an hour high, the fog burned off and we saw, just half mile away, Maniakes's tents, his banners and standards, his wagons and his horses and men, thousands of them, stretching along the road and on the hillsides that rose above it. They were preparing for the day's march and they were as astonished to see us as we were to see them. I formed up my Varangians in a shield wall across the road, with the mercenaries, mostly archers, slingers and javelin men, behind us. We were a pitiful force, there was no disguising it.

Presently, Maniakes cantered down the road toward us on his great black charger, followed by a score of Khazar bowmen on their ponies. One of them was Moses the Hawk. I recognized his lean, scarred face at once. And he looked right at me, but gave no sign.

By this time, the day had turned unseasonably hot. Pergamenus, heaved his sweating bulk out of the palanquin and came forward to parlay. "You damned rebel," he cried. "In the name of God, I order you to surrender at once and throw yourself on the Emperor's mercy."

Maniakes let out a bark of contemptuous laughter. "They sent *you* to fight with *me*? Monomachus should have saved himself the trouble." Then he glanced around and his eye fell on me. He leaned down from his saddle and peered at my face. "Odd Thorvaldsson, is that you? By Christ, it is! Join me, man. You and your men are fine soldiers, you'll have a place of honor with me."

Don't think I wasn't tempted. This was suicide, what we were doing. And for what? To satisfy the spite of Monomachus's mistress's brother? Gorm was standing beside me, holding my standard. He put his mouth to my ear and whispered, "Maybe he's right." I'm sure all the men were thinking the same thought.

"Will Harald be happy to see me?" I replied. "Bring him here, I want to see him."

"Harald? Harald is—occupied." There was a moment's hesitation in his voice.

"Then the answer is no, General. I have my duty. Turn your men around and go back to Italy. If any word of mine can spare you the consequences of this rash act, I will do my best."

He looked almost sorrowful for a moment. "Pity," he said, "to die out here for nothing."

"Varangians don't fear death," I answered him back in a voice loud enough to be heard by my men, hoping that they would roar their assent, clash their axes against their shields.

But the ranks were ominously quiet.

Maniakes wheeled his horse around and rode back to his lines.

"If any man wants to pray," I called out, "let him do it now." Some of the men knelt quickly and crossed themselves. The few priests who had marched with us sprinkled our standards with holy water. I sent up a swift prayer to Odin to strengthen my arm.

Then, with a blare of trumpets, the Greek cavalry leveled their lances and charged us, first at a trot, then a canter, then a gallop. The ground shook under their hooves. Pergamenus, moving faster than I'd ever seen him do before, fled to the rear.

"Form the swine array," I shouted to my men, "crouch behind your shields, let the archers fire over you, strike at their horses' legs. Hold the line!"

I'd been in battles like this before and I knew that even well-trained warhorses can't be made to charge into a solid barrier of shields without shying at the last moment. It's only when the defenders break and run that the slaughter begins. Harald's Varangians worried me more. But I could not see them anywhere. Was he holding them in reserve for a final blow? Or had he lost control of them? But I had little time to think about that now.

The thrusting lances, the maces and sabers flashing up and down, the snap of bowstrings, the screams of horses and men, the ring of steel on steel, the reek of sweat, the groans and the curses. My Varangians, once engaged, fought with grim steadiness. Still the enemy drove us slowly back on our heels; they overlapped our flanks; we had nowhere to turn. If we broke, it would be all over for us. A horseman trampled Gorm, who stood beside me. I hooked the man out of his saddle with my axe and drove the spiked butt into his face. Maniakes was fighting in the front rank, flanked by his Khazars, striking left and right with his mace, shouting his war cry. He came straight for me. He *wanted* to kill me—I saw it in his eyes. He brought his mace down on my shield, splitting it in two, a second blow landed on my shoulder, knocking me to the ground. He lifted his arm to strike a third blow that would crush my skull. *Here it ends*, I thought, *death in a desolate place far from home—a viking's death.*

My life was saved by Ingimund, a huge young Swede, one of my new recruits, who stepped over me, snatched up the broken half of a lance and thrust it up, catching Maniakes in the chest. The point pierced his heart. He toppled backward and crashed to the ground like a great tree falling. Moses, who was right behind him, leapt from his mount and threw himself on his body. An instant later, another Khazar sliced off Ingimund's head with a sweep of his saber. But the lancer who carried Maniakes's pennant wheeled and galloped away, crying that the Emperor was dead and then the others turned their horses around and followed him by tens, and then by hundreds. Our side let out a cheer and began to chase them. I swung myself up onto a riderless horse, got in front of my men and did my best to turn them back, shouting at them to let the Greeks withdraw. With an effort, I got them back under control. Gorm untangled himself from a heap of bodies and hoisted our standard again.

I rode back through our ranks, past heaps of dead and groaning wounded, to where Maniakes lay. Moses crouched beside his body, bleeding heavily from a wound in his right arm. He looked up at me with pain in his eyes. Not physical pain—he never showed that— but the pain of a faithful guard dog that has lost its master.

I told two of my men to carry him to the rear and bind his wound. "Take good care of him, he's a friend."

And now here came Pergamenus, sweating and wheezing. "Damn you, why did you halt the pursuit?" he snarled at me. "Treachery, I call that."

"Call it what you like. They still outnumber us five to one, there's no profit in driving them to the wall. And I want very much to talk to Harald."

The eunuch came closer and touched Maniakes's corpse with the toe of his silk shoe. "Damned rebel. Cut off his head, Commandant."

What a pointless death this was, I thought. *Maniakes had his faults, God knows, but he was driven to this by people who weren't fit to wipe his shoes.* "Cut it off yourself," I said, and turned away.

When I found Moses later, our surgeon was binding up the stump of his right arm above the elbow. "Had to take it off, sir, it was hanging by a flap of skin. Cauterized it. Should be all right. I offered him opium, he would only take a little. Here, give him more if he wants it." He handed me the flask, left us and moved on to other casualties.

I squatted down beside Moses. "This is an unhappy day, my friend. I would rather your general had lived."

He held up his hand to silence me. "It was his life or yours. He wanted you dead, not just beaten."

"But why?"

"You're too dangerous to their plan. Listen, Tangle-Hair, I have much to tell you. Harald and Halldor, with Ulf and five or six others left the army a week ago, in disguise, on horseback, heading back to Constantinople. They must have slipped past you on the road at night."

"For what reason?"

"Treachery. I was outside the general's tent on the night they made their plan, Halldor talking pretty good Greek—I didn't know he could. I heard everything. The general knew he couldn't take Constantinople by storm. It's never been done, he said, unless someone inside opened a gate. Harald volunteered to do it. Said he still had plenty of friends in the Guard. Said he would kill you if you got in the way. They never even thought you would come after us. Harald and his men would hide out in a little farmhouse he has in the fields on the north bank of the Lycus about three-quarters of a mile inside the Fifth Military Gate. He drew a map for the general, you'll find it in his tent. When the general got close he would send a man to alert them. And then—"

"And then Harald would be Commandant again under Emperor George Maniakes." *Harald and Maniakes*, I thought bitterly. *But didn't they hate each other? That was the reason for sending him. Harald swore an oath to me on the body of Saint Olaf and I believed him. What a simpleton I am!*

A shudder went through Moses's body. I gave him the flask of wine and opium and this time he took a long drink. "Maybe it doesn't matter now," he said when he could speak again, "we aren't marching on the city."

"But Harald doesn't know that yet. I'm sure he believes Maniakes has defeated our little force—he very nearly did. But when he learns otherwise, he'll steal everything he can and escape to Gardariki. If I let him get away from me this time, I will hang myself for shame."

Moses's eyelids fluttered and his head sank on his breast. I covered him with my cloak and ordered him carried to a tent. I was needed elsewhere now. I went among my wounded—there were dozens of them—calling each man by his name and praising him. As usual, we Varangians preferred to patch each other up, using the methods we'd learned from our mothers, rather than trust a Greek doctor. My own wounds—my injured shoulder where Maniakes had struck me and assorted cuts and bruises—could wait until later.

The most pressing question was what to do with Maniakes's army. Pergamenus was for executing every one of the senior officers. I put a stop to that. In the hour that followed I went to their camp and settled things. The Varangians all crowded round me and swore they'd never taken an oath to Maniakes or, if they had, it was Harald who made them. And when they saw my dragon standard floating above our ranks, they refused to attack us, though Maniakes threatened to flog them. And I took them at their word. What else could I do? I gave orders that the army was to elect a new commander and march back to Italy without delay. There was still a war to fight. I chose only one cavalry regiment, the elite Scholae, to return to Constantinople with us. Pergamenus swore and blustered but I ignored him.

Later that night, I went back to look in on Moses. Too late. Some of his Khazars were gathered round him, chanting words in their language and tearing their clothing, which is a thing the Jews do when someone dies. "What is an archer without his arm?" he had said, and turned his face away and died.

Early the next morning, Gorm and I with six other Guardsmen and a captain in the Scholae (a man known to Harald), all of us mounted and leading pack mules, set out at a fast pace for Constantinople.

45

ÐREAM NO MORE

My men and I crouched under the shadow of the wall. The night was quiet, save for the whisper of the Lycus flowing sluggishly past us. A crescent-moon hung low in the sky, half-hidden by cloud. A mile to the east, the domes and towers of the city were a black silhouette. I peered into the dark, hardly breathing, gripping my sword. It would be soon now. Soon. And—yes—there it was, the glimmer of a lantern coming toward us at a walking pace; the soft chink of armor. Harald walking into the trap I had laid for him.

Two weeks had passed since we set out from Ostrovo. We entered Constantinople dressed as ordinary travelers, our weapons and armor covered up and bundled onto the backs of the pack mules. We followed the Mese through the wide swath of farmland, dotted with barns and houses, that stretches between the ring wall and the city proper until we came to my old country house. We didn't risk going into the city, I dared not even send a message to Selene. We could not take any risks that might alert Harald that we were nearby. Of course, we were noticed by my curious neighbors, but I handed out purses of silver to buy their silence for a day and a night. That was all the time I needed.

According to Moses, Harald and his men were hiding in his little farmhouse near the Fifth Military Gate, where the stream of the Lycus runs under the ring wall and meanders toward the city.

The land fortifications of Constantinople are massive and impregnable.

A line of double walls thirty feet high and fronted by a deep moat that runs for three and a half miles from the Golden Horn to the Propontis, making a virtual island of the city. The walls are punctuated by enormous square towers and entered through a dozen gates. Some of these gates are splendid constructions of marble and gilded iron, others are smaller and merely utilitarian. The Fifth Military Gate was one of these. It was the weakest spot in the wall because at that point the land dips into a valley and the moat drains into the river. The gate does not lead to any public thoroughfare and there are no monasteries in the neighborhood. Harald had chosen it carefully.

That afternoon I had sent my Greek cavalry officer to Harald's farmhouse with a message purporting to be from Maniakes. I'd written it in camp after the battle and sealed it with his own seal. The general (it said) was nearing the city with a flying column of cavalry. Harald and his men were to go to the gate at moonrise tonight, overpower the garrison—manned only by a few ill-paid mercenaries—and open the inner and outer doors. Then Harald would show a lantern from the top of the wall and Maniakes would charge in at the head of eight-hundred lancers, trumpets blowing, banners flying. With the city stripped of soldiers, he could seize the palace with ease.

While the officer was delivering this message to Harald, I went to the gate, just at dusk when the guards were bolting the doors, identified myself, and warned them to be ready. All I needed them to do was hold the gate, we would do the rest.

When Harald and his men were almost close enough to touch, we leapt at them out of the dark, bellowing all around them to make ourselves sound more numerous than we were. "Maniakes is dead!" I shouted, "throw down your weapons. You're under arrest." Gorm and I together tackled Harald, threw him down on the ground and bound his arms and legs with ropes we had brought.

He thrashed and bared his teeth. "Kill me then, Tangle-Hair. You wasted your last chance. But you haven't got the guts, have you, you coward."

"Cut your throat now? That's too easy a death, Harald. When the Greeks finish with you, you'll wish I had killed you." I drove the pommel of my sword into his teeth and then hauled him to his feet.

Halldor put up a fight but we overpowered him. The others

surrendered meekly. When the fighting was safely over—and it was over in a moment—the garrison soldiers emerged from their blockhouse and offered to help us guard our prisoners. I made the mistake of letting them. And it was then that Ulf Ospaksson kneed one of them in the stomach, wrenched free and dashed away into the night. *We'll catch him later*, I remember thinking.

Ten days later, Pergamenus and the army returned, marching in triumph through the Golden Gate. The whole city poured out to cheer them. Maniakes's head preceded them on the point of a lance. Six of his officers were tied backwards on the rumps of asses with their heads shaved and their faces smeared with dung. Monomachus rode out to meet the procession dressed in full regalia and mounted on a white horse, as though this were *his* victory instead of the product of his weakness. Sclerena, of course, was there with her brother Sclerus, whose foolish spite had nearly brought down the dynasty. After this, the celebrations went on for days with pageants and parades and public banquets and basketfuls of coins showered on the crowd—all paid for out of our dwindling treasury. Pergamenus was rewarded with Maniakes's Anatolian estates. I was honored with the ceremonial sword of a *manglabites* and the rank of *protospatharios*—the same rank that had been given to Harald once.

Harald.

What to do with him? We argued over it in the Emperor's council chamber. He and his men were now prisoners in the underground cells beneath the Baths of Zeuxippos (the same in which he had once tortured Zoe's servants). Would we let them rot there? No one wanted to charge them with sedition. We could not afford to admit publicly that Varangians, for the first time in their history, had joined an insurrection against an Emperor. But we could, at least, charge Harald with theft: all the purloined gold that had been discovered in the well behind Constantine's house. If Harald hadn't actually stolen it, he had spent it freely. Constantine could be dragged out of his monastic prison to give evidence against him. So that was decided. But how to punish him?

"Blind him!" cried Zoe, stabbing the air with a shaking finger. "Cut off his ears and nose and send him to a monastery." Poor, put-upon Zoe. Years of bitterness were finding their voice at last. Pergamenus and Sclerena agreed with her and so did Theodora, who was acting less like a nun every day.

"And what is your opinion, Commandant?" the Emperor asked me.

I'd been brooding over this for days, of course. Harald mutilated and humiliated? What a tempting thought. But the shame it would bring on the Guard—no, I had a responsibility to protect their honor. "Better a quick and quiet death in his cell," I said finally. "Halldor too. Release the rest and dismiss them from the Guard."

But Psellus, who as Logothete cared most about foreign affairs, reminded the Emperor that Harald was a royal prince of Norway, and did we want to bring those savage people down on us? Didn't we have enough enemies without that?

"Norway's far away," I said, "and King Magnus has no love for Harald."

But Psellus insisted, "Harald has connections with the Rus, too, and God knows those people have done us great damage in the past. No, it's too dangerous."

"More dangerous than leaving him in prison? To do nothing is cowardice."

"Tangle-Hair, to do nothing is sometimes the better course," he replied sharply.

Psellus and I rarely disagreed but we were both angry now.

"Enough," cried Monomachus, holding up his hands. "I do believe it's time for lunch. We'll take this up again another day." Argument always upset his digestion.

But the weeks went by and that day never seemed to come.

✝

One night around this time I awoke from a restless sleep. I rose from bed, pulled a fleece around my shoulders, shuffled into my shoes, and went out onto the terrace. We lived now in a handsome two-storied mansion on the Horn, near the Gate of Saint John. It had once been Harald's. I leaned on the balustrade and looked out across the water, dappled with moonlight. Beneath me, the city slept. This city of burnished gold and rotting filth, of beauty and cruelty, of piety and cunning. The city guarded by God, the Greeks liked to say. No. Guarded by *me*, with *my* life.

Selene came up quietly and stood beside me; she put her arm through mine. "You were talking in your sleep."

"Saying anything I shouldn't have?" I tried to smile.

"In your language. What were you dreaming?"

"Something to do with my mother, I think. Doesn't matter." Jorunn Ship-Breast. It was her face I had seen, tear-stained, half-hidden by her streaming hair, leaning over me, the night she sent my brother and me to find our sister's killer. I had woken up with my heart pounding. "It's gone now, whatever it was."

I felt Selene stiffen. "Your mother is your native land, that's what the dream books say. You do want to go back, don't you?"

"Selene, hush." I put my arm around her waist and held her close. "This is my home. There's nothing for me back there. That's all past."

"Dearest, we think we leave our past behind but sometimes it reaches out and pulls us back when we least expect it."

"Not me."

"Then what did it mean, your dream?"

"No idea. I don't believe in dreams or sneezes."

She gave a little laugh. "You're a bad liar," she said. "Come back to bed now. Make love to me. And dream no more."

46

YELISAVETA'S TALE

SPRING, A. D. 1043

Yelisaveta Yaroslavna kicks her stallion to a gallop, splashes across a stream and through a stand of birches just coming into leaf, her long yellow hair streaming out behind her, her hawk riding on her fist, the greyhounds racing beside her. Ahead of her is her dacha, a neat little house of painted shingles and pointed eaves, her own house, where she never has to lay eyes on Ingigerd, her mother. Behind her rides her brother Vladimir and the others of their party. It has been a good day, her first hunt since the snows melted; she is bringing back ermine, weasel, hare, a baby fox.

Inside the garden gate she leaps from her lathered mount, tosses the reins to a groom, and runs into the house. With one motion, she flings off her cape and takes a proffered goblet of hot wine from Ala, her dwarf.

"Mistress, you have visitors," Ala says. "Two foreigners came this morning, Varangians they said. They wanted a bath, I sent them to the sauna."

"Then fetch them out." She slaps the foolish girl on the cheek.

Varangians! She feels her heart beating. Can it be? At last?

She tosses down another draught of the wine, trying to calm herself. Meanwhile, her brother has slipped in through the door. Vladimir, at twenty, is five years younger than she. He is the only one in the family she loves.

"Volodya, it's him!"

But it isn't him, after all.

Two blond-bearded strangers appear in the doorway, shepherded by Ala, their faces red and hair damp from the sauna. Bolli Bollason and Ulf Ospaksson; they introduce themselves, speaking in Norse, a language she has hardly spoken since the day Harald fled from Novgorod, leaving her behind, a heart-broken girl of fifteen. She cannot hide her fear.

"Harald Sigurdsson? He isn't ..?" Her throat is tight.

"He isn't dead, Princess," says the one called Bolli. "But he soon may be, or he may be blinded, or castrated. He is a prisoner these eight months. Sometimes he gets a message out to us—"

"So long!"

"We couldn't come sooner. Storms at sea, your Russian winter. Take us to your father now. Only with his help is there a hope of rescuing Harald."

Yaroslav the Wise, Grand Prince of Kievan Rus, is in his study, as usual, hunched over a book, a fur cap on his balding head and a rug over his knees against the cold. He is called 'The Wise' because he owns dozens of books in both Slavonic and Greek, and has even written a book of laws for his turbulent nation. But as a husband and a father? Perhaps not so wise. He looks up, blinking his watery eyes, as his children and two strangers enter.

"Young Harald in prison? But how can it be?" His hands flutter, he touches his white beard.

Bolli and Ulf, both speaking at once, pour out their well-rehearsed story. How the noble Harald was accused—unjustly—of rebelling against the Emperor, betrayed by his best friend, Odd Thorvaldsson, who schemed to get the post of Commandant for himself. At the mention of that name, Yelisaveta and Vladimir exchange a swift look. That youth with the shaggy black hair and glib tongue, Harald's skald, clever at languages. A pagan, and didn't care who knew it.

And their mother's lover.

"Dear God," cries Yaroslav. "Of course, we must rescue him ... my daughter ... and he ... but how ..?" As the old man struggles with his words, there is the sound of a hacking cough from the doorway. Ingigerd, his wife, stands there, steadying herself with a hand on the jamb.

Yaroslav winces. "Yes, well, come in, my dear, we've just had some terrible—"

She takes them all in with a cold stare. The woman is more than fifty years old, the mother of ten children; she is bone thin, her skin like paper, and she has a sickness in her lungs. How much longer can she live? Only willpower keeps her going. Willpower and rage. She already knows what news these Varangians bring. She has a spy in her daughter's house.

"Harald Sigurdsson in prison? Let his great carcass rot there. We haven't heard from him in so long I dared hope he was dead." A coughing fit overcomes her and she sinks onto a chair.

"*Why* must you hate him so, Mother?" Yelisaveta screams at her, making white-knuckled fists of her hands. "He came to us just a boy, seeking refuge with us, but you treated him like an enemy from the first day."

"You know why," Ingigerd hisses.

Yes, they all know why. All, that is, except innocent Yaroslav. As long as Harald lives, Magnus Olafsson, the young King of Norway, will never be safe on his throne. Ingigerd will do anything to protect Magnus, whose father she loved.

"I am nearly an old woman already, Mother. If I cannot marry Harald I will die, unloved, a virgin. Is that what you want for me?"

"You a virgin? Don't tell me you haven't had lovers, you little slut."

"No, Mother, I have not, not like—"

A warning look from her brother stops her before she can say, *Not like you and King Olaf, you and Odd Tangle-Hair.*

"Please Inge," Yaroslav raises his hands to heaven, "in Christ's Name, or course we must do what we can for Harald in return for all the priceless gifts he's sent us, and for the girl's sake, or else see her gloomy face here forever. And yet—and yet I don't know what."

But Ulf speaks up now. He and Bolli have a plan to free Harald and their friend Halldor from prison, but it can only work if there is a diversion, and a friendly ship for them to escape to. And as the Varangians talk, young Vladimir's eyes catch fire.

"Yes, Father, do it! And not one ship but a hundred ships, five hundred. We have them, and we have the men, eager to plunder these Greeks. We will do more than rescue Harald, we will avenge his suffering." Vladimir is captain of the druzhina, the elite warriors of the Rus army. "My druzhiniks grow fat and lazy. And it has been a hundred years since your grandfather Igor laid siege to Constantinople—"

"And what a disaster that was," Yaroslav wails. "Those devilish fire-breathing machines. Who can stand against them?"

"But his time *I* will be in command."

"And I will be with you on the deck to receive my bridegroom," cries Yelisaveta, embracing her brother and kissing his cheeks.

"Yes, all right, yes, my son." Even in Yaroslav's old breast there still beats a warrior's heart, though faintly. He pulls down a dusty volume from his shelf, opens it to a map of Constantinople.

And while they plan, Ingigerd, coughing and clutching her chest, staggers from the room.

47

SAGA'S END
[*Odd resumes his narrative*]

The booming note of the cathedral's great bronze gong, invaded my dreams with confused images of swirling robes and flickering candles. Suddenly, I sat bolt upright.

Today wasn't Sunday. This was not the call to prayer; it was an alarm.

I threw off my covers and groped for my clothes in the half-light of dawn. Selene snored and rolled on her side. I took my sword from its peg on the wall and ran downstairs to the foyer. Someone was pounding on my front door. I opened it and Gorm rushed in, almost knocking me off my feet. More of my men milled outside.

"Ships," Gorm panted, "hundreds of them anchored offshore."

"Whose ships?"

"We don't know. Best wear your armor."

Upstairs, while I struggled into my mail coat, Selene and the children watched me with big eyes.

"What is it, Odd?"

"No idea."

"I'll come with you."

"No, you stay here. Keep the children indoors. I'll send word back when I know what's happening."

Outside, the streets were already filling with frightened people. We pushed our way through them to the palace. There panic reigned: clerks and servants, women and eunuchs, their voices shrill with fear, rushed this way and that like a terrified flock of gorgeous birds. Gorm and I mounted to the upper gallery of the Daphne, where we found the Emperor, still in his nightshirt and slippers with a cloak thrown round his shoulders. Psellus and the other senior officials were with him, all of them gazing down upon the stupefying sight. Boukoleon Harbor and the sea beyond for as far as you could see were filled with dragon-headed long ships, their sails furled, oars at rest.

"How in Christ's name..?" Monomachus demanded.

No one could answer him. How had this alien fleet rowed down the Bosporus, right under our noses in the dark of night without making a sound? Incredible. Yet here they were.

"Thank God for the chain," murmured Psellus, meaning the chain of massive iron links supported on buoys, that was stretched across the mouth of the Horn every night. "But for it, we'd be surrounded."

"Have they sent a herald?" I asked. "Do we know who they are, what they want?"

"Obvious what they want, Commandant. We're under attack." This was General Theodorocanus who spoke, turning to me. A tough and capable man, he had replaced Maniakes in Italy and had only recently returned to take command of the home forces.

Now, as we watched, one of the long ships rowed in close, within hailing distance of the shore; a warrior standing in the bow shouted to us but we were too far away to make out what he said. We ran down to the quayside. The warrior cupped his hands around his mouth and shouted again and now there was no mistaking his words: they were Slavonic.

"Greeks! Prince Vladimir Yaroslavich greets you. You are rich, you Greeks, and you are all cowards, hiding behind your walls like women. I come to demand a ransom from you—a thousand gold *solidi* for every one of my ships, five hundred and twenty sail. Pay me and I will spare your fine city. If not, I will burn it to the ground. We are the Rus. No one can stand against us. You have until tomorrow morning to bring the gold." His ship backed water and swung around.

Vladimir! I remembered him as a handsome youth, whose mother I had bedded back in Novgorod. He knew I had dishonored him and he hated me for it. I wondered if he recognized me now: it would be the worse for us if he did. I translated his words for the Emperor.

"A thousand gold pieces for each ship," Monomachus bleated. "There isn't so much coin in the city. If we melted down the statues, the throne..?"

But General Theodoracanus gripped his shoulder and shook him roughly. "Courage, Majesty. We will pay them nothing. We will fight." There was a moment of shocked silence. To handle an Emperor like that, even to touch him, was almost sacrilege.

"Yes, courage," Monomachus repeated with a quaver in his voice. "Yes, yes—fight."

The general released him and turned again to me. "Commandant, order one bandon of your Varangians to stay with his majesty, station the rest of your men along the sea wall. I'll bring up reinforcements as soon as I can. I'm putting you in charge here."

The sea wall runs along the Propontis for a mile and a half from the mouth of the Golden Horn to the monastery of Studion. It is only a single line of fortification and not as high or strongly built as the land walls. The city's garrison was under strength, as usual. Even if we sent every soldier to the wall, we would be stretched too thin. I sent a runner to the Varangian barracks and at once my men poured out, with shouts and war cries, racing down the streets to the harbor. I didn't doubt their courage, but there weren't enough of us.

The next hours were filled with frantic activity. The city was in a turmoil. Frightened people, carrying whatever belongings they could, massed at the gates, fighting to get out, while at the same time others were trying to bring wagonloads of provisions in, in case we were besieged. Meanwhile, Patriarch Alexius and his clergy processed along the wall, chanting, swinging censers, and carrying the *Hodegetria* on high—the icon of the Virgin painted by Saint Luke's own hand, the talisman that had always preserved the city in times of peril. More to the point, Theodoracanus and his officers worked desperately to put together a squadron. Many of our ships were unseaworthy, others were scattered in faraway stations. We had only a few vessels that were fit to sail and armed with fire siphons.

Evening drew on. I paced the sea wall, checking on my men, and then helped to bring catapults and missiles from the arsenal and hoist them onto the battlements. And all that time—I confess it—I spared hardly a moment to think of my wife and children. As night fell and it seemed that the Rus would make no move, Theodorocanus told me to go home and snatch a few hours' sleep.

The front door was ajar. The door slave must have forgotten to close and lock it. I would punish him for his carelessness, I remember thinking. I climbed wearily up the stairs to the bedroom, calling Selene's name.

The blow to my head was so hard that I blacked out. When I came to my senses, I was on my back. A face hung over me—a haggard face, the blond beard long and matted with filth, the eyes bright with hate. Harald! And behind him Halldor, equally dirty and unkempt, and at their side Ulf and Bolli in Varangian uniforms.

"I couldn't leave without saying goodbye," Harald snarled through the tangle of his beard. "It's for me the Rus have come. While you and the Greeks were distracted, Bolli and Ulf came to the prison and told the guards that you'd ordered them to go to the harbor. It took only a minute to pry open the bars. Outside they had cloaks and swords ready for us—and here we are."

So this was why the Rus had held off their attack. The ransom demand was only a trick. Oh, they'd take any plunder they could scoop up, but that wasn't why they were here: they were here for Harald.

"You won't get away."

"I think we will." Harald grabbed me by the hair and pulled me upright. "Look around you, Tangle-Hair. See my vengeance."

I groaned. Two of my servants sprawled dead by the doorway. Selene lay writhing and twisting on the bed, bound and gagged. And Gunnar— my son—lay crumpled in the corner in a pool of blood.

"Brave lad," said Harald, glancing at him. "Came at me with his little knife. And your woman fought hard too, for such a scrawny thing, it took all three of us to hold her down. I'm taking her with me. If anyone tries to stop us, I'll kill her. If she behaves herself, I'll sell her in Kiev. Otherwise…"

I spat at him. He hit me in the face, breaking my nose. The blood ran down my chest.

"Harald, hurry up for God's sake," Halldor urged.

"And now, Tangle-Hair, you are going to the deepest pit of Hel, where Black Odin reigns." With one hand he dragged me to my feet, with the other he plunged his sword into my breast—once, twice, splitting apart the steel rings of my shirt—a searing pain, I couldn't breathe. He drew out his blade and a spurt of frothy blood followed it. I sank to my knees. "You came to Miklagard to cut off my head, Tangle-Hair, remember? To send it back to sweet Ingigerd. Now I will cut off yours and drop it at her feet." He drew back his arm, lifted his sword high.

I raised my eyes to his, expecting the stroke. "What do you want from me, Harald?"

"Your life, you black-hearted liar. You were *never* my friend."

"I could have killed you—twice."

"Then more fool you."

"Let my wife go, you bastard, she's done nothing to you."

"She's our safe passage out of here."

He slashed at my neck just as I lurched forward, as though someone—something—had pushed me from behind. The blade landed across my shoulders, twisting in his hand so that it struck only a glancing blow. Was it Odin who saved me? Or my father's ghost? Or only the Norns, who did not want my death to come so soon? I cried out in pain and fell on my side. Harald reached down to drag me to my knees again.

"Harald, for Christ's sake leave him, he's a dead man already," Bolli shouted from the window. "Varangians are running this way, we'll never make it out."

Harald hesitated. I saw his face working with hate. Then he sheathed his sword, grabbed my wife and threw her over his shoulder like a sack of meal. The last thing I saw was Selene's streaming hair, her face white as bone, and her eyes big with fear. Pleading. They haunt me still.

They ran out onto the terrace and down the steps to the water's edge. I dragged myself after them, leaving a smear of blood on the floor tiles. Somehow, I pulled myself up on the balustrade and watched them climb into a waiting skiff and shove off. In a moment they were enveloped in darkness. But I heard the sound of their hull scraping over the chain, that enormous chain that had defied invaders for centuries. To anyone but Harald it would have been an impossible feat; I don't how he did it.

Then black night covered my eyes.

The next thing I knew, Gorm was bending over me and the room was filled with my men. They had come to tell me that Harald had escaped. One of them knelt beside Gunnar. "The boy's breathing," he said. Another was holding my screaming daughter to me. "We found her and the nurse under the bed in the other room. She half-smothered the child to keep her quiet."

"Gorm, bind my wounds," I whispered, "help me up."

"Lie there, you've lost—"

"Help me."

They stripped off my armor and tunic, stuffed wine-soaked rags in my wounds, and carried me on a litter down to the harbor just as dawn was breaking.

Theodorocanus led our small fleet out to battle the Rus, driving straight for Vladimir's flagship. I drifted in and out of consciousness and remember only flashes of what happened next. The Greeks will tell you that the Virgin saved us, true to the promise of her holy icon. I can only say that after a brief fight, in which we did the Rus some damage with our siphons, a sudden storm blew up from the sea. Psellus said later that he had never seen a storm move so fast or blow so hard. Our ships retreated into the shelter of the harbor but the Rus were caught in the open, swamped and scattered all up and down the coast and smashed on the rocks. Our side cheered, raised their hands to heaven, and thanked God. But I could only think, *She is out there somewhere.*

In the days that followed, thousands of dead Rus washed ashore, thousands more were taken alive and blinded. In fact, very few escaped back to Gardariki. From my bed, I ordered my men to inspect every corpse and captive: none was Harald, Halldor, Bolli or Ulf. None was Vladimir. None was Selene.

The Emperor ordered a week of thanksgiving, with parades and prayers and races in the hippodrome. The populace went mad with joy.

But there was no joy for me.

For weeks after that I hung between life and death. The Emperor moved me and the children to a suite in the palace where his personal physician could tend my wounds and Gunnar's. Psellus and his wife came to see me every day, as did Zoe and Theodora. Zoe, grieving like a Greek mother over a dead daughter, sobbed and tore at her hair. She really had come to love Selene like the daughter she never had. Psellus wrung his hands and apologized again and again for being the one who argued against executing Harald. I forgave him.

It was myself I could not forgive. If only I had given a thought to my family that day. If only I had killed Harald when I had the chance. The feeling of guilt that I thought I had buried forever, from all those years ago when I blamed myself for the death of my mother and brother, returned a hundred fold to torment me now.

When, days later, I was able to stand and walk a little, I spent hours at my son's bedside, stroking his forehead, speaking softly to him. Harald had hacked off his right hand. He lay in his bed, not speaking, seeming not to know me. It broke my heart. He would never be a warrior now, never wear the proud livery of a Varangian.

Day and night, as the weeks went by, I thought of Selene: Where was she? Had Harald taken her back to Kiev or had he just thrown her overboard? Was she alive? Was she a slave? Psellus put every man in the Office of Barbarians at my disposal and every ambassador, every agent was queried. None of them knew anything except that Harald had returned to Kiev along with Vladimir and the remnant of the Rus fleet. Weeks became months, months during which I hardly slept or ate, but only dragged myself restlessly about the room, and drank myself into oblivion at night to snatch a little sleep.

At last, when I could walk and ride again, although still in pain, I made up my mind to go searching for her. Psellus pleaded with me to stay, the Emperor and Zoe too, but I would not listen. There was no peace for me there.

They all came down to the quay one morning to see me off on a Black Sea merchantman bound for Cherson. Gorm asked to come with me. But no. Instead, I appointed him captain of my old bandon. I would have recommended him to be Commandant but he begged off, saying it was too grand a post for him and besides he was thinking he might go home to Sweden soon anyway.

Psellus and Olympia took charge of my children—Artemisia seemed all right and played happily with Psellus's daughter. But little Gunnar, pale and sickly from loss of blood, still would not speak. He stared silently out of vacant eyes. Finally, I closed up our house and gave Selene's clothes and jewelry to Olympia for safekeeping. I kept only a small portrait of her painted on an enamel plaque. The artist captured her beauty and her intelligence: the big, serious eyes, the half-smile on her lips. I took that with me. It is all of her that I still possess.

I went first to Kiev. By the time I got there, Harald had married Yelisaveta and taken her back to Norway. Young Vladimir refused to see me. Ingigerd gave me a brief interview and treated me with a mixture of pity and contempt. But she told me that Harald had sold my wife to an Arab trader in the town, just as he'd threatened to do. Where she was now, Ingigerd neither knew nor cared.

After that, I wandered from city to city, following the slave caravans—Cairo, Baghdad, Damascus, Isfahan, Bokhara, and other places I cannot even name—until my money was gone and my clothes turned to rags. I froze in winter, burned in summer, was robbed more than once and left for dead. And always and everywhere I thought I glimpsed my beloved in the crowded streets, or standing naked and chained on a slave block. I approached women, convinced that they were she, and got many a beating for it. I consulted seers and fortunetellers, too, who sent me off on fruitless chases.

And as I traveled, despair, like a black tide, rose up and enveloped me, and I sank by degrees into dumb melancholy; the melancholy—the madness—that is in our blood, the same melancholy that had sickened my father in his last years when he would sit in his chair by the hour, staring into the fire, as silent and solitary as a stump, only his hands moving as he carved the runes. For the first time, I understood something of his pain.

I never went back to Miklagard. What life was there for me now in that city of evil memories? Psellus would provide for my children better than I could. And I never pursued Harald to Norway. What chance did I, still crippled from the wound he dealt me, stand against him, a king, surrounded by his housecarles? And anyway I had lost the heart for fighting. Harald had bested me, he was the better man. Eventually, I heard a rumor that he had invaded England—the world was never big enough for him—and died fighting there. And what did I feel? Anything? By that time, it almost didn't matter.

There passed whole years that I cannot account for. And then one day I saw my reflection in a glass and realized I was an old man. My hair white, my face creased, my eyes dim. Surely, death's hand was on me. But if so, I wanted to die in Iceland, in my old home, where my father and his father lie buried. It was just as the old noaidi in Lapland foresaw all those years ago; I knew when the time had come. And so I came back. And here you see me, waiting for death, and, while I wait, telling you my saga, for no other reason but to pass the time. It's a poor tale and of no profit to a pious young deacon like yourself, Teit, or to the bishop, your father. Frankly, I'm surprised you've stuck it out this long...

POST SCRIPTUM

Odd pushed himself away from the table where we sat and stretched his broad back.

"You've had my story, Teit Isleifsson. T'wasn't what you wanted to hear, was it? Well, time you were going back to Skalholt. Leave me alone now."

I sat clutching my quill in my inky fingers amid the heaps of parchment that covered the table. I tried to speak and couldn't. At last, I knew Odd's secret—what had driven him back to Iceland and brought him to this pitiful condition, and my heart ached for him. I had no words. I searched his face in the fading light and, as I often had during these days and weeks, tried to see in it the proud, laughing, black-headed youth that had once been Odd Tangle-Hair. A priest should give comfort, but he wanted none. Absolution, but of what sin? He rose and walked to the far end of the room where he stood watching in silence while I gathered my pages and bundled them up.

"What will you do with it all?" he asked at last.

"We have a scribe at the monastery," I answered. "His name is Brother Ambrose. A skillful copyist. I will have him make a fair copy and bind it in calfskin. It will go in the library."

"Alongside your psalms and your saints' lives?" A bitter smile crossed his lips; he was mocking me, of course, as he always did. I didn't mind. "Calfskin, eh? Your father will balk at the expense."

"He's still in Rome."

"Your older brother, then."

"I don't care what Gizur says."

"How you've changed!"

I didn't know what to say to that. But he was right. I mumbled my farewell and hurried out the door into the summer twilight. As I mounted my pony, I cast a glance up at the brooding bulk of Hekla, the volcano where Odd's forefathers slept. Soon he would sleep among them, I thought, if there is any sleep for the damned.

✝

A month later I knocked upon Odd's door again. This time I had brought a visitor with me.

"You again, boy?" He peered through a crack in the door. "Have you not troubled me enough?" Surly, as always.

"There is someone I want you to meet, if you're willing. An old friend of yours."

"Of mine? They're all dead."

"Except for one."

After a long moment, Odd pulled the door open. I stood aside to let Brother Ambrose precede me into the dim interior. He was a man of Odd's age, tall and very thin, stoop-shouldered. He threw off his monk's hood, showing a tonsured head fringed with white.

"A black-robe?" Odd muttered. "I've no friend among them."

Ambrose took another step into the room, leaning on his crutch, dragging the shriveled leg that hung uselessly from his shattered right hip. I knew now where he'd got that injury.

"Did I do right to come, Odd Tangle-Hair," Ambrose said in a soft voice. "Will you welcome an old shipmate?"

"Kalf Slender-Leg?" Odd gaped. "It can't be you."

Ambrose—Kalf—ventured a shy smile. And Odd's face—how can I describe the change that came over it? The hard lines of the mouth softened. The eyes filled with sudden tears.

"Kalf!"

The two old men gazed at each other in silence, each, I think, shocked by the ravages that time had wrought. Then Odd threw his arms around his boyhood friend and dragged him inside. They stood with their arms wrapped round each other, remembering, I think, what they had meant to each other—how, as boys, they had left Iceland in a stolen ship to go a-viking; how Kalf had saved Odd from his mutinous crew in Lapland, and how they had quarreled bitterly in Norway when Kalf turned pious and joined King Olaf's army; how Odd had carried him half dead from the field of Stiklestad; and how, at last, they had become friends again. (All this I had heard from Odd, of course, but also from Kalf—and, as people do, they remembered many things differently.)

Odd drew him down onto the bench with him. And I, watching them, could not hold back my tears. I withdrew to a far corner of the room to give them privacy, but I overheard what they said.

"I left you behind in Nidaros, at Bergthora's inn, still weak from the wound that Glum dealt you with his ax. Nearly fifty years ago. How have you..?"

"Oh," Kalf chuckled, "I've dragged this leg over half the world. Rome, Compostela, Monte Casino, Jerusalem, Bethlehem. Not a shrine that I haven't visited or a hospice that I haven't lived in. And then finally back to Iceland, oh six years ago now, where it suits me to live a quiet life as Brother Ambrose. The family that hated your father, and my grandfather for helping him, is still powerful in this land. Halldor and Bolli are old men with long memories. I've been careful not to say that I know anything about you."

"Six years." said Odd wonderingly. And only a day's ride away. Both of us living like hermits—"

"And neither of us knew it," Kalf replied, "until I was given your saga to copy. Odd, I weep for you. How you have suffered, my friend."

Odd's expression froze. He frowned and turned his head away. "I ask no one for sympathy. If you came here only to pity me you can turn around and go back. I left Miklagard because I could not stand the pitying looks of my friends."

"I know. I left Nidaros for the same reason. Odd, God's will is at work here. Even if you can't forgive yourself, He can, he has."

"And that's what you came to tell me?" Odd shot back. "You Christmen. You're drawn to misery like a cat to cream—you want to soak your whiskers in it. You see me brought low and you think now you will convert me—but you won't. By the Raven, you won't."

Kalf looked down and smiled. "I know better than that, Tangle-Hair. No, I haven't come to convert you; I've come to beg a favor of you."

Odd's eyes narrowed. "Of me? What sort of favor?"

"I'm a restless fellow, a wanderer, even at my age. My health is still good, I have a little money put by, and there are places in the world I haven't seen."

"Such as?"

"Such as Golden Miklagard."

Odd leapt up in anger. "Ah, I see what this is! You and the young deacon, scheming together. To lure me back there. Why? To see a son and daughter who no longer remember me if they're even alive? To find a new Emperor on the throne, who owes me nothing. To find that Psellus, all my friends, are dead, or, worse, embarrassed at the sight of me? What would I do there? How would we live when your little money runs out? I won't beg."

"Then I will. Odd, you *must* go back. You owe it to your children to show them who their father was—what a warrior, what a poet, what a fine man. They deserve to know it, Odd. Let us go together. And who knows what we may find? When you and I were sixteen and we stole Hrut's ship, we and Stig and the rest, and we sailed away into the wide ocean with the glacier twinkling behind us and dolphins in our wake, we didn't know what fate had planned for us. No more do we now. Odd Tangle-Hair, let's be those boys again. What is there here for us but bitter old age and poverty?"

✝

A year has passed since the day they sailed away on a merchant ship bound for the south. Two old men, but they could work their passage. Odd is a steersman and a navigator still, and Kalf can speak the dialects of Spain and Italy. I went down to the coast to see them off. For all their wrinkled skin and white hairs I saw in them the brave faces of youths, alight with the fire of adventure. How I longed to go with them, to walk those streets and gaze upon those gleaming towers, to see and do all the things that Odd's words have conjured in my imagination. But no, I am no warrior, no sailor. My path is a different one, but it is the one I've been given and I must follow it.

In the end it was Odin—Satan, as we Christmen call him, though I have come to the opinion that God is God, whatever we call him—who made up Odd's mind for him. He consulted the runes and they spoke to him. (He would say no more about this, and I didn't press him.)

And did they ever reach Miklagard? you will ask. Did Odd find his children alive? And was there still a bosom friend to welcome him and give him comfort? I can only believe that a merciful God granted him his heart's desire.

Teit the Deacon
Skalholt, AD 1081

AUTHOR'S NOTE

If Odd returned to Miklagard in the 1080's, he would have found his friend Psellus still alive. Philosopher, orator, historian, polymath, Imperial secretary, Psellus was not only an actor in the events narrated in the novel but is our primary source for them. No other Byzantine chronicler of the age imparts the richness of detail and shrewd insight into character and events that he does. It is to him that we owe, among other things, the description of Zoe's perfumery, her color-changing figurine of Christ, and her preference for comfortable clothes. His history, the *Chronographia*, can be read in the Penguin Classics translation by E. R. A. Sewter, *Michael Psellus: Fourteen Byzantine Rulers*.[†] Psellus is silent, however, about the early stages of his own career, and it is only my notion that he served in the Office of Barbarians. Under Constantine IX, he became one of the most powerful men at court. We do happen to know that his daughter died in childhood and that he adopted another young girl (Odd's ?) to take her place.

A tale of adventure needs not only a hero but a villain. My villain is Harald—no doubt, unfairly. He wasn't called *Hardrada*—'the Ruthless'— for no reason, but I have ascribed acts of villainy to him that the real

---

[†]Although Constantine was his birth name, Psellus entered holy orders during an enforced hiatus from political life and took the monastic name of Michael; it is under this name that his works have come down to us.

[‡]The Penguin Classics edition by Magnus Magnusson is one of several available translations.

Harald certainly never committed. Patriotic Norwegians are entitled to take umbrage.

Nothing about Harald's career during his Varangian years is beyond dispute. Did he or did he not blind an emperor, as we read in *King Harald's Saga*, and if so, which one? Why was he imprisoned and how did he escape? And how is this related to the more-or-less simultaneous Rus attack? For all this, I refer the reader to the invaluable *The Varangians of Byzantium* by Sigfus Blondal (Cambridge University Press, 1978). What is clear is that Harald returned with Yelisaveta to Norway, where he briefly shared the throne with his young nephew, Magnus, until the latter's death in 1047. Thereafter, he ruled alone over an empire that included Norway and Denmark. By 1066 he was the most feared Viking warrior in northern Europe. In that year he invaded England (William the Conqueror was invading it too, at precisely the same moment). Harald's death at the battle of Stamford Bridge marked the end of an era.

Halldor Snorrason, Harald's right hand man and fellow Varangian, returned with him to Norway. But Harald soon found Halldor's blunt manners disagreeable and the two parted ways. Halldor returned to Iceland, where he lived to an old age. The same is true of Halldor's brother-in-law, Bolli Bollason. Of all the Icelanders in the Guard, only Ulf Ospaksson stayed with Harald, in high favor, until his death.

Setting a historical novel in Medieval Byzantium comes with peculiar difficulties. The complexity of Byzantine ceremonial, the bewildering multitude of officials with unpronounceable titles, the great number of men all named either Constantine, George or Michael—these pose problems for the novelist who wishes to convey the flavor of court life without overwhelming the reader with needless detail.

Almost nothing survives of the Great Palace. There are numerous reconstructions based on the literary sources, none of them convincing. The astonishing flying throne was seen and described by one Liutprand, Bishop of Cremona, who in the tenth century went on an embassy to the Byzantine court. The passage is worth quoting at length:

In front of the Emperor's throne [he writes] *there stood a certain tree of gilt bronze, whose branches...were filled with birds of different sizes which emitted the songs of different birds corresponding to their species. The throne of the Emperor was built with skill in such a way that at one instant it was low, then higher, and quickly it appeared most lofty; and lions of immense size (though it was unclear if they were of wood or brass, they certainly were coated with gold) seemed to guard him, and, striking the ground with their tails, they emitted a roar with mouths open and tongues flickering … Thus prostrated for a third time in adoration before the Emperor, I lifted my head and the person whom earlier I had seen sitting elevated to a modest degree above the ground, I suddenly spied wearing different clothes and sitting almost level with the ceiling of the mansion.* [§]

Liutprand, a man of no curiosity, had no idea how any of it worked. My explanation is merely a hypothesis, which owes something to the way that a stage magician levitates a woman on a couch. Hydraulic engineering was certainly well understood by the Greeks.

The Khazars are one of history's most fascinating vanished races. In origin a nomadic Turkic people, they ruled an immense empire that stretched from the Volga to the Caucasus until they were defeated and scattered by the Rus. Subsequently, many of them served as mercenaries in the army of Byzantium. While neighboring peoples were converting to Christianity or Islam, the Khazars, or at least their ruling elite, somehow converted to Judaism. That they are actually the ancestors of modern Ashkenazic Jews seems improbable, though it is still an open question.

As for the Varangian Guard—the 'Emperor's Wineskins', as they were fondly called—I again refer interested readers to Blondal's book, which collects every scrap of evidence on the subject and engages in complex (not always persuasive) argumentation. They were recruited from Scandinavians and Rus. Originally, they may have numbered six thousand, but I found that number unwieldy for my purpose. We don't know where their barracks was, how their command structure was organized, nor what they did in their off-hours. All of that must be imagined. But, of course, therein lies the fun.

Finally, Teit Isleifsson, Odd's amanuensis, is a real character. The son of Iceland's first native born bishop, he lived to teach Latin and theology to the grandsons of Vikings in the cathedral school at Skalholt.

[§] Translation by Paolo Squatriti, *The Complete Works of Liutprand of Cremona*. Catholic University of America Press, 2007

ABOUT THE AUTHOR

Bruce Macbain grew up reading history and historical fiction and eventually acquired a master's degree in Classical Studies and a doctorate in Ancient History. As an assistant professor of Classics, he taught courses in Late Antiquity and Roman religion and published a few impenetrable scholarly monographs, which almost no one read. He eventually left academe and turned to teaching English as a second language, a field he was trained in while serving as a Peace Corps Volunteer in Borneo in the 1960s.

Macbain is also the author of historical mysteries set in ancient Rome, (*Roman Games*, 2010, and *The Bull Slayer*, 2013) featuring Pliny the Younger as his protagonist. Following *Odin's Child* and *The Ice Queen*, *The Varangian* is the third in his Viking series, *Odd Tangle-Hair's Saga*.